EXPLODED VIEW

EXPLODED VIEW

SAM **McPHEETERS**

Talos Press
NEW YORK

First Talos Press edition 2016

Talos Press books may be purchased in bulk at special discounts for sales promotion, corporate gifts, fund-raising, or educational purposes. Special editions can also be created to specifications. For details, contact the Special Sales Department, Talos Press, 307 West 36th Street, 11th Floor, New York, NY 10018 or info@skyhorsepublishing.com.

Talos Press® is a registered trademark of Skyhorse Publishing, Inc. ®, a Delaware corporation.

Visit our website at www.talospress.com.

Visit the author's website at www.sammcpheeters.com.

10 9 8 7 6 5 4 3 2 1

Library of Congress Cataloging-in-Publication Data

Names: McPheeters, Sam, 1969- author.
Title: Exploded view / Sam McPheeters.
Description: New York : Talos, 2016.
Identifiers: LCCN 2016018039 | ISBN 978-1-940456-64-5 (paperback) |
ISBN 978-1-940456-65-2 (ebook)
Subjects: LCSH: Murder--Investigation--California--Los Angeles--Fiction. |
Women detectives--California--Los Angeles--Fiction. | BISAC: FICTION /
Technological. | FICTION / Mystery & Detective / Police Procedural. |
GSAFD: Science fiction. | Mystery fiction.
Classification: LCC PS3613.C5872 E97 2016 | DDC 813/.6--dc23
LC record available at https://lccn.loc.gov/2016018039

Cover design by Michael Heald
Interior artwork by Jason Snair
Author Photo by Lisa Auerbach

Printed in the United States of America

“In other words, seeing is believing. But does anyone really believe that any more? Believing is believing.”

—Philip Gourevitch

I
ZILCH PATROL

"I said, 'It's tough.'"

Done talking, Terri folded her arms and leaned back into the freeway center divider, a shock of cold concrete on her hip jolting her upright again. It was an awkward confirmation that she was actually here; standing in the middle of the interstate, watching several hundred festive cops loiter on a freeway blocked to traffic, the mob made all the merrier by bumper-to-bumper congestion in the opposing lanes. Where westbound was a parking lot, eastbound held a tailgate party.

Every New Year's Day since she'd joined the department, Uribe Steakhouse opened early for a police-only champagne brunch. But with Jack Uribe still cleaning up smoke damage after a Christmas Eve kitchen fire, someone had had the bright idea to stage this year's gathering in a corner of Los Angeles State Historic Park. That site had proven so inhospitable—trash, dogs, stray hypos—that when a quarter-mile stretch of the I-10 had been shut down to search for a shell casing, the 300-strong group had simply migrated wholesale to the freeway.

Quickly glancing over both shoulders, she registered that traffic hadn't budged. She'd been arguing with the driver directly behind her, each having come to rest on either side of the center divider, directly under the boxy arch of the freeway signage scaffold. With her back to him now, Terri was struck by the uncanny feeling that she'd been speaking with an imaginary friend the whole time. Seemingly in response to this thought, a voice behind her said, "Yeah, Terri, it *is* tough. Tough seeing my tax dollars pay for your bullshit."

She sighed and turned, looking down on a balding, beet-faced man leaning out of his car, the edge of the divider perfectly level with his open window. He was a type: the powerless bigmouth.

"Uh-huhn," she said. "You don't really continue a conversation with a cop by using their first name."

"Half the goddamn police force is having a freeway party, and you're lecturing me, Terri?"

She twisted and took in the scene, seeing officers in uniform doing a clean sweep farther down, but closer more officers, some uniformed, some in shorts and jerseys, everyone chatting and laughing, most with their shades perched up on scalps, nearly everybody holding open containers. She had to admit, it didn't look great. All they needed were a grill and some lawn chairs.

"Our goddamn taxes pay your salary, Terri."

"First of all, it's 'Detective Pastuszka' . . ."

"We pay your paycheck, and you repay us by shutting down the goddamn freeway. That sound about right, Terri?"

From behind, a voice said, "Who's your buddy?" She turned again to greet Sergeant Carlos Jaramillo, his ponderous gut supported by a faded T-shirt for Meat Wagon Steakhouse. Perhaps he'd slipped it on as some sort of half-drunk protest against Uribe; most of the guys out here were still boozy from last night. There'd probably be some chest-bumping soon.

"Loudmouth citizen number 8,001," she said. "Guy's mad at us because he has to sit in traffic for ten minutes."

"Hey buddy, we just shut down eastbound," Carlos said. "Westbound is all Juggernaut. We got nothing to do with that."

"Hey buddy, I saw you over at the Kangaroo Room."

"Oh yeah? How'd I look?"

"Like you, but less of an asshole."

Carlos licked his lips, locked fingers, and stretched his arms with the palms out, then reached up and pulled down the shades resting on his own scalp. From a distance, cop glasses—PanOpts—looked like any other pair of store-bought EyePhones. Seen up close, they were the ultimate expression of authority, a more potent symbol than even a badge or gun.

"Okay. Franklin Herrera of 466 West Broadway in Glendale," Carlos said with a pleasant little smile. "Age thirty-six, divorced, employed by Totonga Graphics. Uh-oh. Oh no. I'm seeing some unpaid littering citations, Detective Pastuszka. Seeing some missed child support payments." He was almost definitely making stuff up on the fly, no one being stupid enough to mouth off to cops with an open offense hanging overhead. But sometimes it rattled the lippy.

"Carlos Jaramillo, who lives in the Woodbridge Arms complex, 8360 Sunland Boulevard," the man in the car announced, reading Carlos's face through his own shades. "I'm seeing some serious CopWatch citizen citations."

"Nice try, dipshit. My ex-wife lives there now."

Terri saw a change come, Carlos darkening, preparing to take this harmless sparring to a different level.

"You got something to say about her, dickwhizzle? That woman's a *saint*."

The man in the car swallowed nervously, looking to her and then Carlos with a sudden solemnity, saying, "Are you aware that in Sweden they have citizen policing now?"

"Ayo! Call it!" Carlos raised up and cupped his hands, yelling out to the multitude. "We got a Sweden!" The crowd cheered.

Nearby, a uniformed officer said, "Damn. Eight hours into the new decade."

Carlos leaned back over the concrete center divider and stuck his entire head into the car, probably stinking up the interior with hooch breath.

"Bad news, Frank Herrera, age thirty-six, working some bullshit job at some place no one cares about. Sweden's in the opposite fucking direction."

"Hey man!" The next driver back leaned out his own window. He was young, crazy-eyed.

"Hey man! Hey man! That's harassment!"

Carlos straightened up, amused again, the man in the first car doing his best to appear righteously vindicated.

"Hear that? Carlos? Terri? The people have spoken."

"Harassment!" The second man shouted out to the world. "It's harassment!"

She realized the second guy was drunk, the crowd's guffaws only spurring him on.

"Harassment!" The second man continued, shrieking now, craning his neck around as if the real cops might show up any minute.

Carlos looked down to his captive audience with a determined smile, tapping the space in front of him. From the way he wriggled his fingers, Terri could tell it was all bullshit, but the guy in the car appeared concerned.

"Hey. Hey. Don't tag me. I'm within my rights."

Zack Zendejas emerged from the crowd, offering one broad hand to Carlos, placing the other on her shoulder. His big slab of a face showed no hangover. Zack was a family man; he'd probably fallen asleep by twelve thirty. In six years as her partner, he'd packed on some weight, Jocular Jock slowly fading into Jowly Jock, probably hitting genuine portliness by retirement time. For now, he could still impersonate the body and bearing of an ex-military man, although he'd only segued into policing, years ago, from a job moving furniture.

"Terri P. Looks like you found some action. You see *this* shit?" Zack nodded up, at the overhead freeway signage, toward the three huge green rectangles hanging over the stalled westbound lanes. "See it?"

"The bag?" Some miscreant had tossed a ratty old gym bag up onto the sign's metal catwalk ledge.

"Keep looking."

On the furthest rectangle, past the arrows directing passengers to Santa Monica and Santa Ana, she saw an extra smudge in white. Seen from this foreshortened angle, it wasn't clear what she was looking at.

"Is that . . . graffiti?"

"Blast from the past."

"Wow. Someone actually found the one surface in the city without paint-resistant paint. Quite a feat."

"More like witchcraft." He pointed lower, to the looped coils of razor wire, draped like foliage over both sides of the structure. "Seriously. How?"

The yelling behind them intensified, and they turned into the morning sunlight, realizing that both drivers were shouting at each other now, oblivious to Carlos, who had doubled over with laughter. She heard the first man yell, "I don't need your help! Just shut up!"

Wincing from the glare, they turned back toward downtown, taking in the skyline's clustered skyscrapers.

"Is this what you thought the fifties would look like?" she asked.

"Ugh. This is the decade I *turn* fifty."

She realized she would too.

"So. Day One." He sounded sympathetic.

"Day One? Oh, right. No more overtime Day One."

For the last sixteen months, overlapping city and state budgets had poured modest surplus cash back into law enforcement, politicians at all levels desperate to get a handle on crime rates. It'd been a golden age of fractional overtime, with plenty of extra cash for motivated cops. Terri had been one of the most diligent devotees of the extra workload.

"You're certainly taking this better than I'd expected."

"I have no idea what you're talking about," she murmured, hypnotized by the gleaming skyscrapers, realizing this was the one truly good time of day to view them, sun hitting dead on and making the buildings appear important and powerful.

Carlos Jaramillo joined them, motioning back toward the arguing drivers. "The fuckin' downfall of civilization. Get a good look."

Zack turned back, squinting. "Creeping chaos."

"You want to talk about *that*? Last week, me and Luis Mahoney were going to that barbecue thing? We're off duty, off PanOpt, Honest Injun not looking for any kind of trouble. We come around a corner in this nice neighborhood by Verdugo, we see two nudists going at it on their lawn. I mean, full on, triple-X action, not a stitch of clothing to be seen. Behind them? Draped across the front porch? They'd made this big banner that said 'Just Try And Stop Us.'"

Zack lit up. He loved tales of broad daylight debauchery. “Sophisticates.”

“Yeah, well. That’s the way of the world. Forget *those*,” he pointed toward the skyscrapers. “The whole city is turning into one big ghetto garbage dump. Trash people on all sides. Look at this crap.” He was getting himself worked up again, pointing to the flat stucco apartment complexes overlooking the east-bound lanes. “These ugly-ass shitboxes, full of tacky, ignorant people. You live in a trash can, how can you be anything but trash?”

Zack met Terri’s eye, grinning, enjoying this. “Yeah, Carlos? How trashy *are* they?”

“Trash-bag hose-monster motherfuckers.” Carlos licked his lips, laughing tentatively when he saw how hard Zack laughed.

“What?”

“You just pointed at Terri’s apartment.”

“Oh shit. Hey, ah . . .”

“No, hey.” She glanced over at her building. “I’m certainly not fond of the place.”

A whoosh came, each of them rotating to watch the west-bound traffic shocked back into action, cars zipping off as if the road itself had suddenly yanked them into the distance.

“Not much of a New Year’s celebration,” Carlos said.

“Pretty appropriate for a year without overtime,” Terri said.

Zack gave another amused side glance, this time directed at her. “I thought you didn’t care about that.”

A shout came from the crowd.

“Pan *up*!”

She pulled down her own shades, the moment of transformation like the instant between holding and wearing a piece of clothing. PanOpt, the network, materialized through PanOpts, the hardware. The world blossomed with captions. Rounded byline boxes sprouted over every head, speech balloons in an endless comic strip. In her margins, a welter of informative keywords, links, transcript, and audio options flourished. These glasses peered back at the eye, gauging nuances—focus, depth of field, iris contraction—and rendering their images faster than human perception. It was a new trick aping an old trick: two lenses fooled the eyes into seeing information in stereo, two eyes fooled the brain into seeing depth. Captions appeared as solid as the people they floated over.

A small clock floating in her lower left field of vision told her it was 9:51. She had the whole day ahead of her, the new year and the new decade after that. A lieutenant addressed the troops, sounding as if he stood next to her, offering a condensed version of the underwhelming speech cops got every New Year's Day. Maintain. Persevere. Overcome.

At least this new year had provided one cinematic moment that would've been impossible inside a crowded steakhouse. It'd been an impressive sight, everyone putting on their PanOpts at once. Although she'd caught the slight self-delusion to the scene. Cops wanted to see themselves as an army, when really they were something far more dangerous: an organism.

Five minutes later, her requested car crept onto the outer shoulder as if trying to sneak out of a party, parking more or less equidistant with her own apartment block. Five minutes after that, she was cruising slow through her domain, Central Bureau, Central Division, four and a half square miles enclosing Little Tokyo, South Park, Historic Core, Olvera Street, the train station, and the Jewelry and Fashion Districts.

Oddly, the central crisis of the Central Bureau wasn't her problem. The commercial skyscrapers of downtown Los

Angeles, having been abandoned and then repopulated with refugees a generation ago, existed in a perpetual legal fog. The city claimed they were a federal issue, the federal government repeatedly bounced the problem back down, housing cops addressed violent crime, and fire marshals staged periodic, unwinnable raids. Immigration had placed the issue in an endless holding pattern. There was nowhere else to put anybody. The situation only became her division's problem the moment a tower dweller died. Which was still a lot of people, maybe half of the 691 total murders last year, with no reason to think they wouldn't top 700 in the year now before her.

The Holy Grail of LAPD intelligence would be a comprehensive, real-time layer showing every single living person in every single skyscraper. They'd tried just that a decade earlier, seeding buildings with mapping drones. The program had been technically legal, skyscrapers being squatted commercial space, but logistically impossible. There were too many warrens, too many changing faces, too many increasingly sophisticated drone detectors. The opacity of the downtown towers galled all cops. At night, it was the darkened skyline of a conquered city.

It remained strange to her that these mighty structures, engines of revenue, could have been felled by mere math. But it was just that simple. Once the price of online real estate dropped below the price of commercial real estate, there'd been no going back. Online offices dispensed with commutes, insurance, utilities. Their square feet were actually cubic feet, open to any workers in the world. There was no incentive for any businesses to maintain a physical office. And with 50 million square feet of commercial skyscraper space in downtown, there was no governmental body that could attempt the tax incentives to lure companies back.

Aimless, she had the car continue up Stadium Way, just outside her Bureau, directing it to pull over at a shady lane in the park. Terri knew that a new case would absorb her civilian life sooner or later, although she'd hoped for some overlap before New Year's, a more graceful transition into this new decade and its blocks of enforced idleness. She wanted as much work as possible because she didn't have anything else to replace working as much as possible.

From her desktop—the invisible plain that appeared to hover just inches from her face—she opened the folder perpetually suspended in her lower right field of vision. A series of documents fluttered into the air before her. With one careful flick of the wrist, she fanned each page out in space, making the assortment of papers appear suspended in the ether. Tapping a spot in the margin, she oriented these pages with the car seats, so that, for all practical purposes, these documents were physically in the vehicle with her, as real as she was.

None of the pages held any promise, the most recent case having gone cold before Christmas. A pensioner had been found face down, stabbed by someone he'd let in to his shabby little single room occupancy in a block of low-income housing fashioned out of converted warehouse space in the Horn, itself a weird little micro-neighborhood fashioned out of the thin wedge where Baker met Spring, at the northern tip of the Bureau. It'd been one of the worst cases of postmortem lividity she'd ever seen. The body had slid halfway off the bed and come to rest on its forehead, pooled blood basically putting the guy in blackface, every responding officer having to suppress giggles as the buddies of the deceased sobbed in the hallway outside.

Straightforward non-refugee domestic homicides were a rarity in Central, there being so few legal residences left in downtown. The other cases were more typical: a seemingly random refugee murder-suicide outside the Main Library; a social worker who'd stabbed one of his clients; the renegade heir to a pallet company fortune; a withered bag lady who'd turned out to be a long-ago corporate attorney. Terri took in the neatly arrayed stacks of information and sighed.

Somewhere in the cases before her, she'd probably committed Overseer Oversight. This was the persistent misconception that somebody must have already made the obvious observation, or that the system itself would have connected the dots long before any person could have made any obvious observations. Although PanOpt had a top-notch backstop program, offering all sorts of after-the-fact analysis and perspective and research, it offered almost nothing in the way of intuitive analysis. Overseer Oversight was all the more irritating because so many other networks and systems within Los Angeles watched and listened for inputs and gestures, knowing when to pay attention, when to act, when to disregard. So why couldn't the police do this?

Seven hours later, an empty stomach finally pulled her out of her forensics maps. She'd missed dusk, and now a flawless symmetrical half moon sat over a stand of trees to her left, so perfectly centered it might as well have been an advertisement. Her stomach grumbled again.

"Right."

She pulled up a web box—a seemingly physical cubby that appeared to hover above her lap—using the Overlay to call up the Internet, the two networks competing but connected. Terri was grateful that she could access both systems through her PanOpts, the cop's extra network being a private system. Viewing the world ad-free was a colossal perk of the job. In the box now, she looked up supermarkets still open on New Year's

Day, finding the physical representation of one up in Burbank, already picturing all the forlorn shoppers on a Saturday night.

So, no more overtime. So what? How bad could these weekend nights get without work? What, was she going to have a breakdown, start sobbing? She glanced up and saw something glitter under a nearby streetlight, unsure if it was a moth or part of the ecosystem of drones, one more roaming eye among millions.

Terri lived in a three-story apartment block built straight into a steep slope on Marengo. It was actually four stories, if she counted the ground floor garage bay, a space where cars once parked and which was now used for mobile trash units that came and went on their own schedule. Across the street, a dirt decline held scrub that had grown from waist high to eye level in the three years she'd lived there. Beyond and below this was the freeway, and past that the tracks for the JoyRide commuter trains. She liked this noise. Her entire life, Terri had never lived more than a mile from train tracks.

As soon as she entered the apartment, that weird exhaustion hit, a heaviness that crept into her limbs whenever she had downtime, or was alone by herself in her own space. In the bathroom, in the smart mirror she'd never bothered to set up, she caught glints from her scalp, as if her hair were slowly transforming into Christmas tinsel. A sprinkling of powdered cleanser on the edge of the windowsill offered proof that she had once half-heartedly attempted to clean the room, to ward off the ants that marched in for her blood every month.

From the jute bag of groceries on the counter, she produced a sandwich and a bottle of Jim Beam, mixed the booze with the last of her soy nog, and plopped down on the living room couch. Her first night in the apartment, she'd fastened a flimsy television screen to the wall with blue painter's tape, and it'd never seemed necessary to formally re-hang it. Despite the room's heavy curtains, there was always a gap that let in sunshine at dawn, so that the smooth rectangle constantly caught the morning light, leaving little purple crescents in her peripheral vision as she made breakfast.

Terri carefully perched the mug on the cloth arm of the couch, letting the ice tinkle and melt for a minute. Still wearing her PanOpts, she brought up a control box, then made a circle-point gesture with her index finger to link it to the TV. Opening a separate box, she went online, to a webroom cubby, selecting all six *Thin Man* movies from the 1930s and 40s, then dinging the Randomizer button.

The chosen moment came up as a still photo of Nick and Nora Charles in formal attire, seated at a nightclub on a boat, one delightful cowl-head ventilator poking up behind them like a giant musical instrument. One wag of her pinkie started the movie. Nick and Nora were mid-discussion, attending some sort of gala social function with armed cops disguised as ship stewards. The Charleses were a rich couple—a socialite and her never-quite-retired detective husband—but their world was also safe enough that they could leave their young child at home, guarded only by a tiny dog.

"Now all we have to do is sit quiet and keep our fingers crossed," Nick said.

"So many fingers crossed now I can't lift my drink." Nora said.

"Uh-oh." Nick lifted his own drink and looked off into the crowd. "Some shiny eyes in the jungle."

Terri watched across the expanse of a century. Men in tuxedos escorted women in furs. In the distance, a cartoony skyline showed the outlines of apartment buildings and skyscrapers, each lit window a tiny, inviting square of light. It was a nation in love with itself, in love with jazz, and electricity, and the night; a world where the darkness was still inviting and romantic. As some caper unfolded within the story, Nora said, "Nick, if you saw something you *knew* wasn't there, what would you do?"

She loved Nick and Nora. She'd seen one of their films when she was very young, and for years the mysterious memory had stayed with her. When she rediscovered these films as an adult, it was one of the few bits of culture she'd brought to her marriage, and one of their few common joys that still carried over into single life.

Part of the mystery had involved her first pre-sexual crush. Terri remembered sitting on the couch at her parents' house, watching one of the films on a flat screen in their old living room, luminous snow outside somehow heightening the enigma of her new stirrings. She'd been captivated by Nora Charles; those almondine eyes, that scrunched nose, the reserved bemusement. As an adult, she'd commanded Nora to strip naked in front of her, but each time it hadn't seemed quite right, something always inauthentic with the gestures of compliant undressing, the different renderings of a bare body. Nora Charles was sensual in her remoteness. The slinky outline of her true form—meaning the body of Myrna Loy, the actress—was back in the past, remote and inaccessible.

She loved Nick Charles with equal force, loved his chipper buoyancy, his snappy jackets and effortless alcoholism; tough like Cagney, suave like Astaire. Nick was a detective able to rise above the grit of the world, dispatching the horrors of crime with patrician enunciation. Terri was a fellow detective, even if she was public and he'd been private, and she identified with him, with his entire smooth worldview.

In the movie, a layer of intrigue played out one level above her comprehension. A jazz band performed on a rotating stage. Men in the audience tapped at cigarette cases. Nick Charles took the floor and made his denouement in front of everyone, elevating the craft of detecting to theater. It fascinated her how much respect police used to command. Even Nick, not police himself, could direct an entire room simply by his air of authority.

A man was shot to death in front of the crowd. A few women raised hands in shock, but no one seemed that disturbed. In most old crime films, someone was always pulling a gun on someone else with no psychological consequences for either party. Had this been a real thing? Were people simply tougher a hundred years ago? She thought of World War II, a conflict that had required actual fighting. She'd never known anyone who'd fought in her generation's war.

She made a fresh drink, steadying herself on the kitchenette counter. Returning to the couch, she remembered to set her Dupe, lest someone call her work phone after hours. Opening a Duplicado Box in the space before her, Terri saw herself smiling. Her Dupe looked like what it was: an oblivious idiot awaiting commands. The effect was unnerving, like glimpsing a mirror in a dream.

"Hey, uh, if anyone calls, I'm out of commission until tomorrow at noon."

"Okay," Terri heard herself say.

"Unless it's an emergency. So, if it is an emergency, make sure they use that word. 'Emergency.'"

"You got it," the Dupe said. In the lower right corner of the box, a small red letter D hovered in space.

"And then, if it is an emergency, but only then, set off the emergency call alarm in the speakers."

"Will do."

What else? "Hey . . . you're set to respond in third person, right?"

"That's correct."

"Good, good." This conversation was threatening to derail the night's good cheer. "Because first person Dupes are creepy."

"Got it."

Mind clouded, Terri struggled to remember anything else she might be forgetting. In the paused silence, she heard her upstairs neighbor tromping across the ceiling, the footsteps headed toward Terri's bedroom. There was another pause, and then she heard the distinctive sound of urination. For some unfathomable reason, the upstairs bathroom had been built over her bedroom.

She hit the randomizer again. Although this brought her to an entirely different movie, she'd landed on a very similar scene. Nick Charles had again gathered a motley troupe of suspects, this time in an apartment, sniffing out the one true villain in a crowd of rascals. Irish cops broke up scuffles and intimidated anyone who cracked wise, no one questioning the lack of legal council.

Terri pinged the TV control box, opening a second box for Soft Content as Nick Charles confronted a young Jimmy Stewart, asking, "But where did you expect to get cash on New Year's Day?"

Terri chuckled: the question made no sense. She tapped the Soft Content box and said, "Nick, punch Jimmy Stewart."

Nick Charles executed a perfect left jab. Jimmy Stewart stumbled backward, clutching his face.

"My nose!"

"With cussing," Terri said.

"You . . . you broke my goddamn nose!"

"More cussing."

Jimmy Stewart straightened up, eyes wide with righteous indignation. "You broke my fucking nose, you fucking ass cock!"

"*That*," Nick Charles said with defiant good cheer, "was for being a piece of shit little rat fuck."

This was enjoyable. "Dance party."

A burst of big band music sounded and the crowd gyrated in place. Jimmy Stewart dropped both hands to his knees and did the Charleston, blood dribbling from his busted nose.

"Increase the party." A cascade of brightly colored balloons and streamers fell from the ceiling. Terri realized she should've done this before having her first drink, the creative part of her mind now muddy. If she were industrious and sober, she could recreate the story as she saw fit, using the template of the film as a canvas, reordering this world with nothing more than skill and voice commands. Not that she'd ever been great at remixes. It required a certain perversity. Her ex had excelled at this; a pleasant memory ringed with hostile, jagged edges.

"Um. Zero gravity."

The entire group rose up off the floorboards, still dancing, arms and legs getting tangled up with the party decorations, the entire scene a little too visually chaotic to follow.

"Okay. Reset to where I started. And pause it." The players dropped back to the floor and took up their original positions, a theater company awaiting direction. In the TV controls, she brought up a Views box, selecting a position and then clicking Immersive. The real room around her dissolved, and she saw herself standing in a corner of the apartment, inside the world—monochromatic but photorealistic—of Nick and Nora Charles. The scene reminded her of one of those murder-mystery plays where the actors roamed from room to room.

"Everybody out. Go on." The characters hurriedly exited through several doors, leaving her alone in the apartment.

She glanced down at the little *R* icon in her lower left field of vision, amused with herself for always forgetting to look at the precise moment this changed. Right now the *R* was a hollow red, indicating altered fictional footage. When she'd started the film, it had shown as a solid red letter. If she'd been watching non-fictional footage—news or otherwise—the *R* would have come up solid black. If she'd then altered that news story, the *R* would appear as a hollow letter, outlined in black. This was by far the most important symbol on PanOpt's desktop, the only guarantee that a given scene was an actual representation of objective events in the physical world, and not some gradation of simulacra below that.

Terri floated through the rooms of the abandoned apartment. When she'd been a kid, one could "lose" themselves in a film only emotionally. Now it happened literally. Even ten years earlier, it had still been possible to occasionally stump the little red *R*, to think up a scenario or visual that confounded the boundaries of Soft Content. These days, there was nothing that couldn't be shown in real time, the networked shades of humanity able to rummage through the collected filmic works of humanity, culling and extrapolating any detail or plot point imaginable.

A scream came from the street. She didn't take the bait, instead watching the breeze slowly suck the curtains in and out of the window frame. This was the story asserting itself, wanting to get on with it, to pull her back into a narrative. The Story was still king because of that one universal asymmetry in all viewing experiences: the human addiction to storytelling. Most people just wanted to be steered back to a good tale. Terri was a rarity, content to stand in an empty black-and-white apartment and just listen to all the obsolete traffic noises of a lost era.

The drink needed freshening, although by now the thought of navigating the refrigerator was clearly too complicated, seeming potentially dangerous. Pulling off the PanOpts, she saw the bottle of Jim Beam resting on the kitchenette counter, and she rose and gleefully toddled over to snatch it with both hands. Then she was back on the couch, in a different movie, making everyone fight, dispatching huge wild boars to tear into whoever happened to have the misfortune of being onscreen, exploding people's heads, howling and howling with laughter.

She woke with a snort in the utility alcove, near the bathroom door, huddled on a pile of dirty clothes. The sad laundry unit, the one luxury of the apartment, loomed above her. Seen from eye level, its circular door and two childlike knobs resembled a huge face perpetually shocked to see her back here again. From this angle, the machine appeared ominous and industrial, its thin gray wiring, normally hidden by the molding of the bathroom door, snaking up through the ceiling to the solar array on the roof, as if an old-timey spy had snuck into the place and bugged her.

Terri rose to a crouch, squinting and groaning from the harsh sunlight of the exposed living room windows, realizing she'd made a nest on the floor with the curtains. She stumbled up, stiff legged, one hand shielding her eyes, finding her PanOpts on the Chinese table, slipping these on with another groan. She called up the Preferences box, found Display, then Variables, then Creations, ordering the system to overlay reality with the appearance of rehung curtains. The living room seemed to magically restore itself. She crossed past the couch, to the small bedroom, not caring if someone zipping by on the freeway got a split-second peek of her in her underwear, feeling the incongruous warmth of sunlight on bare skin where her eyes told her there was none.

In the fridge, one of the three legs of her anti-hangover trifecta was absent. At her old house, she'd always kept a rasher of bacon for just such emergencies. Now she had only eggs and coffee, and as she turned on the scratched kettle, a wave of nausea passed through her with such intensity that she had to pivot over to the sink and stand with arms locked on the countertop, willing herself to not puke all over the dishes that had sat unwashed for the last week. Her body produced one long, quivering belch, but nothing else. Where were all those barf bags she was always taking from cop cars?

As the eggs sizzled, she heard a peep, a blinking telephone icon in the upper-right corner of her vision drawing attention to itself. Terri preferred PanOpt's bone-conduction audio, but she'd never bothered to figure out how to disable the temple speakers. After her breakfast plate had been arranged, there was another wobbly crossing to the couch, the entire apartment building seemingly riding the crest of an ocean swell, then she was down on the edge of the cushions, propping up her elbow, bringing up the TV on the wall.

Nick and Nora had just woken up as well. The television showed them paused in their bathrobes, her seated at a small vanity, him standing, posing suave, frozen in a backward glance. Terri restarted the movie, having no idea which film she'd stopped on last night.

Inside the film, a butler entered their bedroom and stooped to deliver a silver tray of food and newspapers, informing them that they'd slept through the entire day.

"The morning papers aren't out yet, madam. These are the evening papers."

"That doesn't seem right, the evening papers with breakfast," Nora said with a darling poutiness. Terri opened another Soft Content command box while the butler, still stooped, pointed toward the bedroom door, explaining that a policeman just outside wanted to speak with Nick.

"Ah, show him in. He probably wants to question Mrs. Charles again," Nick said.

"Don't do that," Terri said.

"You know what? *Don't* show him in. Me and the wifey will just have a nice breakfast," Nick told the butler, doing a quick double-take. "Excuse me, dinner."

"Very good, Mr. Charles," the butler said, exiting the bedroom still stooped.

Terri cleared her throat and said, "Nick."

"Ah, yes, Terri." He looked straight at the camera, making eye contact with her on the other side of the screen.

"Please read me the news."

"Certainly. Ah, *our* news, or . . . *your* news, young lady?"

"My news."

Nick unfurled one of the newspapers.

"Let's see here . . . Sunday, January 2nd." He glanced back out at Terri. "Headlines?"

"Sure."

"Ah, well then . . . 'Busan, Nagoya, and Quezon airports shut down for twelve hours by vector control over Marburg scare.' 'Turkish rebels advance within ten miles of the Izmir airport.' 'Unnamed sources inside TF Pauling say an initial public offering could come as early as March.'"

He bent the paper at the fold and continued with the lower-front page.

"'Worst storm in fifteen years pummels New England.' Oh, and this headline says, 'GAO predicts a $39 billion cost overrun for Navy.' And, ah, 'Inquiry into Berlin stampede resumes.'"

This intrigued her. "Read me that story."

"Yes, that does sound interesting," Nora said.

"Alright, don't everyone *gang* up on me." Nick squinted and shivered his shoulders in mock annoyance, looking back down to the newspaper. In a semi-stentorian voice, he read, "'Berlin, January 4th. After a break for the holidays, the Bundestag investigatory committee resumed emergency hearings into last year's deadly midday stampede at the city's busiest U-Bahn station. Even with the recess, emotions ran high at the three-hour meeting . . .'"

She pulled up a transcript in the margins as Nick read.

"'. . . While the chief of police defends his office's chronology, forensic inconsistencies continue to plague the investigation, with three dozen crucial discrepancies casting doubt on both . . ."

Terri paused him, double-wagging her finger toward the screen and importing the footage into her PanOpts. She minimized the Charles' household, and then clicked on the words "U-Bahn station."

A mosaic of photographs from the Berlin subway station stampede filled her field of vision. She selected a shot from the entrance, the steps already cordoned off by police tape, the faces of two bystanders twisted into fantastic masks of anguish and loss. This she minimized as well, searching the wall of photos for something from the actual footage of the hell below.

Toward the bottom of the grid of pictures, she found what she was looking for; the heart of horror. This photo showed the stampede at one of its visible crush points. In this picture, a wall of clothing and flesh had been forced into a caged enclosure, pushed, by the flow of the crowd, into a locked cul-de-sac meant for maintenance workers. Arms and fingers had been smashed into the fencing. Faces pressed into chain link like soft clay, tongues lolling, eyes rolled back. She probed this photo even as it seared her. Having found this image, she couldn't look away.

Stampedes were the mystery of the day. At first, these stories had come from far-flung megacities with names she barely recognized: Durban, Kano, Jabodetabek. But in the last two years, people had stampeded in cities with clearly recognizable names: Berlin, Caracas, Winnipeg. The unspoken conclusion was clear. They were getting closer. No one had a handle on what caused these mass tramplings, although the problem seemed like the logical successor to the political psychoses of twenty years earlier. It was as if the entire world had PTSD.

Stampedes once had causes. Even the ones rooted in flimsy rumors—like the long-ago Pacific Rim salt riots, those days and weeks of the young trampling the elderly, everyone convinced iodine could ward off radiation—were better than stampedes caused by spooked crowds. And even those stampedes seemed better than these stampedes, which defied logical explanation even as they slowly metastasized from continent to continent. Creeping chaos. She shrank the picture and exhaled, shaken by just a single flat, still image. She was grateful that, on this one subject, she was too flat-out chickenshit to view the footage in immersive.

Terri closed the Berlin photos and maximized Nick and Nora back on the wall TV, both still frozen in a world of class and spacious living. She pinged the talk channel and said, "Okay. Go on."

"Well, let's see. Those are the top stories."

"Maybe she wants to hear the local stories, Nickie," Nora said with a seductive slyness.

"Ah, yes. Local." Nick cracked open the paper and began reading from the same page. "'A four-alarm fire at an apartment block in Lynwood leaves twelve dead.' 'A fight between teenagers at the Pasadena Tournament of Roses leaves four dead.' 'Reseda City Council schedules an emergency meeting over fresh allegations of corruption.'"

Nora turned and smiled at Terri, and for a moment seemed real, an entity reaching across the decades for communion.

"Isn't he just the best reader, Terri?"

She paused the set and finished her breakfast in silence. Fortified, she dinged the circling phone icon and heard a message from her niece, Krista Sprizzo, returning Terri's call from New Year's Eve.

Krista picked up on the fourth ring. "Heyyyyy . . . hold on?"

"Yep."

There was a quick fumbling noise and then Krista's VT—her projected public self—materialized on the other side of the couch. She looked just a bit older, the slight curvature of her chest a brand new development. Had Krista redone her profile, or had she actually been visited by the puberty fairy in the week since Christmas?

"Hey."

"Hey yourself. How's it going?"

"Good, good. Except school's back tomorrow."

"That stinks. Early."

"Yeah. What's up?" she asked in a rush, as if Terri were frittering away her precious free time.

"Oh. Well, I just called because I think you left your EyePhones over here when you came over for that shopping trip." She lifted these up to show her niece.

"I didn't leave any shades there." Krista's head bolted, and she suddenly stared off through the closed front door of Terri's apartment, as if she were actually present and had just heard something distressing in the hallway.

"I *have* my school glasses, Mom! I didn't leave them *anywhere*! *God*! Hold on, Aunt Terri," Krista's VT froze as the real Krista, fifteen miles away, rose to slam her door in Valley Village. Terri pictured this bedroom. She had peeked in when visiting over Christmas, and had been genuinely surprised to see all the old posters of horses and soccer players removed, usurped by the images of young boys with long, curly hair and steely stares, nothing in any poster to even make clear what particular human endeavor the young men excelled in. Perhaps each was the president of a poster company.

"Okay. Sorry," Krista said. "She's just . . . nnnn!"

"Yeah, sure. Listen. I didn't want to bring it up, but now I'm thinking I'll feel dumb if I don't. You want to talk about what happened?"

"Nothing happened," Krista said with a cool reserve, momentarily all adult.

"Well . . . if you got suspended for three days then, yeah, something did happen."

"Two days, and it's an in-school suspension. Gina says we'll just have to clean bathrooms or something. It's a joke."

"Your mom didn't think it was a joke," she said, suppressing a wince at her own tone.

"She just likes to overreact."

"So this was, what, a game?"

"Yeah."

"Any one I would've heard of?"

"Maybe. 'Strangers on a Train'?"

"Wait a minute, *that* was the game you were playing? Isn't that the one where that teacher in Seattle got paralyzed?"

"But, we weren't *do*ing it like that!" Krista whined. "All you do is, you tag the worst teacher at your school. Like at Millikan? Somebody tagged Mr. Ballesteros, the Spanish teacher, because he's so gross with girls. Like, he's always staring at everyone's chest and making this gross sucking sound with his teeth. But even that's just, like, a level five out of ten. So if someone from a different school sees him outside of school, they can only do something from level five. Like, maybe they pour a milkshake on his shoes or something. So when we were at the mall, we saw this guy with a level two. I think he's like a math teacher in Hollywood? But his level was so low that we had to do something small and sneaky. So we followed him to the food court, and when he put his shopping bag down, she snuck in a pamphlet on gum disease she'd gotten from the dentist thing. That was it."

"That *doesn't* sound like that big a deal," she agreed. "But you have to understand why everyone was so freaked out. After that thing in the news."

"We didn't do anything like that! It's not *fair*."

"Hey, that's the way of the world," Terri said, feeling a little pukey all over again.

"Anyway, I have to go in a second."

"Hot date?"

"Yeeeaaah," she said, still recognizably a kid. "Hey, we should get lunch sometime."

"Absolutely," Terri said, finding herself suddenly alone on the couch. She looked back up to the TV, Nick Charles paused with his newspaper, realizing that Krista's generation seemed to have skipped the PTSD part.

Krista at the mall; the image wouldn't gel. Kids just didn't go to physical stores to buy anything. That was the generational chasm in a nutshell. Terri's peers drove places to shop, or they went online and shopped in webrooms. Krista's peers shopped in the Overlay. The Internet was already too much work for them, requiring the illusion of travel. If Krista needed shoes, she'd just bring up a sales layer and have it show her the shoes as they would appear on her feet, or scattered around her bedroom, or floating in physical space, as if she were a sultan's princess having slippers brought before her by an army of ghost servants.

Terri thought of the mystery EyePhones, her mood darkening. This was a problem. She couldn't bear to peek at their archive, lest it contain some fragment from her past life. But she couldn't afford to lose them for the same reason. It didn't seem plausible that these could actually be her old EyePhones. After the divorce, Terri had spent a huge sum to fly home, back to Jersey, for a weekend of self-diagnosed closure. She'd fit all the most important totems of her marriage into a single shoebox, then slid the shoebox into the darkness of the rafters of her aunt's garage. Or had she? Maybe her desire to have included the shades in the shoebox had placed them there in her mind.

She twirled the shades between two fingers, seeing the Zeiss logo on the temple. In PanOpt, she pulled up a Zeiss company directory and dialed tech support.

"Assistance," a cheery man's voice said in audio only.

"Yeah, hi. I found a pair of EyePhones in my apartment, and I can't remember if I purchased these a long time ago, or if a visitor might have left them by accident. Here's the footage."

"Okay."

"And, ah, I don't . . . I'm wondering if I can obtain an index or something, remotely, without having to turn them on myself. Because if they don't belong to me, I don't want to violate, you know, someone else's privacy."

"Of course, I get it," the man laughed. "We've all been there. Let me see what I can do."

This seemed somehow off.

"Hold up," she said. "Are you a real person?"

"Well . . . I'm *really* interested in providing you with quality customer service."

"No. Nope. Please put me on with an actual person."

The voice sighed with good nature, saying, "Okay. One moment, Ms. Pastuszka."

She muted the hold music and rose, wondering if these slender EyePhones actually contained any footage from the old house. She and Gabriella had lived in South Pasadena, in a 1920s craftsman they'd bought and fixed up over the course of a decade-long marriage. Terri still dreamed about that home at least twice a month, its surfaces, with groaning floorboards to tiptoe past at night, the way her bare feet had gripped the wood, like she could stay there forever.

A few years before the divorce, their dog Congo had died. Grief had colored their shared world for months, a private sourness that survived like a virus requiring only two hosts. After the divorce, her own unending sadness seemed a continuation of this grief, a one-person anguish that followed her, an odor that refused to abate and which only she could smell.

Solo, Terri had had to decide how best to expunge her ex from her networked life. The options were endless, up to and including a full delete—entirely erasing all traces of her ex from her world—with proximity warnings if there had even been a threat of them running into each other in a public space. But then Gabriella had moved, first to Mexico, then overseas.

A voice said, "Ms. Pastuszka. I understand you have an indexing issue?"

"I have some old EyePhones, and I don't know if they're . . ."

"No, yeah, I've got all that up here in my case file. I'll just need a little more info before I order the indexing."

"Oh, great."

"Let's see . . . you want full transcripts?"

"Jesus. No. What would I do with that? I just need an overview of contents."

"Alright then. Sounds like you want the one-time Basic Index. That runs $625 without any abstracts, $80 for each additional . . ."

"Wait. What? That's nuts. Look. Is there just a way you can tell me the purchase history? That's really what I need."

"Sure, I can do that. Gimme just a sec . . ." She wondered if this was the same disembodied operator as before, disguising its voice, adding a few pauses for plausibility.

"Yeah, you bought these two years ago, at the StadiumStomper webroom. Need to see the receipt?"

"'StadiumStomper'; I've never even heard of that. Are you sure it was me?"

The voice laughed. "You used your face to pay, so yes. These were bought January 25. Looks like this was . . . a pop-up room for Super Bowl supplies. Ring any bells?"

"Oh," she remembered: someone had invited her to a Super Bowl viewing party. She'd bought these shades because using PanOpts for a sports event seemed ostentatious, and her old ones were back in Jersey, safe from her own prying eyes. She hadn't wound up going to the party because she'd given herself a nasty sinus infection from sobbing.

"Thanks. All I needed to know."

"Excellent, Ms. Pastuszka. And while we're talking, I'd like to real quickly tell you about our . . ."

She dismissed the caller with a single finger swipe in the air. This was the exact reason she never used civilian shades. Her resistance to sales was low after the divorce. Using PanOpts, she was all cop, except when she placed a call out. It would be a silly distinction if it wasn't real.

She spent the afternoon at the Tujunga Farmer's market. On the drive home, a text announced,

LORDY LORDY LOOK WHO'S 36
COME HELP MUTTY RING IN HIS NEW YEAR
UGANDA, 9ISH

Approaching her apartment at the tail end of dusk, she saw the building's dark bulk silhouetted against its hill, and the thought of staying in for another night filled her with a dread close to out-and-out fear. She tried to remember the last time she'd been out for purely social reasons, realizing she'd already decided to stop in at Mutty's party. Her upstairs neighbor had a cat or cats, and as she reached her landing, she detected the faint but unmistakable tang of ammonia drifting down the next stairwell, as if to emphasize the dangers of becoming a recluse. Producing her house key, she instinctually glanced down to make sure she was alone. Once, a gray drift of cat fur had followed her in and set off the drone alarm.

The only piece of furniture she'd kept from her marriage was the three-legged Chinese table. She'd just moved it from one front door to another. This table had had a vital function in the old house, being the place where professional glasses were left, a symbolic gesture made literal, neither of them tracking the muck of their professions back into their shared sanctum. Now it was just muscle memory, the one place she kept her PanOpts when they weren't on her person.

Terri placed the PanOpts on this table and thought, *I'll need to look nice*, laughing when she realized she'd said this out loud. There must be something here snazzy enough to wear to a birthday party. She smiled, remembering the fitted three-quarter sleeve with the fat blue and purple lightning bolts she'd gotten as a college sophomore, some weird homemade thing she'd bought at a crafts fair on a freezing afternoon, back when bright zigzags had somehow been in fashion.

She'd kept it maybe because she associated some fun nights with that shirt, and perhaps because she'd been borderline chunky in college, always in the cafeteria with its endless meal plans, and had only slimmed down later, after graduation and the few years of hardship. She'd always suspected the shirt would still fit her as she got older and wider.

The shirt wasn't in her dresser. It wasn't dangling in the closet, where it wouldn't be anyway, among her work clothes, and it wasn't, obviously, in the hamper. She hadn't worn it for years, although it seemed like there'd been plenty of times when she'd yanked it out and dismissed it with annoyance. She stood in the living room, staring out toward the rapid lights of the freeway, chewing her lip in annoyance, some of the tingle of expectation draining out of the room. Back in the bedroom one more time, she grunted to lift the surprisingly heavy dresser, finding only two mismatched socks. She stood, feeling another bolt of post-hangover head pressure. She didn't have an apartment macro because she'd never seen the need, now that she was on her own. This was pretty much the exact thing that people set up Life Recorders for. The force had monitors in the hallway and stairwell for her benefit, and for a weird moment she contemplated calling up someone on The Wall and asking if they'd seen the shirt. Instead, she grabbed her PanOpts from the table and did a quick voice search that came up blank.

All calls would be archived. In the kitchenette junk drawer, she found and donned the old shades, finding the shirt after three searches. She'd been sitting on the couch last April, talking with Tammi in that dreary, familiar way of family members slipping in and out of verbal autopilot. She saw herself from her own perspective, eight months in the past, staring down at the blue shirt on her lap, fingering its seams in disinterest and hearing herself mumble, "I guess that all, you know, gets eaten by the co-pay anyway." She considered deleting the conversation, then decided to mail it to herself, so at least she'd have this memory of her shirt, one bit of her own life slipping through her fingers.

Poltergeist might help. She contemplated digging up her old password and posting footage of the shirt, seeing if anyone out in the world somewhere had spotted this in the garbage or being worn by some thief. She'd known a cop in Van Nuys who'd used Poltergeist to find a guy who'd stolen his rhinestone jacket right off the hook of a Denny's men's room, just reached right in over the stall door and snatched it. And Gabby had successfully used the service once, years ago, after she'd left a shopping bag full of expensive cosmetics in a dressing room somewhere.

Terri had set up an account but had never figured out how to use Poltergeist anonymously, always getting tagged as cop from the get go, not being savvy enough to know how to conceal her identity. And anyway, Poltergeist was notorious for creeping trolls. Even if she could get on incognito she'd still have men sniffing around her public VT. She'd have to learn how to get into these services as a four hundred-pound Samoan guy. Somebody in her circle of acquaintances must know how to do such a thing.

The refrigerator door made a cool surface to lean into. The only light came from the living room, and as she surveyed the silent apartment that had so thoroughly bested her, someone far away—a teenager or crazy person on the train tracks or beyond—squawked once, a forlorn, high-pitch whoop of glee or defeat or primal terror.

Riding over to Uganda, she'd suspected that the thing for Mutty was really just an excuse for a smaller core of detectives to continue the abridged New Year's Day party. When she arrived, however, she was surprised to see a small thicket of cardboard birthday hats by the bar. Mutty Posada himself emerged from the crowd, wearing two hats at angles, like pointy demon horns.

"Alright. Pastuszka on the spot. Somebody here owes me $50. Said you weren't gonna show."

"Who said that?" she said, secretly a little pleased that anybody had thought enough of her social life to include her in a wager.

"Um," he turned back and peered into the crowd with bewilderment. "Somebody . . . um . . ." For a second, he appeared to raise a tube of lipstick to his mouth. She realized it was a portable vaporizer. "*Man* . . ."

It had taken her a while to figure out that Mutty's perpetual gap-toothed grin was the result of ongoing highness. So many cops stumbled through the profession permanently fuzzy, although booze remained the drug of choice. Back when she'd joined the force, many of the older cops still remembered having to drive themselves around the city. "The Battle" had originally been a term of derision aimed at her bracket, the generation of cops for whom cop cars were chauffeurs. It was only later that the word had taken on a stoic quality, The Battle being the fight against chronic drunkenness or highness. And something providing joyful balance to their daily slog. The Job vs. The Battle.

As the lone black detective on the not-so-newly reformed housing division, Mutty probably had to deal with his share of both, Job and Battle, many of the adult refugees still harboring deep-seated racism from their own rural hinterlands. Although by all outward appearances, he was as serene as the Buddha. In a profession full of storytellers, Mutty was a rare good listener, able to sit back and tease out interesting details. He was probably the closest Uganda came to having a mascot.

Not quite sure what to get, she ordered a whiskey sour. Two detectives from Juvenile eased over, Kirk Delacruz and Marilee Havers, Kirk saying, "Just the tiebreaker we need."

"Oh yeah?"

"Tell Mary I'm not crazy. We did see graffiti on the 10, right?"

"I don't remember seeing that."

"Not *on* the 10. On the freeway sign. Remember?"

"Oh yeah. Yeah, that was weird. I didn't see what it said."

"Who cares what it said. But we saw it, right? And it wasn't some group hallucination?"

"It was real. Yeah."

"It said 'Imsane'," Steve Cruz said from behind the bar. After spending thirteen years on Homicide and Robbery, Steve had retired to serve drinks and butt into any conversation within earshot.

"Hey, c'mon Steve. You weren't even there . . ."

Steve shrugged. "Grooper sent me footage. I'm telling you what I saw."

"'Insane'?" Terri asked.

"No, I-M-S-A-N-E."

"What the fuck does that even mean?" Terri said.

"Vandalism," Marilee said. "Nihilism."

Terri nodded vigorously as a hand clasped her shoulder.

"'Sup, Terr," Zack said, looking past her, toward the end of the bar. "Surprised to see you here."

"I was going to say the same thing."

"I had to come. I'm the hat man." He pointed over to the birthday party contingent.

"Janice bought them for the party next week." He raised his voice, projecting down toward the merry makers. "So I'm going to need them back at the end of the night."

She smiled and squinted. Janice Zendejas was absolutely the kind of mom who would buy birthday hats a week early. When she'd been raising their twin girls, Ashley and Audrey, she'd gone overboard on the pink-and-pony-themed everything. Now that the girls were nearly adults—fifteen or sixteen, stern go-getters lost in academics and athletics—she'd poured that maternal energy into Wade, a spastic little man already halfway through first grade. Wade was a walking drum solo. Mutty approached from the rear.

"Zendejas." They clasped hands, and Mutty pulled him in close to loudly whisper, "You owe me fifty *bucks*, son."

The five of them grabbed a table. Mutty, odd man out, sat a distance from the group to receive well wishers. Marilee said, "Speaking of nihilism . . . tell them about the movie, Kirk."

"Shit. We were down on South Grand two nights ago, going . . . I don't even remember where now . . . and I see they're showing a movie on the side of the old AT&T center."

A few times a month, someone in the opposing skyscraper trained a projector out of one of a thousand windows to beam a film on four stories or so of blank wall on 420 South Grand. Terri remembered these showings being loud, booming off the glass canyon walls, someone having lugged concert speakers up into one of the skyscrapers as well. Some cops got pissed off by movie nights, but nearly everyone recognized their value as pressure releases for the community. Especially in the summer.

"We already had some popcorn from one of those minishops, so we're both like, 'Why not?' It was that movie, um . . ."

"*North By Northwest*," Marilee said.

"Yeah, that was it. Except in this version, Cary Grant was a private eye, and it was set in modern day LA, and there were these crazy Bollywood musical numbers. It wasn't half bad. So we're sitting there on the hood of the car, I know everyone can see us, everyone knows who we are, probably a million eyes on us. But then, the movie just got . . ."

"Fucked," Marilee said.

"That's the word for it. Cary Grant starts killing people, doing drugs, screwing amputee hookers, and I'm getting really uncomfortable. Then there's a whole scene where he goes on a rampage in a police station, and afterward, he's got maybe a hundred heads on spikes out in front of the station, and he's drinking this big chalice of blood. And then, Mary leans over and says, 'Is that you?'"

"It was," she confirmed. "Both of us. They'd stuck our heads on sticks. In the movie. Someone saw us in the street, and inserted us into the film."

"I'm not thin-skinned, but man. Creeped me out, seeing myself dead like that. And the worst part? How many thousands of kids do you think were watching this?"

"Psssht," Terri said, mad, taking her drink more seriously.

"Hell of a message to send these kids. Total nihilism. The meatballs are literally using our own buildings as canvases to project their twisted little psychodramas against us."

Terri laughed at this without knowing exactly why, her own concentration a little fuzzy. She'd planned on taking it slow with her whiskey sour, and then suddenly realized she'd killed it. She'd forgotten how strong the drinks were here. She closed her eyes, as someone said, "Didja catch the game last night?"

"I got bored by the third quarter, so I made all the players drop trou and take a shit on the court."

She smiled. Every boy cop at Uganda kept a game or fight up in the corner of his vision. All these guys were probably only half here as well, secretly cheering or lamenting some private score. Probably most of them weren't even real teams to begin with. She opened her eyes, seeing that a fresh beer had materialized in front of her. A pal of Mutty, Willis the Narcotics Guy, had taken up a backward chair at their tightly packed table. He asked, "What do you guys think about that thing at the Tournament of Roses?"

"What about it?" Zack said. "Wasn't it nine kids got into a street fight or something?"

"I heard it was twelve."

"You're thinking of the fire in Lynwood."

"Isn't that you guys?"

"Tournament of Roses stuff is Pasadena, not us."

"Yeah, but it's all in the county."

At a certain point, she gave up trying to follow the conversation, happy to be here and not on her couch. Zack was laughing and then he slapped her on the back and said, "This round's on you, lady."

She nodded and rose, carefully crossing through the crowd, catching sight of herself in the one long mirror behind the bar and seeing that someone had placed a birthday hat on her head.

When she returned with draft beers for her and Zack, Willis was holding court, recalling some overheard story of carsurfing carnage. She smiled, feeling her own tipsiness, not quite able to follow who was saying what.

"These guys jump like they're human mountain goats or something. Except mountain goats don't slip."

"Hey, every mountain goat slips when it's leaping from car to car at 140 miles per hour."

"How does someone convince themselves that a boosted glove box is worth instant spaghettification?"

"Stupid doesn't need convincing."

"'Spaghettification,'" Kirk laughed. "More like 'Darwinism in action.'"

Zack looked annoyed. "How the fuck is it Darwinism if each of these idiots leaves behind six kids?"

A chirpy alarm sounded at six fifteen a.m. She was still clothed, still wearing her PanOpts, slowly focusing to see a tremendous angry man standing over the bed, glowering down at her wretchedness. This was Boris. Boris was a man-shaped apparition conjured in an app for drunk people. She must've been destructively hammered to have triggered Boris. He would have assisted her home last night, yelling at her like a drill sergeant, coordinating with the battle taxi, forcing her to take step after step, helping guide her house key out of her pocket and into the door.

Terri dismissed Boris with a hand swipe, sat up, moaned in dizziness, and dropped back to the pillow. Grunting from the effort, she placed herself in the morning briefing. Seeing a room at eye level, when her inner ear told her she was flat on her back, was still somehow less awful than the vertigo that would come from sitting upright.

The department being decentralized, briefings and roll call took place in a simulated lecture hall modeled on the old Parker Center auditorium. Presence was mandatory, and she wondered how many in the hundred-plus audience of detectives, officers, and sergeants were similarly miserable, slumped in beds or car seats scattered across the city. A floating almanac box told her dawn was still forty minutes away. She pulled up a traffic box, seeing the Rolling Juggernaut—that eternal traffic jam—creeping up the Santa Ana Freeway and expected to head east. Some Lieutenant she didn't know was droning on about boosting response times, perhaps deliberately trying to put everyone back to sleep.

Zack called and mumbled something as she placed him in audio, not wanting to see or be seen. Terri muted the briefing, letting the transcript unfurl in the margins, so that she appeared to be staring out at a still gathering of cops, perhaps during a long moment of silence. She tried to speak, growled, cleared her throat, and said, "Say what?"

"I said, I quit. I'm *out*."

"Oh yeah? Finally gonna pursue the life of a scholar? Good for you."

"Seriously, you ready?"

"Ready for what?"

"Did you not check the big board?"

"I'm barely, barely, barely awake, Zack."

"We just drew Zilch Patrol."

She exhaled loudly, wincing from sinus pain. "Where?"

"Swap Meet, forty-five minutes ago, refugee cadaver littering the parking lot. I'm done with this Mickey Mouse shit. Seriously. I'll retire, screw it. I'm heading your way right now."

"I'm not even dressed," she said, realizing this was a lie.

"Come down in your PJs, I don't care. No one cares. First catch of the goddamn decade."

"What, in the city?"

"I meant for me, my first catch. This stupid bastard couldn't have kicked off a day later? Let me get a real person?"

"Yeah, that is tough on you," she said, forcing herself upright. "Would you honestly be happier if it was some Oregon hobo in the Swap Meet lot?"

"If it was a made-in-the-USA corpse? Yeah, I would. 'Gee, I wonder where *this* guy lived?' 'Golly, how did he wind up here?' 'Shucks, who would have a motive to bump off this poor little fellow with his one brown tooth and a knapsack full of pinecones?'"

"Sounds like you've cooked up quite a back story for your guy. Maybe they'll let you switch cases." She closed her eyes, letting the spins settle. "At least urgent response gets us out of roll call," she croaked.

"I'll take roll call," Zack said as a car honked outside. "And I'm here. Hurry," he added in mock impatience. "God forbid the maggots and buzzards get this idiot first."

"Listen, I need to brush my teeth, find a hangover pill, change my shirt. Give me like five minutes."

"I thought you said you weren't dressed."

"That was a metaphor."

He made a snoring noise that sounded more like an oink.

They arrived at 6:40, South Figueroa Street looking like a surrealist painting, the blazing streetlights competing with the sky's pre-dawn glow. It was easiest to have the car pull up on the southbound side of the street, depositing them onto a sidewalk already clogged with buyers and sellers. A pill kept the worst of the hangover at bay, but Terri still felt the pull of vertigo, extending one hand to steady herself on the car and almost falling when it abruptly zipped off. A teenage refugee kid selling pre-rolled joints on the street caught her eye and froze with a half smile. She frowned and pointed toward the Swap Meet wall, meaning toward the rabble just inside.

"Take it indoors, Hiawatha."

It was strange to her that something so colossal didn't have a formal name, but there it was; the Swap Meet, a 950,000-square-foot sports arena that had itself been dwarfed by the more modern Itaú Unibanco Arena in Carson. Before it'd been repurposed by refugees, the building had been an early, catastrophic casualty of downtown's commercial collapse. Now it was the only major abandoned structure in Central Division that wasn't used for human habitation. Instead, the space served as a massive indoor marketplace, every bit as labyrinthine as a Middle Eastern bazaar from a thousand years earlier. The Swap Meet was the main venue for selling to refugees. At least half the vendors were citizens looking to make a buck.

They crossed the street, both slipping on rubber gloves. The parking lot ran along two blocks of Figueroa, divided in the middle by West Twelfth Street. The entire space held 1,500 merchant-leased cars, give or take, most vehicles parked in tight formations. Their body was halfway up the northern lot, ten feet from the sidewalk but hidden by a concrete divider. At the far north edge, two huge buses, each bound for megacasinos in Rosarito, sat stalled by a small squadron of uniformed officers taking statements from every passenger. Zack chivalrously held up a yellow band of crime tape, Terri still feeling dizzy as she dipped her head to pass under. As they approached the actual scene, they were both careful to view everything from every possible angle, dipping and weaving in the dance of all homicide detectives.

A slender, middle-aged Indian man lay face up between two tightly packed cars, having selected a deathbed so narrow that his shoulders hunched up against either tire. There was some salt and pepper in his mustache, but nearly none in his tousled, matte-black hair. By appearances, he was just shy of fifty, although any number of factors could easily have added decades to his true age. His face had that expression of slack-jawed shock Terri had seen so many times before, no one ever looking as if they'd made their final stand with a hint of dignity.

He'd been shot once in the heart at close range. The entry appeared well-placed, the shooter probably having used some sort of anatomy layer to get a clean kill. An overhead byline box read "JHADAV, FARRUKH" followed by a twelve-digit number—imported from India's vast biometric database years earlier—as if he could only afford so many lines on his tombstone.

"He is wery died," Zack muttered to himself in a fake accent as he did a squat and grunt to retrieve Farrukh's wallet. She leaned against one of the cars for a moment, a swell of nausea rising and fading.

"How come *you* don't have a hangover?"

"Because I weigh eight hundred pounds?" He straightened, red-faced, fishing through a deeply worn vinyl wallet that was probably a family heirloom.

"Nothing but cash."

"So no robbery."

"Hold up." He fished out a pair of disposable EyePhones, a flimsy, curved rectangle with one triangular cutout for the nose. They were cheap, probably not comfortable, certainly not built or priced for long-term use.

"Why wasn't he wearing these?" she asked.

He shrugged and held the rectangle out between two fingers. "So . . . I assume you want to limit your outdoor movement? And loud noises? And fresh sunlight?"

"That'd be great," she said, taking the disposables, slipping the evidence into a baggie and then zipping that into a side pocket on her coat. "I'll get the basic itinerary and then take off to deal with the shades."

Zack squatted again, half-rolling the body to search for an exit wound. When that turned up no bullet, he did a quick scan of the pavement, his shades finding it ten feet away. He stood, wiped both temples against a forearm, circled around one of the cars, and retrieved this, standing to examine it like a jeweler with a diamond. They'd linked forensic boxes, so they both saw the same identification at the same moment.

"Browning HP, Mark I, nine-millimeter" she said. "*That* narrows it down."

Zack looked back at the body. "Hey, at least this dipshit got popped by a real gun. Some dignity in that, right, Farrukh?" If no progress occurred, Zack would tire of this particular case after only a few days. At best, Farrukh Jhadav had a week. Probably less.

She did routeline while he worked the crowd. Of the two floating PanOpt boxes used most, cops generally set their sign box, that universal menu, to appear at elbow height, and their call box, the window of visual communications, to appear at somewhere close to waist level. Many rookies learned this lesson the hard way, setting both boxes at eye level—all the better to intimidate by pointing a finger directly in a perp's face—and developing tired limbs, "monkey arm," halfway through an arrest.

Terri kept her own boxes horizontal, at waist level, sliding them into new positions on a case-by-case basis. In her sign box now, she scrolled through menus, finding the Routeline controls. A bright red tube appeared to materialize from Farrukh's chest. The tube rose perpendicular to the pavement, like a piece of playground equipment. Six feet up, it bent and continued parallel to the ground, its squiggly path tracing the route Farrukh had walked—as recorded by civic surveillance—crossing back over South Figueroa to disappear into the Swap Meet. They'd try their luck inside, but the place was a notorious warren, the perfect setting in which to ditch a weapon or hide for a day. Tens of thousands of people would enter and exit in the next few hours.

She glanced around the sidewalk, taking in the staggering excess of public information that accompanied all citizens: age, address, family, occupation, associations, degrees, estimated income, average rent, frequented haunts. Four years earlier, courts had ruled in the LAPD's favor that face-tagging comments could remain delinked from police records, and thus inaccessible to citizens. Ever since then, face tags had taken on a Wild West, tell-it-like-it-is quality. A severe-faced black woman strode past with two little boys in tow. Overhead, a cop tag read "COUGH DROP STEALING DOO DOO MAMA / CONSIDER SHOOTING ON SITE." She wondered if the officer of record had intended the weird misspelling.

Terri removed her PanOpts for a moment, always careful to take in faces as they were, to exercise her own intuition whenever possible. She scanned the crowd for feigned indifference or dawning horror, thankful that the days of families IDing bodies were long gone. People surged past on the sidewalk, murmuring, selecting, purchasing, debating, spying, cooing to children, flicking at unseen objects, punching codes into the air, instructing or cajoling or laughing with partners eternally offstage. Even the passing refugees, most without eyewear, seemed lost in their own private hustles. She was never sure why this surprised her. A hundred million people were still looking for a soft landing, two million squatters in southern California alone.

Her car shot up the freeway. Vehicles swooped and coasted with the rhythm of sync and release, taking advantage of slipstreams, cars beholden to their ever-changing cargo, weaving gracefully to the contours of their shared master map, recording and re-recording every obstacle or pothole or sharp turn. Cars used to serve as extensions of the human nervous system; now people were just specks inside an infinitely larger nervous system.

The car synced with a battered jalopy sporting a primer-gray quarter panel, its closest window covered by a thick cut of plywood. For a moment, the two vehicles moved like one unit. There was a click and a knock and then the other car dropped out of sync and zipped off at the interchange, having physically transferred some bit of cargo from one auto to another. Terri tried to visualize what kind of ghetto-ass nastiness might be in this particular glove box, as if the car itself had passed part of its essence instead of offering itself as a node in a vast decentralized network.

If it had been her glove box, she would have retrieved her personal items from the panel next to the front seat. Instead, this car would switch packets with another, the cargo moving on and on to its final destination. She was old enough to remember a time when packet switching had been a luxury. Now it was something closer to a courier service.

Just past the 101, her car caught up to the Rolling Juggernaut. The Juggernaut was a drifting, mile-long traffic jam, the granddaddy of all annoyances. Its solitary traveling wave moved across the freeways of Los Angeles, a chaotic entity that defied predictive models. In its persistence, the Juggernaut was both complex and chronic. There wasn't a passenger in the city who hadn't fumed against the irony. The same progress that had liberated cars from traffic also contained an error that enshrined a bit of this congestion for all time.

Terri's car, containing an on-duty cop, accelerated as she approached the stalled wall of traffic. Zippering through the Juggernaut may have been one of the more minor perks of the job, but it was also the most thrilling, and a great way to scare the bejesus out of a cuffed perpetrator. Even now, having experienced this action so many times, she felt her hands dampen as the car shot toward seeming death. Only in the last few seconds did she finally see the zipper, the passageway formed as the cars in the traffic jam edged aside, her own car shooting into the narrow channel between vehicles, doors and windows and bumpers whooshing by within an inch of her own car.

Slowing to exit, she passed a freeway sign on which a Caltrans worker was in the act of scrubbing off graffiti, every other traffic marker in the city apparently hit in a blitz. Swooping down onto surface streets, she glimpsed a public health banner featuring a shirtless, glistening boxer, the caption next to him reading "K.O. CHOLERA," and for a moment she thought that was the fighter's name.

Even though it was only in El Sereno, going to the Networks And Retrieval building felt like trekking to Arizona. A concrete bunker framed the entry, surrounded by a teardrop-shaped parking lot bordered by hearty scrub and spiny, Jurassic-looking plants. Downstairs, she found the office of Carla Morales, the door already open, exposing a desk cluttered with instruments that looked like a cross between soldering irons and dentist tools. A vintage table lamp with a paper shade cast a warm glow over the workspace.

Carla emerged from a back storeroom. She was a squat, bulldog-faced woman with an overgrown crewcut and PanOpts set to show her weary eyes. They'd met once before, but it'd been long enough ago that Terri wasn't quite sure if she should reintroduce herself.

"Hey, I'm Terri . . ."

"Disposables, right?"

Carla took the flimsy wraparounds, vaguely reminding Terri of a bartender she'd once known, not so much in appearance as in sheer ugly depletion. Both women gave out a signal that they'd never fully figured out how to make their lives work with any efficiency or joy.

Carla wrapped the disposables around a faceless wooden hairdresser's dummy and clipped two mystery tools to either end.

"So. Your first step is what, memory or draggage?"

Carla shrugged. Terri looked around the confined space for a place to sit, seeing boxes and papers piled on the room's lone chair and sofa. Zack called in VT, materializing as if standing inside a stack of banker's boxes.

"Okay, you there?"

"Yeah, lemme punch you in." She tagged and flipped Zack's VT into the room.

"Hey . . . this is my partner, detective Zendejas."

Carla looked over her shoulder, nodding at Zack's apparition.

"So, ah, we're just seeing what the memory and draggage are," she said, semi-embarrassed by Carla's lack of social skills.

"The baggage you draaaaaag around," Zack sang to himself, taking in the flamboyant slovenliness of the office.

Draggage could solve a case in minutes or it could provide weeks of unrewarding grunt work. Everyone kept different items on their private desktop. Some people brought a few photos and shopping lists around with them. Some people lugged around their entire lives. Everyone she knew kept some representation of their finances floating nearby. In general, the brass were okay with cops keeping draggage on their PanOpts desktop, as long as it was in one tidy folder and you didn't let the physical manifestations of your outside life in any way interfere with the Job. Zack waved a hand in front of her face, pointing to himself and mouthing, "Mute me."

Terri tagged him, muting his audio to Carla as she bent over the wooden head, tinkering with unseen panels in her own PanOpts.

"Why did you pick Carla Morales?" he asked, the small red M floating next to his face her only assurance that they weren't being overheard. She texted,

Doesn't she have good rep? I thought she'd been on The Wall forever

Zack smiled with a malicious edge. "Yeah, and you know why she's not on the wall now, right?"

I hadn't really thought about it

"She used to be a raging goddamn drunk. Isn't that right, Carla," Zack said.

U just lost mute privilege

She tapped the little red M as Carla looked up from her seat.

"Nothin'."

"Nothing, meaning? Nothing of consequence?"

"Nothing as in, he just bought these. There's a ten-second recording from the convenience store where he bought them and a receipt folder with one receipt. For this. No draggage. Your victim didn't have the chance to use these yet."

Zack gave out his thin smile of annoyance. "Why exactly did Detective Pastuszka have to go all the way out to your office for this info?"

Carla stood, rubbing the back of her neck. "Because if these hadn't been new, who knows what kind of nastiness your guy might've stashed on them."

"I don't know, I've seen some nasty footage in my day." His smile faded. "If we're running against the clock, I don't see why we can't swipe a victim's EyePhones with an alcohol swab and check it out our own selves."

Terri wasn't quite sure what to make of this back and forth, although Zack's question had crossed her mind more than once.

"First of all, most systems will be viewer-locked, so . . ."

"Disposables aren't."

". . . so you'd need an eye cracker just to get inside. Second . . . you ever hear of Jimmy Nakamura?"

"Nope."

Carla sighed, exuding weariness.

"There are two types of illegal EyePhones. The common ones are the closed systems, the Calleciegas. After IIPACT, no one manufactured Calleciegas, meaning the best you could buy back in '36 was maybe, I don't know, a five hundred-terabyte system. With good money, maybe eight hundred terabytes. Either way, without networking, it's a self-secure loop. Meaning if you're a pedophile, or into snuff stuff, you might have a big dungeon to work with, but it's still a dungeon of finite storage space. So these guys found themselves needing harder and harder images, while at the same time having to store all that generated footage on eyewear they couldn't afford to break or lose. Every year that passed meant that much more accumulated nastiness.

"Maybe five years ago, detective Nakamura answers a domestic violence on a place in Topanga. In the basement, he finds an off-network pair of EyePhones. They confiscate these, and when they get back to their work station, they realize they've found one of the last of the old-time Calleciegas. Because Nakamura found them, he volunteers to put them on and see what they're dealing with. Ten minutes later, he takes them off, leaves the station without saying a word to anyone, goes home, shoots himself in the head.

"After that, the department only lets root viewers go down. Automations being able to handle content that most people cannot."

"The plumbers."

"Yeah, I've heard them called that. It's the root-viewer programs that go in, the plumbers. They hunt around for illegal footage. Whatever bad stuff they find gets distilled into black-and-white outlines, like a coloring book. They pass the evidence up to us, and only then can we go to the DA with charges. I've seen some of these outlines, and it's bad. Bad. Stuff you've never thought of before and, trust me, don't ever want to see. That answer your question, Detective Zendejas?"

"What's the other one?" Terri asked.

"What other one?"

"The other type of illegal EyePhones?"

"Oh. Bypasses. Open systems."

"That thing in Tarzana," Zack said, his interest barely still there.

"What thing in Tarzana?" Terri asked.

"There was a bank robbery maybe ten years ago. Maybe longer now. Those guys knew they couldn't get to all the tellers quickly enough, that somebody was probably going to get to 911. So they used a bypass. When somebody did call the cops, it only looked like they were talking to the cops, when actually they were talking to one of the robbers' girlfriends. That's what a bypass does."

Zack caught Terri's eye long enough to make a face of boredom, winking out.

"What happens when your office gets a bypass?"

"We have a few here, under lock and key. I think the Tarzana guys got eight to ten for the robbery, and another thirty years for possession of the bypass. It's serious shit."

"Hopefully under serious lock and key."

"I got bumped down here six years ago, and I've seen the bypass collection exactly once."

"So you've never handled any fresh catches?"

A momentary look of puzzlement crossed Carla's face.

"How would I? We don't find them any more. No machine built in the last twenty years will present unauthenticated content as real content. Even the Manila PD finally got serious about that one particular problem. When they did the big switch, it was just a matter of time before they rounded up all the problem equipment."

"Big switch?"

"Before the Overlay got standardized, everyone operated on just a few computer monocultures. That made everyone vulnerable to all kinds of malware and reiteratives."

Terri rubbed her chin, no longer sure how to contribute to a conversation she didn't understand. She pointed toward Farrukh Jhadav's disposables, still wrapped halfway around the head-shaped block of wood.

"Can you dispose of those?"

"No next of kin?"

Now it was Terri's turn to shrug, not caring enough to even say that she didn't care.

An hour later, she was still in the parking lot, reviewing her own footage to dispel that nagging feeling that she'd forgotten something. The compulsion to second-guess herself had only emerged in the last three years. She called up Zack, seeing that he'd hiked all the way over to the northbound 110 on-ramp, having deputized two uniformed officers to help him gather a group of refugee teens into the graded no-man's land between access road and freeway.

"Yo, yo, yo," he said, corralling the handcuffed boys into the center of the dirt rise. "Who's the killingest?"

"Hey," Terri said, flipping herself into the scene. Behind the group, she spied the saddest of all makeshift memorials: actual flowers that had lived and died, plucked and placed in a netherzone to honor a nobody.

"Okay, whoever wants to be not arrested, raise your hands," Zack said, turning to face her VT.

"You see this?" He pointed up to the green freeway sign looming above the low hill. Over the names of the downtown exits, someone had spray painted the word "IMSANE" in huge white letters.

"Here's what *I* don't get. Is he appealing to our sense of decency, like 'I'm sane?' Or is he so fucking banana-time bonkers that he can't even spell the word 'insane' right?"

"Are you asking me to guess?"

"I'm a bit more scientific than that." He turned back to the kids, spreading his arms wide.

"Any of you guys give up the shithead who did this"—he made everyone turn and take in the defaced road sign, like a teacher chewing out a class—"You get a thousand dollar re-ward. Straight up."

She squinted. "Really?"

"Yeah," he answered, oblivious to the kids in front of him, "Me and like twenty other guys did a pool."

"You didn't do a pool for that Williams kid murder, but you do a pool for this?"

"Yeah, well, Williams was a done deal. This is a mystery. You! Moose McGillicuddy!" Zack pointed at the largest kid in the group, a sweaty monster of a fifteen-year-old. "Want a thousand bucks?" Before the kid could think up an answer, Zack was back working his captive audience, stuffing business cards halfway down each kid's waistband.

Terri turned, scanning the other street corners, seeing a family scurrying behind a stand of trees, above this the backside of the Ritz, the behemoth Wilshire Grand building looming beyond that, the thought of all those *people* making her angry, the huge tower one mini-Calcutta out of many. She said, "Huh," and rewound what she was seeing. Her gaze moved backward, back down to the trees and the family that had darted away so quickly. She froze and zoomed in, realizing the youngest girl, a toddler held in the arms of her mother, had no byline.

Refugee girls made it off the grid far longer than refugee boys. On raids, she'd come across Indian women in their twenties whose faces still came up unregistered in PanOpt. Some women lived entirely feudal and indoor existences. Muslim women had it the worst. In the Swap Meet, she'd once glimpsed hennaed fingers dart from under a faceless black robe to squeeze a pomegranate. It had lasted only a second.

No one would compile data on these women. Their lives were absolute solids. She sometimes thought of these surplus people as she rode through the city, glancing up at blackened skyscraper windows. Women never allowed from their rooms. Women without history, who survived only as desperate scrawls on drywall, as whispered names or tiny grooves scratched into windowsills by fingernail. Some women departed the world without even these records or remains, like animals built of pure cartilage. No bones.

On Tuesday morning, she woke with a vague sense of gratitude, the aftertaste of some dispersed dream victory, or maybe just her own body thanking her for not drinking herself to sleep for the third night in a row. After breakfast and a shower, she drew her curtains against the slanted sun, grabbed the PanOpts from the hall table, aimed the portable fan at her face, and arranged two big pillows under her knees. At eight on the dot, the phone rang with a shrill chirp. She slid down her shades as Zack appeared in her living room.

"Yo."

"Yo to you. Everything correct? Got your coffee?"

"I'm good. Got the goddamn house to myself for once," he said, tagging a space in the air above her head and then flipping them into the Basement.

She found herself seated before an austere office desk in an otherwise empty room of luminous walls, each papered with the faint, huge watermark of the LAPD. Her couch had vanished, so that she saw herself floating on air, legs still bent at the knees, propped up on invisible pillows. She tried to remember what she'd set as her public VT, then decided it didn't really matter if she was just going to be down here all day. Pearly Rodriguez appeared behind the desk. He was a pasty, balding little man with a hairline starting on the top of his head and the thin cardigan of a librarian.

"Pastuszka and Zendejas", he said, beaming. "The dynamic duo. What's shakin', kids?"

"Fightin' crime. How're you holding up, Pearly? Still doing the Friday night Risk marathons with, who was that? Salcedo?"

"Oh, I wouldn't know," Pearly said, smiling like the Buddha. "I'm not Pearly. You got his Dupe."

"I thought you just got *back* from vacation," Zack said with a surly edge.

"Pearly did. Like I said, I am not he. I guess he decided he liked it so much he went on the big vacation. He retired just before Thanksgiving. You're looking at the captain of the ship now."

"No shit," Terri said, feeling a little thrown off. "So it's a Duplicado-run basement from here on out?"

"Yeah, they made some tweaks, decided they didn't need a real person, so here I am."

Zack glowered. "Jesus Christ. This whole operation is on autopilot?"

"'Fraid so," Pearly said with jovial delight. He'd always seemed to treat the world as one big joke when it was actually him. Why wouldn't his Dupe act even more amused?

"Hey, weren't you working on that thing with the pallet king last year, Detective Zendejas?"

"Yeah," Zack said with a curt undertone.

"Whatever happened with that?"

"Nothing happened with that. Let's get on with *this*, okay?"

"Hey, it's not like this thing's gonna start up without you, right?" he said, making a few high squawks of laughter, as if all three of them were in on a joke that was also somehow at their own expense.

"Okay," Pearly said, smiling broadly, not taking his eyes off Zack. "So I have you both starting just inland from West Twelfth and South Fig at 5:28 yesterday morning. Sound right?"

"That's the one. Where's the consent box now?"

"Just your lovely face and this conversation, my dear."

"Oh, you mean we won't have to sign in with you each and every time now?"

Pearly beamed again. "Nope. Come and go."

"Good," Zack said, too late. The room dissolved and they were back in the Swap Meet parking lot an hour and ten minutes before they'd actually laid eyes on Farrukh's bewildered corpse. They'd seemingly arrived at the crime scene at the moment a drone located the body, having itself been alerted, roughly a minute earlier, by the ShotSpotter network. For all the hassles and drudgery of Basement work, she always enjoyed this moment of drop-in, that feeling, fleeting in its magic, of being a time traveler.

In actuality, they'd each entered a frozen simulacrum, an immersive visualization of Los Angeles constructed from a million eyes: camera nests, traffic control, drone footage, smart surfaces, and the nonstop rolling feed of every personal macro carried by every officer on the force. In the arsenal of LAPD forensic intelligence, the Basement was one of the heaviest guns, a private vision of the entire city in which cops could sleuth through public footage, stopping, starting, rewinding, or speeding time as needed.

Zack had set his VT to show him as he would appear if they'd been physically standing in this actual spot, and as he surveyed the crime scene, she saw him shake his head as he'd surely be doing in the living room of his actual house, many miles away.

"Fantastic. Blindsville."

She nodded. The space between each narrowly parked car appeared solid, filled with a geometric wedge of fluorescent pink: the blind. The blind represented any portion of the physical world not surveilled. Public spaces such as parking lots were thickets of blinds, full of crevices and undersides unrevealed by the forces of civic detection. Only the between-car gap that held Farrukh's body was illuminated, lit up by the twin eyes of the drone dispatched to locate the site of a shooting. She looked up now and saw this drone lit up for identification, appearing here as bright and significant as the star of Bethlehem.

Where were her old presets? It hadn't been that long since her last serious visit, back in September. A forger of casino chips had spiked his partner's celebratory margarita with coolant and then chopped the body into bits, which he'd distributed in bite-sized chunks across the streets of downtown, the poor vic wolfed down by stray dogs. She'd followed that scavenger hunt in the Basement, painstakingly tagging every glistening nugget. It was only when she'd retold the story to her sister's family, over Christmas dinner, that she'd realized how grisly the whole case had been.

Zack tagged and linked her, and then the city around them sprang to life. Traffic lurched into reverse, birds flapped backward, lone figures strutted jauntily back down the sidewalk. The space occupied by Farrukh's corpse filled with a bright solid pink. As they watched, a hooded figure popped up from this blind. A second later, corpse rose to face killer, both of them emerging from the solid pink above the shoulders, the perp coming out at chin level, Farrukh jutting out at the collarbone, the goofy shock of his death mask mirrored in his last moment of life.

"Meat marionette," Zack said to himself, halting playback. He stepped to the left of the moment of death, so that his own head appeared to jut out from the roof of one of the parked cars. She floated over to the other side, bringing herself up close to the shooter. He was four inches shorter than Farrukh, wearing shaded EyePhones, a dust mask, and a green-and-blue-checkered sweatshirt with the hood up and tightly drawn. Only a one-inch triangle of nose gave any indication of a general skin tone.

"Little guy," she said.

"So . . . huh." Zack's hand emerged from the roof of the car and stroked his chin thoughtfully. "Came up from under a car, and then . . ."

He hit play and Farrukh collapsed back into the blind. Almost imperceptibly, the killer glanced down at his handiwork. Then he dipped back down into the blind as well.

"That's a new one," Zack said, meaning the opposite. Every stick-up kid and would-be criminal mastermind knew to travel under parked cars to avoid detection. Zack stepped back out from the vehicle and said, "You check south, I'll go up by the buses." She nodded, floating back down toward West Twelfth as the world started back up. She passed a half-dozen cars, each connected to the next, and the asphalt below, by a solid block of pink.

"Anything?" he asked, still sounding as if he were standing next to her.

"Naw," she reached the end of the row. "There's no way he came up over here. It's wide open. Those buses were probably too inviting. Want to wager that it's all blind between the two?"

He grunted as she raised herself up twenty feet to get a full overview of the dreary lot, its somber array of battered cars parked in tight formations, the swift flow of traffic on Figueroa and then the more complex flow of the human crush starting on the sidewalk past that.

"Yeah," Zack said from the end of the buses. "All pink. Surprise, surprise."

"Should do a daylight request on that hoodie."

"Okay," he said, appearing to type in space. "Fingers crossed."

The world sped up. Car traffic blurred into a transparent river. Shadows shrank and then elongated, and as dusk approached, a comic, high-speed mass exodus spilled out from the Swap Meet, the parking lot clearing out in what appeared to be three seconds. These were the outside vendors, non-refugees, upper-middle-class merchants with leased vehicles. These people knew to get out of Dodge before nightfall, downtown being a very different world after dark. The lot was bare; if the suspect had made an appearance in the blur, the system would've caught it. He paused motion and sighed.

"So our guy's only escape route was between those two buses. He comes up, changes, makes a casual getaway."

"Unless there's a burrow hole we don't know about."

Zack turned up the brightness, bathing the lot, now free of all cars, in an eerie half light.

"Gotta be sure," he agreed.

They moved over the surface of the lot at what would be 6 p.m. yesterday, him on foot, her floating on an invisible couch. They both knew they weren't going to find any getaway holes, their search being just one more pantomime of Cover Your Ass. You never knew who was going to be watching the playback.

"Fuck that swizzledick busybody," Zack said.

"What? Who?"

In a squeaky voice, Zack said, "'Catch the pallet king yet?'"

"You're getting yourself worked up over a Duplicado, idiot."

"I'm gonna go find the real Pearly and rip the rest of his hair out. That molester."

"Didn't the real Pearly have some serious health problems? He's probably dead now."

"Yeah? Good."

She yawned and took in her environs: an empty lot in a motionless city. It was too early in the investigation to have hit such a complete dead end.

"Okay. Rock paper scissors for high-low."

"Loser's high," he said as they shook fists, him keeping his while she flashed two fingers.

"Damn it."

"Hey, you think I like going low?" Zack asked. "Just get up there and let's one of us find something quick so we can get back to being actual cops and not walking dog shit detectors, okay?"

He vanished into his own viewing session. She opened a control box, resetting the world to noon and then sending herself aloft. No matter how slow she made this ascent, going high always gave her a bad combination of vertigo and carsickness. Thirty stories up, she pulled off her shades and rubbed her eyes, undergoing one more flush of queasiness as she found herself back in her own living room, seated and motionless. After a minute of this, she pulled the PanOpts back on, seeing herself floating a quarter mile over the city. From this vantage point, she could view the entire skyline, and the distant county edges where the basement ended in vast walls of solid pink. She was glad she'd remembered to set up the fan. In the Basement's street level, her fan's breeze provided a gentle gust in the canyons of downtown. When viewing the city from overhead, it was a puff of stratosphere.

She called up the same routeline she'd run the morning before, in front of the Swap Meet, opening another control box for this and setting the duration to two weeks. Next to this, she opened a separate control box for all of Los Angeles, reducing the city to black and white and lowering the opacity to 50 percent, so that she peered down at a vast diorama of smoked glass. Everywhere the late Farrukh had traveled in the last half month was now represented by the red line—thread-thin when seen from this altitude—that curved through the streets and alleys containing his life's routines. When she dropped back down to nine hundred feet, she had to clutch at the soft throw pillows below her legs to ward off that nagging sense of free fall.

Farrukh's daily schedule showed a hub on West Second Street. From here, he left every morning between 5:00 and 5:10, returning every night between 8:50 and 9:20, each exit and entry clearly time coded on the routeline with multicolored tabs. His daily routine fanned out in westward patterns made visible: Koreatown, Hollywood, Wilshire. In the margin, she opened a text box for Zack, typing,

The deceased was a delivery boy. I'll get in closer, but I'm guessing taco walla

As she dropped down to five hundred feet, he replied by text,

Bullshit. What kind of taco walla earns an assassin?

She shrugged. It was a good point, maybe. Zooming down to fifty stories, she peered at the hub, squinting in curiosity, like a child examining an insect. At twenty stories, she saw where the multiple lines seemed to converge on a bush. She slipped down to street level, annoyed at herself for not doing this part last and sparing herself another ascent. She brought the city back up to full opacity, seeing the many lines indeed dipping into a large, overgrown hedge that, on closer inspection, had been yanked from its roots to clumsily cover a three-foot chasm in the sidewalk.

She opened a call box and dialed the housing directory. Billy Bustamante came up first. She'd dealt with him a few times before, and couldn't remember anything wrong with the guy. He answered on the first ring.

"Howdy, Terri P."

"Hey Billy. Question. I got a meatball dead in the Swap Meet lot, and when I do his routeline, it looks like his daily comings and goings are through a hole at Second and Grand. I'm assuming this guy isn't burrowing down into the ground, so . . . where does this go?"

"Beats me."

"Come again?"

"What's your duration at? A week?"

"No, two."

"Set it for a month and you'll see what I mean. Before this hole was opened, your guy was probably crawling up out of a shaft behind the old law library. Go back to Halloween, and he was using one of a half-dozen holes under the 110. We gave up trying to map all this crap."

"Since *when*?"

"Since last summer, when the meatballs discovered the old pedestrian tunnels under Grand Park. These guys have hundreds of displaced engineers and architects and nothing but time, so I'm kind of surprised this didn't happen a decade ago. When they were doing just teeny rabbit holes, yeah, sure, we could totally track those. But these new tunnels plug into existing passageways, some of them a hundred and fifty years old and blocks long. In August, we discovered a full underground railroad. I don't mean Harriet Tubman style, I mean a working miniature steam engine, like, for kids, that somebody salvaged from an old shopping mall. Some skyscraper folks found the sealed tunnel under the Hall Of Records, expanded it another six blocks, laid down tracks and lights, different station stops, the whole deal. It was impressive."

"That's insane. That would take boring machines, trucks, generators . . ."

"Or an unlimited amount of manpower. Sorry to be the bearer of bad news, but yeah. Your guy went in at Second and Grand, there's a quarter-mile radius for where he might've actually called home. Maybe more."

She puckered her lips, saying, "Got it. Thanks."

"Hey, if it's any consolation, I wouldn't be surprised if downtown collapsed in five years. It's probably Swiss cheese down there now."

"That would be nice," she said, hanging up.

Three hours later, having tagged every dreary way station on Farrukh's daily itinerary—retail, work-at-homes, a few anomalies she'd have to check out in person—she pulled off her glasses, stretched, and made herself a sandwich. After lunch, she slipped back into the Basement and dialed Zack. They met in the Swap Meet lot. He hadn't bothered to change the creepy twilight.

"Whatya got?"

"Yeah," he looked around, seeming exhausted. "Let's, ah . . . hold up." He typed in the air, the world brightened, and the street and sidewalks snapped into focus, showing them one split second, everyone halted in place.

"Okay. 5:29 a.m. Three rings. First-tier potential witnesses, here, here, here, and here," he said, pointing to a row of motionless pedestrians, each tagged with colorful overhead boxes displaying their names and addresses. Zack had nicknamed each: Big Nose, Fatso Tits, No Neck, Cheese Whiz.

"Already long odds except for Fatso . . . Beverly Gutierrez, over here. She maybe made some kind of a face at the gunshot, although ShotSpotter says the whole thing was under 120 decibels. Maybe the shooter pressed close, used Farrukh himself as a silencer."

"Does that ever really happen?" she asked.

"Then ring two, here." He pointed out two cars whizzing by in the northbound lane, both neatly tagged. Zack beckoned her over to a passing car, its elderly passenger paused, mouth open in conversation, seeming delighted about something. Caught by eye-level spot cameras, he appeared to be sitting in a vat of day-glow pink fluid, the blind obscuring everything below the window line.

"Maybe," she said. "G-Cars aren't known for their side macros."

"No, I mean maybe *he* saw something."

"At eighty-five miles per hour."

"Yeah. Okay. Touché. I'm trying. Fuck."

"Third ring?"

"Whatever. This kid on the far side of Fig." He pointed without enthusiasm toward one motionless teen leaning against the concrete wall of the Swap Meet like he was James Dean.

"Over a hundred feet away, no shades."

"Yeah," he made a quick smacking noise. "And then three cars, here, here, and here, in southbound. One's a Mercedes. Good side macros. I looked up the specs."

"And three lanes of northbound between them and the shooter."

"Hey, you never know. I ran some sightlines, and there were a couple split-second gaps." Zack stared off at something. "Also. Check *this* out."

Floating, she followed him diagonally southwest, over to the gleaming black Mercedes captured in mid-motion. "See the son?"

She maneuvered herself around the car and stared into the starboard window. A mousy older gentleman sat in the seat closest to her. Next to him, a young man with Down's Syndrome slumped with his tongue slightly protruding. The only developmentally disabled people she'd ever interacted with had been children; she found Downsy adults somehow unnerving.

"Check out the ownership box," Zack said.

She pulled this up, reading "OVERHOLSER, RICHARD JR."

"Yeah?"

"The guy next to you is Richard Overholser, *senior*."

"So the car is registered to the son?"

"Yep." Zack walked over and leaned across the windshield. "Asshole probably thought no one would ever notice."

"Right." She floated back to the center divider, staring out at the world and its dearth of clues. Zack was on the verge of an exhausted rant about the rich guy and his disabled son, she could feel it, like they were an old married couple with de facto ESP.

Instead, he turned to her suddenly, saying, "So, what if *Pearly* got bumped off, and we got to come down here and rub it in his Dupe's face?"

"Go get some lunch, Zack."

In the morning, she ran. Terri only wanted to jog when she wasn't able to. But the moment she did set out, there was always a relief tempered with gratitude that she'd made the right choice. She ran down Marengo, away from her building, hair secured by a Hidden Drive brand sweatband, a stats box in her upper-left field of vision showing each step, each calorie burned, each muscle group used, offering endless options for other joggers to run with or against, the motivational possibilities infinite.

At forty-three, she was fit from running, her old back injuries now nothing more than a passing stiffness. But her age was beginning to show, in the stubborn slack below her jaw, the slight folds below each eye. Her flat stomach wanted to sprout a little belly, one she wasn't sure she could run off forever. Worst of all was the sun damage. She and Gabriella had been religious about the beach, Terri because she'd grown up in a state where coastlines were either ruled by goombahs or covered in snow, Gabby because she had a spectacular figure and liked to show off. They both had been avid sunbathers, and now her arms had taken on a deep olive hue, and her upper chest was spackled in large, ominous freckles; from certain angles, her skin reminded her of dried apricot. Terri looked older than she was, although it was a well-maintained older.

The endorphins usually kicked in before Boyle Heights. By the time Terri approached East Cesar Chavez, life felt good. She made a right onto this main commercial thoroughfare, passing faded murals, dogs tied to fresh, skinny trees, minibikes chained around larger trees whose fat roots pushed the pavement up from below, so that she had to make little jumps over the skewed slabs of concrete.

Then she was jogging down crowded sidewalks, through awninged sections of trendy restaurants that had been allowed to metastasize outside their buildings, running past annoyed diners who failed to recognize that they were the interlopers, not her. Past this were the street vendors selling potted herbs, ghost pepper, tarragon, other kiosks offering henna body art or hand-designed purses. She was in Posertown.

When she'd moved to Los Angeles, this neighborhood still held the remnants of its former character: pawn shops, liquor stores, hair salons, check cashers. Now it was full of ridiculous arts and crafts boutiques, pottery and woodworking seminars, and hand-tooled shingles for useful trades championed by dilettantes. Above all else, it was a subculture obsessed with furniture. Posers gushed over their sofas and end tables, the "culture" of craftsmanship, which lathing and wood-planing classes they'd attended.

She jogged past business after business peddling time wasters to a generation that loved wasting time. In front of King Taco, the former neighborhood's lone holdout, a street vendor sold decals of comical faces to cover electrical outlets. Two doors down, there was the flavored popcorn store with a front door that changed color based on clientele. Next to that, a store sold nothing but binaural headphones shaped like deer antlers. She could understand twenty-somethings living lives of deliberate folly. But the thirty-something posers mystified her. These people had known childhoods of deprivation. How had they so efficiently adapted to the foppery of people who had grown up without hardship?

Posers posed with the trappings of the past. These days it was all modern vaquero style, white cowboy hats and neckerchiefs worn over bolo ties. At least that was better than five years ago, with flabby white boys shaving their heads and wearing wifebeaters with red or blue doo-rags. Vaquero style must be a reaction to those earlier posers. At least that was a little perk of working Central Division, not having to deal with all the skyscraper knuckleheads, real-life gangsters, coming into Boyle Heights to prey on stray posers after hours.

Tony Collazo called, a small picture box of his head opening in the upper-right corner of her view.

"Ayyyyyy. Woman of the hour!"

"It's my day off, Tony," she lied.

"Yeah? Ours too, now." He sounded jovial and slurry. "I'm just calling to thank you for getting us off dogshit detail."

"Huh?"

"That nobody you drew? Turns out he's the shooter on *our* nobody. You just solved us an assload of hassle."

She came to a halt, standing low with her hands on her knees. "Farrukh?"

"Yeah, whatever the fuck the name is, he's the guy that popped our boy Froggy Sarin on the Glendale bridge. We got a pic of his leg scribble from a street sweeper on scene. And that is that, and now we are drunk."

She remembered the tattoo, just below the knob of Farrukh's right ankle, something amateurish in Sanskrit she hadn't deemed worthy of translation.

"How do you know it's not a common tattoo?"

"Hey, because we crossmatched it with three freckles from your crime scene footage, okay? Jesus, you should be happy too, especially considering the news. One more reprobate safely expunged from the realms of malfeasance."

"Glad I could help?"

He hung up, cackling.

She stood and checked her pulse, trying to recalculate the case with Farrukh as a murderer. She didn't look forward to telling Zack. It was the first catch of the decade, and she'd already gotten it wrong.

"Especially considering the news." In the lower margin, she enabled her news crawl, reading "DAUGHTER OF LA DISTRICT ATTORNEY SANTOS KILLED IN POSSIBLE SEX CRIME." She shook her head, murmuring, "This ghetto garbage dump of a city," as she started running back toward her apartment.

After showering and dressing at home, she put on her shades and saw Zack had texted,

Got a lead. Car your way in 5

She peeked out the front window, seeing the car already there, calling Zack back in audio only while hunting for her jacket in the debris field on her bedroom floor. He picked up as she was out the door.

"Okay, where are you?"

"I'm just leaving my place."

"You haven't left yet? I've got something to show you."

"Let me stop walking first," she said, already seeing a display box in her right-hand field of vision, an expectant screen accompanying her down the stairs and out into the waiting car.

"Where am I going?" she asked as the car accelerated.

"Fourth & Olive. So, I went back to twenty minutes before the Swap Meet thing and just walked around the crowd for a while to see if anything looked off. Check this out."

He'd culled footage from the basement into a 2D viewing box, so that she was looking at a scene of a teenage refugee boy bopping down the street. He was fit, with bare, wiry arms and ridiculous permed-out hair, and it was early enough that his EyePhones weren't darkened, so that his nut-brown irises were visible, making him seem even younger and more innocent than he probably was. Although the fact that he owned EyePhones at all marked him as a hustler of one sort or another.

Suddenly the kid looked off in the distance, got spooked, and bolted. Zack had paused and rotated the scene here, drawing a dotted line from the kid's eyes to one of the between-car blinds.

"This guy saw our shooter. And he knew our shooter."

The footage swung back to the kid's face, over which she read GOSWAMI, SANJIV.

"I took the liberty of hunting for a face request, and the kid hasn't popped up since. But in Known Pals . . ."

Three high-relationship names scrolled down. One popped out immediately: Ravi "Bottlecap" Rajagopalan. She didn't know him, but nicknames were always good news when seeking a weak link in a chain. Sure enough, his Relationships box listed the sixteen-year-old as an associate with the 2K SSKs, a couple of outstanding warrants still tagged.

"'Bottlecap,'" Zack said with a slight laugh. "He's down outside the Two Cal plaza right now, milling around in a gaggle of jerk offs. I got a couple eyes circling overhead and some housing contacts in the vicinity, so I think we should be good if he tries to take it back indoors. We squeeze this kid, he gives up Sanjiv, Sanjiv gives us the shooter, boom."

"Hey, yeah, about that. I got word from Tony C. Our boy Farrukh shot and killed, presumably killed, an SSK last week. So, you know, uh, the plot thickens."

"Oops." She could hear him grin in validation.

"I guess I eat it on that call."

"I'm not surprised. Your notes said the guy had EyePhones, and I more or less took that as pre-confirmation that he was indeed a flaming asshole."

She'd seen these shades in random shots pulled from his half-month routeline, Farrukh ditching his actual, non-disposable EyePhones just three days before the shooting, on New Year's Eve, as if he were turning over a new leaf. She'd assumed that this marked Farrukh as a different sort of hustler, a hustler of labor. Even if he made only a hundred dollars a day, he could have still scrimped and saved, maybe found a Swap Meet dealer who did layaway. She'd heard of crazier things.

"He's an asshole just because he had shades?"

"He's an asshole because he killed another asshole. That's the Law of Assholes."

She didn't care for his tone of victory. "That's not an ironclad law."

"How does one of these nobodies afford shades without gang connects?"

"He worked as a delivery guy."

"I'm confused. Our boy's a stone-cold killer. You just told me that. If you're still defending him, what exactly do you think happened?"

"I'm *not* defending him," she said, feeling defensive herself. "I just want the facts kept straight."

"What *are* you saying?"

"That if . . . that just because the guy had shades and at one point a gun doesn't mean he was gang. Maybe he killed in self-defense . . ."

"What?" Zack sounded genuinely incredulous.

"Maybe this guy he shot, Froggy, was blackmailing him, or threatening a family member." Her face went hot from the absurdity of her argument.

"And where do you think he got the gun if not from a gang?"

Terri looked down at her ragged cuticles, paused, then said, "Maybe he made the gun himself. Any meatball can walk into any Office Plus, plunk down $500 for a three-way printer and a tub of Flexum. All he'd need is bullets."

"And five hundred bucks. Which you're saying he would have already spent on a pair of EyePhones."

"Well . . ."

"And where's he going to put a three-way? No gang is gonna let him print up his own arsenal."

"Then maybe he bought the gun from a banger."

"Really. So far the only gangbanger you have him crossed with is this Froggy fellow he shot. You think Froggy gave him the gun?"

The car zipped through the South Olive tunnel, popping the side door as it emerged into sunlight and pulled to the curb.

"I think there are a lot of ways to go on this," she said, stepping onto the narrow, crowded sidewalk, "so just keep an open mind."

"Let the record state that *you* are telling *me* to keep an open mind."

"Yeah, let the record do that." She looked straight up at Two California Plaza, one of the few downtown skyscrapers still referred to by name, its mirrored skin a dull matte from years of unwashed grime. The building's fifty-plus stories always made her nervous this close.

"I'm at the corner," she said.

"Yeah. I see you. Which housing guys are down here now?"

"How the hell should I know?" Zack stood at the foot of a steep staircase teeming with refugees, no one adhering to one side for up or down. Past him, in the opposite direction, she could see the AT&T building that served as a movie screen, its long-removed corporate markings still visible as faint stains.

"I mean, which housing guys are you dealing with on this thing?"

"Oh, uh. Mutty and whatsisface. Hawley."

"Alright." Hawley was probably up for sprints, if it came down to it. "You have a fix on this guy?" She was standing in front of him now.

"Heart of darkness." He pointed across the street, to the overgrown knoll. They strode over to the park, traffic routing around them. John Hawley, limber and bald, emerged from the shade. Behind him, she could make out the dark figures of a half-dozen young men sitting cross-legged, arms behind backs.

"He's still here," Hawley said.

"Good, good. No pointing, so nobody gets the scent, but, down there?" Zack nudged toward the sloped clearing beyond the thicket.

"He's just hanging out with his buddies, smoking joints, picking up girls. He's not going anywhere. Hey," he nodded toward Terri.

"Where'd Mutty get to?"

"We originally came over to pick up some shithead on an attempted murder thing, and then I ran across the boner patrol over here doing hobo fights with rocks. So Mutty's back there with the main guy, waiting on a warrant revision. Back in the thicket," he said, laughing as if he'd made a joke.

She crossed behind them, over to the group of miserable miscreants seated in the shade. The arrest was Zack's thing, so she'd wait for his pacing, follow his lead. Plus, it was good to act nonchalant. If cops barged in to nab him, he'd have enough warning to bolt. They'd need the cover of Mutty to get close. It was classic cat and mouse bullshit, but she wasn't going to be the one to spoil the play for her partner.

As she approached the group of arrestees, Terri frowned at that familiar refugee stink. They smelled like sweat and hot dogs, with a sickly sweet scent of infant: many refugees used baby powder in lieu of showering. Two young uniformed officers stood guard over the bunch. Seeing the face she made, one said, "Stay away from the end."

She followed his stare to the furthest member in the group. He was a dirt man, so thoroughly drenched in filth that he'd been rendered ethnically unrecognizable. All he needed were cartoon stinklines, which, she vaguely remembered, was an app somewhere in PanOpt's sandbox. The man was crying, rocking on the ground, holding his head between two soot-blackened paws.

"How come he's not cuffed?"

"That guy? He's not under arrest. He's just a bystander. Said someone stole his wheelchair."

The other cop laughed. "Who the hell would want to sit in *that*?"

When she made her way back to Zack, she overheard Hawley say, "It was probably just a jump-in gone bad."

"Are you guys talking about Farrukh?" Terri asked.

Neither man spoke, each holding back a smile.

"He was forty-six," she said, guessing an age out of anger. "The guy *worked*."

Hawley looked over her shoulder then gave a thumbs up to the air. "Hey, he's done. Let's go down all casual like, so as not to disrupt the wildlife. Zack, you got a ventriloquist thingy?"

"Yeah, I'm good."

The three of them set down the steep grade of the small park, through the thin stand of trees to a large clearing filled with milling refugees and tangled, ankle-high wild grass. This was a small pocket of heavy gangland. Any one of them coming down here on their own would have been a dangerous act. Even Mutty's solo deal with his catch was problematic, although he'd made clear to everyone that his partner was twenty seconds away, meaning the airborne cavalry—both real and mythical—was less than a minute after that.

They found Mutty halfway down the dirt slope, surrounded by a small flock of steely-eyed middle-aged refugees, all men, muttering and shaking their heads in outrage. The attempted-murder kid stood with hands cuffed behind him, mumbling through tears, "I just wish I could go back and . . . I just wish I could do everything different. But I can't. I can't go back."

"Arrow of time, man." Mutty said, not really listening, moving something invisible in the air before him.

Zack texted,

2 o'clock

She yawned as she turned, seeing a balloon holding the byline for Ravi "Bottlecap" Rajagopalan over a young man standing thirty feet away, one of a half dozen. He didn't have shades, which was a stroke of luck. Yawning once more even harder, she reached into her sign box, pulling up a dozen Affiliation boxes over everyone within Ravi's immediate social circle. For good measure, she expanded Affiliations to label everyone in the park. Terri counted twenty allied SSK sets represented in their immediate vicinity. She turned for a moment, mesmerized by the sheer variety of stupid gang names.

SSK stood for Sky Skraper Krip, a sweeping title appropriated by hundreds of divergent and sometimes-warring gang sets. The range of gang names, in this one division alone, still astonished her: Alpine Disaster SSKs, Knuckle Row Underworld, all the varied Rollin' Figs sets. Then there were the sets named for their buildings; 633 South Fig Sky Kriplas, 505 South Flower playa SSKs, 445 W. 5Th Kop Killa Krips. For every one set whose name nearly rose to witty—Thugee Life Deth Squad, Viet King Kong SSKs—there were twenty with titles so brainless they defied belief. And it always seemed like the sets with the stupidest names were the deepest in membership.

The Sky Skraper Krips lifted their name and aesthetics straight from the lore of gangsta rap and decades of filmic Los Angeles underworld. The SSKs were, in a way, the antithesis of the posers: they'd appropriated their host culture, and mutated the perceived values into something far more potent than the original. In all her dealings with old-timers on the force, she'd never heard any pre-war stories rivaling the sheer barbarity of the newcomers' gangs.

Although the worst of it had been over by the time Terri had made the force. In the old days, warfare raged floor by floor, block by block, replicated outside downtown, on a neighborhood-by-neighborhood basis. After the relative success of the LAPD's targeted drone attacks on automatic weapons—and then all firearms used by labeled gang members—the gangs had reverted to more primitive weapons; slingshots, knives, home-printed zip guns. One industrious set in Century City built a working medieval siege engine, capable of catapulting two hundred pounds of projectile a full city block.

Russian roulette was the most perverse form of jump-in for the SSKs, searing the inductee's psyche from the outset, while simultaneously pruning down the swollen pool of humanity. She'd heard these jump-ins referred to as "decimations," after the Roman military punishments from two millennia earlier. But that form of military killing had at least involved one-in-ten odds. These kids, some not even teenagers, were shooting themselves with home-printed revolvers, so their odds never rose above one in six. Probably even less than that, once you factored in the shitty makes of some of these guns.

Among male refugees ages fourteen to twenty-two, Russian roulette fatalities edged out homicide as the leading cause of death. The ratio was probably higher than that, since some of the bodies were dumped in the middle of nowhere with no explanation. Cops hated this phenomenon only because it further swelled the city's unsolved murder rolls. Zack texted,

In 10, 9, 8 . . .

She braced herself to run.

"Los Angeles police. Down on the ground, Rajagopalan," he said without yelling. She saw Bottlecap look up, as if the voice had come down from the Heavens, and realized Zack was using a public address drone, literally talking down to his target as he approached. "Down. Now."

She and Zack and John Hawley speed-walked out in their best rendition of a pincer movement. All three kept their weapons holstered but hands at the ready, careful not to rile up the crowd any further.

Bottlecap sighed and dropped to his knees in melodramatic slow-mo, raising his arms behind his head in a well-practiced gesture of resignation.

"Man, this is *bull* shit."

Zack was behind him now, the gaggle of teen cronies frittering away nonchalantly as if their buddy had simply been called off for lunch by his mom. Although no one frittered away too far.

"I gotta *go*. I got an important meeting I got to be at!"

Zack laughed and looked at Terri, saying, "I hawing a wery im-poor-tant air-and."

The words came out brittle, Zack fluttering his hands like a Bollywood dancer and then producing a pair of zipcuffs as if he were a stage magician.

"Yo man, that's not what I sound like!"

Bottlecap was right. Skyscraper kids, having grown up without a nation, had no such Old World inflections, their accents instead culled from a century of American movies and songs.

"If you please," Zack continued for his own amusement, "you doing a wery bad im-per-soo-nation of me."

"Pshhht," Bottlecap looked off, unimpressed. "You know in Sweden? Everybody a cop."

"You wouldn't last a second in Sweden, idiot," Hawley said.

Bottlecap looked baffled. "What does that even *mean*?"

Terri took in the crowd, realizing they'd been quickly and efficiently surrounded by the older refugee men. No one had shades, meaning the group was running on unchecked emotion alone. One said something behind her, his words coming out in an unintelligible rush.

"Excuse me?"

He repeated himself, the mellifluous roll of his speech completely undercut by his bizarre stresses.

Zack looked over his shoulder as he hoisted Bottlecap to his feet. "What are you trying to say?"

The man spoke a third time, his anger making his words faster still, triggering subtitles in the lower margins of PanOpt. Terri tried to suppress a snigger as John Hawley laughed out loud. She read,

You can't come down here any time you choose and just drag people off without rhyme or reason!

"Hey, we've got plenty of rhyme," Zack said, grinning, one hand clamped on Bottlecap's elbow, snapping his fingers with the other hand, coming off a little manic.

A second refugee chimed in, older, gray bearded, but with clearer intonations. "This is totally unacceptable. You can't pick people at random from a crowd and drag them off to God knows where."

"You know," Hawley said, "maybe you should take this as a sign from Vishnu to pick a better caliber of city park to relax in."

"What other park?" the man demanded.

"I dunno. Maybe check the directory of 'places not infested with gangland wasteoids?'"

Subtitle Man chimed in,

There is no such! Where are we supposed to go?

"How the hell is that my problem?"

How the hell is that your problem? You run this city! You are the ones in charge!

Hawley darkened. “I never told you guys to come here!”

“And where are we supposed to go?” the older man demanded, his words coming out quick now as well. “Huh? You tell me? Where are we supposed to go? Huh? Where?”

Terri grabbed Bottlecap’s other elbow and said, “Next time, don’t blow up your own country then, moron.”

Among the younger refugees milling in the background, she heard an “oh shit,” and saw several boys staggering off, hands over mouths, suppressing laughter. But the words hit the older refugees like a unified slap in the face. Each stepped back, stunned, unable to make eye contact.

She and Zack brought Bottlecap up the slope and into a waiting cruiser. The car sped off toward the 110, giving them time to interrogate, maybe make the kid nervous if they had an opportunity to zipper through some cars at high speed. Zack had placed him on the jump seat, so that he’d see the rush of the freeway between his two interrogators. Zack wiped his brow and removed his shades for a moment.

“Kid, you are in a world of fuck if you don’t tell me exactly what I need to know.”

Abruptly, Bottlecap started bawling, backing his legs up onto the car seat in sheer terror.

“Don’t put those things on me!”

“What . . .”

“Don’t do it! I’ll talk!” He was snorting back tears and mucus, having gone from nought to a hundred in just a few seconds.

Zack looked down at his PanOpts. “These?”

The kid stared wildly at the shades, as if Zack held a poisonous snake.

“Okay, calm down,” Terri said, hands outstretched. “No one’s putting anything on you. Zack?”

He placed the shades back on his face. “Look. Happy?”

Bottlecap sniffled and nodded, smearing his wet cheek on one shoulder.

Terri retrieved a handful of tissues from her jacket, quickly swiping his face, stuffing the nastiness in the car's waste slot with disgust.

"Jesus, kid. We're going to take a few minutes and when you've got yourself together, we are going to have a friendly discussion. Got it?"

He nodded once without making eye contact.

Zack texted,

What?

She shrugged. The car sped up, hooking onto the I-5, starting into the arc of a citywide loop. They passed through a cloud of animal stink, and Bottlecap looked up, more or less composed again, saying, "Ooh, skunk."

After they'd dropped off Bottlecap on a street corner—but before she'd marinated in the Basement for hours—Terri had waited while Zack bickered with his wife. Five blocks away, they parked below an oak tree obscuring a huge, Mexican-style mural of Gandhi and Nehru, then spent several hours back in the Basement, following leads. When she finally took a break, the sun had already swung to the other side of the street and her leg had cramped enough that she had to exit and do some ham stretches on the sidewalk.

Looking back through the car window, she saw Zack hunkering down, manipulating the air, guiding himself through unseen regions, and Terri grasped that she'd unfairly misjudged her partner. Justice would almost certainly elude Farrukh Jhadav, but it wasn't either of their faults. Throughout her career, cops talked wistfully of the Slide, that stat-obliterating surge of humanity into every American city by the former citizens of its late ally. Even though it had the tone of permanence, some cops still treated the Slide as a temporary condition. But people made more people, and when those new people grew up angry and hermetically disenfranchised, the Slide kept sliding. Every year it got a little more entwined with the other capitalized missions: The Job. The Battle. The Slide.

The initial crisis had reduced Los Angeles to a tide pool; the Slide chipped away at the city's recovery. Convictions for mayhem bumped up by 2%–4% every year, one of a dozen Slide stats that cops continually studied and swapped, like baseball fanatics. The sheer glut of people strained every agency. Mental illness went masked under varied violations—assault, disorderlies, drugs—but everyone knew it was on the rise. Just in the last two years, it had seemed to infect the ranks of first responders, mutating from absurdist gallows humor to something darker. "I've lost my inspiration," one paramedic had told Terri after she'd caught him pissing on a corpse.

Sometime in the late afternoon, Zack slapped his knees and said, "Liney time." He had the car drive them to an alley behind an industrial laundromat, one of several public spots used for meetups, the clang and the billowing steam pretty much obliterating any chance of getting overseen or overheard.

Liney dawdled up ten minutes later. He was a wizened old-timer, a paid informant who tattled on fellow refugees in exchange for restaurant credit. Liney was notoriously unclean, his silver hair glued to his scalp through sheer grime, the creases and crags of his face filled with deep furrows of grit. She'd once glimpsed Liney without his shirt on, in the street, and had been surprised at how sinewy the guy was, beneath the sheen of filth and the thick gray fur of his caved-in chest.

Zack stepped out for their meeting and she heard Liney clap his hands in delight, his greeting lost under the machine noise. She'd always been amused by the guy's speaking voice, both his proper British accent and his weird, third-person delivery. The last time she'd seen him, he'd been wearing bowling shoes, having made the comical, bright-green leather seem almost elegant.

By the time Zack returned, the day had turned overcast, drizzly, and when she pulled up a second weather box, she saw the forecast directly contradicted PanOpt's own row of cartoon suns.

"Maybe my man will finally get a shower," Zack said.

"Anything of consequence come up?"

"Just seeding seeds." He shrugged. "You never know. He's come up with the goods in the past."

At dusk, they both realized they'd never eaten a proper lunch. Five minutes later, they were in Food Truck Alley, Zack ordering some gloppy orange something, Terri getting chicken vindaloo, thinking just for once, she'd love to eat someplace that didn't include chutney or some dank plastic bowl of warm cucumber yogurt. Zack motioned her toward an empty picnic table chained to a tree, then said, "Nope, bird poop, forget it."

"You could just sit away from it."

"Would you say that if a dog did it?"

They agreed on a railing bordering a useless strip of concrete, finding a length where some frustrated vagrant had pried off the bird spikes. Terri tried to balance her meal on her lap, finally giving up, keeping the paper bowl in front of her and placing her tea on the ground, hoping the ceramic mug wouldn't read this as abandonment and report back to its food truck. From this angle, they could view the last strands of dusk across a lot framed by boarded-up buildings. The sky faded without reds, its hues of blue fading straight into pale gradations of gold, and she felt perched on a mountaintop, Olympus, looking down on a vast ocean.

Terri was halfway through her meal when Zack murmured, “The Accursed.”

“Huh?” She glanced down the sidewalk as three figures approached. Two were known vice detectives. When she’d joined the force, vice was just one more division, with all the beats and downtimes of any other unit. Now it was a portal into the inferno. In the wake of the Slide, vice detectives saw the true floor of the city. Most cops she knew used PanOpt’s tweaks and content walls to shield themselves from the raw horror that vice cops wallowed in every day. Within the force, they were a sad caste: The Accursed.

“Hey gang,” Zack said, greeting Carlos Moisey and Trinh Nghiem and a young guy, fit but clearly green about the gills. Carlos was a giant, nearly a head taller than Zack, with colossal hands and forearms. Trinh was a compact, slender blonde. The few times she’d run into them, Terri had always been struck with how utterly in sync they seemed as partners, both operating with that quiet reserve of all Accursed.

“Hey Zack. Hey Terri.” Carlos had a surprisingly gentle voice. “This is Chuck. He just came in from Philly last week. We’re giving him the grand tour.” She and Zack raised their mugs in salute, a measure of pity in the gesture. If this guy got sent to vice straight out, he must’ve severely pissed off someone somewhere. Carlos and Trinh both ate churros; Chuck looked like he might puke.

“So what’s new out there?” Zack asked, making Terri cringe. Asking any questions about the day-to-days of the Accursed seemed hopelessly tone-deaf.

"I was going to ask you how the DA's daughter thing was going. That's all anyone wants to talk about on our end. Must be some scrambling going on for you all."

"Nah, that's Pacific. We're just on dumbass duty until some pretty little college kid gets bumped off in Central."

"I hadn't even been keeping up." Terri finished her tea. "Big story?"

"Yeah, of course. Got all the elements." Carlos's voice was so pleasant and soft, he should've been a therapist. In the air to her left, she brought up a web box and found a photo of Stacy Santos. Zack was right: she was pretty—had been pretty—with a big mane of frizzy brown hair and barely-there dimples. She hadn't just been attractive, but *fresh*, vibrant, the kind of kid you'd want on a college brochure.

Carlos shifted slightly and blocked the streetlight behind them, so that all three were suddenly backlit, like a ghost trio sent to deliver a message. "I heard Juan Santos was supposed to give a press conference at noon, but he was too broken up to even get to the podium."

"I heard they found multiple footprints from the same boots outside each window," Zack said. "That means the shooter cased her house for days, just peeking in like he was watching a TV show."

"It's like *The Walker*," Terri said, always nervous that she'd say the wrong thing around one of the Accursed.

"Yeah," Trinh agreed. "Creepy."

Chuck the Trainee cleared his throat. "What's that?"

"*The Walker* . . . you never saw that show?" Zack asked. "Huh. I guess it's set in LA I'd just kind of assumed everyone had seen it. It's this program about . . . shit. How do I describe it?"

"The Walker is a person who walks through walls," Terri explained. "The whole program is shot from the Walker's perspective. The Walker just walks around. Sometimes the Walker walks through buildings. Sometimes the Walker walks through fields. Sometimes, if you watch at night, you'll catch the Walker walking through empty businesses, libraries, kitchens." Goose bumps rose on her forearms.

"It's like those drones that float around in Asia," Trinh said. "Making new drones, sending their reports back like someone was still watching." Carlos shifted again, and in the fresh streetlight, Terri saw a look of utter desolation on Chuck the Trainee's face.

"Hey, yeah." Zack took a bite of his orange glop, continuing with his mouth full. "I'm supposed to ask. We had this weird thing where this banger wannabe started crying when he saw my shades. You have anyone do that to either of you?"

This time Terri actually made a face at Zack, trying to convey that he needed to quit it with the cop talk, to let the Accursed be.

Trinh said, "Oh yeah. The blinding thing."

"What blinding thing?"

"It's the new rumor going around. Someone somewhere got it into his head that we've been getting gang kids alone and using our PanOpts to blind them."

"Blind them how? Huh?"

"I think the rumor is that PanOpts are set to blind anyone who isn't the assigned user. You know, if someone finds a pair in the street."

"Even if that was true, I wouldn't place my shades on any of these nasty meatballs." Zack belched lightly, patting his stomach. "Get that shit testing cootie positive? No, thanks."

She arrived at her building just as a warning spritz burst into rain. The apartment, dark, silent except for water slapping windows, seemed to be someplace she'd found temporary shelter for the night. The lethargy was here, a mystery fatigue that hit whenever she was in her own space with no clear-cut goal. Tired without doing anything, she tried to figure out why she felt so horrible. The news about Froggy wasn't it, although Tony Collazo had done a decent job of ruining her morning run.

After they'd dropped off Bottlecap on a street corner, Terri had waited while Zack bickered with his wife. She'd gone into a bar to use the john and stumbled into a round of mid-afternoon karaoke, refugees and unemployed citizens mauling their favorite tunes in front of each other. When she'd come out of the restroom, an overweight black lady in mismatched goodwill clothes had taken the stage. The woman had sung an old, slow-tempo soul song, something about someone she'd loved who had done her wrong. And although her delivery was halting, she'd had a nice voice and real sense of conviction, as if the woman had picked this song out of millions because it resonated with her own backstory, so determined was she to tell her tale in song, at least once, here in this mid-day beer den. Something about that faltering insistence had moved Terri, shaken her, and when she'd emerged back out onto the street she'd felt that familiar wobbliness, the rug of life pulled out from underfoot once again.

Terri kept thinking about the look on the face of that trainee, Chuck from Philly. Whatever it was he'd seen had clearly shattered him. She'd give the guy a month, tops, followed by twice as long on the Blue Dot. She kept returning to the riddle behind the expression. What had he seen? Her fascination was the fulcrum so many horror films should have used but seldom did: never show the scare. She imagined it would have to be something involving a child. She herself had witnessed some deep horrors on the job, accidents, burns, suicides, crooks crushed or impaled in the act of wrongdoing, shut-ins left to decompose or get eaten by their own starving pets. But nothing had ever stuck with her the way just a half-dozen child abuse cases had, images so circuit-trippingly terrible that they registered as comedy, several times actually eliciting belly laughs from her and other responding officers, although they lingered in eternal afterimages.

She slumped on the couch, drained, counting backward from twenty to will herself up and into bed. The rain came down harder now, lashing the windows, again leaving her with the impression that she'd crawled into an uninhabited culvert somewhere for the night. Terri involuntarily thought of the old house, the house she'd put so much of herself into and was now exiled from forever. She'd never set foot inside that house again.

She couldn't bear the thought that every year, little by little, her memories of the house in South Pasadena were slipping away. Of course, the entire house was still there, in her old shades, which now sat uncharged in a box in the rafters of her aunt's garage, getting frozen every winter. Maybe her aunt could ship the box back. Terri could take them to a service, get the footage scrubbed of Gabriella, so she could just look at the house again. But how could she ever bear to look at it again?

Pulling up the coverlet, she thought about falling asleep in that house while it was raining. She remembered listening to the drizzly aftermath of a storm from the back bedroom. There'd been an acoustic depth to the unlit enclosure behind the house, an unexpected complexity of sounds. She'd laid perfectly still, concentrating on the nearby rhythms of dripping eaves, beats and pats on the roofs, further gurgles from new furrows in regions normally thought of as flat, droplets falling from leaf to leaf, rendering one uniform region—the blank canvas of a dark backyard—in sudden, unexpected, exploded view. In her apartment now, there was only the rain, flat and unwavering.

On Thursday morning, Bottlecap was forty-five minutes late.

"Good," Zack whispered when they finally saw him speed-walk toward the car, parked in a shaded red zone downtown. The kid read their faces before he got the door open.

"Wait. Let me explain."

"He's got two open warrants," she said to Zack, as if it were still just the two of them in the car together. "And don't get me started on that thing he did last summer. I've got a busy afternoon, so I vote we take him in now."

"Last summer?" Bottlecap said, eyes wide, his mouth a tight little circle.

"Yeah, last summer, Tonto," Zack said, winging it, seeing over Bottlecap's head only two warrants for who-gives-a-shit assaults, both against gang members. "You really think we don't know what you did?"

"Look, I had to get Johnny down here! That takes *time*," he whined.

"Who the hell is 'Johnny'?"

"Sanjiv. He owes me money. So I had to like, call someone and then have that someone call someone. But he'll show. Just, he's going to be in like a mask and shades, so you'll need me to point him out." It took Terri a moment to remember the name, Sanjiv Goswami, the kid who'd allegedly seen the shooter.

"When," she said.

"Soon. Maybe . . . an hour."

"How far away?"

"Four blocks from here."

"You know we're going to be watching your every move, right?"

"I know that."

"And if you screw this up, if you try to run, if you deviate in any way, we're going to sick a SWAT team on you," she said. "I mean that literally. We will literally use precious city resources to apprehend you with a specialized paramilitary platoon of two five-man units. For that thing you did last summer."

Bottlecap nodded with ridiculous eagerness, suddenly the best kid in the class.

"So *go*." She watched him scurry out and across the street, tagging him for real-time surveillance.

"Why are these guys so suspiciously susceptible to bullshit?" she asked.

"Christ, I'm sick of negotiating with losers. Tricking losers for loser intel on loser corpses," Zack said. "Why couldn't a hot naked celebrity have stabbed another hot naked celebrity?"

"Uh-huh." She was following Bottlecap's progression around the corner.

"With a sharpened Oscar statue."

"Yuh-huh."

"Instead, we got the worst of both worlds."

"What worlds?"

"Take that vice team, last night. Carlos and whatserface."

"Trinh."

"Yeah. So, okay, they're not dealing with any glamour killings. Fine. But at least they're down there in the real shit. If you're going to deal with scum then, you know, do it. Get dirty. Don't waste time with bums like this Farrukh guy."

"Yup. Scums not bums," she said, seeing that Bottlecap had slowed to a leisurely strut as soon as he'd cleared the corner. Did the kid really not understand that she was watching him?

"And then fucknuts like Babylon Johnson get Stacy Santos?" Zack continued. "Where's the cosmic justice?"

"Probably a lot of pressure on Babs right about now. Think about that."

"What pressure? You and I know who did it."

"We do?"

"Yeah. Farrukh killed her."

She whistled a high note. "Postmortem homicide. I'd never considered that angle."

"I'm serious. Some other Farrukh out there got tired of collecting cans, hiked out to a nice neighborhood and cut this girl's throat for kicks."

"Open and shut."

"This isn't a goddamn joke. These guys are *laughing* at us, watching all of us spin our wheels." He motioned toward two barefoot Indian men speed-walking down the sidewalk, a rigid stretcher hoisted across both sets of shoulders and piled high with food cartons.

"I don't think any taco wallas are laughing at us."

"You're not even listening to me."

"Yeah," she said, not listening, always slightly entranced by these worker-ants of the city, ceaselessly performing the repetitive, anonymous functions of food transport.

The taco wallas had evolved from the dabbawallas, men who'd once delivered lunch throughout the offices of urban India. After the war, the system had reorganized itself in the new world with a fierce tenacity, offering two things Americans could not offer themselves; a tireless work ethic and superhuman punctuality. The taco walla system was vital to the new economy, hundreds of thousands of home or workstation employees being situated far from restaurants or food truck corridors. But where the walla profession had once served as the first shallow step toward upward mobility, it was now only a means for barebones survival. A glut of labor had boiled all the profession's innovations and offerings down to one crucial variable: price. It was one more race to the bottom.

Lacking costumes, these men were known by their wares, cylindrical metal containers for home-cooked meals and the increasingly frequent box lunches from caterers. It was a network entirely outside the networks, using color-coded tins for routing, so that the meals could slip from courier to courier, regardless of literacy, never slowing the supply chain. The only other system that could approach the cruel efficiency of the taco wallas was automated, the amazing-that-it-actually-works glove-box packet-switching network of cars. "The awful freight of the world": where had she heard this phrase?

"We're probably gonna be cooped up in this car all day."

"No one's keeping you in this car," she said. "Let's walk a beat around the block. Maybe you'll come across an Oscar stabbing."

They exited into the sun. She trailed Zack as he instinctually followed Bottlecap's path across the street, even as she kept the kid's whereabouts active, seeing the pictogram pulse in the distance, visible through buildings. Approaching the curb, she saw with amusement that Zack faced a route choice. To their right was a convenience store, pitting his strong love of snacks against his deep-seated need to do everything clockwise.

They walked north, away from the store. Halfway down the block, they passed a pair of uniformed street cops she didn't recognize. The officers had stopped two adolescent kids, both black and both seemingly bored. One kid's T-shirt showed Arnold Schwarzenegger as the Terminator, with new wave glasses and a short, punky haircut, the words below this image reading COP KILLER. The second kid was taller, his shirt reading HIGH

ON HATE. The street cops seemed more amused than anything else, pointing from one shirt to the other, presumably alerting any of their coworkers who might be watching. As they passed, Terri heard the bigger kid say, "It's a restaurant, asshole," with a surprisingly deep voice. She wondered who else was watching this disrespect unfold in real time. She thought of the stores down by the bus station that sold cop piñatas.

Even before the next intersection, they could smell the toilet tent. In Central Division alone, the city had built a dozen latrine shelters; sprawling, squalid enclosures under cheery sea-green-and-white-striped canopies, with separate-sex bathroom, washing, and bathing areas. She'd entered one only once, chasing a kid who'd set an animal control van on fire. The stench had hit her as something physical, like chemical warfare. The skyscrapers had hundreds upon hundreds of bathrooms, but it was nearly impossible to monitor or control which gang used those facilities as rewards or punishments. Although it was really the city that was being punished. The last mayor had even set up a toilet tent in City Hall park.

Turning the corner, the stench hit full-force. A young woman walked toward them, holding her long black hair over her nose, like an air filter. Terri took in the lengthy lines of men—women and girls being on the far side—some refugees, some homegrown homeless. The paved half lot next to the tent had become parking for every manner of human-powered conveyance. Three-wheelers, pedal cabs, Bodaboda bikes; all types of personal transport were represented. Or were they? She'd heard of human rickshaws operating in the maw of Watts, sinewy, desperate men essentially offering long-distance piggy-back rides in the street.

At least none of these people had to worry about toilet spies. All LAPD-facility toilets compiled personal health info from the leavings of their users, tallying gut flora and precancerous cell counts and blood anomalies. The information was pull and not push—revealed to officers only when asked for—but it was still unnerving. Bathrooms at LAPD workstations were among the cleanest in the city. No one ever used them.

"Hey, if you don't want to chance it, here's your chance," she said. "No smart toilets in the TP teepee."

They'd arrived back at the Oxxo, the same convenience store she'd seen from the car. Even at the far end of the block, the stench, or the sense-memory of the stench, slightly turned her stomach.

"All that walking, I deserve a treat," Zack said. "Want anything?"

She shook her head as he continued into the store. Peering in the window, she saw all the sales notices were written in an odd and oddly popular font, with each letter composed of cartoon bones.

"Detective Pastuszka?"

She turned, ready to deliver another lecture on Proper Etiquette For Approaching A Cop, realizing instead that she faced Chandrika Chavan, the public representative of the Refugee Advocate Of Los Angeles. Chavan was around her age, plump but pretty, if one could somehow ignore the fat red scar that ran up the left side of her throat. The scar seemed perfectly positioned over an artery. On her sari, one large metal button read RECOGNIZE.

"Yes?" Terri had never spoken with Chavan, but the lady's reputation loomed large.

"Detective, I'd like to know what you're doing about the murder of Farrukh Jhadav."

Her accent was unreadable. There were cops who claimed to be able to place older refugees within three sentences: Bengali, Gujrati, Punjabi, which group were mumblers, which group would give attitude, and who would come off as emotionally unreadable. But of course there were so many other variables to consider: who was Hindu, Muslim, Christian, or Sikh; who'd come from Mumbai, or Delhi, or the crushing sprawl of Uttar Pradesh; who was a former mogul, or middle-class, or semi-literate, or street flotsam; who belonged to what caste, and who still obeyed the phantom gravity of the castes; who had pollinated what convoluted political beefs from the doomed country, and which of those beefs were state-level, and which were national. The matrix of permutations was vast. Somewhere deep in PanOpt was a world-class learning program, complete with glossaries, charts, overlays, and dialect guides. She didn't know a single cop who'd ever bothered to check it out.

"Now, you know I can't comment on an ongoing investigation. So why even ask?"

"I'm asking because we're very concerned that a thorough investigation be conducted. Do you know how many refugees were murdered in Los Angeles last year?"

Terri sighed, calculating that it was easier to see her way through this conversation than to dismiss it. "Not off the top of my head."

"Three hundred and eighty-eight. Do you know how many cases were solved?"

"Again, not off the top of my head."

"Twenty-two. These are people with families, communities . . ."

"Tell me something I don't know, lady."

Chavan had prepared for this, raising one finger in the universal gesture of lecturing. "Okay. Let me tell you a little about Farrukh. He got out of Kolkata two days before the war, made it onto an IACA boat convoy, wound up in Malaysia, then Darwin, finally ending up in the Santiago aid camp for six years. Six years with no word from his family, no home, no job. Eventually he meets his brother and three nieces, gets his gold card, tries to find work. But of course there aren't jobs for forty million extra people in South America, and there are jobs in Mexico. So the five of them set out on foot to Toluca. That's a three thousand-mile walk."

"Yeah, how'd they get across the Panama canal? Doggy paddle?" Terri resisted the urge to point out that Farrukh had seen more of the world than she had.

"No, they sold one of the daughters for passage. The next-oldest died before they reached their campsite. He lived and worked there for eight years, mowing lawns, each year making a little less than the last because Guatemalans and Hondurans can work cheaper. Did you know Farrukh had a master's degree in civil engineering?"

"Izzat a fact."

"Eventually they get priced out, his brother dies of strep, Farrukh goes north with the last daughter. He got into LA four months ago."

For a moment, Terri seriously considered letting slip that Farrukh also shot a gangbanger and pushed his body off a bridge. Instead, she said, "Despite what you may or may not think about the investigative abilities of the LAPD, let me assure you that I am doing everything possible to locate and then apprehend the killer or killers of Farrukh Jhadav."

"Really. Because . . ."

"Yeah, really. I take this case as seriously as any other on my plate."

" . . . because it would be a shame if someone were to get ahold of the comments you made at Angel's Knoll yesterday. Something about 'next time, don't blow up your country.'"

"That would be a real shame," Terri said, taking a half step into Chavan's airspace. "Seeing as how it'd be a felony violation of state anti-wiretapping statutes."

"It would be interesting to see what would happen if they ever tried to enforce that law. Look, I'm not trying to threaten anything . . ."

"Damn straight you're not."

"I want to offer my services." Chavan held out a cream-colored business card. "If there's any way my office can help, just give us a call."

Terri took this and decided not to say anything else, tucking it into a jacket pocket and turning abruptly, walking the twenty feet back to where Zack stood with his large soda, having watched the encounter go down with his mouth slightly open. He waited until Chavan had walked off, back toward the toilet tent.

"What the hell did *she* want?"

"What do you think? She knows we're on the case and wants to know why it hasn't been solved yet."

"Why? Just because I stopped in here for a drink?"

"Yeah. *That's* why."

"Huh." They watched Chavan stride off, one shoulder of her sari flapping in the toilet-tent stench. "Maybe *she* killed Farrukh," Zack added.

They continued back to the car.

"Pssht," he said. "'R-A-L-A.' They don't even have the human . . . dignity to stick a plural in there. 'Advocate.' Like they're the one and only."

"Right." She felt strangely drained.

"And does RALA do squat for Turkish refugees?"

"In LA? All three of them?"

"You know what I mean."

An hour and a half later, Bottlecap finally called.

"I'm here in Pershing Square, near the . . ."

"I know," she said. "I can see you, remember? Also, that's a lot farther than four blocks."

"Yeah, well, I had to call my boy Sup, on account of . . ."

"I don't care. No one cares. Is Sanjiv there?"

"Yeah, he's here. So, he's wearing this kind of brown jacket with . . ."

"*Tag* him. Jesus. Just blip a tag on his head and flip it to me. We'll do the rest."

"Yeah, yeah. Okay, yeah . . ."

The car pulled out, Zack jolting up from a nap. At the park, they circled a few times, seeing Sanjiv Goswami in dark shades and a dust mask. She'd come up with a contingency act to get them close without raising suspicions, but on the second pass around the park, Sanjiv moved to cross the street at the same moment they passed, walking right up to the car without knowing what he was doing. All they had to do was slow down and pop the side door, Zack lunging out and grabbing the kid like it was a political kidnapping in some third-world country.

Sanjiv struggled in the back seat for the five seconds it took to figure out who they were, one flying punch coming perilously close to Zack's chin. Zack ripped off the dust mask and slapped him across the face, hard enough to knock the EyePhones off.

"Sanjiv Goswami, you witnessed a murder on Monday morning and you didn't report it to the authorities," Zack said, worked up into a bullying fury. Terri always secretly enjoyed these rare transformations, Zack channeling all his bulk and resentments into something approaching theater, a type of drama as over-the-top as Nick Charles's suspect gatherings. She thought, *Didn't this kid only witness a shooter?*

"What? Naw, man!"

"Yeah, you did. Put those back on," Zack said, motioning to the shades. Sanjiv did this, his hand fluttering.

"You watch old cop movies?"

"Yeah, okay," Sanjiv said, impatient in his desire to say the right thing.

"You know 'good cop bad cop'?"

The kid nodded idiotically.

"I'm the good cop. So what happens now is, you go back to Monday morning at 5:14 a.m. You were on South Fig, walking home after a long night. You're going to retrieve that footage and then you're going to link me on the playback. If I see any funny stuff—seizure-flash, booby traps, snuffy-crush films, *anything* I might find personally objectionable—my partner here is going to take off her PanOpts, place them on your face, and blind out your eyeballs. We clear?"

He nodded slowly, mouth pinched tight.

"Let's do this then. Monday morning. 5:14."

Sanjiv reached up into the air, his timid hand gestures birdlike as he called up his own playback. Zack said, "Good, good . . ."

She nudged Zack in the ribs for a link. He tagged her back and then she was looking at the same pre-dawn Swap Meet scene he'd already shown her, but from a first-person POV. She wondered if he'd memorized which cars they were supposed to be looking at. Under a streetlight, something fluttered, the POV suddenly shifting, following a dimly lit moth as it passed overhead and then trembled down into a space between two cars. Then the footage was of running, first-person bolting down the street.

"Oh Christ," Zack said. "Is this Monarch? Are you doing Monarch? Pull up your desktop."

The running footage was now overlaid with dozens of ridiculous civilian apps. In Sanjiv's upper-left field of vision, she saw a box reading MONARCH WARNING. She pulled up her PanOpts as they slowed and pulled to a curb, Zack having already commandeered the car's control box.

"Out."

Sanjiv exited, looking both bewildered and crestfallen, as if he'd failed an initiation.

"What? What happened?" she asked as the door closed back up, Zack palming his face.

"It's a *game*. For housewives. Monarch. Janice plays it. They get points for doing things, like if you do certain tasks, more butterflies show up. It's fucking stupid."

"Huh?"

"He saw the 'black butterfly of death.' If it touches you, you lose points. That's all. No shooter."

"Wow," she said, placing a hand on the back of her neck, trying to come up with some witty punchline to the morning and then thinking better of it.

They stopped at a workstation, and while Zack was in the men's room, Krista called to say she'd gotten the day off from school, asking if they could meet up for lunch. Terri agreed a little too quickly. Every month she worried that her hold on Krista's respect seemed more and more tenuous. When Zack emerged, he seemed taken aback.

"You're going to let a ten-year-old girl ride alone into downtown?"

"Krista's thirteen."

"Since when?!"

"What kind of question is that?"

"She good thirteen or bad?"

"What's the difference?"

"Good thirteen is 'kissing is gross.'"

"I don't know. Which were Ashley and Audrey?"

"Those two idiots were on their second marriages by thirteen."

Krista had chosen Jazz Hands, some fancy restaurant of unknown, high-end cuisine, just two long blocks down from City Hall. Maybe her niece had thought she was being considerate by picking someplace close by, but on the three-minute ride, Terri realized she should've steered them toward someplace outside her jurisdiction. There were too many street scums who could recognize her, too many chances for people from her one life to make a cameo in her other, better life.

As the car brought her down from the state park, it had to shoot through the human gauntlet, the ever-present scrum of protestors outside the front entrance to City Hall, swamping both sides of the street. Sometime in the last decade, these scenes had solidified into a daily scenario: outraged citizens, victims' families, clashing advocates demanding whatever undeliverable version of justice they felt would keep the earth from flying off its axis in outrage.

The public's capacity for self-delusion never ceased to amaze her. Citizens allowed themselves to accept the most amateurish of footage; faked political exposés with bad dialogue, continuity errors, time codes that made no sense, impossible police interrogation scenes, nighttime phone calls between investigators, even courtroom testimony—which any adult knew was not recordable—showing officers discussing framing suspects, sometimes so clumsily executed that the forgers left in the swells of background music from whatever movie they'd cribbed from. It was all fantasy, a million fantasies, tens of millions, the unrestrained psychic canvas for the entire city and the connected world beyond. She kept remembering that, how many of the world's eyes were on them, even now that the Southland had abdicated both its entertainment and aerospace thrones.

Making everything one shade more confusing, every now and then an actual bit of real life got mixed up in the ocean of falsity. Five years ago, someone actually obtained three-angle, immersive footage of Bob Delagarza spelling out the framing of a small crew of go-nowhere stick-up kids in Morningside, fessing up to his misdoings in language so expository he sounded like a comic-book villain. Perhaps he'd thought the absurdity of his dialogue would have covered him in the event that anyone taped anything, although no one would ever know for sure. The day after the indictment came down, he had his car drive him into the Mojave, took a fire axe to the dashboard, and climbed into the trunk with a bottle of Cutty Sark. By the time his wife had the force do a search for him the next afternoon, he'd been cooked.

Her car pulled up to the restaurant, and she was shocked to see her niece standing aimlessly on the sidewalk. Daytime streetwalking wasn't really a thing this far from West Ninth, and Krista's jeans and hoodie weren't the standard candy girl getup. But her pensive body language and lack of a backpack radiated vulnerability.

"You should have waited for me inside," Terri said as she stepped onto the sidewalk, masking her annoyance.

"Oh, it's okay. I like the sun."

As she held the door open for Krista, she instinctually looked for a No Cash sticker, finding it discreetly placed on the wood frame of the door itself; a small circle showing a red slash over George Washington's head, a wordless warning for illiterates. Years ago, there'd been a fizzled federal effort to force retail businesses to accept cash, which had meant accepting refugee business. In those days, No Cash signs had been actual signs, not stickers, able to be quickly removed if and when an inspector came. These days, no one even acknowledged the law. Accepting cash meant tapping into the vast refugee economy, but between the hassles of dealing with actual refugees and the hypothetical risk of vandalism by anti-immigration groups, most ground-level shops and eateries in Central didn't bother.

An unsmiling young man in a black apron seated them toward the back and brought menus and thin glasses of fizzy water. The walls sported smooth butcher paper covered with elegant, swooping line art drawings of celebrities that fell somewhere between caricature and respectful portraiture. Krista sat down with her back to the wall, flanked by Jackie Chan and Humphrey Bogart. Oddly, autographs accompanied both drawings.

"Fancy place you picked."

"Grammy Jane gave me some money for Christmas."

"So how'd you get the day off, anyway?"

"There was a gas leak in the gymnasium. Mr. Leverence threw up in front of an assembly, but I didn't see it. Everyone got sent home."

"Sweet," Terri said, feeling dumb for saying it. There was some relief that Krista was still a kid, not as developed as her VT had led Terri to believe. She wondered if her niece had set up her own online representation to show her more grown than she actually was. Perhaps this was a service telecom companies provided to their adolescent clients. Or maybe it was the new default.

"How's Rex?"

"He's okay," Krista said with a drop on the last syllable.

"Meaning . . ."

"Uhn. He's always asking me questions. Like, 'How was your test' or 'What do you want for dinner?'"

"What a nightmare."

Krista studied her menu with pursed lips. After they'd ordered, she said, "Aunt Terri, did you hear about the girl from that college who got killed?"

"Girl from that college. Stacy Santos?"

"Yeah, her. Do you know anyone working on that case?"

"No. Not directly."

"I thought maybe you did."

"Why, you have a hot tip?"

Krista hesitated, then leaned in across the table and half-whispered, "I heard she had her head cut off. And the guy who did it? He shipped it to her *dad*. On his birthday."

"Huh?"

"And it was wrapped up like a present, like in a box with gift paper and a big ribbon on top. And there was a card, with the present? And the card said, 'This is the only way I could get your attention. Please catch me. Don't let me kill again.'"

"That makes zero sense."

"Oh." Krista leaned back, looking disappointed. "I guess it doesn't."

"Sorry. Good rumor. But yeah, I can guarantee it didn't happen like that. And the father is the District Attorney, not the chief of police. So he prosecutes criminals, he doesn't 'catch' anybody."

"Yeah. Who knows what happened, I guess."

"Well . . . just not that."

"I mean, maybe she wasn't even killed in the first place."

"Say what?"

"Most of the news is fake anyway."

"That's not true," Terri said, genuinely distressed. "Do you think that?"

"Sure. Everyone knows it."

"I don't."

"There's all kinds of fake news. You could see one show with something about a bank robbery, and in the next news show, the bank robbery could be completely different. Like, maybe the guys were refugees or from Brazil or something."

"Yeah, but . . ."

"And then, really, it's just whoever made that news show, they're the one changing or making up the footage because they're prejudiced."

"I don't think that happens as much as you think it does."

Krista widened her eyes. "It happens all the time!"

"Look. When you watch the news, you really have to look out for two things. First, what's the agenda? Nine times out of ten, really ninety-nine times out of a hundred, they're going to be removing things, not adding them. An Orthodox Jewish news feed might remove women from news stories, or a Scientology feed might take out politicians they don't like. Then there are the business interests. You ever watch any of the Odeon networks?"

"Sometimes"

"Okay. So their parent corporation is owned by one of the biggest shipping companies in the world. Which means when there was that strike a few years ago at the Port, Odeon just didn't cover it. Or if there's something about, I don't know, shipping lane piracy in the Philippines, they probably won't cover that either. But it's not a problem. Because I know that other news outlets will cover it."

"But how do you know who owns what in the first place?"

"Well, that's the second part. There are plenty of news outlets that are trustworthy, and if you pay attention to their media coverage, they'll spell out a lot of the details about who owns what, and who covers what. The *New York Times* has a great webroom. Which you'd probably never go to, right? But that's fine, I'm sure all the same content is available in the Overlay. The point is, they're a reliable outlet. Same with Viscera, and CSM and MCVN. They make money because they want people to be able to trust them. They need people to trust them."

"*Yeah*," Krista said, coming off almost sarcastic. At least she wasn't itching to peek at her own shades, like every other kid her age.

"If you have a question about a news story, you know you can always call me, right? The police department has the best news feed in the country. Or maybe second best. Chicago's is pretty good."

"Well, how do the police know what's not fake?"

"We have an entire division dedicated just to the networks. The Wall?"

"I know that."

"Well, then you know that a big part of what they do is verification work. We have to have accurate information, because our lives could depend on that information. So the people who work the Wall make sure we have reliable intelligence from verified news sources and surveillance."

"But how do you know the information *those* sources give you is real?"

"What do you mean?"

"If someone can fake a news story somewhere else, why couldn't someone fake the information that the police get?"

"Because . . . because they can't."

"But why?"

Terri rubbed an eyebrow, groaning softly. "Because there are safeguards, for starters. The little *R* in your EyePhones, in the corner? That means what you're watching is real . . ."

"I know *that* . . ."

" . . . so if you see that *R*, you know it's real."

"But couldn't someone just fake the little *R*?"

"Where would they play their faked footage? There's no machine anywhere in the world built in the last twenty years that will present unauthenticated content as real content."

"Why can't someone just build a pair of EyePhones that could play anything?"

"Because it wouldn't be possible."

"Why not?"

"It's sophisticated equipment. You'd need a warehouse, and network components, and secrecy . . . it just wouldn't be possible to get all the parts you need to build something that could bypass all the mechanical safeguards."

"Why?"

She flashed back to conversations she'd had with Krista back when her niece was a large toddler, meeting every patient explanation with that word—*Why?*—trying to break the world down into its atomic components. Terri sighed.

"Basically, it comes down to trust. Why do we trust the power grid, or the traffic system, or that trains will transport food to supermarkets? A madman could poison the water supply, and yet we still use our sinks and showers. For that matter, the waiter could poison our food now. But what would be the motive for someone to poison us? How could they do it and not get caught? There are a million safeguards out there so that we all trust the system we need to, you know? Look, take your volumetric telepresence—your VT—as one example," she said, inwardly wincing that she'd just tried to make herself look smart to a thirteen-year-old.

"When I call you, you could have your VT set any way you want. You can sit, you can stand, you could float around the room. You could even set your own appearance any way you want. You could be Abe Lincoln if you want. I had to deal with a guy once, for a case, who would only answer the phone as a cartoon hippo. True story.

"Point is, no matter what or how your VT is set, I still know it's you. The system tells me it's you. And because I have faith that this system is safe, I'll continue to use it. Otherwise, no one would use it."

"I guess."

"Or take money. What is money? It doesn't have value in and of itself. If you get a hundred dollars from Grammy Jane, it's still just a number with a value attached to it. You can't hold that hundred dollars in your hand. But you know it's in your Geist account, and that it has value, and that the bank will honor that value, and anywhere else you want to spend it, it will have value. We all believe in it, so it exists. If these systems don't work, then the systems wither and die and people establish new systems. If you think about it, that's really all we have. Without that basic human trust, people would just go around killing each other."

"Like someone killed Stacy Santos?" Krista said, smiling slyly.

Terri rolled her eyes, letting her gaze stay at the kitchen door, its narrow view of spotless tiles and stainless steel. Finally, she said, "Yeah, but we're going to catch this guy. Thus reinforcing public trust."

"Do you really think he'll get caught?"

"Yeah. I do."

"But aren't there lots of unsolved murders and stuff every year?"

"Sure. And this one is different."

"Why?"

"Because Juan Santos is the District Attorney. And the police work extra hard to catch someone who kills a family member of the District Attorney's office."

"That's not fair! What about all the other people that get killed? They're not as important as the District Attorney?"

Thinking, *Tell me about it*, she said, "Hey, I'm just the messenger. But that's a big part of being a cop. You have to make compromises, every day."

Krista sighed. "That's what Rex says."

"Rex says that about being a claims adjustor?" Terri sighed and took in the room again. "Just don't believe everything you see on *Mind Narc.* Real-life police aren't that exciting."

"Yeah, okay."

Two weeks earlier, over the long holiday dinner, Krista had described the entire plot of *Mind Narc* to Terri as if she'd never heard of the show.

"You know, when I was your age, girls weren't that into science fiction. Is this just something you like on your own? Or is this something the girls at your school watch?"

"I don't know. All *my* friends watch it. Stacy, Jean, Paula . . ."

"I guess that's good news."

"Good news? Why?"

"Back in old timey times, kids who were super into sci-fi were the last ones to wind up kissing other kids in a closet."

Krista smiled but didn't blush, saying nothing.

Terri rose for the bathrooms, saying, "The correct answer is, 'kissing is gross.'"

In the bathroom, the over-lit faux-depression tiles hurt her eyes, and she found the first stall so spectacularly clean that she wanted to just stand there and admire the toilet for a moment. Not that she trusted public toilets. Hadn't there been an Overlay magazine, a while back, dedicated just to the excreta of celebrities?

She arrived back at the table to see their food had arrived. Krista sat hunched over. Terri thought she was laughing at the portions until she sat, seeing the tears streaming down her niece's face.

"Hey . . ."

"They want to kick me off the swim team," Krista blubbered.

"Oh. Why?"

"Because . . . of the stupid game . . ." she sniffled. "With the teacher."

"Strangers on a train."

"Yeah," her shoulders hunched once in a sob.

"Wow. That's a rough break."

"They had a guy come from the school police, and he took me out of class in front of everybody."

"Yeah, that's what they do." A wave of anger flashed over her—anger at the LAUSD cops for humiliating a thirteen-year-old, at the poor kid's teachers and administrators for presumably allowing this sad scene to unfold—so that it took her a moment to process when Krista looked up at her with tear-streaked cheeks and said, "Do you know anybody in the school police? Is there any way you could, maybe, fix this?"

That afternoon, back in the Basement, Terri called up the shooting of Deo "Froggy" Sarin, wondering why a gang member would pick or accept a nickname far less scary than his real name. He'd been shot on the bridge that turned into Glendale Boulevard. Replay started at 4:20 a.m. on December 30, the bridge empty except for Froggy and a lonely street sweeper on its sad, eternal mission to make the city a little less dirty.

Froggy walked south, a scrappy little guy hunched over in the rain. In the margin, his rap sheet and associations showed ties to two different trafficking groups, both managed by the IKDK SSKs, a mid-level gang set based around Pico-Union. He looked angry, probably brooding over whatever sorry set of circumstances had him on foot in the middle of the night. Below him, the dark waters of a storm surge rushed by in a blur.

Farrukh approached from the south, dressed in a hoodie and face mask, impersonating his own future assassin. He walked directly up to Froggy, only drawing the gun in the last few seconds. The gun wasn't homemade, meaning it surely would have had its serial number filed off. Froggy said something lost to time, there being no audio on the bridge. Farrukh raised the gun, firing once into the other man's chest or shoulder.

Froggy stumbled backward, tottering against the low pedestrian wall. Farrukh simply walked up, placed one hand against the wounded man's chest, and gently shoved him headlong into the dark, rushing waters. Collazo had been right: there was probably no way anyone could survive a drop like that.

She realized a lone coyote had padded halfway down the bridge toward them. The animal took in the troubling scene with a cocked head. She'd heard their calls almost nightly, back in South Pasadena; not the distant cinematic howls of wolves, but childlike yips that would set off all the dogs in the neighborhood. For an instant, the animal seemed to glance past Froggy and Farrukh to look directly at Terri, as if she really were a time-traveling ghost. She felt that familiar disconnect, momentarily forgetting where and when she was, watching the coyote turn and trot back to its own realm, wondering if she'd just been given some strange mystical message.

ShotSpotter had caught the gunshot, but the hooded Farrukh had sprinted off a half minute before the first drone arrived on scene, skipping over the bike path and then doubling back to make a getaway under the bridge itself. She crossed over to the other side of the bridge, soaring downriver to see if there were any glimpses of anyone fleeing or floating. It was far too dark to make out much of anything. As had happened so many times before, she found herself wanting to stop and redo this scene, to give it a different ending.

Remembering there'd been some tags on the shooting itself, she rewound again, placing herself back at the moment of murder, Froggy's expression still one of startled rage. The first comment, by Collazo, was surprisingly professional, making an official note of Froggy's rep file, noting his involvement with a punch-out crew a few years earlier, that he'd apparently been promoted to sex trafficking in the last six months. Then there were the follow-up comments, each tagged to the subsequent moment when Froggy fell into the unlit river:

no muss, no fuss

somebody should make a public service announcement out of this

Self-flushing feces. I love it.

For a half decade after the war, precipitation had almost stopped in southern California as the Earth grew dryer and colder. When the rains had finally returned to Los Angeles, they'd returned in force, the bizarre weather patterns of a wounded planet being one of the few realms too large and too complex to be fully understood or predicted. Storm surges became an annual trauma, conspiring with increased snowpack on the San Gabriel and Santa Monica mountains to convert the paved Los Angeles river into a channel for raging brown floodwaters four months out of every year. A news crawl at the bottom of her vision read TOURNAMENT OF ROSES CONFLICTING ACCOUNTS, 18 DEAD.

Terri called Carla Morales, hoping she wasn't waking her.

"Not Carla," Carla's Dupe said.

"Yeah. Tech question, Not Carla. Can EyePhones survive getting wet?"

"Theoretically. It depends."

"On."

"It depends on how long they were wet, what was the context, what brand they were."

"Good to know."

The Dupe hung up on her.

"Oh-kay." She called up a Department of Water and Power engineer, yawning as she tried to phrase her river questions correctly.

"In flood surges, tons of debris is going to come down the LA river," he explained, "Chairs, shelving, tires, aluminum siding . . ."

". . . I actually need to know about what *doesn't* get through. What could a human body get snagged on?"

"Yeah, that's what I'm trying to tell you," he said with irritation. "All those things are inorganics. With surges, we don't get any non-wood organic material larger than a rat, and even that not so much. In fast-moving water, hard objects do a great job of battering soft, cellular objects. A human body would disintegrate long before it hit Long Beach. Maybe a foot might pop up, but unless it comes free of its shoe, we're never going to notice it. And past Compton Creek, water speed is upward of ten to twelve miles per hour at over sixty pounds per cubic foot. So even if someone were looking directly at the outflow, they probably wouldn't see anything, and even if they *did*, they certainly wouldn't be able to retrieve anything they saw."

"Stupendous. Thanks," she said, already disconnected, flexing her jaw in impatience.

Terri stared at the wall. New conclusion: Froggy's shooting was pride-based. Froggy had disrespected Farrukh, Froggy had died. No muss, no fuss. She'd seen this scenario enough times to know there were few boundaries to what a refugee man would do when sufficiently compressed. There was a sub-subgenre of cop films known as the "I Am A Man" video, with male refugees tearfully or insanely asserting their manhood; snapping, shrieking, kicking over pathetic chai kiosks, attacking cops with puny fists, collapsing in the street, devoured by the disgrace of their social emasculation. All her poking and prodding around Farrukh's last days easily supported this theory.

She liked this about Basement work, that it allowed her to ponder problems four-dimensionally, adding duration to width, height, and depth. But there were frustrations here as well. For one thing, there was that strange powerlessness, the unfulfilled desire to act on history, even immediate history. It felt like something close to a trap, nearly philosophical in its revealed truth. The past is always more solid than the future is fluid.

The next morning, she had herself driven to the Good Sam Medical Complex. She followed PanOpt's curving blue arrows down a long, brightly lit hallway to a first floor conference room clearly bustling with pre-conference hubbub. In the welter of faces, she located a plump, dark man with a white overcoat and steel-rimmed EyePhones. Even if he hadn't been wearing his uniform, even if she'd run into him on the street, she'd have known he was a home-grown American just by the way he carried himself.

"Doctor Singh? I'm homicide Detective Pastuszka," she said from the doorway with a broad smile, knowing that everyone's shades would show her shield somewhere overhead. Can I ask you a few quick questions?" He returned her gaze with a bold formality.

"Detective, this actually isn't a good time . . ."

"I know, and I'm sorry about that, but I just have a few questions about Farrukh Jhadav. You met with him here three weeks ago?"

"I don't recall him specifically, but I know exactly what this pertains to," Singh said, nodding. "He'd gone to one of those web rooms that allows you to trace any relatives you may have. He found out that we were very, very distantly related, maybe fifth cousins or something, if there even is such a thing. I don't remember, and it doesn't matter. He was looking for money. They're all the same." The dozen or so other doctors in the room went about their own hushed conversations with showy nonchalance, examining the colorful wall charts, the floor, looking everywhere but at the two of them.

"'All?'"

"Any doctor of East Indian ancestry will tell you the same story. Refugees try to establish some sort of familial connection with us to get a handout for money. Or food, or shelter, or clothes . . . anything, really. These guys are a dime a dozen."

"Anything about this particular guy that stood out?"

"Really, I don't remember. It was a quick conversation. I told him I couldn't help, and that was that."

"Oh? Well. Huh. You know, my records have you two speaking in your office for twenty-eight minutes," she said, trying to put it light and sweet, making it sound almost like a question. No need to drop the hammer in front of the man's colleagues unless necessary.

Singh looked momentarily startled, probably having assumed LAPD surveillance wouldn't include window shots from public streets. It was a common misconception, a willful delusion. If you do something in full view of a public thoroughfare, when has that ever been off limits to law enforcement?

"No, that's incorrect," he said. "But I'd be glad to show you my room macro."

He excused himself, and an older woman, also in a white coat, tapped her wrist. Terri beamed, hamming it up, saying, "Great, great, that'd really help clear things up for me."

They headed back down the hallway, but before they got to the stairs, he beckoned her into a side conference room, running his fingers through his hair.

Singh paused a moment, then said, "A long time ago, maybe eighteen or nineteen years, a guy showed up at my office saying he was my second cousin, just arrived in the US on one of the airlifts. Turns out he really was my second cousin. He'd met my dad both times he'd gone over to visit before the war. We spent the afternoon talking, got some beers, I loaned him five hundred dollars to get on his feet. My wife nearly crucified me, even though the money wasn't an issue. Turns out she was right to be concerned. This cousin started coaxing more and more money out of me, showing up more and more frequently. One day he arrived at my house—not here, which is where we'd always met—and it was clear he'd been drinking. I told him to ease off, and he . . . he didn't exactly threaten me, but he sort of . . . lunged."

"Lunged."

"He, you know, took one menacing step toward me really quickly and started laughing. It was nothing, really, but my wife was in the room, and she wanted me to contact a bodyguard service. Then it didn't matter because we found out he was dead."

"Found out how?"

"My wife had already set up a face alert, so she got the notification and called me at work." A trio of doctors passed in the hallway and Singh grew quiet.

"Look," he said, nearly whispering, "I did talk with Farrukh for a half hour. But I did tell him I couldn't help, and that he was not to bother me."

"Must've been an awkward half hour."

"That was at the end. Before that, I just listened to his story, listened to his current situation, tried to coax details out of him about his daily life, his routines."

"Why listen if you're going to kick him to the curb?"

"Are you familiar with The Hand Of God?"

She thought about asking if that was the church in Crenshaw, felt stupid, and instead shook her head.

"It's a charity group. A very select charity group. It's for situations like this, so that a handout doesn't look like a handout."

"Say what?"

"If someone shows up, someone like Farrukh, someone wanting something, I dismiss this person with sufficient rudeness to make sure they don't come back. Make it crystal clear. No handouts. Then I tag this person in Hand Of God and set up an account for a one-time windfall. Maybe they find a wad of cash in the street, or a winning scratcher, or someone reverse-pickpockets them. You'd be surprised at how many ways there are to help someone out without them ever figuring out what's going on."

"And how much did you give him?"

"A grand."

"That's a lot of money for a remote relative you're never going to see again. What made this guy so special?"

"Nothing. I give away a grand, on average, once a month." Seeing the look on her face, he shrugged. "I'll make that much this afternoon. Look. Barring some kind of calamity, I'm going to retire in May. My wife retires in July. Our house goes on the market, our furniture goes to one of those auction places, and we are gone. We have a sixty-four-foot yacht that'll get us to Polynesia. We're going to spend the rest of our lives far, far away from all this." He motioned to the hospital, and the city. "And when I do physically interact with civilization, it's going to be at marinas or ports of call where there won't be any refugees. So why not help while I still can?" He paused, then said, "Is he dead?"

"I'm homicide. So, yeah. Shot dead in a parking lot, Monday morning."

"Huh," he said, as if she'd told him the elevator was out of service. "He was a hard guy to say no to, I'll say that for him. Worked his ass off. No days off. He told me about what happened in Panama."

She played dumb. "What happened in Panama?"

"There were five of them, him, his brother, his brother's three girls. They walked up from somewhere ridiculous, maybe . . . Argentina? I forget. Camped by the side of the road, got robbed more than once, foraged and raided dumpsters along with everyone else flooding north. This went on for months, so by the time they crossed over into Panama, one of the girls was already sick. Probably, from what he told me, either malaria or HVFV. They camped out within view of the canal, and he set out to find a pharmacy, to try to scrape up something for the sick girl. When he got back to the campsite, there was a note to meet them at such and such a dock. When he got there, there were only two girls, the sick one, and the youngest, the one born in an aid camp, Rujuta. The brother told him, rather matter-of-factly, that he'd sold the oldest daughter for ferry space and a Red Cross parcel. They only had fifteen minutes before crossing. Farrukh went crazy, racing around the docks looking for her, but when it came time they just had to leave.

"He said he had nightmares about her every night. Those were his words. 'Every single night of my life.' He was a hard guy to say no to. And then the sick daughter obviously died, and I don't think the brother was doing so well by the time they'd settled. I think he died of strep."

"I wouldn't know," she said, dropping some of the sweetness. "Farrukh had a tattoo on his ankle . . ."

"That was her. The daughter."

"Did you catch a name?"

"Like I said, Rujuta."

"Wait a minute, he had the name of the remaining niece? The one who's still alive?"

"They're very close. Or were very close. That's too bad," he muttered. "Now, if you'll excuse me, Detective . . ."

"Hold up. Do you know anything about this daughter, Rujuta?"

"Really, I've told you everything I know."

"There's nothing Farrukh might have said to you? No clues to her whereabouts?"

"I'd be glad to send you the macro, Detective," he said, meeting her stare. "But I know far, far less about these people than you do. I don't even care about them." He smiled, stepping around her. "Helping them just helps me sleep a little better at night."

Doctor Singh's debriefing turned out to be the high point of a go-nowhere day. Another six hours of dead ends had combined with Zack's lack of enthusiasm into a toxic brew of apathy and sluggishness. When they walked into Uganda after dusk, she dragged a dozen open boxes with her, including three Basement views, a coroner's report, and five transcripts. Each felt like a mystical weight, something her spirit would be chained to in the afterlife.

Inside, she experienced a familiar type of déjà vu, where the bar, with all of its camaraderie and laughter, seemed like the only thing that was real, and the sidewalk, city, and planet outside all dull counterfeits. She took off her shades and the illusion evaporated. Only two tables, each flanking the front door, generated all the camaraderie and laughter. It was hard to tell if they all knew each other, although it looked like some sort of ongoing birthday celebration. From a booth in the corner, Miguel Hull waved them over. He sat sandwiched between two overweight Gang and Narcotics guys whose names she'd forgotten, everyone together but talking to others.

Miguel had been Zack's previous partner until he'd gotten busted, seven years ago, for borrowing an air compressor from an evidence room. He'd since done penance and re-made detective in Western. Every now and then, schedules would overlap and he'd meet up with them at Uganda. There'd been a time when she'd acknowledged a twinge of jealousy whenever the two men got together, as if Zack were making time with an ex. Then she realized Miguel could be a better conversationalist.

Terri and Zack each took an edge of seat at the end of the two booths, facing each other. His shades chirped and he rose, saying, "Auuuhhhggggg. Round three. Excuse me, gang."

A fight with Janice had slowly come to consume the afternoon and evening. She had a hard time picturing what the Zendejases would fight about. Janice was neat, clean, and kept her cards close to the vest. If she had ever felt her own twinges of jealousy over how much time Terri spent with her husband, she'd never shown it. The two cops continued scrolling through the air in front of them. Miguel said, "We were just discussing your boy, Dorothy."

"Owen Dorothy? *I'm* not on his mailing list." Three weeks earlier, Detective Dorothy had sent out Christmas cards featuring three prostitutes found in the refrigeration locker of a shuttered convenience store, each shot once, in the head, their threadbare saris soaked with blood. The card's caption had read, HO HO HO.

"Hey, I get it, Terri. I'm on your side. Totally out of line, he completely deserved suspension. We're all just hoping this doesn't close the Godzilla pipeline."

She growled. For years, cops had traded altered Godzilla movies, redoing the beast's battles as absurd pornos: *Godzilla Does Rodan*, *Godzilla Pounds King Kong*, *Godzilla Bangs Mechagodzilla*. These remixes were less appealing to her than fantasy sports championships. It made sense that Owen Dorothy was the mastermind, although lots of other cops had a hand in the redo world, constantly mining lower and lower into the depths of carnal subgenres for new shocks.

"C'mon. The work that man does? Pure art. Isn't that right, Jack?"

One of the overweight cops grunted.

"You can't deny the artistry, Terri."

"I've never seen any of his handiwork, so I wouldn't know."

This got the table's attention.

"Are you kidding me?" one of the heavy strangers said. "It's some of the most sublime artistry done by the human hand!"

She was about to ask, "Do I know you?", when Zack swung by the booth and deposited two sandwiches as he walked, still engrossed in his argument. As he stalked off, she heard him say, "Uh-huh. Meaning what, exactly? That I *don't*?"

Uganda offered a fridge of sandwiches and other last-resort bar food. As she looked down at her paper-and-twine-wrapped bundle, she faced the sudden and absolute knowledge that she didn't deserve such a bounty when so many had died. It was a fleeting experience, universal for every other adult her age, although she'd never once discussed it with anyone.

Miguel was talking about his own redo, some project he'd labored on for weeks. She snapped out of her trance.

"This is this thing you were telling me about last time? With, uh, Mary Pickford and Robert Redford?"

"Yeah."

"As cops, right?"

"Cops in the future, yeah."

"What happened with that *Dragnet* redo you were working on?"

"It's sort of a crowded field with that one. So I back-burnered it for a little while."

Cops' obsession with *Dragnet* had never abated in all the years she'd lived here. It was an odd twist of local history that the cops had become custodians of the city's filmic past. Everyone she knew pored over these old movies and programs, dispatches from a time when law enforcement had infinitely fewer tools but infinitely more respect. Other American police forces had undergone similar declines of prestige. But only

Los Angeles had once owned a police force so memorialized throughout more than a century of cinema. All those LAPD archetypes—besieged, brutal, corrupt, heroic—lived on in the endless, eternal mash-ups of police culture. One more private world among many.

The two overweight Gang and Narcotics guys said, "Oh shit" at the exact same moment, huffing up out of their seats and rushing out the front door.

"*Some*one's in trouble," she said.

"That? They've been waiting on that Shep guy. He's supposed to help them crawl out of The Loop."

"Shep Lyra? That idiot freelancer?"

"I don't think he's so freelance anymore. I think he graduated from a *Times* stringer to a salaried reporter."

"And he's the guy who's going to get them out of The Loop?" She snorted. "Good luck."

The Loop was an echo chamber, a hermetically-sealed alternate reality of false reportage that attempted to swallow all cops. Some police lost their careers in The Loop, others just had their blood pressure raised by it. Reporters who fed The Loop referenced other sources from inside The Loop, supplying the largest media market of all; people who needed to have their opinions validated.

Officers on the Wall went after false footage with all the resources the department could bring to bear. But there were a million needles in a vastly larger haystack, all that citizen footage and raw data requiring sifting and analysis, everyone watching every move of every cop, or so it felt, some footage apparently generated just for the fun of it; SWAT standoffs, businessmen freakouts, skyscraper suicides, sometimes slipping from witness footage into pure action movie, sometimes satirical.

"Man. He looks bad. Is this a new thing?" Miguel motioned toward Zack. She wolfed down half her sandwich, then rose and approached the table where Zack sat seething, Miguel cautiously in tow.

"Wanna take your mind off whatever? And compare notes?"

"Whatta you think," Zack said.

"There's still some halfway potential foot and car witnesses you tagged."

"It's a bunch of crap. You know it, and I know it."

"There's the Mercedes. That one's driver-owned and probably has decent side macros," she said with a light lilt, realizing how dumb it sounded now that she was saying it.

"What's the point of doing any of the southbounds if there was another however many lanes of traffic between them and the lot?"

She contemplated pulling at the thread—what's the point of being a detective if you lose interest four days in?—then thought better of it, she really being in no position to cast stones, after all the various go-nowhere cases she'd let dissolve after a week or so of waning enthusiasm.

"Where's the guy live?" Miguel said.

"The dead guy? He lives in a trash bag at the landfill," Zack said with a growing testiness.

"Okay, calm down," Miguel said, smiling at Terri, raising his eyebrows and then bumping his chin up. "Where's the Mercedes guy live?"

She drew up the list in her margins. "Stone Oak."

He whistled. "Mulholland."

"Oh yeah?"

"Yeah. Nice. If you're doing any tonight, pick that one."

"You been up there?"

"No, but my nephew did some contracting up there and he let me look over the footage one day, when I was sick with the flu and had nothing better to do. Only time in my life I've ever been jealous of a roofer."

"Who? Stu?" Zack asked.

"Yeah," Miguel said with a half chuckle.

Zack chuckled at some old in-joke, so Terri did too, happy to see him momentarily escape from his funk. One of the tables near the front door burst into a mass volley of applause and laughter.

"On that note," she said, "I gotta take a whiz."

"Gotta do a two," Miguel said from behind, following her down the long hallways leading to the restrooms. For a moment, she thought he wanted to speak with her in private about Zack's morale problem, but then she heard the men's room door slam. Miguel had never been her partner.

Returning from the ladies' room, she saw that the far two tables had abruptly cleared out, leaving the space with a slightly mournful, closing time vibe. Uganda was spooky that way, even on Fridays. In a half hour, it could be standing room only. She put on her shades, reading that it was only a little after nine. Zack sat at their table clutching a beer with both hands, staring down into the settling bubbles with an expression close to total blankness, his head hung low enough to give him a stubbly double chin. She thought of her father, seated at the kitchen table of her childhood, lost in the invisible vice grips of debt and bills.

"'Sup, killer."

He sounded a weary grunt.

"Going home?"

He sighed, took a long, thoughtful sip, and then said, "No, gonna wait it out a few hours."

Terri considered asking him if he wanted to talk about it, then realized she wasn't currently interested enough to act as a responsible therapeutic ear.

She looked around the somber room one more time, then said, "Hey, if you want a diversion, it's just ten minutes away."

"What's ten minutes?"

"The Mercedes place. Get some fresh air, see how the other half lives?"

"Jesus, you're a pip, Terri. Why don't you ever give up?"

"How about I just check and see if the Mercedes is even there?"

He took another slow slurp, wiped some froth off his chin, and glanced at her sideways. "Yeah, great, do it. You're going to anyway."

She brought up a surveillance box over his head, punching in a drone order as Miguel emerged from the men's room and said, "The fuck? The Rapture happen?"

She shifted focus, looking through the semi-translucence of the hovering Surveillance Box to the wall next to him, where a faded poster for some beer she'd never heard of featured two muscle-bound idiots in lederhosen hoisting their steins to the Heavens. She must've seen this poster a thousand times and never actually looked at it. Miguel made a bored sucking sound and finally said, "Hey, I forgot. Guess what I ran into? Zack?"

Zack groaned.

"Guess what I ran into? Over at the Haseley?"

"I have no idea who you ran into."

"The lonely boner."

Zack suppressed a small smile. "No, you didn't."

"Yeah. For like thirty seconds. I was out in the parking lot, Kip was still inside, I felt this, like, sixth sense, and I looked over,"—he did this now, his face crumpling in glee as he stared over to the space where her surveillance box hovered, seen only by her—"and it just sort of . . . *floated* . . ."

Both men burst into laughter.

"Is this one of those guys-only things?" she asked.

"Naw, it just . . ." Miguel was laughing too hard to speak.

"It just floats around," Zack offered, trying to keep a straight face. "And you never know where it's gonna strike . . ."

"It's like a . . ." Miguel was doubling over with laughter, his voice a squeak. "It's like this . . ."

She walked past several empty tables to the bar, shaking her head, catching and then losing the eye of the unsmiling bartender who, wearing shades, stared straight through her, off into the visualizations and problems of his own life.

She said, "Just water," as a chime sounded and a text box in her upper-left-hand field of vision signified that the drone had spotted the car at the residence. Year after year, the response time got a little quicker. She kept the drone in a holding pattern in case the Mercedes took off again, then dinged a request box for a ride of her own. A pictographic car materialized over the bartender's shoulder, a red neon cartoon indicating that her ride was eight blocks away and closing, as if it had been racing toward her all this time.

Another volley of laughter came across the oddly desolate barroom. She turned and saw it was Zack and Miguel, still chortling over their private joke. In her apps sidebar, she called up and clicked Hospice Style, so that the two men appeared to grow old and feeble, their backs bent, gray hair and beards descending to the floor, until they finally collapsed in on each other in a death hug, dying in each other's arms, melting into dust, which an imaginary gust picked up and scattered into nothingness. A car honked outside.

"Yo!" She raised her hand and snapped her fingers. "Zendejas! Vamos a rollo!"

Out on the sidewalk, the air had cooled considerably, the sky lit by a fullish moon to an eerie, portentous gray, a strong gusty breeze shaking the palms that lined the block. Far overhead, a fleet of mammoth, silvery cumulus rolled in from the coast like battleships. She stepped to the curb and leaned against the car's side, waiting for Zack with folded arms. All cops took full advantage of this prerogative of the force—keeping an automobile waiting for as long as they wanted—and she wondered now how many minutes and hours of her life she'd wasted standing in this exact same position. Surely more than her partner.

As she watched, a sunburned drunk in a sleeveless T-shirt shuffled down the pavement with a cheap BMX, trying simultaneously to balance the bicycle against his arm and himself against the bike. He crossed between the car and building in quiet concentration, and she thought, *Mulholland: How could this all take place in the same city?*

The two finally emerged, Miguel saying, "Hey, Terr, you left your drink."

"I'm good."

Zack looked up and said, to the night sky, "You coming with, Migs?"

"Nah, I got a traffic meeting at eight. Early night."

The three waved goodbye and as she and Zack climbed into the warm vehicle, she had to consciously will herself down from sparking an argument over his shitty attitude—as if his ex-partner could just snap back into position whenever Zack felt like it—instead saying, "What the fuck is a 'traffic meeting'?"

"Beats me."

The car slid into motion. Uganda had been named after a group in-joke, Culver City being a punchline of alleged remoteness, a place no one actually went except to go to sleep. Cops might make a bit of noise on the sidewalk outside, but a strict local ordinance kept vehicles under sixty miles per hour within city limits. As they moved toward the freeway in silence, the car passed under a lone, long-decommissioned traffic light, bobbling on its metal pole like an animal perched in the dark. It reminded her of the blackouts, the bad days. She probably wasn't the only one who made this association, the memory surely jarring every cop who had passed under its arch over the years, a specter of bad tidings that would register with even the wooziest of booze brains.

The car jumped onto the freeway and accelerated, a particle in an artery. They passed huge mounds covered by worn black plastic tarps, stalled construction machinery, dark stacks of massive concrete tubes reduced to smears by the speed.

"You're not sucking me into your thing," he said, looking out the window with one foot propped up on the jump seat, staring out at the blurred center divider.

"Which thing?"

"The thing where you spend your weekend nights hunting down crumbs," he said.

She pursed her lips, knowing she should feel insulted but somehow secretly pleased. Long ago, she'd realized that her reputation for being thorough, for putting in time far above and beyond what was called for, did not necessarily work in her favor. Some cops probably viewed her as a pain in the ass. But it was nice receiving any sort of acknowledgment toward how much labor she actually put in.

"I'll tell you one thing, though," he continued. "I'm gonna blast that bigwig."

"Mr. Overholser," she said, hoping this wasn't about the son.

"Putting the car in his son's name. I'll put a boot up his ass."

"Yeah . . . maybe don't do that."

"I am doing that."

"Sure. But maybe don't."

"Too late."

"Right. Only don't."

The car continued to pick up speed, shooting through a narrow channel between a formation of tractor-trailers, five wide and at least ten deep, slightly terrifying in their immutability, the moonlight between each one strobing off the windshield.

"You don't think it's disgusting?" he said.

"That he gave his son a car? Maybe it was a Christmas present. Maybe it was a reward for not pooping on the floor, I don't know. People have all kinds of crazy motives. What I'm saying is, if this guy's car is the issue, let's keep our eyes on the car. No reason to go all the way up there and not get the recording."

She recalled the conversation with Chandrika Chavan, and thought that it also would be nice to skip any more bad public relations this week. No matter how creepy or demented someone's living arrangements may be, there was probably no scenario where it would look good for a cop to chew out the parent of a grown developmentally disabled child. And who knew who recorded what.

"First of all, he didn't *give* his son anything. It's still his car. He just put it in his mongoloid's name. The issue is that he's evading taxes or title fees or some other kind of fee," Zack said. "He's obviously evading something. He's found one more loophole that he can juice us all through, and he thought no one would ever notice."

"So?"

"So, I *pay* my taxes. And this joker probably pays nothing and rides around town like he's the Monopoly Man? It pisses me off. So yeah, he can fuck off into the furnaces of hell. But I won't tell him off until we have our useless recording. That'll appease you?"

"Sure," she said as the car slowed for the exit and banked left, up into the hills that marked the borderline between the overlit world of everyone and the secluded world of true financial power.

The car ascended and further slowed, accommodating the road's switchback twists. Besides a few streetlights illuminating small patches of shoulder—stage sets—this was a shadowy patch of rural seclusion, elevated and forever separate from its governing metropolis. Over one set of high, well-trimmed hedges, she could make out the turrets of a hulking nouveau riche Brazilian manor.

"You ever come up here?" she asked in a slightly awed hush.

"Once. Me and Janice did some sightseeing back when we were dating."

The car turned a bit too sharply, and a deep pit opened in her gut.

"Ugh."

"Huh?"

"Queasy," she said, registering an undeniable surge of saliva.

"Mind over meat, Pastuszka."

A car passed in the opposing lane, the headlights of each dimming in respect for their human cargo. "Yeah. Janice got a little green too."

Car sickness bags were standard issue in all police vehicles, but they were usually considered last resorts. And they certainly weren't intended for actual car sickness. She'd only needed them a few times that didn't involve drinking, usually in the moments when swooping or soaring in the Basement messed up her inner ear. In general, cops relied on Dramamine or wristbands to ward off carsickness. She had neither.

"Um. Where're the barf bags?"

"Seriously?" A wave of alarm crossed Zack's face. "Do not puke."

The car took another tight corner.

"Yeah." She doubled over. "Yep. Yep. Okay. *Yeah*."

"Oh shit. Oh shit. No no no . . ." Zack intoned as he fumbled through the paraphernalia in the jump seat pouch.

"Okay. Here's one," he said. "Just *wait*, until we get . . ."

She grabbed the bag and neatly snapped its waxy sides open, involuntarily leaking tears as the remains of her dinner came lurching up. When she'd finished, she heard an odd echo of her own retching, catching Zack hunched over his own bag. This made her gag for another instant, although nothing else came up.

"Shit." He wiped his eyes.

She made a deep moaning sound, wiping her mouth on her sleeve before catching herself in disgust.

They sat in silence for a moment, one hot little baggie between each set of shoes. The car had stopped, perhaps disgusted at their frailty.

"I think we're here," she said, noticing that the windows had fogged up.

Terri leaned forward and rubbed one elbow on the windshield, switching arms when she remembered the mouth swipe.

"Give me a minute," he said.

She gave a feeble chuckle. "Where do we put these?"

"Unh." He ran a thumb along the seal of the baggie. "I don't know."

"Yeah . . ." All she could see through the patch of unfogged window was a wall of shrubbery. Tossing trash in the bushes would've been a serious thing, if anybody caught them.

"Just, uh." She felt in the small snap pocket of her jacket sleeve, relieved when she produced a small tin of breath mints. "Just, ah . . . let's just leave them, and we'll see if Overholser has a trash bag or something."

They stepped out through the jump door, seeing that the car had parked on the thin dirt shoulder flush with an immaculate wall of hedge, trimmed to an inhuman perfection. Light showed from a gap in the landscaping ten feet away. Zack led the way, Terri clacking three mints around in her mouth.

The recess opened onto a gated driveway. A discretely lit call box, inset in the shrubbery, offered a single button. Above this, an illuminated sign read The Wig Wam. Zack pressed the button and a display pad blinked to life, requesting a phone number in a serene green typeface.

"That's ballsy," she said.

He punched his number into the keypad, his PanOpts chimed, and then he said, simply, "LAPD," crisply enunciating each letter.

The wind picked up, tousling the tips of bamboo that peeked out from the other side of the steel gate. Each leaf was a healthy green: all the bamboo planted next to her apartment building had burned, brown tips. The gate clicked and opened inward with the soundless ease of a bank vault door.

They crossed an enormous driveway on white pebbles that crunched softly underfoot. Far overhead, recessed lights dangled between towering limbs of oaks. Moonlight squiggled off a half-dozen glossy sports cars parked to their left. Zack pointed off into the shadows to the right of the house, saying, "Thar she blows." She squinted, just making out the Mercedes in a dark bower that held another half-dozen cars.

Two colossal wooden cigar store American Indians flanked the front door. This door did not swing open. Zack reached out and slammed the brass knocker once, hard, saying, "'Wig Wam.' Jesus."

"How come your house doesn't have a name?"

"It does," he said. "We just . . ." The door clicked, paused, and then swung inward, revealing Richard Overholser. He seemed smaller and sadder than when frozen in his speeding Mercedes.

"Mr. Overholser, I'm Detective Zendejas, of LAPD Homicide. This is my partner, Detective Pastuszka."

The little man's hands drooped at his side. "How can I help you?"

"We have reason to believe that your vehicle may have recorded a crime on Monday morning."

It took Terri a moment to process the interior visible from the open doorway. From a foyer of dark stained wood and Mexican terracotta, a sweeping staircase curled up and out of their line of sight. Another two colossal dime store Indians flanked the railings, and she could see another two more wooden Indian chiefs standing guard in the thin wedge of majestic living room beyond Mr. Overholser's shoulder. She could just make out the rounded hump of a grand piano, an overall impression of opulence so forceful that it hurt to see, vexing her that they could share the world, much less the city, with a residence like this.

"Which car would that be?" the older man asked quietly, looking more like a butler than someone who would reside in such splendor.

"The Mercedes," Zack said, pointing back out into the leafy murk of the car park. Perhaps because there was no way to tell how many Mercedes might be parked on the premises, he added, "The H1H. We'd like to have a look at the car's side macros."

The man frowned slightly. "Oh. That's my son's car."

"Really," Zack said, rocking on his heels. "Your *son's* car."

"Yes. This is probably something you should speak with him about."

"Excuse me?"

From somewhere past the sweep of the staircase, a deep, man's voice bellowed. "What the hell is going on down there?"

Mr. Overholser turned dutifully. "It's two police officers."

"De*tec*tives," Zack said.

The voice bellowed. "Perhaps you might explain to them that nine o'clock at night is an intrusive time for investigations?"

"They want information. From one of the cars."

"Jesus Christ on the fucking cross!" Loud stomps followed, and Terri saw the younger Olverholser tromp down the stairs, her brain doing a skip as it tried and failed to reconcile the authoritative voice coming from the huge, squashed face. She turned and saw Zack staring with an open mouth.

"Are you kidding me with this Gestapo crap? Do you know what time it is?" the colossal man asked, as if they hadn't heard him bellowing. He was dressed in a tuxedo shirt and cummerbund, and the two ribbons of a bow tie dangled around his neck. His fat, squat limbs swung at either side and then opened wide, as close to a physical challenge as anything she'd seen go down in front of the skyscrapers. "Well? Here I am."

When Zack didn't say anything, she glanced at his slack-jawed stare and said, "Mr. Overholser, we were just telling your father here that we have reason to believe your car recorded a crime scene in downtown Los Angeles. A murder."

"So. What."

"So, we'd like to look at the recording macros. Now we can . . ."

"Lady, I'm an *entertainment* lawyer. Crosley, Johnson, and Overholser? You ever heard of Danny Dex and the Donkey Dong Crew? *I* put that together. I make both your salaries combined every three days."

"Sir . . ."

"No. You've said your bit, now you're going to hear me out." He extended one huge, flat hand into the air between them. "You two bust in here in total violation of the fourth amendment, you badger my father, and about what? My car? It's unacceptable. I don't accept it."

"Well," Zack said with a surprising softness, "you don't have to accept any—"

"And let me guess," the younger Overholser barreled on. "This alleged murder. Does it even involve a citizen?"

"That's actually not the issue you need to be . . ."

"Yes! Or! No! Is the deceased even part of our legal system? Or is this someone who broke federal and state law to get here, and God knows how many other laws once inside this country?"

Zack glanced away. Terri said, "This is an open investigation involving a refugee murder, sir, and any . . ."

"Then the answer is no."

"No?" Zack said.

"No. I work my ass off, my property tax pays your pension, so no. I don't comply. Get off my premises."

"Sir, we can obtain a warrant in a matter of minutes," she said with what she hoped was a defusing calmness.

"Try it!" he roared, those thick, stumpy arms swinging in rage. "I'll tie you two up in so many IAG misconducts that you'll be working street corners as crossing guards! Don't think I don't have your badge numbers."

The four of them stood there for a moment, and she thought she heard Zack swallow. Terri produced a business card from her jacket pocket, and leaned in to hand it to the elder Overholser, who accepted it with a nod. She and Zack made their way back across the expanse of white gravel, onto the tranquil street, back into the puke-smelling police car.

They drove off at thirty miles per hour, saying nothing. Passing a scenic lookout, she directed the car to U-turn back, holding the top of her vomit baggie with two carefully pinched fingers as they banked. She stepped out onto the windy little overlook, still feeling unsteady and something else; headachy, fatigued, as if they'd caught a strange strain of altitude sickness from climbing too far above their social strata.

Zack walked to the nearby railing and peered over the vast grid of Los Angeles. She pulled up her shades and rested them on her scalp, the image of the lit city seeming unreal when viewed with nothing but her eyes.

"I don't think it's healthy to not frequently see this view first hand," Zack said, tossing his barf bag over the railing. She extended one arm so that her shades weren't in danger of falling as well, letting her own bag drop down into the leafy darkness. Crickets chirped out of season. She'd heard some gated communities imported them by the half ton just for the comforting rural background noise.

"Have you ever seen that before?"

He laughed. "Nope. You?"

"No. I mean . . . what *was* that? Was that the operation?"

"Yeah, I guess. But I've never heard of one without, you know. Someone doing the mind but keeping the body."

"I heard Voehner had it done. But, yeah. He looked like . . ."

"Regular."

"Maybe it gives him a business advantage? Overholser, I mean. Looking like that?"

"I don't know."

"Jesus, the shit you see in this job," she said, instantly regretting having uttered the world's biggest cliché aloud.

"Ah, we've both seen worse." He spread his arms wide. "Five billion people out there, Pastuszka. Lotta room for God to improv."

She dozed after the car dropped off Zack, waking in front of her apartment building. When she made it up the flights of stairs, she was fully awake again, standing in that silent, messy living room, whispering, "Damn." The clock in her lower-right field of vision told her it was only 10:10, the night still young. This would be her first Friday without overtime. No more working at night.

She placed her PanOpts back on the Chinese table with a soft knock and then paused with one finger still touching them, like a chess move she hadn't committed to. No more *paid* work. She could work as much as she wanted. If that's what brought her a scrap of pleasure, why not?

And yet an hour later she found herself bored and frustrated and gummed up, another Friday night down the drain, wasting her time in the Basement by watching strangers attempting to enter one of those chain stores that sold slices of wedding cake, person after person pushing instead of pulling, despite the door's signage. Technically, she was bound to honor the investigative boundaries of this tool, but she'd never gotten busted for farting around. Everybody did the same if an investigation went on long enough. Kenny Voehner had used the Basement to backstalk an ex, and it'd still taken IAG more than six months to catch on.

She pulled off the shades and massaged the bridge of her nose, trying to rub out the soreness. The phone chimed on audio only, and when she pulled them back on, she was surprised to see a rare unlisted number, not knowing that was still possible these days.

"Yep."

"Oh. Ms. Pastuszka. Is this you, or . . ."

She knew the reedy little butler voice.

"Mr. Overholser. Yeah, it's me, I'm up. What's on your mind?"

"Listen. I just wanted to say . . ." his voice grew low, and she guessed he was trying to speak without getting overheard.

"I just wanted to apologize for the way you and your partner were treated tonight. That's all. I just wanted to apologize. It wasn't right."

"We've been called worse. But thanks."

"It wasn't right."

"Fair enough."

There was a silence, and she was about to thank him again and hang up when he continued. "I didn't raise him like this. I wanted you to know that. He was a good boy. It was just after the operation . . ." His voice trailed into a whisper, and for a moment he seemed to be mumbling to himself.

"After that, he changed. That's all. They told me he'd be a new person, and they were right. I lost my boy. And now I have this, I live with this man. What you saw tonight."

"He seems successful," she said to say something.

"It wasn't worth it."

"Okay. Well . . . again, thanks. And if you somehow think you can change your son's mind about that footage, we'd be grateful."

"Oh, there's no changing his mind. Not Ritchie. He's a bull. He was stubborn even before. But now, no. There's no way."

"Understood. Thanks for calling." She'd heard stories of strangers treating investigators as therapists, but it had never happened to her in nine years as a detective. Or was something else going on here? She could still hear the man breathing on the other end.

"Mr. Overholser, is there anything else you'd like to say to me?"

"Well, I'm in the Mercedes. How do I send your recording?"

Ten minutes later, she had the attachment open. He'd sent the last month of footage, and after she'd trimmed it down and corrected for hyperfocal fisheye and boosted brightness, she found herself pleasantly surprised by the richness of the car's video. She could never remember which frame rates were which, but whatever speed this was, it was total overkill. Maybe that was the point with luxury vehicles.

The footage was flat, 2D, eye-level for a toddler. She synced the Mercedes's portside recording with her Basement map and rolled it at 5:28 on Monday morning, the car just past West Seventh, traveling southwest down Figueroa at seventy-eight miles per hour. The setup reminded her of a question from a high school math test. How many seconds before the anonymous assailant blasts the hard-working nobody? Past Eleventh Street, she slowed action to one-twentieth time, teasing out the hidden, heavy metal ballet of bumpers and hubcaps that lurks behind all vehicular motion.

Spotting the first of the casino buses from across five lanes of car traffic, she chopped the speed in half again and called up Zack's sightlines. There were six of these, each a neon green bar strung across the road like a finish line, a half-dozen filaments connecting one particular between-car blind with the view of this passing Mercedes. This in turn called up each of his witness tags, and the far sidewalk now blossomed with a dozen caption boxes floating over the heads of passers-by.

She rolled through the first sightline and paused motion, turning and zooming into an empty space between tightly packed vehicles. Thirty-six cars lay between the corpse and the casino buses. The Mercedes sped from the north, and the shooter crawled up from the south. She had no idea how fast the assailant had moved, if he'd paused under a particular car, if he'd sensed her own watchful eye seeking him out, four days in the future. The odds had to be astronomical that she'd catch her mystery man crawling between two particular vehicles at the precise moment her particular car passed.

She waited out the next sightline, the car flowing through the dreamy choreography of slow-mo. At Zack's second marker, she paused and zoomed in to another patch of air. Motion resumed, and something tiny caught under a wheel two lanes away. As she watched, it exited from under the unhurried pressure of rubber squeezed against asphalt, launching itself into the air and spinning with a weightless ferocity. She paused and zoomed in, seeing that it was a paper clip, one tiny, private detail of the world that only she would ever witness.

At this speed, motion hypnotized. Had Pearly ever come down into the Basement and slowed down the world? He must have gotten bored. Among other serious conditions, he'd suffered from crippling sciatica, all that relentless enthusiasm probably a means of concealing pain. Or maybe he'd set his VT to filter out the hurt, to substitute smirks for winces. If he hadn't been able to maneuver through the physical world, he still had his own private world right here, 24/7. She couldn't see herself ever growing bored with all this at her disposal.

She yawned again, wondering if Pearly actually had died. Had she heard that or assumed it? The third sightline approached with a fluid grace. At this speed the green rod seemed mechanical, a component executing a task with unhurried precision. Maybe this is what death is, she thought. Maybe you get to explore forever and ever, world without end, slowing down time until you can watch each individual photon tumble through space like a dust mote. The sightline arrived and she halted motion and turned to zoom. Maybe you get to replay all the lost moments of your life, searching out every clue and solving every mystery. She pulled into the third space between cars, thinking, what outstanding mysteries would a man like Pearly Rodriguez leave behind?

Terri said, "Oh," the PanOpts up and off her head before she knew what she was doing. She sat perfectly still, finally palming and rubbing her eyes, trying to stop that skipping sensation, her brain doing loops, contradicting itself for the second time in one night. Using both hands, she slid the shades back on, finding herself in front of the Swap Meet parking lot at 5:29 and twelve seconds on Monday, January 3. With the finality of a roulette ball landing in its slot, the sightline led to a space between two parked cars. The figure in the green-and-blue-checkered hoodie squatted just below the line, having crawled up and paused before continuing, scanning the street for witnesses by sheer reflex. The shades and dust mask had already been removed and pocketed, and as the face of Stacy Santos, late daughter of the District Attorney, peered out across South Figueroa in one-fortieth real time, her eyes seemed to meet Terri across the expanse of days, the shock on one face perfectly mirroring the shock on the other.

II
GHOSTING

For almost as long as Terri had been a detective, LAPD headquarters sat on West Temple Street, in the crook of the Hollywood and Harbor freeways, less than one football field outside her own jurisdiction. All cops attempted to refer to the building as West Temple, but more and more it was just called The Temple, usually with a slight shrug and a smile to acknowledge the cheesiness of that nickname. From the outside, it looked like one of the no-name warehouses out by the airport, mirror-windowed shipping hubs surrounded by spooky, deserted parking lots. Even the simple steel plaque announcing Los Angeles Police Department sat low and squat, looking like an oversized grave marker.

A somber blue arrow bid her inwards through the cool lobby and down a long hall to the Chief's office. She placed her PanOpts in a breast pocket, snapping this shut before knocking with one knuckle. The door opened itself into a surprisingly austere antechamber: one small cloth couch, a reception desk, another unostentatious doorframe bordered only by the flags of America and California, a window looking back out onto a perfectly still parking lot. She stood for a moment, not sure what she was supposed to do, who was watching her, thinking about all the perpetrators over the years who'd seemed dazed upon surrendering their shades and encountering the world as it truly was, flat and unadorned.

Laughter leaked from the next room, and then the inner door opened and Assistant Chief Reynoso—young, Jamaican, linebacker-huge—leaned out, looking back over his shoulder, saying, "Next time, he's buying the whole goddamn platter." He turned and used the knob hand to usher her in. Chief Blanco stood behind her desk with a benevolent smile, directing Terri into one of two leather chairs. She had a flashback of getting called into the principal's office.

Reynoso perched himself on the ledge of the window frame behind Blanco, folding his arms, his face passive and unreadable. Both had dressed casually, and Terri took a moment to remember it was Saturday, that most people nurtured lives beyond their profession.

Blanco had come to head the force in the wake of scandal, and if she was known for anything as a Southland celebrity, it was for not being a celeb, for declining the spotlight in politically stark contrast to her immediate predecessor. Oddly, she had far more presence than any chief in living memory, being a stern, physically large woman, well over six feet tall, with broad shoulders and an imposing bustline. Before Terri had made detective, every anonymous jab at Blanco had turned this chest into freakish caricature, enlarging and dehumanizing the woman. Although Terri couldn't remember seeing any of these critiques after the chief had become Chief.

"So," Blanco said. "Quite some detecting there."

"Just one of those, you know, needle in a haystack moments."

Blanco smiled, just as unreadable as her second in command.

"My first question has to be, you've checked into this? There's no—I mean, absolutely none—question of mistaken identity or footage integrity?"

"None. Once I had the face, it was pretty easy to tag Stacy Santos on the scene. She gets to the swap meet twenty-eight minutes earlier, disappears inside, gets picked up again at the southwest and southeast entrances twice, then crosses into the lot and loses herself in the tour buses on the northeast side. It's all in my report. Getting her particular drones is another haystack-needle situation, and probably not crucial. I ran some basics on her traffic the week before. Before that, she was at college."

"At UC . . ."

"Palm Desert. So the only real question is where she got the gun."

"And motive. Because this is, of course, a fairly batshit set of circumstances."

"Yes ma'am."

"Any ideas?"

"On motive? Before Stacy entered the picture, I had some general theories about Mr. Jhadav. I can't imagine any would surprise you. He was the shooter on Froggy Sarin, who was,"—she was about to say a "nobody," then caught herself—"a low-level street thug with probably a minor future in the junior SSKs. Certainly not anyone with enough juice to get on task-force radar. Jhadav shot him just before New Year's."

"So he shot one, she shot one."

"That's where it stands."

"And besides my office, who else have you told?"

"No one."

Terri took in the pause and thought, *Fuck It*, taking the PanOpts from her shirt pocket and leaning forward to place them on the desk with a quiet clack. The red light was off: she wasn't recording their conversation. It was an over-the-top gesture, despite the many times she'd heard of officers and detectives doing precisely this, in situations probably far more trivial. Folded, her shades looked suddenly absurd, cheap.

Blanco dipped her head and smiled to acknowledge the gesture. Reynoso hadn't altered his own slight smile. He might as well have been a wax statue.

"Okay. Good. You get the hazards of this situation. And your partner? Don't be offended, but do you trust him?"

"I do."

"Does he know about this?"

"Not yet."

"Okay. So. That still leaves the question of porousness. Outside this room, the only living person who knows about this is the mayor. I haven't even told Juan Santos yet. I'm sure you can appreciate what a delicate situation this is. This Tournament of Roses thing is probably going to get worse before it gets better. Santos's office can keep on for a while during his bereavement leave. It would be politically . . . *complicated* . . . to go ahead and announce this new situation with his daughter without proper context."

"Context," she said by way of agreement, the word perhaps coming out challenging.

Reynoso cleared his throat and said, "There's no reason to go public with this information until we at least have a motive. Why did she do it? Was she in trouble? Was it somehow self-defense? Maybe Jhadav was somehow threatening or extorting her? Maybe he'd attacked her in the past, done a rape? Like she had some post-trauma and decided to take matters into her own hands? And did she get popped by one of his buddies? That seems like the probable here."

Terri kept her impulse to defend Farrukh in check.

"So," Blanco said, with no hint of precisely how she wanted this steered. "What do we do about this?"

There it was, as overt as the PanOpts lying face up on the desk. An actual backroom deal in which Terri had actual leverage.

"I had an idea. One of our cold cases from two years ago was from a young woman about Stacy's age who was shot in similar circumstances, in Everett Park . . . laundry room, single shot through a small window. I mean, it's not really cold, we know it was the boyfriend. But no one came forward, there was a lot of foliage, and the guy had enough shimmy in his alibi that we couldn't do anything on it. There are enough similarities here that we could play this as a possible serial killing. I mean, it's weak, but with a nudge from your office, I could get attached, work the Santos thing from this angle, and go, you know, on the low."

Reynoso chuckled in approval, "Goin' on the low."

"And Zack," the Chief said, surprising her with a first name. "How does he fit into this?"

"How should he fit?"

"Are you comfortable leaving him out of The Loop? For now? You could always say it was on my orders."

"I could."

"And what do you want in return?"

"I'm sure there will be some resource issues down the line."

"Obviously overtime is no issue."

Terri smiled. Getting her overtime back had never crossed her mind.

She left the Temple only twenty minutes later, but it felt like she'd been inside for hours. For one thing, she must've been sitting tensely, because a terrible ache had settled in her shoulders and neck. Then there were the clouds, which had parted suddenly, brightening reality beyond the lobby's tinted windows in a way that felt a little like another hangover, glints coming at her from the row of expectant cars waiting curbside to ferry the upper echelon of the department to expensive lunches.

She turned her phone on halfway across the lawn, hearing a message from a Central officer who'd located one of Farrukh's coworkers. A cop car double parked itself and popped open a door. Stepping inside with a little spring, she realized she was back on the clock, back on the mighty teat of sanctioned OT after only a week in the desert, appreciating the grand irony of this. She was probably the only detective in a twenty thousand-person organization who'd been willing to detect for free.

The car drove her to Lincoln Park, one of the rare eastside success stories below Pasadena. Up until last year, the space had been an open-air refugee camp, its drab lake known as the Ganges of Hollenbeck Area, refugees frolicking and pissing and doing laundry in it, a total mess. But some whipped-up civics group had staged a countersiege of the grounds over the course of just a few months, and their efforts had reached enough of a critical mass that the force had been obliged to offer matching effort, redeploying to an area they'd written off a decade earlier. She'd been irritated at the shift when it happened, the spillover of humanity slopping into the rest of the city, foot traffic coming under the Alhambra Avenue Overpass and raising the overall shit level in Northern Central Area for her and everyone else. In all likelihood, her own neighborhood would've been rendered unlivable if it weren't for the mighty barrier of the San Bernardino Freeway.

She saw now that it was a halfway decent park again, regretting her default to cynicism. Even if civic space was zero-sum, it was nice to have somewhere people could bring their children. As she shot past the park's southern border, there were flashes of paddleboats and bobbling kites and then a glimpse of a baseball game. The car swung into a lot near a colorless assortment of two-story municipal operations buildings, rolling to a stop near a small crowd gathered in one leafy corner. An officer was already walking over as she stepped out.

"That's him."

A miserable-looking, middle-aged refugee sat on the curb at the edge of the lot. He was leaner and darker than Farrukh, legs bent and splayed, arms behind his back. On either side stood two tiny girls, barely more than toddlers in pigtails and faded pink saris, both in different stages of hysterical bawling. Behind him, the low, sloping hill rippled with the wild, waist-high prairie grass that overtook lots and sidewalks every winter, so that he appeared perched on the outer lip of civilization.

"Jesus, you cuffed him?"

"He's a murder suspect, right?"

"The guy's a resource," she said, walking over, reading the byline over his head as she said, "Mr. Bhanghoo, I apologize for this mix-up." She hoisted the man to his feet, always surprised, when making physical contact with refugees, at both their lightness and lack of body fat. It was a well-muscled arm. No name accompanied either of the squalling girls, so far off the grid they might as well be space aliens.

"Please. I have my daughters. I'm on a schedule. It's very important I make the rest of my deliveries," he said through a thick, over-enunciated accent, inadvertently doing a spot-on impression of Zack's own impression of every refugee ever. Bhanghoo motioned toward a jerry-rigged three-wheeler with pedals and no visible motor, stacked high with paper lunch boxes the officers had left baking in the sun. She winced.

"Excuse me one moment," she said, striding over to the nearest uniformed cop, a young redhead guy with no apparent interest in this scene.

"What were you guys thinking, cuffing him out here?" she said with quiet rage. "And what the fuck were you planning on doing with his two kids?"

"We called social services. I don't know why they haven't shown up yet."

"Social. Un-fucking-believable. Cancel that. *Now*. You," she said, pointing to the other cop, both of them probably half her age. "Get those cuffs."

Chastised, one officer fumbled behind Mr. Bhanghoo while the other pointed and gestured into space as if manning a switchboard in an old-timey movie. The two girls tapered off to whimpers, hypnotized by the young cop's frantic, indecipherable hand gestures. Mr. Bhanghoo whimpered softly.

The wind shifted and Terri rotated, like a dog hearing a high note. A strange roar came from somewhere just past the municipal buildings, and as the noise intensified and swelled, she realized the roar was human. She was hearing screams: an entire crowd, screaming in near unison. A feeling close to pure dread settled over her, froze her in place, even as she glanced from one officer to the next, then to the cuffed and miserable refugee, wondering, *Am I the only one hearing this?* She lifted a trembling hand and flipped through View options to rise up, over the park, gazing down at her small, insignificant assemblage of people and finally seeing, just past the building complex, the baseball diamond teeming with life, the cheering crowd already settling down. She dropped back to ground level, shaken not only by the initial sensation but by a dual realization that something had inexplicably unrooted her, that she'd allowed a beam of pure horror to shoot through her body. She closed her eyes for a long moment, willing herself to calm down, resisting every urge to walk back to her car and sit to collect herself.

When she opened her eyes again, Bhangoo stood in front of her, rubbing his wrists. Another volley of whoops and laughter swelled and faded in the distance. The two officers conferred off to the side, their uniformed authority still absorbing the tiny girls, one of whom stood sucking on a pair of glistening, fat little fingers. She heard the redhead cop say, "Log it, tag it," his soft voice conveying the wound of a professional drubbing at the hands of a higher up.

Bhangoo moaned again, even though he hadn't opened his mouth. Their eyes met in confirmation and both turned away from the officers and the girls, back to the source of the moaning, which she now realized was in the foliage, not far from where Bhangoo had sat. Something low stirred in the underbrush. Thinking of dogs, she instinctively placed one hand over her holster.

A strand of reeds rustled and then a dark human face popped out at knee level, like a practical joke. The face was shiny with grit, another filth-drenched dirt man who raised his head and snuffled up the power to use his vocal cords.

"Please . . ."

She stared mutely, as if the terror from just a moment earlier had manifested itself in the dark underbrush.

"Please," the man croaked. "Please. Please. Doctor." He reached a hand toward her, almost close enough to clutch at a pant leg.

She swallowed and heard herself say, "Sir, let me just *deal* with one situation at a time, and, and, and then we'll have someone attend to you."

"Doctor," he said, struggling in the scrub. She glanced over at Bhangoo and, seeing an extra dread on his face, looked back down to the man in the weeds. The other arm was outstretched now. This limb ended at the wrist, and where a smooth stump should have been, there was instead a swollen bulb of wet pink and dark purple, the wound flecked with white foam. She stared long enough to register that this moving whiteness was made of maggots, looking back to Bhangoo, whose face seemed to convey that he had reached the same conclusion: don't let the girls see.

She felt this impulse violently. In the lifetime of hardship and calamity ahead of them, these two kids didn't need one extra image of horror imprinted on their tiny brains. She nodded violently away from the trees and the inhuman figure below as they both turned, seeing the smaller of the two girls was already looking behind her, staring without understanding, and as the other sensed her sister's shifted focus and turned as well, their father had already crossed the three steps between them, palming both faces with each hand, hurrying them back toward his three-wheeler.

"Hey," one of the cops yelled, reaching out.

"Let him go," Terri said, reaching into her side pocket. "Mr. Bhangoo. Hold up."

He didn't turn and acknowledge her until he'd reached the bike, looking back as he hurriedly lifted both girls and placed them in the narrow space behind his seat, eyes bugging out, obeying his instinct to flee.

She produced a pair of disposable glasses. "Take these," she said, trying to keep her voice steady. "This goes to me direct.

Call me within twenty-four hours, or, you know, this unfortunate situation could happen all over again."

He looked past her shoulder and then met her eyes with a look of incredulity, as if to say, *How?* As he mounted up and sped off, she turned back to the two baffled officers and said, "Are you guys blind? Call a fucking ambulance already."

The South Garcetti Street workstation was her closest bet for a fruitful run-in, someplace where she could sit and sift through the best way to contact Babylon Johnson and have it seem halfway casual. Stacy Santos was his case, and she figured it would be easier to try him herself, rather than have Chief Blanco contact him from on high and make Terri's involvement seem something more than informal. Entering the workstation, she found one huddle of a dozen cops, recognizing Dena Cruz and Matt Chessy and Diego Q, everyone sitting together but working separately.

"Hey gang. Anyone have a personal contact for Babylon Johnson?" This got a few chuckles and quick head shakes. She sat, and the gathering used her arrival as an excuse for a group break. Chessy pinched the bridge of his nose and removed his shades. She'd seen a study recently about the alleged harm to humanity posed by a steadily diminishing lack of eye contact.

"Okay. Two men enter, one man leaves," he said. "Babylon Johnson versus Torg. Go."

"Babs is only a foot taller," Diego said.

"Yeah."

"So what's his handicap?"

"You mean Babs?"

"Yeah."

"A backhoe," someone said.

"I'm being serious," Chessy said with mock seriousness.

"A baseball bat. Wait," Dena said to jeers. "A baseball bat that's also a gun that can shoot baseballs."

"So, a magic baseball bat."

"It doesn't have to be magic. Somebody could actually build a baseball bat that shoots baseballs."

"How many baseballs would it hold?"

As the conversation devolved into a discussion of how many baseballs could fit in the chamber of a baseball bat gun, Terri considered sharing her spooky incident from the park, the screams from the little league game. But how would she even phrase it? This was always her barrier to mingling; a lack of socializing meant a lack of social skills, and she always ended up oversharing to compensate. Someone said, "So once he's shot his what, four baseballs? Then what? He has to fight with a hollow bat? Jeez, even I don't hate Babs *that* much."

Diego said, "I dreamed last night my mother-in-law attacked me with a baseball bat. She was pissed off because she'd just found out I'd been sleeping with her daughter. I was all, 'But me and Aricely have been married eight years!'"

Terri laughed politely, relieved she wasn't the only one with a compulsion to divulge.

"So this morning I tried daymaring it, to show my wife," he said. "You ever done that?"

She realized he was talking to her. "Done what?"

"Daymaring."

"I don't know what that is."

"Oh. It's when you go back and try to recreate your dream in soft content."

"I've never heard it called that. Huh. I probably tried a few times, but it never really seems as good as the dream was."

"Don't do that," Dena said.

"I know," he said. "Although I almost got it right a few times. I guess it's not the mentally healthiest thing to do . . ."

"No, seriously. It's not just that it's bad for you. I mean it's *bad* for you. Remember Bruce Quezada?"

"From MCD? I thought he retired."

"Yeah, before he retired. There was this thing at a construction site in the valley, a family business. The eldest son crossed one of the last big-time meth crews, and thought he was going to somehow skip town before they found out. Instead, they showed up at the home office, tied everyone up and threw the whole family into a cement mixer. Then they tossed in some cinderblocks and the guard dog and left the thing on in the hot sun. And it was a long weekend. Bruce was the first one on scene, three days later. They weren't even bodies by that point.

"Afterward, Bruce does everything right, takes his eight weeks, does the Blue Dot, the works. One day he has an especially bad dream. He spent most of the morning trying to recreate it in soft content. Which is already *really* not mentally healthy. And, like you said, doesn't really work anyway. That afternoon he's watching a game when a commercial for detergent comes on. At the end of the commercial, this lady stuffs a collie into her front-loading washer and turns it on. Bruce was horrified, but what could he do? He got tagged."

"Tagged by who?" Diego said.

"There is no who. He just got tagged."

Terri said, "Reiteratives?"

"Maybe not that complicated, but that general type of thing. Some automated marketers decided that Bruce liked seeing dogs tumble around. And once they decided to show him that . . . well, that was that. It's not like there's some central authority he can go to and say, 'Hey, your targeted advertising is deeply messing my shit up.' There probably aren't even any real people left in advertising these days. So he's off network now. The poor guy sits around and reads mystery novels. He has to have his daughter place phone calls for him, because he doesn't want to see any more dogs get stuffed into appliances."

She draped her head over the cloth chair back. Daymaring: she marveled at the beautiful circularity of the word. All those primitive fumblings with shared lucid dreaming—phantasmagoria, kinetoscope, cinema—had found their endpoint in immersive soft content. Film had returned to the days of the nineteenth-century peepshow, seen one person at a time. Even animation had come full circle, all of existence essentially a giant cartoon, to be squashed and stretched at will. It amazed her, the ease with which the average citizen could go through life with their core beliefs upheld by a personalized reality. Even she had done this, in a way, having had Gabriella scrubbed from her PanOpt archives. She didn't want to contemplate how thoroughly Krista edited her universe.

This new generation lacked a common, central event. Terri's generation had been defined by that long, hot June weekend when billions died, everyone watching in disbelief as China and India killed each other. Her own adult life seemed bound by just a handful of afterimages; the night scenes from remote villages, the obscene silhouettes of apartment blocks lit by distant flashes, the sound of thousands of people screaming at once, the moment when she'd pulled off her EyePhones in terror and realized she could still hear the screams, people in nearby apartments screaming, people on the street screaming, an entire networked species howling in horror.

Modern kids had no such common event. They had no common anything. Everyone Terri's age groused about the entitlement of the next generation, people who grew up after the deprivation of the postwar bad days, the American economy temporarily totaled by acts of aggression half a world away. But the difference was larger than that. These kids had never experienced wholesale suspension of belief, the firm sensation that the carnage on the news had to be fake. All the world required of them now was a momentary suspension of disbelief; if everything was fake to begin with, then they'd never had a stake in the world in the first place.

Terri's dad had been a kind-eyed tree of a man who'd put on a lot of weight and lost a lot of hair in the years before he'd died in the shower when she was fifteen. He'd driven two hours a day, sometimes three, for a decent port job. She'd always been grateful that he hadn't been around for the bad days, despite the fact that her mother had to go through so much on her own. At least the Port Authority pension had held, the firewall between the extended Pastuszka household—eventually including her aunt and two nieces—and all the cash-crunch misery of the world beyond their house.

There was a game called Time Tower, or Tower Timer, she never remembered. It was hugely popular and strangely persistent in its popularity. In the game, players traveled back in time to the morning of 9/11, having to perform a series of tasks in both of the burning twin towers. A player could go back again and again, encountering past versions of one's self, altering past actions, looting jewelry from corpses, wandering through smoke-filled corridors, dodging sparks and flames. She'd never played herself, but Zack once let her watch his own game play. He'd stopped on the sixtieth floor and showed her, through a telescope his in-game character had had the foresight to bring along, an earlier version of himself in the window of the opposite tower. It'd been spooky and arresting: she could see why the game was so addictive.

Terri's parents would have been horrified by this game. Her dad had known two transit workers smothered under the rubble. Throughout her childhood, the date had the whiff of death. Now it was just a punchline, or, somehow worse, a plot device. She realized this was just the way of the world. Soon people would divorce the India-China war from its power to shock, laugh at its flattened miseries, squeeze it for whatever jokes and games and puzzles it had to offer. In all likelihood, this had already happened. For half her life, she'd heard the mantra: the dead should not have died in vain. But they already had.

Voices from the other seats made her realize she'd drifted off. She heard Chessy repeat the two-men-enter question, and then heard Mutty say, "Is this because Torg is back up?" Terri opened her eyes and straightened, smacking her mouth.

"Back in again?"

"Yeah. My man's got some more scores to settle, I guess. Hey Terri."

"Hey Mutty," she said, hoping the sleep breath wasn't as bad as it tasted. "You have a contact for Babs?"

On Sunday morning, Babylon Johnson and Ruben Torres picked her up in front of her building. She'd heard of both men long before she'd had the displeasure of meeting either, back when they'd served on the city's infamous fan-out anti-gang unit, two mayors ago. The duo had made a big impression on the powers that be, big enough that both rolled over to homicide when Pacific Area absorbed the Marina Del Rey station five years ago. Climbing into the department minivan, she realized the Santos case was probably the stuff guys like this dreamed of. Terri was just tagging along to see what made Stacy Santos kill, not who had killed her.

"Heyo Pastuszka," Babylon said, extending one firm handshake from the front bench seat, even as she moved away from him, toward the third row. He was muscle-bound, black, with powerful forearms and one signature leather wristband, his shiny baldness offset by huge fuzzy rectangles of mutton chop.

"Babs," she said, nodding, "Ruben. Thanks again for the ridealong."

Ruben nodded from the other side of the front bench seat. He was small, and pensive, and adept at disguising grotesque stupidity as reserved thoughtfulness.

The minivan swung back to the on-ramp and then they were on I-10, shooting east. "Whenever you're ready, I can use that residence footage," she said, partially to give herself something to do that didn't involve talking with either man. Babs was in the middle of a heated conversation with someone unseen, but he flashed her a thumbs up and did a quick V-and-point motion as he laughed and said, "Forget it man, forget it. . . . that entire *zip* code needs to be spayed and neutered."

A one-inch cube materialized in front of her face. She tapped it with her finger and the cube expanded to fill her field of vision, and then she was inside the living room of the Santos house on Captain's Row, a gated community on the western inlet of Marina Del Rey. She fiddled in the control box, delinking her view from the literal footage of what Babs had personally witnessed, hoping he'd done some thorough peeking, already annoyed at the neon pink blinds she could see between a book-lined breakfront and the wall. This was an extrapolation of the Santos house, culled from walkthrough footage and stripped of any other human life. She could wander the space at will, everything set as it was during the time of the walkthrough, roughly two hours after the body was found.

The house had a breezy feel to it, holding a tasteful assortment of stained-wood furniture and spacious couches and throw pillows embroidered with bossy little anchors. The place seemed one level too large and posh for a mere District Attorney. But then she remembered something about the DA marrying a former supermodel, explaining both the money and Stacy's good looks. Terri registered a flicker of sorrow at the destruction of such a perfect family unit, then thinking, *Fuck it, he plays the martyr card right, he can leapfrog City Hall for Sacramento.*

She followed floating arrows upstairs to Stacy's bedroom and found it bare, the discarded quarters of a college girl already four years gone, just a space with a bed and two large rolling suitcases piled on a dresser by the window. A doily sat tossed in the corner. Had Stacy resented her parents turning her old bedroom into a guest room? The other rooms on the floor had been explored hastily, leaving dozens of bright blinds between and under pieces of furniture, Babs and Ruben probably under strict orders to employ maximum tact.

The actual murder had taken place downstairs, in the back of the house, in a small annex furthest from the street. A wall of deep shelves held oars, lifejackets, picnic coolers, and other brightly colored doodads she guessed were boating paraphernalia. The room had two doors, one to the house, one to the dock, and then two windows, west and east, the latter overlooking the marina water and a lower deck that connected, by a long catwalk, to the actual pier for their two boats. Stacy had presumably come back here to change into her bathing suit. The assailant had stood on a narrow landscaped ledge, waited for her outside the west window, and fired one shot clean through her head as soon as she'd entered.

Her body lay on the floor, face down in a bikini top and terry cloth sarong, a mass of glistening black hair covering her head, arms at her side, palms up, a long smear of blood and slop on the wall the only indication that something terrible had happened. As was common with most scenes at the heart of an outsized horror, there was something small and nearly pathetic about the body itself. A floating coroner's tag noted that this footage had been taken by the responding officers and then stitched into the detectives' footage. She remembered hearing that the mother had been so distraught she'd forced the paramedics to perform CPR, despite half her daughter's head having been taken off.

She saw now what she'd already been told by Babs over the phone; there was no sex crime. The shooter hadn't even waited for her to undress, instead firing and fleeing on foot. Terri stepped through the west wall, coming out on the narrow rise that bordered the back of the property. The perp had stood on landscaped wood chips and shot through the open window's screen. No footprints, no fingerprints, no cells, no shells. She called up a Shotline layer, sending a thin purple ribbon through the blackened hole in the screen, across the room, and out through the broken glass of the opposite window. In a control box, she set the entire house for Wireframe View, and then looked through the walls to where the Shotline arced down into the water of the marina. Another LAPD tag read, UDU IN WATER 16:22 1.5.50 NOTHING RECOVERED.

She whistled in marvel, never having heard of divers going in within two hours of first call. But that was the level of attention the force had brought to bear. How could it be otherwise? Not that it would do them any good. If they hadn't gotten a break by now, they wouldn't. The rich paid for privacy, and now they were going to pay because of privacy. Captain's Row prided itself on a lack of surveillance, relying on foot security instead of drones or macros or even reliable ShotSpotter sensors. All the killer had to do was scramble down to the water thirty feet away and swim off in any of a half-dozen different directions. Maybe he or she had drifted away atop Froggy's stiff corpse.

She floated back toward the house, reentering through a kitchen wall. Turning, she saw a slender tree growing outside the window, and she thought of the skinny tree outside her old kitchen window in South Pasadena, an on-and-off-ramp for the agitated squirrels that used to gallop across their roof. Before moving to California, she'd never known that squirrels could cluck. But they did cluck, pausing at eye level on the tree to make eye contact with her and tut angrily, enraged at the beautifully arranged pots and saucepans dangling from the ceiling rack and the gleaming marble countertops Gabriella had so painstakingly selected.

The car angled upward and Terri felt a pit of queasiness. She pulled up her shades as the freeway sloped up the hilly pass into the inland valley, peering out the back window to align stomach with inner ear. In the distance, downtown's tightly packed skyscrapers perched on the horizon, like the Emerald City of Oz. Her earpiece chimed.

"Hey," Zack said, "Calling you back."

"Yeah, gimme a second." She pulled up his VT and did a circle point to the seat next to her, so that it appeared to her and her alone that he sat in the car with them.

"You at home?"

"I got Wade's birthday party all afternoon. There's about five hundred seven-year-olds everywhere."

She heard a rush of high-pitched squawks and squeals in the background. "Hold up. I'm going onto the patio." Unaligned, his presence on the bench seat spoke and swayed with the motion of the car, but itself offered no other evidence that it was supposed to represent a sentient human being somewhere else on the planet. It was as if Zack spoke while hypnotized.

"I saw you got a witness on the case of the guy who got killed in a parking lot that no one cared about," he said, his lack of enthusiasm momentarily matching the torpor of his VT.

"Yeah, I got with them yesterday."

"And?"

"And nothing. Dead end number 846."

She had talked with Mr. Bhangoo this morning by phone. He'd told her what she had already suspected, that he and Farrukh hadn't been friends, hadn't been anything more than grunting acquaintances. Although when pressed, he offered that he didn't think Farrukh had any friends. Both worked for three different walla companies, breakfast, lunch, and dinner. Terri had asked if Farrukh had ever done anything out of line, out of the ordinary, had ever given him any reason to make any possible enemies. "There's no time to make *anything*," Bhangoo had said. "We get our boxes. We give our boxes. We go."

This sounded right. Farrukh had worked sixteen-hour days, seven days a week. The guy was at his maximum earning power, presumably still supporting his niece, and the odds were good his pay wasn't cutting it. She'd heard of skyscraper residents working themselves to death on orders of their floor manager, taco wallas mired in eternal poverty, gangs juicing them for every penny, able to track their movements, and thus their earnings, through the networks. In some skyscrapers, gang middle managers dynamically priced rent in direct proportion to earnings. A guy squeezed this hard would have no problem going to other corners of the underworld for something extra: not work, but maybe a loan, or a finder's fee on something.

Ever so slowly, the pieces were drifting into place. But only if she ignored the Stacy Santos thing. Santos: shit. She realized she was going to have to be careful to keep all notes out of her and Zack's shared data pool.

He asked, "Where are you going?"

"Heading out to UCPD."

"And how are you on the Santos thing again?"

"Similar m.o. as on Hackley. Identical, really."

"So what?"

"So, maybe it's the same doer."

"I thought that was the boyfriend."

"I don't know that we ever landed on that," she said, hoping she was as good a bullshitter as he was always giving her credit for. A gaggle of children squealed behind him at the same moment Babylon exploded in laughter from the front seat. She heard Zack grunt to express skepticism tempered with indifference, which was what she'd counted on.

"That asshole Babs in the car with you?"

"Yep."

"Tell him . . . scratch that. Don't tell him anything."

"Tell him yourself," she said a little too loudly.

From the front seat, Babs bellowed, "Yo, is that my man Zendejas?"

"God, I hate that fucking guy," Zack said, his VT mouthing the words blank faced, like a man-sized ventriloquist dummy. The minivan banked right and a patch of sun lit his VT's face, seen from three-quarter view, so that the right eye momentarily turned a bright, translucent amber and his seated image seemed jarringly real. Babs said, "Put him on! My man!"

"Do *not* put me on with that walking hard-on."

"He says he has to go. He's at his kid's birthday party." Babs laughed, and she realized he thought she was joking.

Zack said, "Don't get raped."

"Wow. Bye." His VT winked out of existence.

Babylon did air punches, yelling, "Karate killa!" as Terri closed her eyes and gently rubbed small circles into each temple, already sick of his presence.

The minivan raced down the other side of the mountain, and she thought back to her phone call with Bhangoo. Neither had mentioned the incident from yesterday. Thinking about it soberly now, she realized she'd heard much worse horror stories of the walking wounded. The city was full of them, refugees unwilling to stumble into the emergency room on the mistaken belief that they'd be summarily deported to Colorado, whisked off to a government camp that, in their eyes, could be worse than anything cooked up by the Spanish Inquisition. One more invisible barrier in a city full of invisible barriers.

Babs said, "Here it comes." He started a countdown, which seemed besides the point. In her shades, she could see it coming: the edge of the Wall. Actually, the edge was itself a wall, the slightly terrifying plane of translucent pink she'd avoided in the Basement, a physical manifestation of the limit of civic law enforcement. Babs belted out his countdown like it was New Year's Eve.

"Five, four, three . . ."

She held her breath for the hiccup. For one long moment, PanOpt blinked, swapped jurisdictions, and then the rounded pentagon logo of the Phoenix Wall appeared to her far west and high overhead, like a second sun, troubling in its lack of subtlety. Even though the PHX Wall extended 450 miles, all the way down to Tucson, it only sheltered six million people, less than a quarter the population of LA County. It wasn't a system known for thoroughness. The hypothetical danger to any LA cop outside their own Wall—something remarkably easy to tune out—had a jarring reminder any time she looked up.

The car picked up speed, whipping by all the vertical trappings of inland autonomy: rooftop generators, private wind turbines, lofty arrays of gold-and-white solar balloons. Many of the older residents and business owners out here remained haunted by shock poverty, by the bad old days when they'd found themselves stranded on the edge of a metropolis. The freeway passed vast cacti gardens of reclaimed mall parking lots, and she tried to mentally superimpose this concept on the city they were leaving, calling up an image of Farrukh lying face up and serene among the dusty succulents and sagebrush.

Somewhere past Redlands, an enterprising vandal had hand-painted SAVE YOUR TEARS FOR HELL on the long concrete wall of a shuttered strip mall. Locals prided themselves on their caustic independence, even as they sopped up the economic run over from the business corridor next door. In the distance, massive wind turbines stood like crucifixes over Calvary. She'd heard of vagrants living inside turbines, squatting in the nacelles—a word she only knew from the program *Squatting In The Nacelles*—occasionally getting themselves killed and roasting in the heat for days or months, the stench making even the most hardened cleanup crews balk.

Near the outskirts of Banning-Cabazon, another switch occurred, this one far more profound than the edge of the Wall. The desert swelled with sprawl, a sea of red-roofed, neo-Spanish colonial apartment blocks and glass-walled condos stretching to the horizon on both sides. This was the long-delayed nanotech corridor, the dominant economic engine of the Southland—and, soon, the rest of the planet—a region flush with so much startup cash that LA County's GDP got a bump just on the overflow. Rumor had it that much of the upper echelon of the urban Chinese nanoengineering elite had discreetly resettled out here months before the shit hit the fan, housed in posh underground quarters, complete with their own private mini-malls and subterranean parks.

She hadn't been out here in years, and the growth was staggering. How could so many people die and yet humanity only lose a decade or two of progress? A wonder set in, vertiginous and breathtaking. Somewhere, out in the blur of fresh development, were the most powerful minds on the planet. Among her generation, there existed a clear sense that many of the traps and indignities of old age would have simply ceased to exist by the time she made it to retirement.

Not that they were affordable yet. The fruits of this new economy—hawked in fluttering cloth banners for augmentation labs and limb clinics, the precursor for the swell of ads in civilian Overlay layers—were terribly expensive. They all heard stories, more and more frequently every year. Jose Minty had three fingers shot off during a foiled robbery in Tarzana. At a clinic somewhere out here, he had three replacements grown and attached, and it'd taken a second mortgage to cover the co-pay. Minty still complained of phantom pains, only half-joking that he could still feel his old fingers out there, somewhere, crawling around in the underbrush, describing the sensation to amused late-night Uganda drunks, wriggling his fingers in the air like a scoutmaster telling ghost stories.

Terri chuckled, realizing she'd been making the same gesture now, occasionally lifting and poking the air in front of her to make herself look occupied and unavailable for banter.

University of California Palm Desert could afford to deck out its campus entry with a lavish display of water-hogging shrubbery and fruit trees. She understood the campus-as-oasis metaphor, but it seemed like a crummy message to send any prospective parents, conveying supreme squander before anyone even entered the premises. As the most successful unit in the not-fully-revived UC system, Palm Desert wasn't a cheap school. UCPD: she pictured a bumbling small-town police department.

As they pulled into the central roundabout, Babs said, "This still winter break?" Ruben shrugged. They stepped out into the warm desert air and a seemingly deserted campus, the only sound a mechanical, arrhythmic clink-clank. It took her a moment to figure out she was hearing two flagpoles, state and nation, each hung at half mast and furiously clanking against their poles, sounding out the university's grief for its fallen student celebrity.

She called up a directory and found the main campus layer. The space surrounding them erupted in Overlay memorials, so many that as she followed Babylon on his walk to Stacy Santos's dorm, the crossing felt like a jaunt through an especially morbid amusement park. They passed crying teddy bears next to candles that twinkled and guttered without need for oxygen. In one spot, an endless rain of rose pedals floated down from Heaven, not far from a hovering forty-ounce bottle of malt liquor eternally pouring itself onto the pavement. She recognized many of the ready-made templates—ribbons, crosses, bobbling wreaths, origami cranes rotating with turntable precision—although she'd never visited any crime scene with such variety and volume, all that hard-earned cash represented by these endless virtual tributes. Perhaps someone in the memorial business had a motive to bump off Stacy Santos.

They traversed a wide commons, offering an expanse of airspace claimed by larger, far more expensive tributes. One house-sized balloon slowly changed from a candle into a valentine's heart and back again, flickering with an eerie energy. Below this, a huge eye cried smaller, tear-shaped balloons that dribbled off into the sky. Farther away, a hot-air balloon shaped like a giant human heart revolved serenely. She wondered how the school allocated airspace in this layer, if it was first come, first serve, or if they charged for the use of even non-surfaces on campus.

The tributes grew both more personal and more anguished as they approached the dorm's quad. Walls featured gaudy spray-paint murals and poignant tributes in fluorescent chalk. The central fountain had been covered in an elaborate wrap-around animated photomosaic of Stacy, presumably made entirely from pictures and videos found online. On any free surface, thousands of strangers had inserted their own charcoal drawings, watercolors, and oil paintings, in all the infinite permutations of projected grief. In public spaces too abnormal for graphics—the curb, bench slats—words took the place of graphics: PEACE 4FER, ALWAYS, LOVE. One floating memorial offered a manifesto, far too much text to take in, although Terri caught the words *my sexual love for the deceased* as she passed. She was surprised that no one had caught this yet, then remembered they were outside LA County and its resources.

She paused in front of the steps to the dorm, turning to take it all in, her eyes smarting from the dazzle and clutter of it all. There were no memorials for Farrukh. He'd passed through the world and left nothing. If she were to go back to the Swap Meet lot, there wouldn't even be a stain.

This entire trip to Stacy's campus had been intended as nothing more than an exploratory ride along. Terri hadn't expected any major surprises. And yet, when Babs pressed the keypad to Stacy's suite and bid them entry, one mystery did indeed resolve itself. Reading through the initial case files the day before, Terri had found herself wondering why a college senior would still live on campus. Stacy had been gearing up to apply for a master's program in Guadalajara. Why would she want to deal with the stresses of roommates, or the noise from on-campus partying? Terri's own dorm experiences had been an endurance test, although she made a point of refraining from discussing college around other cops, lest she offend those whose schooling ended at eighteen.

Standing in the dorm's living room, she had her answer. The suite was a modernist duplex, with one two-story glass wall facing due west, over hilly scrubland the university must've purchased and kept vacant just for the view. She had to remove her shades to confirm that the distant mountains really were real. It was hard to imagine how spectacular the setting sun would look through this window.

Stacy's room was upstairs, also facing west. There wasn't much to go on: unmade single bed, empty hamper, work desk with nothing more than a Lakers pencil caddy. Her father had told Ruben that Stacy hadn't been romantically involved with anyone for over a year, and there was nothing to contradict that here. Turning from the window, she saw that the entire smooth wall adjacent to the door had been decorated with only a newsprint school events calendar and an inspirational meadow scene reading *BATHE IN BLESSINGS*. The attached single bathroom looked unused. Maybe something to that detail, she thought, remembering again that she was here to figure out what had made Stacy kill, not who killed her.

There was one interesting quirk in the closet. Santos had collected novelty key chains, hundreds of them. They hung on an orderly grid of hooks she must've installed herself. There didn't seem to be much rhyme or reason to the collection. Some were probably mementos from past trips, but others advertised sports teams, or long-ago cartoon characters, or hardware stores. Perhaps it'd reminded her of childhood, although when Terri turned off the closet light and stepped back out, the darkened collection seemed vaguely creepy, like the souvenirs of a serial killer. Maybe something to that as well.

She exited into the landing hall, then stepped out onto a second-story exterior walkway that connected dorm suites. Inside, the men wrapped up a thorough look-through, mapping each room and then stacking this map against one made four days earlier, by campus police. She was still marveling at the carnival atmosphere of all the Overlay memorials when she heard Babs make a dismissive whinny, turning to see him examining the door's light-up thumb pad. Appearing to speak to the door itself, he said, "Yeah, they're all light ups. Bet my damn thumb unlocks each one now, too. Some *bull*shit. Where'd you get with that voice coach?"

"You talking to me?"

"Uh-huh," he said, facing her but seeing someone else. "Yeah, yeah. That's it. Don't back down. To her, or her skinny-ass sister."

A college boy exited from the next suite over, eyeing her and Babylon with visible unease. The kid was pale and bug-eyed, wearing a turtleneck and bolo like every other pencil-neck poser back in Boyle Heights. He didn't view them through any EyePhones, but it must've been obvious who they were. The young man turned and speed-walked for the far stairs, making it halfway before Babs called out, "Heyo! Hold up! Hold up! Let me get with you, chief!"

The kid turned and froze.

"That's that shit! You're in it now!" Babs laughed, walking forward with one arm outstretched. She watched this unfolding scene with mild amusement, the poor student looking like a prey animal. She thought about calling up the kid's byline, taking a peek at his back story, then thinking, *Who cares?* Babs caught up with him and held one palm against the young man's chest, even as he looked away, still lost in the heat of his call.

"Naw, man, fuck that! You wait a month? For what? So she can get *another* interest-free loan from your dumb ass?"

They stood like this for a minute. The college kid made eye contact with Terri and she shrugged apologetically. To the wall, Babylon said, "I hear that. But, you know, I'm gonna wanna hear that the *next* time we talk." He chuckled, turning to the kid and saying, "Let me ask you something, chief. How come none of you kids use keys?"

The college boy paused and said, "Are you talking to me?"

"Who the hell else would I be talking to?" Babs said, glancing about theatrically, his open palm still on the boy's chest.

"Okay . . . what?"

"How come none of you kids use keys? You know what a key is? A house key."

"Um. Yes."

"Okay, then. I couldn't but help notice that every single door on this campus is a thumb pad. You aren't worried about how you'll get back in your room if the power goes out?"

"But . . . why would the power go out?" the kid asked as if it were a trick question. Babs sighed and let his head droop in mock frustration.

"And let me guess. You never even bothered to get your driver's license, right?"

The college boy glanced back at Terri again, and for a second looked like he might cry.

She shrugged again, saying, "Well?"

"I have my identification back in my room. If you'll just let me get it . . ."

An hour later, she and Babs and Ruben sat at a metal bench under a fluttering cloth umbrella, not far from where they'd disembarked, three trays of paper-boxed lamb curry and potatoes between them. Out of a hundred tables, only one other held people. But the cafeteria had been open for business, at least to service the cafeteria staff.

"What was the final deal?" she asked. "Is it still vacation? Or did they clear the campus just because someone got killed?"

"Sunday," Babs said. "Maybe everybody's at church."

Over the double doors they'd emerged from, she read JANUS CAPITAL DINING HALL. It'd taken her a little too long to figure out all the buildings had sponsors. She didn't like feeling unobservant. When she looked back at her traveling companions, she caught them glancing over her shoulder with delight, twisting to see the turtleneck boy scurrying off. Babs said, "Do you realize a freshman in college today wasn't even *born* when the shit hit the fan?"

She laughed. "They get the key chains but no keys."

"God damn! Yes! That was messed up, right? Reminded me of, um, what's that guy?" He looked to Ruben. "I don't remember his name, but this guy? Nice house, adobe, in one of the canyons. I don't even remember what got us out there, but we go in? In his living room, he's got hundreds of gas station rest room key holders. Remember those? Keys attached to all kinds of stuff so people wouldn't steal them. Metal kitchen spoons, broken wrenches, lug nuts, bookends. Decades of this crap, hanging all over two walls in the guy's living room. So we get him out on his lawn, seated, cuffed, and we start talking really loud about what a break this is, how we're going to charge him with felony possession for each and every one. He thought he was facing, like, nine hundred years. So he twists around and goes, 'The guns are in the cooler! The guns are in the cooler!' I said, 'Man, I wasn't even looking for guns!'"

Ruben smiled at this moment with pride, as if recalling his wedding night.

She sipped her coffee. A real-life tumbleweed rolled across the edge of the parking lot, thought better of it, and zipped back toward the scrubland. As she watched its progression, her gaze rested on a colorful assortment of boxes and tubes by the edge of the seating area. She'd seen this as she'd exited the cafeteria, and had assumed it'd been just one more memorial to Stacy.

Examining the collection of odd sculptures now, she realized it was a miniature shantytown. A torn banner reading SEGREGATION NATION shuddered in the wind. Five feet away, a colossal cardboard tube at least seven feet long—packing material for some monstrously large piece of machinery—had been planted upright and painted in gray, with amateurish black boxes for windows. She saw the little paper-mache kufi cap on top and realized it was meant to represent the West Fifth Street skyscraper.

"Is this supposed to be downtown?"

The men turned and made nearly identical hissing noises.

"Spoiled-ass pieces of shit," Babylon said. "'Waah! Our Indian brothers have to live in high rises! It's not fair! Wahhh!'"

"All they need are some little meatballs."

Babs bent his flexible spoon backward and flung a ball of curry at the base. When this fell short, he reached into the container, pulled out a fresh glop barehanded, and hurled it with the true aim of a Major League pitcher. The projectile hit not quite dead-on, making a satisfying splat against the thick cardboard.

"And there's the R-A-L-A."

She finished her coffee and said, "I ran into her last week, not far from there."

"Ran into who?"

"Chandrika Chavan. RALA."

"Jesus, that fucking twat slot."

Ruben smiled and said, "Aw, all that lady needs is a good long dumpster fuck." His voice was reedier than Terri remembered.

"A humpster! Face down in the trash," Babylon agreed, adding, "*Monch*," making a quick downward-palming motion and then high-fiving his partner.

"Hey guys, don't hold back on my account," she said, no longer smiling.

"That lady is a goddamn liar, too. After all that shit she talked when they took out the last pay phone downtown, public works still puts in those pedestrian footbridges. Then, when the time comes for her to good mouth us, for once, Reggie Flores goes all the way to her office, says, 'Okay, we held up our end of the bargain. You get the footbridge for the pay phones. Now we need you to keep up your end, and tell everyone that this was the deal we made.' You know what she said?"

Terri realized he was talking to Ruben, not her.

"She's all, 'I never said that. We never had any conversation about that.'"

Ruben murmured something, but Terri was already tuning them out, thinking first about Stacy—Had she ever sat at this table? Was she one of the kids who built this sad shantytown?—then thinking about the name, Palm Desert, best of both worlds. She realized this was the farthest she'd physically been from Los Angeles in nearly three years. She had enough money for a nice vacation. But where would she go, alone?

On Monday morning, Zack picked her up nearly two hours before dawn. Usually he brought her a drink in these situations.

"No coffee? What'd I do to deserve this?"

"I blew up my rotator cuff. I can't really lift anything with my left arm. Let's get some. There's a Coffee Siege up in Feliz that's already open."

"Blew out? Or up?"

"Right. Whichever. It hurts."

"Wade's party get wild?" she said, amused. Terri had an advantage this early in the morning, being able to bounce back to life quickly. All she ever needed was a splash of cold water on her face and she was up. Zack was a cinder in the mornings.

"Oh God, it's too complicated to tell without coffee."

The city was dark and private, and she felt strangely optimistic, passing lavanderias with their tumbling anonymous laundry, a glimpse of a walking couple, the man holding a sleeping child and the woman cradling a tiny sleeping dog. She flashed back on Jersey, being driven somewhere by a parent. Terri always wished she had the correct music to go with these moments. She could probably find the right songs, but it would be too much work, she'd have to get out her shades, turn them on, find a radio app, and tell it to make up its own DJ banter. By then the moment would be gone.

Matching her thought, the car's radio played a squealing guitar solo. She turned up the volume by hand, hearing a husky man's voice croon,

Well I'm high on rock n roll
And ain't never gone be told
What to dooo-a-hoooo-hoooo
So momma off my back
You better cut me slack
Or I'll rock and roll all over you-a-hoooo-hoooo

Zack followed her stare and slitted his eyes, placing a thumb on the radio's tranquil blue button, as if speaking with a tiny band playing just behind the dashboard.

"Write better music."

The husky voice switched gears, busting into a throaty power ballad,

Rock n roll, Rock n roll
It's all over my soul
Gonna Rock n roll overload
To Rock n roll you

"Sorry," Zack said. "It gets in a rut sometimes." To the radio, he said, "Write a song about homicide detectives solving important murders." A jaunty piano and sax number started up, and a different man's voice sang,

Well I'm a rock n roller cop
And baby I won't ever stop
Till I've caught the rotten cock
Who murdered yoo-a-hooooo . . .

He nodded. "Not bad."

The car pulled halfway into the coffee shop's crowded, tiny lot. As they emerged, Zack said, "Hey, I'm out of ghost stickies."

"I'm going to pretend I didn't hear that."

A line of frowning working people waited at the far counter for their drinks, the poser shop being open too early in the morning for actual posers. A quiet underburble of flamenco guitar gave the space a formal, grim air.

The barista, young, not smiling, said, "Yop."

"Yeah, two large."

"Two large what."

"Two large coffees?"

"Regular coffees."

"Yeah."

She traced a finger in the air and said, "Twenty-eight."

"Check it again. I've still got some on my prepaid."

"No, you don't," she said as a drawn-out sigh, as if talking with a child caught in a repeat offense.

"No, actually I do."

"Would you like me to pull up your transactions?"

"Yeah, you do that. This was a goddamn *Christmas* gift, there's no way I killed it this quickly."

She squiggled her finger in the air a few more times, then tapped the bridge of her nose. Zack pulled down his PanOpts as the barista said, "It's in 19, channel 41."

Terri put on her own shades and brought up the public layer, seeing a brightly lit array of small boxes floating over the counter, footage of all of Zack's transactions for the previous two weeks, arranged like rooms in a living dollhouse.

"Jesus, okay," Zack said. "Overkill."

The barista smiled at his defeat, handing over a small square of paper which he signed, saying, "In the old days, management would've just given me a coffee pro bono, you know that?"

As they left, a customer said something while looking over at them and half the room laughed.

The car pulled them back onto the freeway, Zack shaking his head like a dog and then wincing, touching his shoulder with the hand holding the coffee.

"Auugh. Faccckkkkk." Zack sipped thoughtfully, returning to life, growing quick eyed.

"So," he said. "Before the party yesterday, we pick up the first floor, we still have time for a nice Sunday brunch before anyone shows up. I get the nice French press going, some crullers; I'm thinking life is good. I sit down at the big table, I'm about to bring up the *Sunday Times* and Janice plops down a stack of papers. Like, actual paperwork. On my table. On Sunday. I go, 'What's this.' She says, 'Those refi papers you promised we'd do last weekend.'

"So already I'm pissed because A, I don't remember promising anything, and B, if it was so fucking important that the bank had to send actual paperwork, why did it wait until Sunday? We clear off space, spread this crap out all over the table, I'm mad at her, she's mad at me for being mad at her, Wade is already high as a kite on gummi trolls or something.

"I go get the French press, put it down next to me, pour myself a mugfull and instantly—I mean, like on cue—Wade jumps up to grab something and knocks my mug over. So then I reach over to tip the mug up and because I'm wearing that big robe? With the big floppy wizard sleeves? I knock over the whole fucking French press. Now there's this tsunami of scalding hot coffee spreading out in all directions on the table, Janice is screaming, Wade is screaming, I'm furiously trying to blot up everything with the mortgage papers, it's like a *war* movie. Then I realize Hyperion is sleeping in the far chair, and one big steaming stream of coffee is heading right toward him. I mean, what a way to go out, right? A blast of hot death in the snout? I've got handfuls of bank documents in both fists, I'm trying to blot everything up, but it's like I can't *get* to that side of the table fast enough."

She nodded in sympathy. Hyperion's real name was Chaz. He was a mopey, dopey basset hound Janice had owned since before she'd even met Zack. The dog's absurd longevity was due to her strict regimen of ground venison and imported vitamins. But as a young dog, Chaz had been known for his voracious appetite for all things shit: diapers tossed in alleys, any stray animal droppings, including his own. Zack had nicknamed the dog Hyperion Waste Eatment Plant. Janice had painstakingly trained Hyperion to bypass these dark impulses and then banished the nickname from their house. Zack only used the moniker when not at home. These days, Chaz was barely there, a milky-eyed survivor who had to be hoisted up and down from their couch.

"So I did this pretty amazing jump, got the spill just before disaster, totally saved the day. The punchline is, I'm up on the table, robe soaked with steaming hot coffee, ruined, Wade looks at the bottom of the tipped-over mug, reads 'Made In China,' and says, 'Mommy, where's "China"?' And Janice just starts *bawling*. I mean, out of the blue. Happens to all of us, but still."

This surprised her. She'd always found a slight impenetrable formality to Janice, a woman well versed in socializing with cops, but who seemed to match their on-guard formality with her own reserve. At Zendejas barbecues, no cop made Uganda-style jokes.

"It was only later, surrounded by little kids, that I realized I must've really done something bad to my shoulder."

"I'm not sure what to say. 'Wow'?"

"Or 'ouch.' Either one."

The car slowed to eighty-five miles per hour, curved onto surface streets, slowed, and halted at a stoplight in front of the train station, one of the few working lights in Central, passage for the tourists that would flood the block in two hours. In the distance, past the train station, she could make out the perfect silhouette of the decaying crane the city was still in the process of suing the owner of, black matte on lambent night sky. A pregnant woman shuffled across the sidewalk in front of them, her head low with shame or purpose.

Zack took another sip of his coffee and said, "Ha ha, you had sex."

In the years before Terri had made detective, commuter railroad surfing had become an epidemic among the refugee population, rush hour trains chugging along their routes as unrecognizable, train-shaped masses of humanity, thousands of refugees clinging to every possible surface that didn't touch the tracks. The problem had gotten so bad that the Southern California Regional Rail Authority simply shut down for two months to assess their options. Several high visibility and extra-gruesome train deaths in Chicago and DC had given those cities the political leverage to install a variety of people-repellant roofs, including spikes, shock strips, and grip-resistant alloys. Some trains rolled into stations festooned with barbed wire.

Los Angeles trains, being slower, didn't produce such photogenic carnage. So their workarounds had to be creative. And SCRRA's solution was indeed a rare feat of political vision: the First Ride / Last Ride program, adding two extra trains, one at the beginning and one at the end of every route. Refugees got steep discounts in return for the waiving of maximum occupancy rules. The result was a pre-dawn and late-evening crush of humanity at Union Station. These trains rolled along with their huddled masses smooshed safely inside.

Terri and Zack waited in the car for ten minutes, knowing that the 5:38 First Ride had rolled out by the sudden upsurge of racial diversity in the throng of predawn commuters, the crowd transforming from all-Indian to cosmopolitan multicultural in sixty seconds, like an elaborate piece of choreography. As they crossed into the mighty lobby of Union Station, the foyer of a great city, Zack said, "You know they shot *Blade Runner* here?"

She'd come along today because she'd been unsure how to proceed with the Stacy Santos thing, knowing from experience that sometimes the best way to solve a problem was to work on a different problem, give her brain time to process information in the background. Now it felt like procrastination, drifting farther from the real work she'd been charged with. Terri opened a web box in the air between them, pulling up the JoyRide schedule and scrolling over to the San Bernardino trains.

"So . . . first arrival is in eighteen minutes. You want front of house or back?"

"I'll take back. I'd rather stand for a while. Probably easier on my fucked-up shoulder. Also, stickies please. Solly Cholly."

"Yeah, that is some deeply sorry shit," she said, digging in her pocket and producing two thin Ghosting Sticker packets. "So if you were a betting man, what odds would you place on us catching fish today?"

"Good. Maybe. I mean, I have a good feeling about the guy."

"Really."

Last year, Lydia Orozco and her half-blind Cuban lover had killed Lydia's husband, Sid, set fire to the body, drained the Orozco Pallet Company bank accounts and fled to Manila. Her twenty-two-year-old son, Jerry, had apparently aided and abetted the conspirators, but hadn't been able to get out of town before the dragnet had snapped into place. There was no record of his having left the city. Escaping by car or bus was out of the question, the guy couldn't afford a flight anywhere even if he could catch one, and if he'd set out on foot, one of a million automated eyes would surely have nabbed him.

"Yeah, really. That *LA Doings* article on the department came out last night."

"And?"

"And I know for a fact that Jerry Orozco is an avid *Doings* reader. And the article explicitly mentions the end of overtime. The math is so simple, even this numbskull can figure it out. He's going to assume that the force ran out of cash and manpower and thus lost interest in his case . . ."

"And of course no one ever loses interest in a case . . ."

He ignored her jab. "So today's the day he's going to bump. I can feel it. And there's only one way out."

"That's not true. He could hop a freight."

"That's still called a *train*," Zack said, his mysterious solemnity almost making it make sense, setting off for the far end of the station, his audio sounding as if he were still standing next to her.

She meandered halfway into the vast waiting room, feeling something close to love for the beauty of the space, the hard-edged eternal grandeur, the building surely having predated Los Angeles by many millennia, waiting patiently for passengers to arrive. Halfway in, she found a free chair, parking herself in the worn leather seat, wide enough that she could fit both hands comfortably on her thighs with plenty of maneuvering room.

Arm space was important for ghosting. The department issued official Ghost Control fobs, but fewer and fewer cops carried wallets anymore, and they'd become just one more piece of unnecessary clutter. Some cops drew the eight buttons on pieces of paper, but that was problematic, as it meant you always needed to keep your hands in sight. And a few cops still used hand gestures, although she'd never been able to figure out how to do that for more than a few minutes without getting arm cramps.

Yawning, she retrieved her own ghost sticker set from a jacket pocket. From the flip side, she peeled off two stickers and slapped one to each thigh, halfway up from the knee. Each clear square came imprinted with four buttons. On her left thigh, she had up/down and left/right. On her right thigh, she had forward/backward and go/stop. She placed her coffee on the floor between her feet, straightened in her seat, and pressed the up button, thinking of an old-timey elevator.

Terri slid up, out of the top of her head, floating up to stop twenty feet above the station floor. She looked down out of some primal superstition, confirming that she was still there, seeing herself seated below, one stranger in dark glasses among many. Older cops preferred controllers when working out of body. She'd spent a year getting used to working without direct, mechanical feedback, but now she couldn't imagine going back. Guiding her body in the ghost zone—the real-time parallel to the Basement—intuitively felt the most comfortable when using fingertip motion, or, when necessary, full hand motion. But hands and arms tire easily, and once she'd got into the right rhythm of finger gestures, it would have been a needless chore using any other interface. Everyone had their own way of doing things.

With near-absolute coverage, Union Station was a cop's dream. In the few opportunities she'd had to do ghost work here, she'd always searched for blinds and come up wonderfully short. In the entire station, there couldn't be more than a half-dozen spaces not surveilled, mostly confined to the thin wedges above the hallway's light sconces, or in the low nooks below each vending machine.

Sixty-five percent was the general magic number for making faces. A person wearing wraparound shades, EyePhones or otherwise, showed sixty-five percent of their face. But citizens could and did wear protective dust masks with shades. Those people could not be identified, and it was those suspicious citizens that she and Zack needed to watch. Jerry Orozco stood 5'11" and had a small mole on the side of his neck. Any face-obscured male passenger coming close to that description was to be questioned.

She fiddled with a stats box, reading that one face out of eighteen wore a dust mask with shades, although the number fluctuated as she watched, the proportions constantly changing with the orderly flow of the crowd. She zoomed over to the Orange Julius kiosk, turning back to face the main room at eye level, a phantom in the horde. Two young girls passed, each holding pet turtles in translucent portable terrariums, crossing close enough to her that she could catch the shallow water sloshing. Further back in the main room, a loud gaggle of students had gathered before embarking on a trip, legs up on their massed suitcases and sleeping bags. Nearby, a young couple stood holding hands, gazing into each other's eyes as if frozen in a photograph. They hugged and parted, and then a sparrow flitted in one of the open doors and hopped along the smooth, worn terra-cotta toward the coffee before her feet, turning only when she shifted her foot, the sensation of seeing herself move making her slightly uneasy.

Zack texted,

1 2 U in 30. Y WB.

She ghosted over to the middle of the long corridor, spotted the guy, then pulled off her PanOpts and stood with a lingering wooziness. She'd let Yellow Windbreaker Man come to her, let him see her face, that she was cop, knowing Zack was on the ghost end and would be watching to see if he bolted. Not that this guy would be their guy. Otherwise, why would he be walking away from the train platforms?

The man approached on her left. She waited until he was two steps away, gliding briskly into his path and sliding down her shades in one practiced motion.

"Los Angeles police. May I see your identification, please?"

The stranger grunted and yanked down his dust mask. A byline reading DONRIK BARBOZA popped into the space overhead. Zack texted,

nice name, dipshit

"Thank you, sir."

She sat, palmed her eyes, and slipped on her shades, returning to the long hallway. Reintegrating herself as the ghostly eye of law enforcement, she watched a man in a dust mask walk down the long hallway with a stiff formality, his strange, calculated gait seemingly requiring concentration. He was far too tall to be who they wanted. Zack texted,

Yeah, I saw this guy walking like that on the other side. U think it's Eshkol, or perpy shit?

She followed the man for twenty feet, her motion as smooth and cinematic as if she'd been mounted on a dolly for a tracking shot. She wrote,

Eshkol. He's following walking instructions.

Zack texted,

OK. But do me a solid? Go ahead & arrest anyway 4 being a geeky jagoff who is actively making the world 1 person more stupid.

She nodded. Eshkol people used movement notation to govern every possible aspect of life—walking, exercising, eating, the repetitive motions of labor—to ensure maximum efficiency. It veered close to religion for some people. She'd heard that thousands of couples used it for sex. She shuddered slightly, turning and whipping down the hallway and back into the main room.

The mighty crush of commuters surged and receded, leaving the long-distance travelers scattered in its wake. After standing to interrogate a half-dozen annoyed men, she settled into her seat for the long haul, starting a timer to remind her to shift legs, another to get up and walk around. At eight, she rose and grabbed a tea from the bustling little tourist kiosk, admiring all the shiny, unsold souvenir key chains dangling from a counter display. By nine, she was already bored with being a ghost, doing aerial loops around the hall.

She eavesdropped. Union Station's mapping included acoustics, and she could drop herself into the airspace of any unsuspecting traveler she chose. Near the south side entrance, a little boy paused to take in the yawning chamber, looked up to his distracted mom, and said, "Are we taking a train to see Daddy?"

"No. I told you, Daddy's in Heaven with the koalas now."

Terri floated down the hallway toward Zack, finding him slumped against a wall and looking genuinely angry. She moved the aural net cursor over his head.

"Seriously. Seriously. You're being serious right now."

He paused and tensed his mouth. She couldn't imagine he was fighting with anyone but Janice. She was always curious about the inner structure of their marriage. Janice invited speculation, being so good-naturedly neutral. How would a couple like that fight?

"You did not say that. In fact, that's the fucking opposite of what you . . . no. Nuh-uh. Wrong."

His right hand extended, as if to ring an imaginary doorbell. After wagging his index finger furiously in space, opening one unseen window after another, his hand suddenly found what it sought, poking sternly at nothing and then rapidly waving up and down. He was scrolling through something. Suddenly the finger halted and pointed downward, as if accusing someone.

"Jan, I'm in the transcript right now. You want to know what you said? What your exact goddamn words were? You . . . LISTEN! I am trying to tell you this."

Any time anyone resorted to digging up transcripts of old conversations, the fight had gotten ugly. She floated off back down the hall. Being cops, their public personas were especially open for abuse: perhaps Zack should have been reminded about the dangers of talking in public. In the main waiting room, she called up one of the cheap civilian programs that aggregated public tags. Sure enough, they were both listed. He already had fourteen comments. Being female, she had ninety.

Terri stacked these comments like a totem pole over the head of her sitting self. She read:

Man, I'd get that piggie so fucking preggers

no way to old NEXT ha ha oinkers

orange ass skin eewwww

Nice rack, nice shitcutter . . . I'll take it

She wondered how this conclusion had been reached, since it was posted fourteen minutes ago and she'd been sitting for the last hour. Then there were the more sinister notes:

Good try puerco, but we see you

u can run but u cant HIDE

ICU COP

The tone of these comments was always a surprise, the overt implication that she, as a police officer, had somehow been caught trying to deceive someone. She'd read in the news somewhere that one out of every four online comments was now made by a machine. She thought of her fake customer service rep. Was he leaving notes somewhere?

The totem pole scrolled upward, losing her interest as text and instead resembling something artistic. Halfway up, she saw a three-dimensional animation of a cartoon elephant mounting her from behind, naked, bent over the chair she was sitting in. Above this—meaning, lower in chronology—someone had redone this same animation with the cartoon elephant wearing a top hat and a star-spangled vest with the word *GOP* emblazoned in glittering rhinestones. From there, the thread degenerated into political flaming between commenters, something so esoteric and boring that she couldn't be bothered to read it to the end.

She wasn't fazed by commenters, although a stray bit of depravity might occasionally take her off guard. In general, comments were zero sum. Every second a real person spent trash-talking an officer was a second not committing a real-world offense. What got her was the knowledge that Krista generated comments as well, even as they had sat together at lunch less than a week ago. It was leering made corporeal, part of humanity's accrued archives.

She was up by the ceiling now, peering down at the entire waiting room. Some people were already sleeping in chairs, citizen refugees, with their belongings crammed into backpacks. Not quite below her, the group of students remained huddled around their luggage. Maybe their field trip was to the train station. As she watched, one leaned over her own seat to say something to a classmate, then reached back and scratched her lower back. Terri felt a stab of déjà vu, an occupational hazard. You couldn't float, as in dreams, and not have this happen.

Increasingly bored, she propelled herself higher still, through the station's ceiling, emerging into the sun. A patchwork of advertisements and photos covered most of the original station roof. She'd talked with cops old enough to remember when rooftops had been painted with street numbers, creating a useful grid for overhead surveillance. Now it was all ad space, every building owner in Los Angeles complicit in the drone trade, legal or otherwise. She kept floating up, a weightless entity soaring over the city, rotating to take in the freeway,

Olvera Street, a distant, tiny band playing in a public square. She pictured a supervisor looking at her essentially goofing off and got spooked, tracing a path line in the air to control her descent without queasiness.

She drifted back to earth at a curved forty-five-degree angle. The mechanics of unreal motion, she realized, were weighted toward the next generation. No one propelled themselves. All she did was move her phantom self through space using hand gestures. The sensation was of the world moving to accommodate her, not the other way around.

In front of the station at eye level, a family had gathered between the two huge Saguaro cacti flanking the outer doors. These iconic landmarks drew visitors from all over the planet, and as the clan gathered now, a man on the curb said, "Say cheese!", raising one finger to the sky and then dipping this finger to signify that a photo had been taken, randomly tagging one instant among the multitude being recorded. She texted Zack,

This job is turning us into tourists.

They pulled into Uganda well after dinnertime. Benny Cuevas acted as a greeter from one of the small round tables up front, sitting across from a slumped young guy she realized was Carlos the vice detective. Benny was several serious drinks into jolly, probably off duty by hours now, and with his button down open to expose a beige undershirt, his fat gut rested on his lap, like a housecat.

"Hey, Detectives. How the hell ya doin', Terri?"

"I'm good, same old. Still Central."

Once, way back when she'd been a rookie and eager to network, Terri had signed up for some community outreach neighborhood thing, drawing Benny as her one-night mentor. All she could remember about him was that he'd talked nonstop in the car, talked nonstop to a roomful of obliging seniors, then talked nonstop on the ride back to the workstation. And nearly the entire time he hadn't taken his eyes off her, one part or another.

"Zack too, awright!" Benny said. "Hey, pull up some chairs. You both know Carlos Moisey?"

"I'm going to grab a beer," Zack said, walking off.

"I was just telling Carlos about this bullshit thing with this armoire I tried to sell on Emporiumpire. You ever deal with that place, Terr?"

"No," she lied. Before the divorce was finalized, she'd posted a few small furniture items in their webroom. When two college girls came by to pick up the stuff, she'd been so dejected she'd just given them everything for free.

"Yeah, well . . . don't." Benny laughed, recalling some tale of minor woe, Terri palming her face and nodding when it felt appropriate. Looking up, she spotted Trinh Nghiem farther back, at the bar. She didn't see Chuck the Trainee. Maybe he'd gotten eaten. When she returned to Benny, she saw that he'd put his shades back on. Even though they were PanOpts, something about his sly little grin put her on edge. She'd seen somewhere that 50 percent of all men were running some sort of naughty program at all times, and that the other 50 percent ran at least one background program to dissuade themselves from naughtiness; nudity blockers, ugly filters, the shocked, semi-transparent ghosts of their dead relatives materializing in moments of weakness. It was a different case with cops, whose workspace was under constant supervision. But there were always exceptions, or aging guy cops who simply didn't care who knew. Years ago, she used to confer with female coworkers over their strategies for figuring out who was and wasn't running these apps. Now she mostly didn't care, although the first thing she had any male suspect do was remove his EyePhones.

Benny seemed like a good candidate for Guy Cop Who Didn't Care Who Knew. If she had to guess, she'd say he used Harem Builder, an app that allowed men to build fake, private harems from even one glimpse of a woman. But there were lots of options. There were the countless layers that visualized women naked, or tried to determine who was menstruating. Then there was Gynovore, an app that enveloped the wearer in a world of graphic sexual carnage. She had no idea what exactly this entailed; it only worked for men.

Terri looked back toward the bar and said, "Why is there a TV out?"

She rose and walked over to the handful of cops gathered in a crescent of chairs with Trinh and Zack and Chuck the Trainee, who looked slightly less shell-shocked, but still clearly out of his element. The TV was a poster of plastic that'd been rolled up long enough that it wanted to curl inward, its four defiant corners lashed to a rolling sandwich board with packing tape. On the screen, a heavyset woman stood on a street in old town Pasadena.

"Everyone was just screaming and running, and I got separated from Dylan. And then . . . and then I saw him there . . ."

The camera cut to footage of a row of bodies lying in grass. As she talked, the actuality anchor, the little solid black letter *R* icon, winked out and was replaced by a question mark, the producer's way of presenting their unreal footage as something yet-to-be-verified, coyly misleading viewers that there might be some gray area.

"Hey, why are we watching this K-Cal bullshit?" somebody said.

Someone else said, "I'd rather watch K-Cal bullshit straight up than some aggregator rehashing K-Cal bullshit."

"Can you please?" an older cop said, motioning to the TV. He was narcotics, Norm or Norman something, she'd met him once.

The small crowd hushed as the woman in the story said, "I don't understand how this could happen. And why the city isn't following up on this."

To the cop next to her, Terri half-whispered, "Is this the Tournament of Roses thing?"

"Yeah."

"What are they saying it's up to now?"

"Thirty-nine bodies and counting."

Another alleged witness came on, describing in low tones how his brother had gotten trampled in a melee. "Where are the police in all this? And why is all this footage just coming out now?"

It was the power of images laid bare. Mobs were moved by footage, regardless of veracity. The city grappled with potent rumors of scrubbed watermarks, of powerful institutions trying to pass off the real as the unreal. Then there were the testimonials; actual footage of people, alleged witnesses, looking into a camera and soberly describing something that they didn't actually see. This footage actually was real, required no scrubbing of watermarks or adding of watermarks. It was actual footage, of actual people, describing actual bullshit.

"Sand trap," the guy next to her said.

"Naah. This is on Pasadena. If they try to wriggle out of it, there's still a whole sheriff's department between us and them."

"This thing is growing. It'll be county before the end of the week. That'll make it the Wall, meaning our problem. Wait. Terri?"

She glanced over and saw she was speaking with Billy Bustamante. In all the times she'd consulted with him about some housing matter, always choosing him out of sheer alphabetical laziness, she'd never actually met the guy face to face. In person, he looked larger and rounder. Zack and Trinh crossed behind the half circle of chairs toward them, followed tentatively by Chuck the Trainee. "Sand trap, sand trap, we're gonna get sand trapped," Zack sang. "Somebody should start a pool."

Trinh said, "I'll put a C on Thursday."

"What's Thursday?" asked Chuck.

"Thursday is when the big ball that is your job goes into the sand trap." Seeing the confused look on Chuck's face, he added, "You Philly guys have a sand trap. Don't even tell me you don't have that."

"Is that like a thing with the Wall?"

All three of them stared at him, and then Trinh explained, in the calm tones of a mentor, "Yes, Chuck."

"Philly's still under Delmarva for another few years. So that wasn't really my department back east."

"Well out here, when the public whips itself up into a sandstorm of flying bullshit, you feel it. Expect a marked difference in every civilian you speak with all throughout the week. By Saturday they'll be egging us."

"No one believes cops," Trinh said, "because anybody can make footage of any event involving cops. People make fake footage because they don't trust cop footage. And they don't trust cops because of all the fake footage."

"The endless waterwheel of bullshit," Terri said, looking back at the TV, the same shot of bodies on trimmed grass, a title graphic reading "ALLEGED COVERUP?"

"They're repeating this footage today," Trinh said. "But in six hours, there'll be hundreds of fresh scenes. It's like it's a . . ."

"A feeding frenzy," Zack said. "And since they know they can't get away with rehashing obviously jacked pass-along crap footage, they'll do it with real footage of 'witness testimonials.'"

". . . a lot of which are just people describing what they *feel* when they watch . . ." —Trinh seemed to search for the words to match her disgust —"the bullshit footage."

Chuck looked like he was struggling with the concept. "But . . . what about the forty-one people they said died?"

"You see any last names? You see the bodies? I'll shed some tears when I see some bodies." Zack glanced back at the screen. "Eyes edit stuff. People see what they wanna see."

Benny stalked over to see what the fuss was about. He glanced at the TV and pronounced, "No artistry."

"Exactly. Exhibit A," Zack said. "You fake something, fake it. Don't do this halfway crap."

She put her shades back on, wondering if she could discretely pull up an app that might give her some clues if Benny was viewing all women naked.

"It's like that graffiti guy, hitting all those freeway signs? All that work scrambling up past the barbed wire, you get to the one graffiti-proof surface in the whole city, and for what? Just to scrawl your name?"

"Kids look up to that jackass," Zack said, staring hatefully back to the TV set, its loop of outrages.

"They have to," Benny said, chuckling to himself.

Terri glanced from Carlos to Trinh, struck by how utterly unruffled both seemed.

Benny added, "Now, throw some *God*zilla in the mix . . ." She and Trinh exchanged eye rolls.

"You catch that one? Um. Hold on." Zack fiddled in the air, scrolling through his mail. "'Godzilla Plows the Statue Of Liberty.'"

"You had to look that up?" she asked.

"Hey, he plows a lot of large ladies. I wasn't sure who got top billing."

Carlos and Trinh wandered off in opposite directions, and Chuck, their ward, seemed momentarily lost as to who to follow.

"Pure art," Benny said, slightly shiny-faced. "Hey. Richie Guerrero. There was some talent. Remember that guy, Terri?"

"Huh," she was still scrolling through an Overlay menu box, trying to find a naughty detector.

"New guy," Benny said to Chuck. "You ever hear of 'Richie the Itchy'?"

"Who?"

"Infamous. Richie Guerrero uses the men's room in a restaurant. Takes off his PanOpts to do a two, and because he doesn't want to set them down on any filthy surfaces, he perches them on the branches of a fake tree in the corner of the room. We've all done the exact same thing in times of lower GI distress. Finishes, leaves, gets halfway to the street when he remembers he left his shades back on the fake tree. Richie runs back, but someone is in the men's room now. Richie's pounding on the door, yelling, 'Police! Let me in now!', and the guy inside is yelling, 'I'm using the john!' Richie couldn't call the cavalry even if he wanted to, so he starts yelling through the door that he's going to break the door down. The guy inside gets mad, starts yelling about his constitutional rights this, due process that, how he's gonna flush the PanOpts down the toilet if Richie doesn't cool down."

Chuck seemed to be following the story as if he were going to get graded on it.

"Richie kicks the door in. You ever had to do that?"

Chuck shook his head solemnly.

"It sucks. Doors are tough. But he gets his shades back. End of story, right? No. Turns out the restaurant owner is an ex-con, some hard lucker made good, and, for whatever reason, the kicked-in door was the final straw in his life. So now the owner makes footage of Richie going nuts, assaulting wait staff, setting the building on fire, having a drug freakout. The footage takes off. Half the city is making its own mashups, but the originals were so good that it didn't matter that the spinoffs were subpar, so that by two weeks later you could see the tree in the corner with sunglasses singing a blues song and it didn't matter, that's how much time and energy went into the production values. And of course you'd see footage with that just playing on a TV screen in the background and it would ring true with the actuality anchor. That's how they sandbag you, kid."

"Sand trap," Terri said.

"That's how they sand trap you, kid."

"What happened to the guy?" Chuck asked. "Richie."

"He quit, moved to Mexicali, probably makes twice his old salary as a paralegal."

She strolled over to where Zack stood, catching a low-level group groan from something said on the TV. Terri was about to inquire on his game plan for tomorrow, remembering he'd already told her he was going back to the train station, hearing him say, "Maybe if you hadn't spent your whole day reading, you wouldn't have forgotten that."

She veered off, back toward the bar. Long before Zack had met his wife, Janice had dated an older man, one of the leading experts on palm trees in the state. After he'd died, she'd inherited his library of tree books, hundreds of them, enough to fill two floor-to-ceiling shelves she'd had built in the hallway at the Zendejas home. Over the years, she'd slowly slogged through the collection, and Terri kept trying to remember to think of some questions about palm trees. They didn't have much to talk about otherwise. The odd hallway in their otherwise bookless home was a little off-putting.

Zack wandered over to the bar a few minutes later, sunk in a funk, not seeing her.

"Bad times?"

"Don't ask." He motioned to the bartender. In the low illumination from the backlit bottles, he appeared prematurely haggard.

"Listen," she said. "When was the last time you took a day off?"

"Yeah." He stared at himself in the long, wide mirror above the lit-up liquor. The bartender took his order and he looked down to his hands on the smooth counter. "What?"

"Benny was talking about sick days."

"I don't listen to that foolwad."

"Well, he was saying how he didn't want to take any sick days because he was probably going to need them, being in as bad shape as he is."

"Yeah. And?"

"And you're not in such bad shape, yet. Have you ever even taken a sick day?"

"I don't know. Probably."

"Not in the time I've known you. You've probably got a shitload. Go on a vacation."

She realized what she was doing as she was doing it, trying to steer him out of the picture while she cracked the Santos case. No: this was heartfelt advice. She ignored the conflicting thoughts.

"What? Where?"

"Wherever you want. Or wherever Janice wants. Take a break. Skip town for a few days, I don't know. Go up the coast."

"Yuh-huh."

"Think about it."

He looked at her with barely amused suspicion. The bartender handed him his drink and Zack lurched off toward an empty table, revealing Trinh Nghiem in the space behind him. Maybe Zack wasn't in such great shape. His bulk had completely hidden her.

"Hey," Trinh said.

"Hey," said Terri.

Later, in Terri's bed, Trinh said, "What's that large scar?"

"Which one?" Terri whispered.

"The big one. On your thigh."

"Oh. That." She thought of her lunch at Jazz Hands: keep it simple. She'd had a tendency to overtalk things in the past. "Um. I got thrown down a flight of stairs in my first year, by a meth head. A large, crazy meth head. They didn't realize how bad my leg had gotten ripped up until I was in the ER with two cracked vertebrae. We were never sure what cut me. I mean, it was a flight of stairs. Stairs aren't sharp."

Trinh murmured, "Those stairs were," lightly brushing a fingertip along the raised scar in the dark. Terri smiled and shivered, looking up at the rows of streetlight slatted through blinds and steamed-up windowpane, wondering if she should add the only interesting part of her rookie ordeal. She hadn't lost consciousness during the fall down the stairs. Afterwards, lying in a heap on the lower landing, she remembered looking up at the silhouette of her assailant and thinking that she was peering *down* the staircase at him, that somehow she'd just killed him and his body had landed perfectly. It was a spooky disconnect, a sensation that had stayed with her over the years.

"I had to deal with one of those in my first year," Trinh said.

"One of what?"

"A large, crazy overlord head. He'd been popping them all day, like candy. Sublinguals."

"Yikes."

"Yeah. By the time I crossed paths with him, he'd thrown a refrigerator . . . remember that neat little bistro on Main, South Main? I think it's that pub now, with the tree in the window?"

"Yeah."

"Okay. So, in that place, he somehow pushed the refrigerator out of the kitchen, hauled it into the dining room, and shoved it through the front window."

Terri snickered, then caught herself.

"No, it's funny," Trinh said. "Although I think that's why they eventually closed. The employees were so bummed out they just gave up. Anyway, I'd gotten off shift, and I was going to meet some friends there for drinks. I showed up maybe thirty seconds after it happened. All the customers and the staff were just frozen in terror, waiting to see what this guy was going to do next. I knew it was going to be three or four minutes, at best, before backup arrived. Did I mention he was naked?"

"You did not."

"Okay. So he's naked, out of his mind, high as a kite, mile-high boner, laughing and pointing at the maître d'. I've got one hand on my heater, and I say, 'You're going to have to come into custody with me, sir.' And he says, 'I'm not going to jail.' So I say, 'No, actually, you're not. I'm taking you to Rivera Mental Health Facility.'

"This guy looks at me and says, 'You're gonna 5150 me? Over this? *Why?*' And I say, 'Well for starters, sir, you're obviously batshit insane.' And he looks off into the distance for a moment, looks down, looks at the fridge out on the sidewalk, and he gets this sad expression on his face. And then looks back at me and says, really politely, 'You know? You're absolutely right.'"

They both laughed at this. Terri shifted to lie on her side.

"And let me guess, when the guy finally came down for real, he was totally baffled."

"I don't think he ever really came down."

"Seriously."

"I mean, he was nice enough on the ride, once he was cuffed and all, but he wasn't what you'd call a rational actor. I remembered to check up on him maybe six months later, after I realized I'd never gotten pulled for a deposition, and they told me he was still at Rivera."

"Jesus. I was only in the hospital a month."

"Just a month? With two cracked vertebrae? You must've had a hell of a nurse."

Terri stared into the middle distance, feeling her bare back cooling, trying to think of something to say that would steer them toward a different topic.

"So . . . any new developments from the seedy underbelly?" she finally said, instantly wishing she'd thought of something else.

Now it was Trinh's turn to stare off, into the darkness on the other side of the room.

"Terri, if I were to tell you how bad things are out there, you'd piss your mind."

They lay like this for a moment in silence, and then Trinh sighed, rising to kneel naked before her.

"Speaking of which. Bathroom?"

"Out and all the way back. Can't miss it."

"*Gracias*," she stood, crossing into the living room, ambient light from the open curtains flashing off her bare torso for a split second as she padded toward the back of the apartment.

As soon as Terri heard the bathroom door click, she stripped off her pillowcase and stuffed this down the side of the mattress. She'd noticed a few days ago that it had taken on a dingy, yellowy hue. When they'd barged into the bedroom, she'd had to maneuver herself over to the light switch, to get them into darkness as quickly as possible. At least she could offer her guest a private bathroom. One of the few things she'd never liked about the Pasadena house was that the smaller bathroom was next to the bedroom and had no fan, so that she and Gabriella had always had to hear each other using the john.

She fell flat on her back, listening to the freeway, trying to pick out patterns, thinking of the 5150 story and smiling to herself. It always fascinated her, all those indecipherable numbers the dispatchers used to use. The world had once been far less direct, unable to provide visuals for every situation. Her mom, a supermarket cashier all through Terri's childhood, had told her that she'd had to memorize dozens of random numbers, nearly a hundred, each corresponding to a different fruit or vegetable. It was always odd to her that a few similar numbers had survived in cop slang as vestiges, bits of obsolete code whose digits still held some weird Kabalistic power. 5-0. 187. 911. 5150.

Feet sounded on floorboards, and it took a moment to figure out these belonged to the upstairs tenant. Terri heard him cross overhead and pause. She cringed, hearing the first unmistakable plashing chimes of male urination.

Trinh had returned and stood mesmerized in the doorway, wrapped in Terri's bathrobe. She looked up, at the ceiling, saying, "That *sucks*."

Tuesday morning Terri woke alone, with only a bare pillow to prove she hadn't merely had a nice dream. Groggily prepping the coffeemaker, she tried to let her thoughts drift, to come up with something from her lingering subconscious to pry this weird case wide open. But the smell of coffee only reminded her of coffee. Throughout all the privations of the four-years-long Bad Days—all the shortages and brownouts and dread—losing coffee had been her biggest struggle. A week after the war, she'd tried to quit cold turkey, to get a jump on the impending food rationing, finding herself completely unprepared for how hard her body would take the cutoff. All that death, and the worst she'd had to deal with was a crushing caffeine headache.

The nagging suspicion remained after breakfast. This was generally the worst part of any case, that old pang that could be either self-doubt or her subliminal sleuth. That the feeling lingered meant there was probably something to it. But what was the feeling? She thought back over the last few days, the hospital, the college, the train station. Something had been like something else. She tried to remember objectively. The paper-mache shanty town; had there been something there, something she'd let get obscured by Babs and Ruben? No, that wasn't it. The kid in the turtleneck. Maybe. No. But something to that. She frowned, hating this familiar, unscratchable itch.

Zack was going to be back at the train station all day. She had nowhere to go, nothing else to do except attempt to scratch this itch. Terri called up yesterday's footage from the station, deciding to start there both out of logic and from a secondary suspicion, a hunch on a hunch. The playback opened in the car, her and Zack again waiting out the crush of refugees before First Ride. The thought of Zack back there for another day filled her with a mix of envy and pity. Hopefully he wouldn't get his man: she didn't need the gloating.

The footage moved forward in eight-speed, faces and name boxes whizzing past, the view zooming up and down the main hall, walking and ghosting about the main room, the catch-and-release drudgery of it all. A half hour in, she was about to take a break when she watched herself shoot up out of her seat, floating up to examine the totem pole of abusive comments. The footage had already darted up through the ceiling when she paused, feeling her index finger perched on her lips but seeing only a paused downtown below her. She rewound, sinking back into the train station. Two stories below, the crowd of students remained huddled around their luggage. She watched as the one student again leaned over her seat and again reached behind her to scratch her lower back.

Smiling, she flattened everything and moved it to the kitchenette counter, the one free horizontal surface in the apartment. She tediously fast-forwarded through the last week of Farrukh's life in 2D, watching him whip through the repetitive motions of his joyless existence in octuple speed. Just after dawn on New Year's Eve, she caught something, rewound and played it back in real time.

Farrukh stood on a street corner downtown, waiting for someone, his wheel-board of food boxes—essentially a painted plank with two casters—perched against a nearby wall. A car eased up in front of him and rolled down its window. He leaned into the door, the gesture suddenly rhyming with the kid at Union Station leaning over her seat. When she'd seen Farrukh do this the first time, she'd assumed the overtly hookerish gesture meant he'd been talking with a potential client, or maybe just a hungry motorist attempting to buy a snack on the go. Scrutinizing now, she saw Farrukh run a hand under the back of his shirt with the insecurity of feigned nonchalance. He was clearly concealing.

"Sum bitch."

She paused, went immersive, and continued playback seemingly standing next to him. Farrukh slowly moved an object around in his waistband, finally retrieving whatever it was from just under the window. There was plenty of blind space on this street, most vexingly the entire seemingly empty car interior below the windowline. But in the half second it took for him to move his hand into the vehicle, she glimpsed the grip and then barrel of a handgun. Farrukh dipped his hands into the blind, clearly stashing this gun in the glove box, then stood and wiped his fingers on his forehead as the car sped off. Terri froze the world when the car was a block away, called up its license and VIN and registry, seeing that it was indeed vacant and serviced by Concierge Glove Box.

She conjured a Superior Court directory box in the air next to the motionless Farrukh, scrolling down to the bottom and selecting Judge Zamora. She'd dealt with Zamora enough times to know she'd probably get the guy's who-gives-a-shit Dupe, hoping not too many other cops had caught on to this same trick. The street faded and she stood in an ornate recreation of Zamora's office, the mahogany paneling and gilt-framed Monet probably not faithful depictions of the man's real-world chambers. The judge's Dupe sat behind an oak desk the size of a lifeboat. For some reason he wolfed down a sloppy joe, using a fast-food bag for a plate. He saw her, smiled, and wiped his mouth on a shirtsleeve.

"Detective Pastuszka."

"Your honor. I need a search warrant for glove box records," she said, bringing up an affidavit template and tapping the Autofill box.

"I trust you're sending me relevant footage."

"Right this moment," she said, bundling the last ten minutes of her life into a neat cube of sound and motion and attaching this to the affidavit. Terri raised her right hand for the affiant swearing, then the room dissolved, depositing her back next to poor immobile Farrukh, a search warrant box icon visible at the bottom of her desktop.

She opened a web box, another hovering windowpane into a false universe. For a moment the square went all white, negative space framing Concierge's bow tie logo. Then this plane melted to reveal a blandly decorated corporate office space. A young man in a sports jacket walked out with the cordial air of an emcee. The odds were good he was a super Dupe, a persona with no real-world counterpart.

"Good morning. Welcome to Concierge."

"Morning. I've got a search warrant for rental records."

"Absolutely, Detective. Please send those over whenever you're ready."

She tagged the warrant icon, flipping it through the window like a beanbag. It was funny: delivering search warrants meant all kinds of attitude and speed bumps from real people. Dupes, having nothing to go on but protocol, acted with unfailing politeness when faced with writs.

"This all looks to be in order," the young man said without breaking eye contact. "Here are the records you've requested." Another little beanbag zipped up from under his side of the window, landing on her lower desktop.

"I wish everything in life were this simple."

"We've all been there, Detective. Is there anything else I can help you with? Did you have any interest in hearing about our new . . ."

She popped the box like a soap bubble. Terri merged the company records with Basement footage, adding one layer of data to the urban still life in front of her. Looking over the rental documentation, she saw a ten-digit number listed in the space where a recipient should have been named. Some companies offered hidden-recipient glove box service—moving dead drops, essentially—although she'd assumed from Concierge's classy trappings that they were above this sort of thing.

She summoned a map box and restarted time in high speed, Farrukh whooshing off, foot traffic surging around her as she stared down at a colorful chart, feeling like a tourist examining a placard as she followed the car's progress through the city. The first glove box transfer came on the Ventura freeway. Eight miles west of that there was another, the cars coordinating with each other, passing off their cargo, the pulsing dot that represented Farrukh's gun moving in a counterclockwise half arc across the city, finally slowing to take the CA-90 spur into Marina Del Ray.

"No. Fucking. Way."

Switching to the actual street corner where the car came to a rest, she steeled herself for another high-voltage mindfuck. But when Stacy Santos actually did emerge from the early-morning crowd, accepting the Glove box contents with a poker-faced alertness, Terri was disappointed to find herself decidedly un-jazzed, having understood and accepted the new reality of this case at nearly the same moment.

So Farrukh passed Stacy a gun. Presumably the same gun she shot him with, although without a serial number she couldn't yet prove this part, or the rest of her hunch. The next step was to see what the college girl did with it. Retrieving Concierge's rental records, she was about to make note of Stacy's anonymous customer number when she felt the jolt that had eluded her just a minute earlier. The ten-digit number was a drop-down; when she tapped on it, another rental record unfurled. Stacy had passed something to someone else.

"Oh shit shit shit."

She called Legal Services, reaching the stern Dupe of a middle-aged male attorney in a featureless gray cubicle.

"Yes, Detective."

"I just obtained a search warrant for rental records on a glove box. On closer inspection, I'm realizing that these records contain additional information, information that wasn't requested but which is potentially vital to this case. Can I look at these additional records without jeopardy?" She hoped Zack would never see this conversation, the strange formality with which she addressed a duplicado.

"Was the information requested in good faith?"

"Yeah."

"Did you uncover the extra information in the normal course of your investigation?"

She had to consider this. "Yeah, I suppose I did."

"Then you're fine. California vs. Hargrave gives you plenty of legal legroom."

"Thanks." She hung up, wondering if there was any way a legal Dupe could be wrong and, if so, if her recording of this brief conversation could somehow protect the case retroactively.

Stacy Santos left the weapon in a different glove box, four hours after killing Farrukh, her own gun-stashing gestures eerily similar to his. Clearly neither had handled a weapon, legal or illegal. Terri watched the car with Stacy's rented glove box speed east on city streets. Twenty-three minutes later, a man labeled QUINTIGLIO, NUESTRO stooped through a car window and repeated these odd gestures of concealment in reverse, taking the gun and quickly stashing it in the small of his back.

At least this man looked like the villain of popular imagination: tall, gangly, with dark sunken eyes and a bald patch fringed with silver hair tied into a swinging ponytail. He was exactly the kind of creep one would expect to find next to a posh waterfront home, peeping in through a window at the pretty young college girl inside. Terri stopped herself. She'd forgotten this wasn't her case. In the Basement, she confirmed another part of her hunch. He'd gone into his house almost four days ago and hadn't come out.

She returned to Zamora, finding him still eating, trapped in the strange existential hell of his office, perhaps doomed to chew at the same Sloppy Joe for all eternity.

"That was quick," Zamora's Dupe said.

"I need an arrest warrant with an extension mail warrant."

"Why the extension?"

"There's reasonable suspicion that my suspect is dead."

"So you want an extension, sine qua non a body?"

"That's what circumstances warrant," she said, not bothering to search the Latin in the sidebar.

He shrugged. She repeated her footage transfer and swear-in, and the second warrant was hers.

She placed precautionary drones on Quintiglio's house, not wanting to call foot officers until she was under way. Rushing to get dressed, it occurred to her that she was still the only actual person in this entire process, a piece of meat among the gnashing gears. If she were to keel over from a stroke on her way out the door, what would happen? The various Dupes she'd spoken with would just go about their days. She pictured the two preliminary drones she'd ordered, circling Quintiglio's house at this very moment. If she never showed up, would they just keep circling?

She zippered through traffic at 160 mph, cars sashaying aside to let her pass, the rush of the road mirroring the rush of the hunt. After sending Babylon and Ruben a courtesy text, Terri pulled up an overview on the property. Quintiglio lived in a Leimert Park backhouse with only one direct approach, through a narrow driveway that let into a little concrete courtyard shared with the main house's back entrance and a one-car garage with its door open, filled to the rafters with a fire hazard assortment of boxes and chairs. One leafless liquid amber tree obscured a corner of the courtyard. She saw three responding officers already on scene, supported by eight eyes overhead in fifty-foot holding loops, two stun-drones in synchronous circles above that. She frowned at this, large drone patterns likely to get picked up by cop watchers.

His neighborhood was a lone bastion of the proud black working class, struggling to stay afloat but slowly sinking under the glacial pressures of the Slide. The car decelerated, passing dingy food trucks and grubby T-shirt stores and several longstanding retail holdouts that had acquired landmark status through sheer longevity. Although Quintiglio's street was a grid of neatly trimmed lawns, every window had bars.

She pulled in across the street from the residence, grateful that nothing was parked in the sad, slender driveway leading to the backhouse. A small gaggle of civilians had gathered three houses down, but otherwise there wasn't any serious onlooker problem. Yet. Two perfect rows of palm trees lined each sidewalk, and she thought of the app that made every palm stalk extend upward into the Heavens, like prison bars for neighborhoods. A young uniformed officer met her out front.

"No one in the front one."

They set their views to show drone positions, rendering the front house as wireframe, nothing more than the see-through blueprint of a house. Another officer met them on the lawn and the trio rounded the main residence into the backhouse courtyard, guns drawn, unified in motion. A pit bull stuck its snout through the bottom of the neighbor's gate just far enough to offer a timid bark. Nearby, an antique satellite dish sat tilted skyward and filled with rainwater, an unused birdbath. The bony tree, in a desperate bid to replicate itself, had scattered sharp, round seedpods all over the concrete, and each cop had to mind their step to avoid crunching one.

A third officer pressed himself against the door frame of the front house's back entrance, making himself perpendicular to the backhouse front door. She did a quick glimpse at each officer's byline, seeing one snicker and flash the other two a hand sign, splayed fingers with a quick double thumb wag: 5-4-5-4. The officer met her eyes and shrugged sheepishly. She friendly-frowned, dialing up layer 54, channel 54, whispering, "That's so *stupid*."

Years ago, some cop with far too much free time had gone into PanOpt's sandbox and set up an audio channel to play Led Zeppelin's "Kashmir" 24/7. When she'd been a foot soldier herself, the channel had been strongly disavowed. But over the years the top brass had come to tolerate and eventually embrace the song: it was a hell of a morale boost in situations precisely like this one. 5454 rendered all audio input as visuals, and as she enabled the layer now, her own visual field bloomed with arrows, lines, and reticles, nothing to read, pure action.

Chorus booming, she planted her feet and pointed, blue-and-red battle schematics extending from her fingertips like lasers. Two breachers buzzed over and attached themselves to each hinge on the rust-flecked metal screen door. There was a pop, and the door fell out into the courtyard with a junkyard crash, sliding a few feet, emitting just the faintest wisps of smoke. She'd thought the drones would have died, insects killed in kamikaze, but then there was another pop and the heavier wood door, not hollow-core, fell inward, landing on carpet with a strange softness.

More drones rushed in, thin lines of red-and-green and blue, illuminating the layout as they went, so that the backhouse also dissolved into wireframe, every room visible as an outline. They saw a seated man in the back room. She set a Public Address drone to read out commands as she followed the lead officer, feeling no suspense, stepping through a cramped front room with one couch, then a second room that felt like a dining area until she saw the twin mattress in one corner.

Nuestro was in the back room, hands upright in his lap, clearly dead for days. He'd been shot through the eyebrow, the eye below intact but eightballed with blood. The four stood for a moment, no one sure what to do with all that adrenaline, and finally the first cop she'd met, out front, burst into air drums, everyone laughing, reholstering their weapons. She ran a shotline up through a broken pane of glass, then pulled off her own shades, breaking the spell of the music, although she could still hear it faintly through the other earpieces.

Drones had given her the full layout of the interior, the brightly outlined shapes of Quintiglio's private sanctum. But they'd done nothing to convey the sheer clutter of the space, every available nook and cranny crammed with piles of books, cardboard boxes, binders, loose papers, photographs. The guy made Carla Morales look like a germaphobe. She was surprised by the sheer volume of notebooks—loose leaf and pocket-sized, dozens or hundreds of each—paper being the least secure medium a reporter could work in.

"From what I understand, this guy was a freelance journalist. Round up all the loose pages and notebooks you can find," she told the officers. "I want a reader here in five minutes."

Stepping back outside, she paused to take in the utter bleakness of the courtyard, then walked a few houses down and pulled up the overhead footage. She first checked out the backhouse's back door, confirming that it led onto a concrete enclosure for recycling bins that was one shade more depressing than the front courtyard, then slowly verifying her suspicions from the initial, aerial footage: between the raised foundation and the narrow, all-blind alley, there was more than enough room for a shooter to sneak over from one block west, or a neighboring yard, or, conceivably, either cross street from north or south. A determined killer would have had a hundred paths through private property.

She returned to the backhouse, surprised to find the reader already parked in Nuestro's meager living room, a coroner team in the room beyond that. The reader was a newer, upright unit of gray metal, the size and general shape of a Union Station trash can. Two of the officers from the courtyard dutifully fed notes of all sizes and formats down its wide metal gullet, the machine analyzing and distilling information with a soft mechanical clap, digesting entire notebooks in a single zap, then excreting neat piles of paper—Nuestro's life work—into a metal pan that had to be continually emptied.

Blanco called in audio.

"We got him, Chief. But somebody got him first."

"Two for two, detective. I'll go through your report with the assistant, so for now give me an overview."

Terri stepped outside and walked as she rattled off all the salient bits: Concierge, Palm Desert, the raid itself. By the time she'd gotten to the particulars of the crime scene, she was back inside her car.

"One more thing, and this requires delicacy. I have every reason to believe that ballistics are going to match the gun that killed Nuestro to the one that killed Farrukh. I think we'd tie this gun to Dio Sarin and Stacy Santos as well if either of those shootings had provided a bullet. It's not my place to do more than point this out."

"That's a hell of a detail."

"I'm still getting my mind around that one, yeah. If I'm right, they've been passing it along in a series of dead drops. I don't have any better explanation at this point. But if you make this detail public, you're potentially back to exposing Stacy's role as one of the shooters. Meaning, unless you keep the ballistic report under wraps . . ."

"Are you suggesting we may have leaks?"

"Uhm."

"Relax, Detective, I'm with you. I'll intercept ballistics. Just as long as we're all on the same page. And do you feel you've covered yourself with your partner?"

"Zack, yeah. He doesn't have a clue about any of this," she said, feeling shitty about her choice of words.

"Excellent work, Terri. Let's talk tomorrow."

A message box softly dinged, and she opened this to see that the reader had sent her a list of possible passwords culled from 17,771 pages of notebooks and loose papers: a lifetime's opus slimmed down to a little over thirty thousand possible words. Having already done some due diligence on the car ride to Leimert Park, she knew the late Mr. Quintiglio had a professional mail account with Segurança, a service used almost exclusively by journalists. Quintiglio would have set up a backup password to complement his face ID. It was antiquated newshound shit, serving both as a legal backdoor for editors and one more way to thumb one's nose at the twenty-first century, just like the piles of notebooks themselves.

She dialed Carla Morales, wondering if she should still feel embarrassed for her call the other night.

"Hey, Terri Pastuszka. Looks like I got the shooter on that Stacy Santos thing."

"Okay," Carla said with deadpan disinterest, probably the only person in the county who didn't care about this news, Terri thought.

"Hey, so, um, the guy's dead. I've got an extension warrant for his mail and a list of thirty thousand possible backdoor passwords . . ."

"Segurança, huh? Journalist?"

"That's what I'm told. How quickly can you cycle through multiple password possibilities?"

"About as quickly as you can send them to me."

"Appreciated."

She hung up and rubbed her eyes, feeling raw and rubbery after the surge of a raid, even one with a nearly foregone conclusion. When she opened her eyes again, Terri saw that a crowd had gathered on the lawn. As she crossed back over to check in, she overheard someone grumble about Sweden and then one of the young uniformed cops say, "Then you'd have to do our job, idiot."

A heavily accented voice said, "Terri." She turned, ready to blast a civilian, then realized she was looking at Kofi Agyeman, a freelancer probably working the same general beats as Quintiglio. He was young, Ghanaian, personable but not someone she'd trust with even a sentence of vital information.

"Aw jeez, Kofi, you didn't know the deceased, did you?"

"I just tracked you here to ask about the Tournament of Roses," he said, glancing around with genuine puzzlement.

"That? Jesus, why don't you ever write outside The Loop?"

"I do! I just did a big thing in the *LA Weekly*."

"I don't know that that counts exactly," she said, looking past him as Babs and Ruben pulled up.

"So, what is this, Terri?"

She smiled, pointing over his shoulder. "You just got the first scoop of the decade and you don't even know it yet."

Hours later, blurry from sitting in a car and poring over Nuestro Quintiglio's correspondence, she pulled up to her apartment building and gazed up at its dull wall of a facade. His mail had conveyed a tireless work schedule, as he'd chased down freelance gigs to the complete exclusion of any kind of personal life. His EyePhones had vanished—just like Farrukh's and Stacy's—so perhaps he'd had a robust social schedule kept carefully partitioned from his work world. But his communications were a depressing read, a window into a life as forsaken as hers. From here on out, any mail sent to the late Mr. Quintiglio's mail account would go straight to her PanOpts; a promise of gloom to come.

She should have gone somewhere, maybe an all-night diner, and just sat by herself to enjoy her fleeting glory. Today's catch was a career highlight. Instead, she'd let herself get drawn back into this silent space: a career highlight without anyone to share it with. Upstairs, she thought about calling her sister with the news, instead falling into the couch with a moan.

How much of her own loneliness was conveyed by the apartment? Trinh had left at dawn with a wordless hug. They'd see each other around, but both knew the deal without having to say it. Terri couldn't help but wonder if her guest had soured on the forced slovenliness of the apartment, the clutter that had to be navigated in the dark. When she herself had gotten up an hour later, she'd seen with embarrassment that Trinh had had to search cabinets for toilet paper.

Terri returned to the one scene that seemed to play on a continual loop under all other thoughts. She'd showered. Her hair had been damp. She'd come into the bedroom, where Gabby was, and had been about to complain about something. But what? An object had broken; an unfairness had occurred; something was overpriced; someone in the orbit of their unified life had said something stupid that required comment. It was a question mark she kept returning to. What had she been talking about in the last moment of her marriage?

She remembered bending to vigorously dry her hair and when she straightened again, seeing that Gabriella sat on the edge of the bed, knees together, hands folded in her lap. Terri had known at that moment that something was wrong, and all she could think was that someone had died and that it must be Gabriella's mother.

"I'm leaving you," Gabby had said in a voice neither soft nor loud. Terri had leaned into the closet door and let herself drift to the floor, the bath towel bunching up around her shoulders. She was still living in the wake of this one sentence, its mystery, still sifting her memories for warning signs. In hindsight, the only clue had come years earlier, when Gabby had surprised her with an elaborate train trip to New Mexico. Terri had been startled at the level of detail and planning that had gone into the vacation. "I have lunch breaks," is all Gabby had said by way of explanation, just the slightest peek into that separate, closed chamber of her personality.

Even that last time in the house—walking numbly through the property with her lawyer, a new set of acoustics to the bare floors, all the equity visible in bright, cheery swoops—Terri searched empty corners of rooms for clues. She liked to think of the house now like all those downtown condos; chemically scuttled, rendered unfit for occupancy by patient investors waiting out the years or decades until downtown property became viable again. Rendered unfit for further human habitation.

Of the two bits of video that had burned themselves into the back of her brain, Terri preferred the nightmare images from the India-China war to the moment when Gabriella had told her she was leaving. She tortured herself for this distinction, even as she knew everyone her age had some similar private shame, some recess of their personality where they hadn't shown sufficient respect to the dead. She unwillingly followed this idea to its next conclusion. She remembered her wedding night, and the relief at actually arriving somewhere in life that could contain such happiness. But she also remembered that relief tempered with a new fear: she'd become someone with something to lose. So did that now make her someone with nothing to lose? She glanced over at the Chinese table, the last vestige of her old life. So she could still lose that.

She thought again of Quintiglio's letters, wondering when she'd last checked her own civilian mail account. Slipping her PanOpts back on, she switched over to the Internet, finding the webroom for the apartment; another bleakly bare space with just a slender half-moon table, eerily similar to her own, holding a stack of letters. She hadn't been here in weeks. Most of it was junk, envelopes that, when pinged, would blossom into vivid circles and squiggles and sales infographics. Toward the bottom of the pile, she saw an envelope marked,

Godzirra!!

Terri opened this without bothering to see which male coworker had sent it, settling back into the couch as the space before her went dark and then lit up with a mighty title, flat and non-immerse but still emblazoned across a terrifying huge screen;

Godzilla Bangs Mothra

The film opened with ominous music over a black, roiling sea, the credits rolling above an ocean storm. When the credits ended, the waters continued churning. She waited for the movie to start, and waited, finally fast-forwarding through another twenty minutes of rain and sea, chuckling at the weirdness of it. She resumed the movie as the storm reached land, as if the camera had crossed such a vast expanse of water it had delayed the film itself. A tsunami crashed up into streets, carrying boats and telephone poles in its wake, the spooky illusion of the intro shattered by all those obvious miniatures.

An immense Easter egg washed ashore. A reporter and his plucky little lady photographer attempted to figure out its secrets while businessmen cooked up schemes around the egg, everything bathed in the effortless, dapper charm of the Japan of one century ago. She fast-forwarded through pastel colors and more cheesy miniatures, yawning, thinking, *One Chuckle*, realizing she was acting just like her niece.

Of course, Krista would have already lost interest in the film. The entitlement of the next generation baffled and slightly scared Terri. Having grown up being able to change the ending of any movie or TV show they liked—no one under twenty watching anything more than twenty years old—they acted like they could alter anything they wanted, in any format. Zack had once told her that his daughters would only watch the new horror films, the ones with different scares for each viewing, and had no interest in any of the films that had scared him as a teen. To kids Krista's age, anything not 3D-immersive was "keyhole." She wondered whom she would talk to if she were actually going to do something about Krista's suspension problem.

Back in the film, Godzilla entered. He stood and roared, that crazy crashing-metal scream that had scared her so much as a child. The beast stumbled through skyscrapers like they were made of cardboard, laying waste to flimsy toy war boats and tanks. Mothra arrived to a flourish of tacky porn music, wah-wah pedals flaring as engorged pistels and stamens sprouted from its fuzzy underside. Godzilla pressed his gray pruneskin against Mothra's monstrous sex parts and the two rolled in the dirt, thrusting, Godzilla using his mighty tail as a prehensile phallus.

"*Ick.*"

Wasn't Godzilla supposed to be about the atom bomb? She'd read that somewhere. Postwar science fiction of her generation had taken a sharply utopian turn, offering stories about jolly civilizations in far-off galaxies, spaceships hovering over lush valley meadows a billion light-years away. Those tales had served as relief from the grinding horror of the daily news. These days, all the science fiction was about people performing strange feats of telepathy. So what did that say about today? Shows like *Mind Narc* projected a longing, she supposed; the stubborn opacity of people's minds, resisting all the advances of the modern world.

The Walker was a different kind of sci-fi show. She wasn't sure what cultural need that one fulfilled. Maybe the human longing to be nothing but an eye. Once, with some cop buddies, she'd rented one of those drones that scoured the Chinese and Indian wastelands for lost loot. She'd drawn a patch of Guangdong, one square mile of the four and a half million square miles now less habitable for humans than the ocean floor. And yet, after she'd buzzed around the pleasantly overgrown rubble, she'd turned to take in the low rain clouds on the horizon, and had been shocked to see a lone figure in the middle distance, one of an untold multitude still trying to carve out a life in the badlands. The tenacity of humanity captivated her. Even China and India themselves refused to completely die, continuing as governments eternally in exile, rootless but not stateless, moving themselves, cobblestone by cobblestone, into an entirely non-corporeal existence.

In the movie, the two monsters were still rolling their erotic horror across hills, flattening villages, smashing through power lines and parking lots and thousand-year-old temples. They kept rolling, through suburban streets, then the streets of Tokyo, colliding with skyscrapers that appeared far more realistic than those at the start of the film, sending cascades of glass down into the terrified crowds below. Godzilla arched his back in ecstasy and roared a plume of flame down into the surging mob, the soundtrack momentarily drowned out by screams.

The camera panned down slowly, leaving the two fornicating behemoths in the background. She was looking into a cavity formed by the crushed lobby of a department store, a wall of rubble draped over racks of clothing and sofas. The camera pulled down farther, resting on the reporter from the beginning of the film. He was kneeling, shirtless, blood covering his head, a huge gash in his back. Before him lay the body of his feisty little photographer assistant, the lower half of her torso torn to shreds. His shoulders lurched, wracked with sobs, the camera closing in on his face. He looked up at the viewer and the camera pulled in even further to follow one tear sliding down the gray dust on his cheek. A title read, *THE END.*

"What?" She tagged the movie with a note,

One chuckle. Try again.

But when she went to send it, the address came up non-deliverable. She hiccupped a second chuckle, trying and failing to recall anyone who had her home mail address.

Terri thought she'd dreamed of Godzilla, but in the morning, she saw it was just the winds crashing through the neighborhood, scattering huge brown husks of palm fronds across the street below. After breakfast, she sat at the kitchenette's lone chair and pondered. Motive. Four victims, three shooters, one gun. On a nearby notepad, she attempted to compile a list of victim similarities, writing, *Lived in county* and then crossing this out when she remembered Stacy Santos. Could there be some way PanOpt could compile any meaningful version of what this list should be? She wrote, *Spoke English* and *Required food*. She scratched her neck, adding, *Biped humanoid*.

Motive. Why did Nuestro kill the District Attorney's daughter, and she kill Farrukh, and Farrukh kill Froggy? Who could profit from this? *How* could someone profit from this? Who could leverage an act of—what? Serial suicide? Back at Rutgers, in her sophomore year, she'd taken a class called One Hundred Years Of Crisis. She remembered reading about the Siege of Mecca, how one group of Muslims decided that everyone else was wrong, marched into the holy of holies with assault rifles and held hundreds of pilgrims hostage. A "malfunction," her teacher had called it. There seemed to be something similar here, although she didn't quite have it sorted out yet. People malfunctioning and then convincing other people to malfunction along with them.

Terri reclined with a sigh and thought again of Farrukh, the crucial link in the chain. She went back to the Swap Meet and caught him as he crossed the street toward the parking lot, headed north to his hole in the ground. Even here, in the last minute of the man's life, he appeared drained, fifteen years older, with sharp crescents chiseled beneath both eyes. It had become her mantra: this was Farrukh's case. Except she'd never before taken more than a passing interest in any of the literally hundreds of hard-luck nobodies that'd crossed her docket in years past. So why him?

Perhaps Farrukh's case held an extra resonance because of their one shared biographical detail. They'd both traveled across a continent for work. The thought of setting out on foot filled her with a strange weariness, her own trip having been made on a Jobs Caravan bus, taking her three thousand miles from Manhattan's Port Authority to the LA Greyhound Station. It hadn't been cheap: almost all of her savings for a trip with a nominal guarantee of safety, three buses with an armed security escort for their pre-arranged food and fuel stops. She'd never been west of Pittsburgh, and spent hours viewing the hugeness of America—its sheer distances, the extraterrestrial vastness of the plains—through a scratched bus window, the caravan taking wide detours around the chaos of Indianapolis and St. Louis. Even though it was late spring, a mean frost had clung to the windows, and the few times she'd stepped outside to stretch her legs she'd been struck by the stinging cold, its rawness, wondering how exactly bad an omen this was for a life-changing trip to Los Angeles. But it'd warmed some in Arizona, and by the time they'd reached California, half the bus of pilgrims was wearing shorts, dazed by the tropical opulence, the orderly rows of palm trees, their own survival after a passage through America's shattered midsection.

The bus trip had been a bittersweet triumph, a fresh start in the middle of what seemed like bottomless ruin. At the time, she'd had no way of knowing that the worst was nearly over, that she was three years into a four-year emergency. Even with all the privations of the Dim Ages—brownouts, uncollected garbage, and encroaching rats, the year summer vanished—the camaraderie of that era was still something she cherished. When America finally proved its resilience, jumpstarting farming and abandoning petroleum, all that solidarity had evaporated with frightening speed. To this new generation, it was as if those years had never existed.

Her mother had bought a handgun the first day stores were open after the war. She'd had to discretely flash it a half-dozen times, keeping it by the bedside when she slept. Those nights in that house still felt dreamlike, bathed in a sheen of dread. She remembered lying on her childhood bed, a cinema studies major with no future, listening to every little sound from the darkness outside. Terri had only left for the west coast after her aunt had moved in. It was funny to her now; she'd found guns so distasteful that she'd never once touched her mom's pistol.

The pass-around gun was key. Where was it? Who had it now? How did Farrukh get it? If Froggy had used the gun, he knew how to cover his tracks. Even his death had covered up for itself. For all she knew, he'd floated out to sea and his stiff, crucifix-posed body was halfway to Hawaii by now.

Farrukh was still up in front of her, paused at T-minus one minute to death. His clothes looked rumpled, slept in. Even after growing immune to so many of life's horrors, she still found herself continually bushwhacked by the sheer immensity of feudal poverty in refugee Los Angeles. If only he still had the EyePhones she'd seen in past footage, not the flimsy disposables he'd died with, she'd be able to get him a morsel of justice.

An insight came to her. Farrukh had been simply too poor to discard his EyePhones. He had a niece: she must still have them. Terri laughed at the obviousness of it all.

She looked back at his face, frozen in its display box, and addressed the deceased directly.

"I need your shades."

As if he'd somehow magically heard her, Zack called fifteen minutes later in VT, just as the coffeemaker made its last final *put-put* noises from the kitchenette.

"Got a buddy here for you."

"Oh yeah?"

"Liney stumbled in. Says he has some intel. I'll leave you two to chat."

"You don't want in? Where are you?"

"*I've* been at the train station since First Ride. You didn't seem particularly interested in obtaining justice for Mr. Orozco, so I'm waiting it out with an LAS Deputy. Thanks, by the way, for telling me you caught the Santos killer. Good work on keeping me up to date, partner."

She blushed, wondering how he'd pieced it together so quickly. "That was supposed to be Babs and Ruben's thing."

"It is, publicly. So extra thanks for turning them into heroes. They'll probably get a ticker-tape parade by the weekend."

"Yeah." It hadn't crossed her mind that she'd transformed two shitheads into champions.

"This is what happens, Terri. This is what happens when you spend all your free time working. You crack a big case without even considering who it is you're making look good."

"Huh?"

"So maybe take this one to heart, you know? Ease up. Don't do other people's jobs for them."

She wasn't sure how to read this. "Okay."

"Just tell me one thing. Santos didn't turn out to do with the Hackley boyfriend serial killer angle you fed me, right?"

"Kind of," she stammered. "It's complicated."

"Yeah, so's this. I gotta get back to the station. Fill me in tomorrow."

"Wait, where's Liney?"

"He's in an interrogation room at First Street. And make sure he understands that he can keep the disposables. No one wants those things back after they've been on his skanky eyes."

She switched to the First Street workstation interrogation booth, finding Liney sitting patiently on a stool. Someone had provided him with a glass-bottle Coke and disposable shades and let him be. He'd apparently arrived wearing a stained polyester Santa hat he'd found somewhere, and a black eye, which she'd assumed everyone at the workstation had had to ignore. He looked perfectly contented, sitting with one leg folded over the other, hands crossed primly in his lap.

She dropped her VT into the picture, saying, "Okay. Whattya got for us, Liney?"

"Ah, Liney has been asking many questions."

"I'll bet."

"Liney has . . . *two* pieces of information!" he said, smiling in a way that seemed slightly demented. She recalled that Zack usually handled these street briefings, wondering how she was supposed to respond.

"That's great."

"Liney has been busy," he said, swilling his soda and staring off in blissful contentment. She sighed, looking back to her open Basement box.

"So. Whattya got."

"You want EyePhones for Farrukh Jhadav."

"How'd you know that? You have them?"

"Liney knows."

"Look . . ."

"Floor and building."

"What floor and building?"

"Floor and building for Rujuta Jhadav."

"That's a good start. Got an address?"

"Floor and building."

"Okay. Time out. I have no idea how Zack handles you, or how his payouts go. So you need to tell me in plain, first-person English what you want for what bits of info. Bearing in mind that overtime no longer exists in my world, thus throwing the supply and demand of our limited relationship way the fuck off balance. Roger, kemosabe?"

Liney made eye contact with a preposterously drooping lip. He pointed down toward his lapel, to a two-inch button for Shakey's Pizza.

"You get paid in Shakey's Pizza credits?"

He nodded.

"Pizza wampum. Really?"

He nodded.

"Okay. You give me Rujuta, I'll give you . . ." She bit her lip. "Two hundred bucks. What's that, four dinners? Two with a date?"

He smiled in contentment.

"333."

"Got a floor?"

"Ah, Liney does his work."

"That pizza is growing little angel wings and flying off to Heaven."

"Forty-six. North East corner."

"Huh. Nice if it's true."

"Liney has more."

"Oh yeah?"

"Rujuta."

"Yuh huh."

"Rujuta scarred. Like so." He drew a diagonal line from his lower chin to left temple.

"No shit." She was surprised that Dr. Singh hadn't brought this up. "Okay."

"And Liney has *more*."

"Testify."

"Froggy."

"What about him?"

"Dio Sarin," he said. "I-K-D-K-S-S-K."

This got her attention. "Okay, you got his name and set right. What else?"

"Froggy trick Nailer."

"Achindra Sankaran? That Nailer?" Nailer was a tough character.

Liney nodded and looked side to side theatrically, as if agents of the underworld could hear him in his booth.

"Froggy trick Nailer," he whispered. "Froggy marked for death by Nailer's people."

She exhaled. His lie detector looked good, and Past Intel Reliability stood at an impressive eighty six percent.

"Well, Liney, I gotta say you're an odd goddamn duck, and I don't really believe you talk like this in real life. But all things considered . . . you eat."

He clapped his hands together in tranquil joy.

"Liney eats."

Reenergized, she called Blanco. The Chief's VT materialized in the messy living room in front of her.

"Any developments, Detective?"

"I'm checking in to see which way I should go. I have good intel on where Farrukh Jhadav's EyePhones might be, but it's forty-plus stories up, and I think negotiation for passage is going to be a trick. So I'm wondering what the best use of my resources is at this stage."

"I don't follow."

"Well, is the primary focus here who shot Nuestro Quintiglio, or finding Farrukh's glasses? Glasses get me motives, but finding the shooter on Quintiglio gets me closer to whatever is happening." She was about to follow up with, "Is this who, or why?", when Blanco interrupted her.

"We don't know that."

"Chief? I'm not sure what you mean . . ."

"There are a thousand different possible shooters. Quintiglio's death may be completely unrelated to the other deaths involved. I don't think it's fair to set up assumptions, and I'm actually very disappointed that you went ahead with the raid on Mr. Quintiglio's apartment without calling me for authorization first. Exigent circumstances or not, you are to check in with my office first, do you understand?"

Terri nodded, baffled, deciding that the best course was to stay mum. Reading into this pause at least that her point had been sufficiently underlined, Blanco continued.

"I've assigned Mr. Quintiglio's case to homicide detectives in Southwest. That thread is no longer your concern. I want you to stay on the search for Farrukh's glasses."

Terri nodded, giving the woman credit for at least having the right names and pronunciations up in front of her.

"And I don't want you talking with any more journalists about this. Even in passing. That clear?" Her face got hot at the minor injustice of this part of the chew out, looking over

Blanco's shoulder toward her dark kitchenette, nodding. The Chief hung up abruptly.

Terri kicked into a box of donation clothes, hangers scattering, something hard in the bottom of the box smashing her toe. She hopped over to the window and placed a hand on the frame to steady herself. The apartment was the worst place to be when pissed off. She stood for a long moment, foot throbbing, staring down at the I-10, then paused motion, merged the Basement with real time, and ghosted herself down onto the freeway, in the westbound lane, surrounded by frozen cars and distracted passengers. Civilians: oblivious, thankless. She glanced up and zoomed in on the gym bag, still stuck on the freeway sign ledge a week and a half later. It would probably be there for years and years, a reminder of Carlos Jaramillo's jab at her life every time she looked out the window. Terri looked back up at her apartment from this angle, disgusted with everything, and was shocked to see herself in this window now, also frozen, looking down at herself, a phantom woman.

A wave of pity came. She didn't mind strangers, or even fellow cops, seeing her building in all its naked ugliness. But the thought of her sister and niece seeing her new place filled her with a sharp sorrow. When living in South Pasadena, she'd felt strangely self-conscious inviting her sister's family over, her own place so spacious and better furnished than Tammi's adequate bungalow in Valley Village. Now she felt a symmetrical self-consciousness, having sunk so low in one move. When Krista stopped by last month to do Christmas shopping, Terri had quickly hustled them right back out the door.

She frowned in realization. It hadn't been that quickly. She switched back to her apartment and looked around the room, all the clothes scattered around the floor. Krista had been left alone while Terri applied eyeliner in the bathroom.

"God *damn* it," she said, bringing up a call box and dialing her niece.

"Hey," she said, letting the anger come out in her voice.

"Hey," Krista said.

"Did you take my shirt? Last month? The baseball sleeve with the fat blue and purple lightning bolts?"

"Oh, no, I'm just Krista's Dupe," Krista appeared to tell her. An orange *D* floated in the lower-right corner. "Can I take a message?"

"Tell her I'm pissed off. Tell her she can't come over here and take whatever clothes of mine she wants."

"Okay, Aunt Terri," the Dupe said with good cheer.

"And tell her I hung up abruptly," Terri said, doing just that.

Up and down, the day taking on a see-saw feel, she fished around in her jacket's many pockets until she found the business card given to her by Chandrika Chavan. The lady picked up after five rings, answering with a curt, "*Yes*."

"Ms. Chavan, this is Detective Pastuszka. We spoke last week about Farrukh Jhadav."

"Of course. Can you hold please?"

"No," Terri said, realizing she was already on hold, glad at least she'd gotten the actual woman and not some mannequin dummy of an answering service. Although she would've preferred that with the Chief. She switched out of audio only and threw Chandrika's profile into a call box, seeing her VT in a flat screen floating over the couch's armrest.

The fact that Chandrika Chavan still had the shiny red keloid on her throat—it being the easiest thing in the world to customize and beautify one's VT—seemed obviously for effect, to play up the victim card. On hold, she realized that she was free to examine this grizzly vertical scar. It looked like a fat red worm, or a leech. How could such a scar even be real? Terri had seen such an injury once, years ago, during a domestic dispute involving two tweakers. One had cut the other, and blood had jetted out in great arterial arcs, the victim still trying to fight, slipping on his own juices. Later, inspecting the body, she'd been shocked at what a tiny puncture it actually was. This scar looked far more severe. How could she have possibly survived such a wound? Terri absentmindedly wondered if it was fake, some kind of plastic surgery.

Chandrika returned, unapologetic for the rudeness.

"I have good intelligence on the whereabouts of Mr. Jhadav's former home," Terri said. "I think the odds are very good that his niece still lives in this space, and I think the odds are equally good that she still has these EyePhones."

"And why do you think that?"

"How many honest-labor refugees do you know that can afford shades?"

"Honest-labor is a politically loaded term . . ."

"And yet you know exactly what I mean by it."

"Where is this home located?

"The 333 S. Grand skyscraper. I'll give you a floor address if you think you can help me locate these remotely."

"'Remotely.' You know I can't sanction any sort of drone incursion . . ."

"I'm talking about human intervention."

"You want me to send a member of my staff into 333 S. Grand? I'm confused. What are you asking here?"

"I'm requesting the help you offered. I need to find Rujuta Jhadav, or at least her premises. She's off the charts, no face, no profession. If you have contacts that can assist in this search, this would be the time to proffer."

"I'm sure you're well aware of our long-standing policy regarding police presence inside the skyscrapers. These are people's homes. As such, the Constitution's protection against unreasonable search and seizure directly applies to these homes. I can't in good conscience offer any assistance in a matter like this unless you first have a warrant."

"And you know there's no judge in the state who will give a warrant on a squatted skyscraper. Politically, I'd burn down a couple of bridges just asking."

"Couldn't I say the same thing on my end?"

Terri sighed. "Look, I'm not asking you to stick your neck out within your own constituency . . ." She paused, unsure if she should have mentioned that hideous neck. "I'm asking you to extend your reach through backdoor channels."

"To get justice for Mr. Jhadav."

"Absolutely." She had no assurance this call wasn't going to be played back for anyone, anywhere, so she was hoping to avoid explicitly stating the implied lie, that she sought a Who and not a Why.

"And if I can't help?"

"If you really can't find it in your heart to assist in an ongoing police investigation," she said, putting the whole thing back on Chandrika, "then we'll probably have to go in."

"Like the constitution doesn't exist."

"Like it doesn't exist inside 333 S. Grand, you betcha."

Chandrika tensed her mouth and looked down at something.

"Pardon my resistance, but I'm sure you're well aware that the timing here makes your own motives rather suspicious."

"I . . . huh?"

"Watch the news. You're part of a larger story."

"I'm not the issue here," she said, controlling the nervous edge in her voice. "Your help is the issue. Why don't we leave it at you will at least think over my offer."

"What *is* your offer?"

"That you help me avoid a full-blown invasion of a skyscraper."

"That's not really an offer, more like a good thing to avoid. Call me any time and I'll talk."

"That the best you can do?"

"Like I said. I can't help with any activity that subverts our core mission. But I'd be happy to raise the matter with my board of directors. Who knows. Maybe one of them would be willing to offer you the backdoor channels that I cannot. So, let's confer before you make any decisions and leave that as an option. Will that do?"

"It's a start."

The call ended, Terri thinking, *Doesn't anybody say goodbye anymore?*

Calling up a news aggregator, she entered her name and said, "What the fuck have I done now . . ."

A series of stories covered the raid from yesterday, on the Quintiglio backhouse. She pulled up a block of footage, viewing herself and the other cops milling around in front of the property, seeing already that the scene had been altered, with Babs and Ruben flanking her and four or five Swatted-out officers in the background. A caption read, "Why Was A Militarized Police Unit Sent To Apprehend One Reporter?"

She clicked one of the text links, reading,

Several key questions remain about Mr. Quintiglio's death at the hands of the LAPD. Chief among these; why was an unarmed citizen journalist taken down by a dozen paramilitarized police officers? And was Mr. Quintiglio targeted for his reportage? In the last few months, he'd written extensively about citywide controversies, including the recent contentious Immigration and Customs hearings, the OBE strike, and the widening Tournament of Roses riot scandal . . .

"But not about Stacy Santos," she whispered, staring at the ceiling and smiling in frustration. In all her years of dealing with public input, she'd never heard or read anyone offering one good idea.

Why didn't she live in a universe where it was okay to crowdsource a murder case? People went public with every other imaginable problem. Not quite twenty years ago, the networked citizenry had linked micro-plots of arable land—lawns, lots, medians—to stave off total agricultural collapse. Ever since then, the Efficiency Revolution had rolled on in smaller and smaller ripples, echoing a new national self-reliance. Vigilant citizens sniffed out wasted food, poor design, misused manpower. Humanity had become obsessed with problem solving.

Of course, only the visible part of humanity solved problems. It was easy to dismiss how much of the world still remained in the dark, sometimes literally. The long emergency, bested by the US in under half a decade, still reverberated throughout the third world. The United States had secured an extension of The American Century only by default, having somehow tricked its two biggest competitors into killing each other, and suffering an almost unimaginable consequence.

There'd been a time when she'd kept abreast of the world's dark pockets. It'd fascinated her, the ease with which some governments repurposed the networks for obscene social control. A multitude of nations—regions—had fatally contracted into self-contained nightmares. And those were the realms that had pulled through the Dim Ages. Large pockets of the world had lost the fight entirely, descending into torchlit autarkies, yielding to deindustrialization, deforestation, the return of slavery. Saudi Arabia had shrunk down to two holy cities abutting a barbarian's wasteland. Other parts of the Middle East were less able to support human life than the Chinese hinterlands. The United States sent probes out into the world's battlefields the way it once used to send them out into the solar system. Terri had followed all this for years; now it was just too depressing.

There were still plenty of stories out there involving human resilience. The Slide meant very different things to different continents. The Americas were overrun with Indian refugees; Europe teemed with the Chinese. Russia wound up unwillingly harboring both, pockets of immigrants sometimes continuing their war from camp to camp, fighting with bricks and pipes. Some refugees repatriated to the new cities being built along the edges of India and China, or tried their hand in the fringe cities that had escaped destruction—Huai'an, Madurai, Quanzhou, Vadodara—still churning out bananas, granite, paper, textiles, all of it untouchable, untradable, cursed, regardless of how many clicks each item did or did not set off under Geiger counters.

Terri returned to the bad aftertaste of the Quintiglio story. She looked up the one public information officer she knew, Linda Ledesma, locating her at the Cadillac Avenue workstation. She placed her own VT on scene, thinking it was best to have this conversation in person, if not actually in person. She materialized near the front entrance, seeing Ledesma's byline over a group huddled toward the back of the room. Terri approached, finding another cluster of chairs in a seeming repeat of the viewing from the bar the other night, everyone staring into one spot in the center of the crowd. This group seemed celebratory. Linda Ledesma high-fived a burly patrol officer.

Terri did a V-slash overhead, making her presence known to the group, then said, “Hey Linda. What’s going on?”

“Terri, hey. They caught that ‘Imsane’ mutt.”

“No shit. That actually makes me happy. What was the magic trick? How’d he get up on all those signs?”

She grimaced. “The fucking guy works for Caltrans.”

“Huh?”

“You ever see anyone cleaning that graffiti off?”

“Just last week, actually.”

“Chances are you were looking at him *applying* the graffiti. The kid would sign out a boom lift, do a little work, do a little crime. It’s ingenious.”

Terri shook her head in disbelief. “Are you telling me that in this city, with all of us hunting this kid, he was somehow able to hide in plain sight? That’s absurd.”

“Overseer oversight. No one thought to look for the obvious.”

Another cop said, “Classic. They’d have put this kid in stocks within the hour in Chicago.”

“Who thought to catch him?”

“Benicio Penny. From Harbor?”

“And does he get the reward pool?”

“Hopefully he’ll get a real pool. Or a statue in a park somewhere.”

“Where’s the kid at now?”

“Now? Got me. Probably Vignes.”

“No, I mean, where’s he at here?” Terri pointed to the empty space in the center of the group.

“Oh, um. 21-20.”

She brought up PanOpt layer 21, finding a large viewing box showing Detective Benicio Penny, strapping and copper toned, holding court in front of their little group and presumably a dozen more huddled micro-victory parties throughout the Southland. Ledesma touched Terri's elbow and said, "Check out the money shot," pointing to a thumbnail box in the corner of the scene. She tapped this, swelling it to fill the air in front of her, showing Penny and the perp. The kid was in his early twenties, handsome, black, wearing the hooded sweatshirt that had served as a villain's cloak for all eternity. In the scene, Penny had the kid corralled in an alley somewhere, hands already cuffed. She saw MANSARAY, DESHAWN over his head, surprised to see he had no adult priors.

"Million dollar question, kid," Detective Penny said. "What does 'Imsane' *mean*?"

"What do you mean, what does it mean?"

"Don't play dumb. What's your thesis?"

"Say what?"

Penny rocked his head back and forth with the cadence of his own questioning.

"Are you saying, 'I'm Sane?' or is it 'I'm so insane that I can't spell the word *insane* correctly?'"

The kid smiled. Terri was struck by the genuineness of the gesture, as if he were delighted to find someone asking.

"Nah man, it's 'I'm sain.' You know?"

"What?"

"'I'm sayin.' You know what I'm sayin?"

Terri groaned.

Benicio Penny raised up to loom over the kid. "I am going to shoot you in the face and plant the gun on your grandmother and do my prison time with a *smile*, you fucking nincompoop."

Terri closed the box with a laugh. "I want to say that's the stupidest thing I've ever heard."

"Doesn't make it not a win. Man, that graffiti shit pissed me off."

The rest of the huddle, watching a different piece of footage, guffawed as a group, and she felt a twinge of pride.

"Hey, so. I actually came down to get some fresh eyes on a situation. There's some new footage in the local news cycle, and I can't really tell if I'm getting sand trapped in it or not . . ."

"Welcome to the club," the burly patrol officer said. "We should make up membership cards." The byline over his head read JOSE ARMENDARIZ, PO II. In all her years detecting, she'd never made the connection that civilian bylines had to be read surname first. Only cops had their names listed in correct order.

"Come again?"

"I saw myself at the Tournament of Roses thing just this morning. I'm riding a water buffalo through the crowd, shooting kids with a Yugo gun."

"Oh *shit*. I didn't realize the Tournament thing had gotten that bad this quick . . ."

"It's not good," Ledesma said. "I've got two dozen different remix issues I'm handling as of last night. But you were saying you're in there somewhere yourself?"

"I'm in the Nuestro Quintiglio footage remixes."

"Oh yeah, Public Information has been handling a bunch of those today also. Multiple fronts. What you should do is send macro footage of your actual whereabouts to Bob Trender over at . . ."

"No, I was there. I was lead."

"Ahhh. That makes things more complicated."

"Just hit the mats for a few days," Officer Armendariz said. "Go low, wear a dust mask. The huddled masses will find something else to bark about by the weekend."

"I hope," Terri said. "I never shoulda spoken with that guy."

"Which guy?" Linda asked. "A reporter guy?"

"Kofi Agyeman."

Armendariz looked off in annoyance. "Pshht. That guy can go *buy* me a cup of kofi."

"Yeah, seriously, Terri." Linda looked concerned. "Never ever talk to reporters. That's Rule One of Public Information."

Up early Thursday morning, Terri jogged to clear her mind, the path forward now obvious. It all came down to EyePhones. Farrukh was the anomaly in the group of killers, the only one who would have saved his eyewear, and the only one with an heir to guard that eyewear. Liney had given up a location. After a quick shower and omelet, she spent the morning and early afternoon trying to reach Chandrika Chavan, calling every twenty minutes, searching the woman out by Ghost. All she needed was RALA's assistance as the lubricant to get a crew into the tower named by Liney. At three thirty, she started organizing a raid party.

An hour later she stood next to a dozen-strong contingent of housing cops, each a known quantity within the downtown word-of-mouth networks. The idea here was to draw as much attention to herself as possible, to call out RALA in their own environment, forcing a confrontation and then negotiating passage for herself and a few bodyguards.

She turned back and was happy to see Zack talking with one of the uniformed officers. She'd left him a message earlier in the day, forcing herself not to ponder too hard how to explain this move to Zack, hoping she wouldn't be forced into pitting the explicit commands of the police chief against the implicit bonds of partnership. As she walked up, he was laughing, saying, "... cowboys and Indians. And the Indians have to be the Indians."

"Glad to see you here, Zendejas."

"Hey, I'm always down for a little excursionary force." He looked off, seeing a growing mass of refugees watching and waiting for their next move. "Some shiny eyes in the jungle. Gotta say, I'm minorly impressed by your dedication to the cause of the hapless nobody. I give you points for persistence, Pastuszka."

In hand-to-text, she wrote him,

this is almost def a bluff. RALA won't budge & I need assistance in getting the guy's shades.

Smiling, Zack texted,

Coulda fooled me. You have enough muscle here to do a full staged raid

She frowned, looking back to the uniformed officers, several already slipping into rubber-edged riot costumes, fetish gear, with a slow, showy pace that would be sure to attract attention dozens of floors up. Where the hell was Chavan?

Terri texted to Zack,

If u have anything offensive 2 say, nows the time. I need 2 get this show on the road, so it'd be good 2 whip up some pissed offedness

Zack smiled, looked around for inspiration, stood tippy-toe, then said, "Why couldn't the Indians have taken the Chinese lead and deserted town? They certainly haven't been made any more welcome. I don't care who was whose ally."

"Yeah, but there wasn't an Indiatown to burn down."

"There is now," he said, attempting to indicate the skyscraper next to them, his finger instead pointing directly at a wall-mounted dispenser offering free swish-and-spit fluoride gelcaps.

"Before I forget," she said, reaching into a jacket pocket and producing some ghosting stickers. "Just in case you need these."

Zack backed off, hands out, unwilling to accept her offering. "Hey, I'm good."

The sky darkened prematurely, heavy rain clouds threatening to move everyone into the lobby. Using the linked binocular app, she and Zack scanned the face of the building, searching for broken windows that could be exploited for drone access. She remembered being a kid, her dad driving her past houses in the suburbs at night, passing window after window lit only by the glow of TV. Later, there were years when EyePhones had this same effect, just the slightest play of light across a nose and forehead at night. Eventually shades became sealed worlds, just like the downtown office towers. There was no way to tell who was looking at what.

The cops milled for fifteen minutes, waiting for instructions, making small talk, Terri catching a group bitch session about how nobody ever received certified documentation from hospital administrators or court clerks. It was the forced nonchalance that preceded action, although she couldn't imagine that anybody believed they were actually going up as a mass. But even as she thought this, Terri caught a subtle shift in the group, cops snapping on rubber gloves, passing out alcohol swabs and wallet-sized soap strips, everyone acting proactive about bedbugs and resistants, infections that would be difficult to treat even in a hospital. Within a minute, the mood had shifted, everyone behaving as if going up were a forgone conclusion.

Mutty emerged from the crowd, slapping hands with uniformed officers as he walked toward her, a replay of his birthday party.

"If you please, mang, you are to be looking at all those pigs down there," he said, an impersonation of Zack's impersonation of a fictionalized Indian gangbanger's impersonation of Al Pacino. She thought about how they would look from on high; would the raiding party appear in any way intimidating? Even with three dozen cops, they'd be outnumbered several hundred to one if they actually went up.

"Is this *real*, Terri?" he drawled.

"Damn straight," she said so as not to alert the locals, making a face, texting him a replay of her communiqués to Zack.

Mutty laughed and said, "Alright, but I got bowling league at eight, so . . ."

A cop looked over Terri's shoulder and said, "What a complete and utter hoo-er."

She turned, switched to wireframe view, seeing—through the momentarily invisible skyscraper directly in front of her—the RALA contingent marching up from the direction of Angel's Knoll, the park where she'd nabbed Bottlecap. Chandrika Chavan headed the group, looking almost regal in her flowing orange sari. The whole unfolding scene suddenly seemed unnecessarily dramatic, the meeting forced upon the envoys of two occupying nations. Terri pulled out of wireframe, striding around the sharp prow of the tower onto South Grand and flipping up her shades to rest just above her hairline, a gesture of good faith.

Terri walked down to meet the group at the footbridge a half block to the north, knowing the whole scene would be watched by the force of cops now massed on the other side of the skyscraper.

"You're a hard woman to reach."

"I gave you my card."

"Lady, I left you forty messages today. So let's get one thing straight. You're responsible for whatever happens here."

"I'm a little unclear what *is* happening here. Are you planning a one-woman excursion into the 333 building?"

"Me and the small army parked on the other side of the building, yeah."

Chavan looked genuinely baffled, her little red scar bobbling up and down, making Terri think of a turkey's wattle.

"Small army. Oh-*kay*. Well, if you are planning on summoning an incursion force, you should know that we are going to picket this action with as much media muscle as we can muster."

"I thought you were interested in getting some justice for Farrukh," she said, truly baffled.

"I don't think Farrukh Jhadav would have wanted this skyscraper turned into a combat zone. There are roughly fifteen thousand people living in this building, Detective. Regardless of what floor your destination is, even one police officer constitutes a major disruption to occupants . . ."

"Who have no right to their occupancy . . ."

". . . causing an extra, unacceptable level of stress to already unbearable stress levels. There are proper channels for negotiating with the residents."

Terri stared with disbelief. "After all this, you want me to, what, meet with a gang representative and make an appointment? All due respect, but are you high? This is an active murder case."

"Here's a better comparison. Would the LAPD have displaced fifteen thousand people in the Stacy Santos investigation?"

"You know what I think? I think you don't really give a shit about Farrukh Jhadav. I think you just want to make a little scene out here, in a public space where you know everyone is watching."

"You're the one who seems intent on public spectacle, Detective." Terri enjoyed the slight hint of disruption in the woman's demeanor.

"Yeah, and we agreed that you'd take this up with your board of directors before forcing my hand."

"I never said that," Chandrika said.

"Excuse me?"

"I never said any such thing."

"Are you being for real? Because, I can't . . ."

A shrill squeal came from the PanOpt earpiece, so nerve-janglingly piercing that both Terri and Chandrika flinched. She pulled the shades down and saw a bright red impact box on the ground, less than twenty feet away, Terri shuffle-jumping backward as something large and ceramic exploded on the pavement in front of her, pieces scattering, her mind shut down by combat fear. Visuals kicked in, the Falling Object Alarm sounding again, people raining objects down at them, PanOpt forcing her into motion. Terri sprinted toward the lobby's main entrance, every cop having seen the alarm, knowing from their own systems that their hand had been forced: Everybody Up.

With Detective Pastuszka in the lead, the incursion force did the human zipper up forty-six flights of clogged stairwells, boring a hole through the endless flow of refugees ascending and descending. Housing had attempted to maintain at least one working contingency elevator in every building, but this plan faded as the sealed shafts had filled with years of garbage, refugee floor captains drilling disposal slots in the stainless steel doors. Zack, Mutty, and the housing cops peeled off at the eighteenth floor, where the projectiles originated. By the thirtieth floor, refugees had cleared out, taking a different stairwell as word of the raid spread throughout the bloodstream of the building.

Even pacing herself, Terri was the first to arrive on the forty-sixth floor. She stood at the top of the stairs, hands gripping knees, heart slamming, waiting for everyone else. Next to her, a badly plastered scar snaked up through the drywall. You could date a skyscraper's abandonment by the presence or lack of these thin seams. Towers deserted before the collapse of the copper market had been systematically plundered of their pipes and wiring.

She spotted the floor's assortment of protein lozenges, another government freebie blasted by taxpayer groups, although this one didn't cost California a dime. The federal government had a strong motivation to keep up baseline nutritional levels within the skyscrapers. Poor diet led to compromised immune systems, which led to quicker and more devastating mini-epidemics. The lozenges had originally come in wall-mounted vending machines that dispensed one per day per person. These went unused by refugees who'd assumed, correctly, that they'd been designed to identify and tag recipients. Now the gray, tasteless tablets sat out in wall-mounted steel basins on every stair landing.

Terri resisted the urge to grab a mouthful. She was feeling her age until one of the uniformed officers, at least fifteen years younger than her, rounded the lower landing and lumbered up the final steps, his face beet red. She pulled up a drone layer, seeing their blue and green swoops throughout the building as they'd sped up the stairwell ahead of the cops.

When her eight-cop contingent had reassembled on the stairwell landing, she clicked a series of check-boxes for the PA system. Eight public address drones had already positioned themselves in equidistant corners of the floor, and as she tapped the final consent box, she heard a boilerplate incursion message, delivered in her own voice, reverberating throughout the nearby halls; *All occupants of the 46th floor of 333 South Grand Avenue are hereby notified . . .*

The group surged through the gray steel exit door, emerging into a hallway far more tightly packed than the lower stairwells, people acting as if they didn't hear her message booming overhead. She assumed some sort of noncompliance order had been given by the floor captain to the two to four hundred people under his command. A realization came: they were far, far outside the protection of the Wall. With nine service revolvers and two stun drones, she might as well be on the surface of the moon.

They set out through a narrow hall lit by emergency lights presumably connected to rooftop solar arrays, the only electricity allowed by the city. She passed an old secretary hutch, and a door still marked "Telephone Room," residents lined up along one wall of the constricted hallway, perhaps to intentionally slow them down. The body heat gave the floor a stifled smell that halfway masked a deeper odor, something strong and briny, reminding her of an aquarium she'd visited as a kid.

Terri passed several open-door warrens of labor. Unpainted plywood berths flanked worn worktables. She saw evidence of printmaking, leatherwork, embroidery, all the tools of Poser Life used here for actual human enterprise. At least SSK sweatshops had the owners and workers under the same roof. There'd been a certain point, years ago, when housing had to choose between fighting child labor or fighting fire code violations. Above one door she saw the red-and-white humped dome of a city–installed fire suppression unit, a stark reminder of which way that question had gone.

The northeast corner held three office suites. Terri dispensed with the PA drones, instead loudly pounding on each door, knowing that word of the police presence would have already arrived. All three doors opened at the precise same moment, as if a Bollywood dance number might break out. Families emerged in a general air of orderly compliance, some of the men giving her funny stares as they passed, perhaps unaccustomed to seeing a woman general in the army of occupation, even though it was the refugees who'd come to occupy her own country. She and the officers fanned out into the three rooms, Terri taking the left suite.

There were no lofts or bunks here. Instead, orderly rows of bags and bundles formed knee-high partitions between sleeping areas. Toward the back of the room, overlapping clothes lines hung between hooks. Past this, the floor-to-ceiling window was entirely obscured by an ancient chunk of billboard someone had dragged up from the city streets, the last three massive letters of a company name reading OJO next to the neck of a rail-thin perfume model.

"Imagine having to see this before you go to sleep every night," one of the officers said.

"If you lived up here, why, why, *why* would you block that view?" she said, high-stepping over mounds of clothing to the far corner, grabbing a chunk of the sign and bending it backward, expecting it to flex and instead hearing the entire piece crack loudly in two.

Where she'd assumed there'd be a glittering skyline, there was only a wall of backlit brown glass. The layers of grime and soot on the outside of the building had obliterated the view of the city. Why was she so shocked? These buildings hadn't been washed in over a decade.

"What a bunch of Charles Dickens *bullshit*," Terri muttered, taking off the shades and squinting into the ambient smudge beyond. Turning back, she saw that the other officers had already moved on to the next room, leaving her all alone in tenement living quarters that had once been a place of business.

PanOpts back on, she conducted a quick walk-through of the next two rooms, cataloging everyone, looking for any female faces in Rujuta's age range without a byline, scar or no scar. Following orders, several of the uniformed officers searched through the scattered boxes and bags of possessions, cataloging each pair of EyePhones. Within five minutes, it was obvious that everyone was accounted for. Emerging back out into the hallway, she surveyed the family members lined up against the two walls in a broken V formation, following their own protocols, seeing that everyone had a byline. Liney had gotten his intel wrong: wrong floor, wrong building, wrong city. "*Pinche ciudad*," she muttered to herself. Zack texted,

Firefight on 18, 1 hit

From the looks on their faces, the other officers must've received the same message, an unfortunate break in protocol. She leaned against a hallway wall, calling Zack with what she hoped was an air of calm authority. Looking down, she saw a neat stack of photocopier paper, detritus from the original tenants.

"Mutty got shot."

She exhaled slowly. "How bad?"

"I'm not sure. They're bringing him down right now. I'm here with the shooter and the rest of the delegation."

"What was it? What happened?" she asked, already reducing the building to glass and bringing up the players twenty-eight stories below.

"It was the kid who'd tossed a serving bowl out the window at us. His floor captain gave him up, and the kid didn't want to be given up. But it doesn't seem coordinated with anyone else."

She fixed everyone's position and zoomed in to see two officers carrying Mutty down the endless flights of stairs.

"I'll call back," she said.

She reviewed the maps. Drones had diagrammed floors 45 and 47, protocol to prevent a between-story ambush, she supposed. She saw the layout of the floor just above her and said, "Fuck it."

Terri ordered two of the uniformed officers back to the stairwell, everyone marching up one more flight, reentering an identical door, rounding several corners and emerging onto a spacious corporate elevator landing. After the murk of the forty-sixth floor, the vividly lit marble here stunned her eyes. Gang leaders appropriated the executive floors and private suites of every skyscraper. Through the back wall, they could see the view that had eluded them one floor below. These windows were spotless, perhaps cleaned by terrified gang associates who'd screwed up. She could see ambient gray helipads, illuminated by the three-quarter moon, the glinting Bonaventure Hotel, the distant Hollywood sign.

Two OG SSKs emerged from some inner sanctum. Each was older, in his late twenties, dressed in Hawaiian shirts, Bermuda shorts, and sandals.

"You fucking assholes think this is over?"

The one on the left smirked and for an instant she saw herself drawing her gun, walking up and pressing it into the guy's gawping mouth.

"We're coming back tomorrow," she said to say something with some meat to it, to have what was rapidly melting into a fiasco not be in vain. "Tenfold. Batten down the hatches." She pulled back toward the stairwell, the baffled officers eyeballing the OGs, then her, both gang executives smiling in amusement.

On the eighteenth floor, she passed a trail of blood.

Back in the gumball, she sat with the calm of total inertia. Having figured out what she'd been doing, the car had set its air conditioning to meat locker-cold, wanting to keep her awake as adrenaline levels crashed. Distant Bollywood music reverberated off the sides of buildings, sounding distorted and monstrous, the war drums of an enemy tribe. She opened up a Medical Status box, seeing Mutty's ambulance as a distant pictogram on a flat plane, his vital signs visible in a little billboard of blips and pulse lines over the racing vehicle.

She whispered to her car, having it drive ten blocks away so she could decompress in silence, PanOpts up and perched on her scalp. She looked out, seeing the street as it was. It was easy to pretend that as soon as she'd taken off the glasses, none of this had actually happened, that Mutty was on his way to get high somewhere. The earpiece chimed, tearing through the illusion's thin tissue. She slid her shades down, descending into reality.

Zack said, "Hey."

"Hey."

"Any updates?"

"He should be at Good Sam in a few minutes. I guess we'll know more in, what? An hour maybe."

"An hour," he sighed, sounding battle-weary.

"Yeah. I don't know. I don't know what else to say."

"We got Mutty's shooter, some shit-scared teen. That's all. Wrong place, wrong time. So don't blame yourself."

"Okay," she said, thinking, *Goddamn right I don't.*

"Okay. Good. I guess, you know. Let's keep each other posted, okay?" Another call dinged in her upper-right field of vision.

"Yeah, let's." She switched calls, seeing an officer, a foot soldier, someone she'd glanced inside, in the scrum of invasion.

"Detective?"

"What's up."

"We clocked the lobby macros, and it picked up one of the guys you were looking for."

"Oh yeah? Who?" she said, trying to remember when she had ordered any such list.

"I just have the name," he paused, reading from his own invisible list. "Dios Sarin," he finally said with undue solemnity, as if the kid were a god of the underworld.

"No shit," she said, wondering if the night might be salvaged after all. "Clip his walk-ons and pass it along."

Three minutes later, she was watching Froggy cross the ground floor of 333 South Grand on December 29, walking with the jaunty swagger of a man who didn't know it was his last day on earth. The lobby had been long-ago seeded with pinprick macros by warriors on the Wall, giving her a good view from every angle.

Something caught her eye. She switched from single camera view and went into immersive, swooping down to eye level with Froggy. When she slowed him down to a slow-mo strut she saw he was carrying a blue-and-black gym bag. Something about this almost jarred her memory. She paused it, opened a side window, tagged Froggy's byline, flipped him into the Basement, and watched his day in high-speed.

His route followed the opposite emotional trajectory of Farrukh's, his appointed rounds occurring on his own schedule, stopping at one notorious Third Street brothel for forty minutes, smoking weed as he exited, looking carefree. It was strange that she was still feeling sympathy for Froggy's killer. He kept the gym bag on his person at all times, sometimes in hand, sometimes tightly strapped around his shoulder.

Blanco called. She paused playback and quickly debated the most respectful form of communication, deciding audio only was probably appropriate.

"Chief."

"So, the latest on this is that Mr. Posada has three wounds. One to his earlobe, superficial, a side entry and exit that looks decent, nothing vital. But the third shot was to his leg, and that clipped his femoral. He lost a lot of blood on the way down. The good news is he's in surgical prep as we speak."

"Okay." She looked out into the open box, the paused image of Froggy in the act of high-fiving some street personality.

"His condition is very serious, Terri. I thought you should hear that from me."

"I understand."

"Listen. How you deal with this is your business. If you feel you need some time to yourself, no one's going to challenge you. I'm just stating the obvious. But I want you to know that you shouldn't blame yourself. This was an unforeseen occurrence in the line of duty."

"Sure," she said, not knowing what to make of this.

"Great. Let's regroup tomorrow. In the meantime, go home."

"Okay."

She unpaused. Froggy continued down Main Street, stopping every thirty feet to shake hands and laugh and slap backs like he was running for city council or something. She sped the footage up. He grabbed a late lunch—or was it breakfast?—at a food truck on North Hill, caught a taxi on Alpine that took him up to a strip mall in Highland Park. Then he was back on the road, going east, to Alhambra, where he met with two teens, underlings, in a small park. She slowed this, their conversation taking on a serious cast but not enough so that she felt the need to piece together lip-synced audio. This was clearly a junior officer laying down the law to rookie foot soldiers. Then he was on the road again, having his car drive him just south of Lincoln Park, not far from the scene with Mr. Banghoo that felt like a million years ago.

It was dark now, raining. He set out on foot, away from the park, feeling confident enough to cross through neutral gang territory, although Froggy's affiliation and the neighborhood affiliations were labeled iffily in PanOpt's database. He kept going, down to the freeway, striding the wrong way along the westbound shoulder, a gutsy thing to do with traffic zooming within three feet. He walked a half mile, his lively demeanor unchanged. Finally Froggy paused below the freeway sign, his face lit a slight green from its ambient glow. She paused and pulled up, realizing her apartment building was directly across the freeway from him, getting an old spooky feeling. Unpaused, Froggy seemed to smile directly at her as he tossed his gym bag with one overhand throw, like an oversized football, landing it on the balcony of the signage ledge.

"Jesus." She'd thought she'd recognized that bag.

She called up the Vignes Detention Center and found herself facing its actual reception room. It was a minor flaw of

PanOpt that cops had to interface the detention system the same way as the public. Everyone—from family to lawyers—started in this same space, either in person or through the networks. There was no pretty splash page, no web room, no informative civic buffer zones, just a 3D smash cut into the outermost circle of Hell. Even with three separate containment doors before the visitation room, you could still hear the distant shrieks and buzzers. All that was missing was the overpowering stench of disinfectants. And sometimes the brain could conjure up this sharpest of phantom smells, so overwhelming was the experience. With the oversized checkerboard floor tiles, asylumish in their connotations, the place was somehow the city's most real destination, regardless of if one went there physically or through a pair of glasses.

She'd wondered why they'd made the experience so brutally authentic. After all, most of the people who came here remotely were just relatives. If someone came here via the Overlay to arrange a self-surrender, they'd probably give a long second thought to going on the lam. Maybe that was the idea; city, county, and state cells were all operating at close to triple capacity.

"Evening, Detective," a heavyset Corrections Officer said from behind a long steel countertop, seeing her as she saw him. His white neoprene gloves, made to cover forearms from splatters, had been rolled up over each wrist, so that he appeared to be wearing chunky bangle bracelets and dinner gloves.

"Officer. Hey, I need to speak with DeShawn Mansaray. Can I get him in a Q&A room, or are those all taken?"

"At midnight?" he laughed.

"Hey, you never know."

She'd heard that overcrowding had gotten so bad they were making men sleep sitting up in the booths.

"Yeah, sure. Assuming there's time. This connected to that special 849?"

"What 849? A custody release?"

"This guy's got some kind of guardian angel. He posted an hour ago. We've been getting calls all night about the kid. Paperwork should be wrapped up any time now."

"Calls from who?"

"Mayor's office. Between you and me, maybe higher. He's got powerful friends."

In the distance, a muffled howl reverberated off a dozen different surfaces and she had to remind herself that she wasn't actually here.

"So. Can I see him?"

"Lemme see what I can do. Come back in five?"

He flicked a spot in the air between them and began typing on the bare countertop. Although he could no longer see or hear her, she said, "Great. Yeah."

Terri turned and took in the room. Only one other person sat in the far corner of the waiting area, some wayward sob story relative the CO must've let rot in place. Despite the soft car seat under her real body, she was more here than where she really was, and in this forced pause, she experienced a flash of emotional fragility and volatile hostility so acute that it registered as déjà vu. Powerful friends: this fucking night.

Looking at this figure hunched over the black-and-white flooring triggered another free association. She opened a web box and then swapped scenes, so that the detention center lobby zoomed up into a small cubby in her upper-left-hand field of vision. In the parked police cruiser she sat in, she typed KANGAROO KORT in her desktop, and then the car interior did a clean dissolve and she was standing in a vastly larger waiting room, a space the general dimensions of an indoor soccer stadium, its floor tiles the same hideously giant checkerboard pattern as the detention center.

She smiled that she'd made the connection about the flooring, that her powers of observation were still sharp. When had she last been here? She checked to make sure she wasn't still logged in under some fake name, and that the webroom hadn't detected that she'd arrived through PanOpts. Any cop lurking here was in for a world of abuse if they didn't bother to conceal their identity.

Terri muted the room's audio, floated herself through a pair of twenty-foot-high swinging doors, and then she was in the Kortroom. Despite the chamber's ornate absurdity—flaming torchlights, animated pirate flags fluttering from pikes, baroque woodwork curlicues reaching up to cathedral ceilings—this was largely a waiting room as well. To her left, hundreds of comically elongated pews reached off into the far distance, each filled with dozens of city cops from every division of every bureau. She'd heard that a third of the force had a Duplicado in the Kortroom dock.

To her right was the Kort itself; the massive railing of the bar, a stage of cracked earth the square area of a professional basketball court, and then the immense raised bench, three stories high and jutting forward precariously. Behind this sat the judge, a twenty-foot kangaroo with steel daggers for teeth and a huge, flouncy powdered wig. As she watched, he thundered against some poor schlub who'd been stripped naked and tossed onto the stage. A crowd of onlookers hooted and hollered, although she knew there must be an exponentially larger audience without visible manifestation. Rumor had it that the LA Kortroom had overtaken the NYPD Kortroom in popularity last year.

She called up a directory and scrolled down to her own name. A downturned neon arrow lit up in the distance, and as she floated over to view her own Dupe, she recognized some of the slack-jawed faces in the seats below; Johnny Gabling, Flaxy Chavez, Maureen Amaya, which seemed in especially poor taste, her dead of an aneurysm two years now.

Terri located herself forty aisles back. She'd been dinged and subsequently sent here years and years ago, the wages of a brutality complaint by some speeded-out nobody whose roughing up she'd participated in. The guy had vanished not long after, and although the complaint had since expired, her Dupe had remained in place, sitting patiently, staring forward as if hypnotized, waiting for its day in Kort.

She called up her Dupe's byline, seeing that her comments list hadn't been updated in months. She was glad to at least read her correct home address listed above her head.

There'd been a stab of sadness, last time she'd been here, maybe a year ago, seeing herself still listed as living at the South Pasadena house.

She heard the CO say, "Okay," and when she swapped locations again she was in one of the detention center's interrogation rooms, barely enough space for two people and a fold-down table. She'd forgotten how small it was. Did any cops still use these rooms in person?

DeShawn slumped casually on the edge of a stool. He'd been given back his tan hoodie and supplied with corrections system disposables. Kids with his circumstances—young, non-violent, barely-felony shenanigans—usually showed a split lip or black eye by this time of night, but he looked no worse the wear for his captivity, and certainly not as tired as her. When he saw her in the space with him, he stiffened formally, an unexpected bit of respect.

"Good evening, Officer," he said. His voice was surprisingly soft and low. Only two ridiculous twin parts shaved into his scalp—perhaps in fashion, perhaps a throwback to some other stupid era in teen fashion—reminded her she was dealing with knucklehead number forty-six million.

"I'm Officer Pastuszka," she said. "Homicide." When she saw that didn't get a reaction, she said, "I heard you have friends up high. Wanna tell me how that came about?"

"I don't know. You work for the city? You meet people."

"You meet people through Caltrans?"

He shrugged, a gesture so casual they might as well be making conversation in an airport bar over drinks.

"Listen. I don't even care. I need some information."

"Okay."

"I need to know . . ." She paused for a moment, trying to think through what she had to ask. "Sometimes people throw objects onto freeway sign ledges. You must've seen a lot of that, right?"

He shrugged again. Was this politeness? Was he baiting her? For a moment she considered that she'd made a serious tactical mistake, not doing this in person. But then, if she'd taken the time to actually go down there, he probably would have been gone already.

"You're shrugging because, what, you agree with me?"

"Yeah, sure."

"Sure, like you've seen objects thrown up there?"

"Uh-huh."

"Like what? What objects have you seen?"

He squinted but didn't squirm. "I dunno, like shoes. Maybe a ball or something."

"A ball? "

"Yeah, like . . . I saw a baseball once."

"Any bags?"

"Bags? Like, a shopping bag?"

A weird lightheadedness came over her. When kids played dumb, it was usually because they actually were dumb. DeShawn knew something.

"A gym bag."

"Naw. Maybe," he said with a sly little smile.

"What I need to know is, is there any way for anyone to get up there if they don't work for Caltrans? If they needed to retrieve a bag?"

"What would I know about that?" Now there was a snicker, at first muffled by his fist, then straight at her. Her eyes narrowed. Denied the prerogatives of close personal contact, officer standing over perp, she could only try to intimidate.

"Do you realize I'm the person that can keep you in this dungeon?" she said, a lie. "You wanna sleep in a box tonight? Hey!"

DeShawn was laughing now, a full-throated guffaw that spilled into tearful snorts.

"Hey!" she was yelling, scaring herself, thinking irrationally that she would be waking the cellblock.

"Hey! Hey!"

She blinked, suddenly back in the reception room.

"What?"

"Too bad," the CO said curtly. "Paperwork's up. He's getting sprung."

"Says who? They don't pull interrogations like this! I'm in an open murder that . . ."

"Yeah, I'll say. It just came down. Mutty died, ten minutes ago. Word is, you're to thank. So congrats." He ended the call, and she was back in the cooling car on an empty street corner.

Terri had the car screech out as she pulled up a fat, three-dimensional Caltrans logo, finding and selecting the green-and-blue directory. Now was not the time to mourn. In the past, she'd found grief possible to defer, having done it twice, once in tenth grade, the afternoon her father died, and then years later, as an adult, during those long shifts in the days and weeks after her dog Congo had expired in her arms. She'd hold off thinking about it until she actually had time to dwell on it, accepting that the grief would engulf her only at that point.

At 1:20, she stepped out onto the shoulder of the westbound freeway opposite her apartment building, having secured a lifter from a city maintenance worker, a sad, round little woman, one of an unseen multitude charged with fixing the city while it slept. The lifter itself seemed kind of morose, its basket drooping in anthropomorphized self-pity. Its control box set directly in front of her, she awkwardly climbed into the basket, raising herself with a lurch, the ascent jerky, mechanical, nothing like the soaring weightlessness of the Basement.

The ledge of the freeway sign was surprisingly narrow, and when she duck-walked over to the gym bag, the grated metal shelf wobbled precariously. Grabbing the bag, Terri steadied herself against the cold green metal of the signage, one hand flat against an arrow pointing toward Sacramento, and when she looked up she was staring at her own apartment building, almost equidistant to the front entrance, trying to remember why she'd left a light on in her living room. Carlos Jaramillo had been right. It was an ugly little building.

Back in her car, prize in hand, the lifter basket once more appeared to droop in glumness as she sped back onto the open road. The car accelerated and swooped onto I-5, as if following the arrow she'd pressed for the state's capital. The route crossed onto a new section of the freeway with no markers, no dividing lines at all. They didn't need markers on the road anymore, she realized. Even headlights were vestigial, unnecessary, manufactured for human benefit only.

Terri looked down to the bag in her lap and turned it over in her hands, feeling something soft inside, seeing no significant product or suspect tags in her PanOpt margins. She ran one finger along the zipper, breathed deeply, and then said, "Stupid." Pulling down the zipper, she reached in and removed the fitted three-quarter sleeve with the fat blue and purple lightning bolts she'd gotten as a college sophomore; something lost and now reclaimed.

III
THE STAMPEDE AGE

"Okay. Let me think," Zack said, standing on the enclosed screen porch of his house in Sherwood Forest. She'd spilled her guts, told the entire story, somehow finding it simultaneously impossible and frighteningly plausible. The exertion of unburdening herself added to the weight of her sleepless night, and she blinked away the urge to sink down into his hard cane lawn chair, meaning the soft car seat that held her true body, many miles away, parked in a desolate alley behind a boarded-up nail salon. Brightly colored toys and blocks littered the porch; if she floated up into space, she'd probably find her own seat filled with toys as well.

"I know you don't have any macros at your place—and I'm going to resist the urge to say 'I told you the fuck so'—but what about your landlord? What's his name again?"

"Mr. Tan? He doesn't record the building, if that's where you're going," she said. "The guy's cheap and he's Chinese. I doubt he's been at the property more than twenty minutes in the last decade."

Zack turned and looked out the screen door and across the lawn, so secluded and leafy that it was hard to comprehend they were both still in the same county. Past the long expanse of well-trimmed grass, a stand of oaks broke the slanting light of breaking dawn into something nearly hypnotic. From her vantage point, she could just make out the dark hulk of their downed Christmas tree, languishing in the gutter next to the trash cans. Terri had never been quite sure how they afforded this house and three kids on his salary alone, but she remembered asking the question once point blank, and him sighing and saying, "Creative use of debt." Or maybe Janice had inherited more than just their hallway library. He muttered, "Tan, Tan, China Man," in a soft sing-song voice.

"So you have no way of knowing if it was Froggy or someone else who was in your apartment."

"I don't."

"But it's a safe bet that even if it was Froggy, it wasn't Froggy, you follow me? I mean, that shitstain couldn't tie his own shoes, let alone execute a flawless B&E. And what would he want with one piece of clothing, anyway?"

"Yeah."

"Another thing. That's your *house*. You remember that thing with Jimmy Montes?"

"Yeah," she said, feeling a swell of exhaustion roll over her. "No."

"He was on that antigang task force back in the thirties, busted up Darrows, Six Sentinels, did a serious number on Lágrimas De Sangue. All those guys wanted him *alive*, you know? But they knew Montes was like the rest of us, he's covered by the Wall. When they finally go after him? Maybe the idea was that they could overrun the safeguards or something. They had probably thirty guys. It was like the end of *Scarface*.

Except that twenty-eight of those guys got knocked out on his lawn and the other two, making it as far as his back gate, got blown up. All those idiots did was provide the force with a perfect system test."

She nodded, feeling a pit in her stomach with where he was going.

"The day you get out of academy, that's it. You're untouchable. All of us. Someone comes at a cop in the street, tries to break into our residences? They can send a blow-dart anywhere in the county in forty-five seconds. Everyone knows it. Fuck with us? You got less than a minute before it's Drone O'clock. As soon as Froggy approached your complex, he would've gotten tracked. And he would've been cold cocked before he got your door open."

"I thought of that."

"And yet, this guy pulls some super-spy voodoo shit, just walks in, takes what he wants, and then leaves. He's a phantom."

"Yeah."

Zack palmed his face, exhaled, and then slowly massaged the creases in his forehead with two fingers. When he dropped his hand, he looked stern.

"This is a fucking setup."

"Yeah."

"Someone inside the force is positioning you to take the fall for something, and I'll be goddamned if I can tell what it is."

The oaks shushed in agreement from across the lawn. She could almost feel the breeze on her bare forearms, wishing she could stay where she was, then remembering she wasn't actually there.

"What now?"

"What now? What now is . . . I don't know what now is," he said, falling into the opposite seat, then saying "Ow!" as he reached under his ass and produced a painted wooden T-rex.

"Who else have you told about this?"

"No one. I was going to go over this with Blanco in person, but it seemed prudent to tell you first." Saying this now, the logic of her decision felt wiggly.

"Yeah. Good. Whatever this thing is, it's vertical. And who knows how far up it goes. You said the CO told you, 'the mayor's office and maybe higher,' right?"

"I can check the transcript. But yeah."

"So don't say shit to Blanco. For now. And don't bother with trying to track down whoever shot the reporter. That doesn't matter anymore."

"Really?"

"Think about it. He kills the Santos girl, she kills our moron, our moron kills Froggy, Froggy kills someone, *that* someone kills someone . . . who knows how far back into the mists of time this chain of shit extends, you know? You already got your man and then some. Jesus, you solved the murder of the DA's *kid*. You're the hero of the city and the city doesn't even know it yet."

"Right."

"So go low. Follow up on leads that keep you off this main thread. Because whatever whackadoo conspiracy shit is in play here, from where I'm sitting, you're only going to get pulled farther and farther in the more you engage. In the meantime, I'll start snooping on the inside, from this end. Get with me later today and hopefully we'll be someplace better than where we're at now."

"Yeah. Okay."

"Where's this old shirt of yours now?"

"I rented a glove box, stashed it in there."

"Good, good." He stood and took in his lawn again, his hearty alertness contrasting her fatigue. "And get some sleep. No offense, but you look like shit."

"Yeah. Sleep is what's next."

Instead, an hour later she stood on the scuffed marble of the first-floor lobby in the Metropolitan Courthouse, a twenty-two-story tombstone that stood even closer to Central Division than the Temple. She was examining a framed collage hanging over the water fountains. It was a forgotten, faded assemblage of celebrities, farm animals, race cars, and basketball players cut out of old glossy magazines and jumbled up with the individual words of the preamble to the Constitution, like a giant ransom letter; the sad exertions of some high schooler who'd surely long since gotten swallowed whole by the very system they'd set out to decorate.

After the bailiff finished his public pronouncements, she slipped into the central courtroom and took a seat on one of the blue-and-gray patterned cloth benches that must've been recently reupholstered. Citizens yawned uncontrollably from their pews, stupefied to be up so early, physically incapable of faking alertness. Men clutched folded EyePhones in sweaty hands, too broke or clueless to wear a dress shirt with a pocket, anxious to get back to their real lives, far away from here, on the networks. A handwritten sign reading Please Check In With Bailiff had been crookedly duct taped to the waist-high divider. It was a perfect example of how the entire county worked, spending money to spruce up the courtroom but not a dime to get a simple laminated sign.

Two women sat in the second row, on the far side of the waiting area from her, their artificial black bobs glinting under the fluorescents. Muslim Indian women had to wear wigs instead of head coverings in court. Terri had been on the force when the rule was enacted, the consequence of a foiled bomb plot by some weird fringe Hindu cult. There'd been uncontrollable protests. Now, no one seemed to care or even remember all the hubbub. It amazed her how quickly the world could heal around grievous injuries. Past this pair, the seal of California hung as a mighty bronze medallion on the wall, like a prize they'd all won, collectively, for being Best State. Third best state, actually. The bailiff strode back in.

Two young public defenders entered from the back. They were both young guys, lean, wearing suits and haircuts designed to underwhelm. She waved to the closer attorney, Josh Closs, realizing he'd lost a few inches of hairline since they'd last seen each other. He smiled, distracted, said a few things to the bailiff, and then circled over for a quick handshake over the partition.

"Hey, good to see you. What're you in the building for?"

She'd need to be speedy.

"I hear Torg Skarpsvärd requested you."

"Word travels."

"I need five minutes with the guy."

"Well, he's downstairs. *I* won't be needing him for the hearing until afternoon, so go knock yourself out. Need me to put in a good word with the checkpoint guys, or . . ."

"Yeah, but he *requested* you. So Minnick v. Mississippi says you have to make the introductions, right?"

He moaned. "Really? Today?"

"Why? What's so particularly crazy about today?"

"Well, for one thing, I got Torg."

"Five minutes, Josh."

"That's four minutes more than I have."

She smiled.

"Damnit. Meet me just outside. *Shit*."

Last March, she'd helped out Josh's sister, a high-powered patent attorney in her own right, by brokering a sit-down with the two officers she'd drunkenly pummeled at a Koreatown nightclub. An apology and some gift certificates had gotten her off the charges, and the incident itself had presumably gotten Josh a large credit in the family favor bank. So now it was Terri's turn.

Josh emerged from a side door two minutes later, nodding for her to follow. They zipped down a flight of stairs, through a set of security doors, then down another, shallower flight of stairs, arriving on a landing where dozens of spare Christmas decorations had been stacked out of sight from the public. Two collapsed fake trees bordered a dozen oversized presents covered in faded red-and-green wrapping, faint lines around the sagging ribbons showing where the paper had bleached from years and years of December sunlight. Behind these, a selection of worn plastic elves stood at eternal attention, like a row of terra cotta warriors.

Once through the main security door to the holding cells, she could smell fresh paint, this basement jail presumably part of the same renovations that had bought new upholstery upstairs. The door led to a tiny antechamber—for all practical purposes, an airlock—between the agents of crime and justice. She turned in her weapon at the Plexiglas window, then waited with Josh in a space not meant for two people to wait in, standing close enough to catch his tang of sweat.

Inside, they walked past a half-dozen holding blocks, each crammed with four or five sad, silent men. At the end of the row, they stopped in a cell holding only Torg. The door buzzed open, Josh signed her in and introduced her, she did the Miranda, and Josh said, "Hey, we're good. There's no way I can stay. Torg, you don't care if I go, right?"

Torg shrugged.

"We even?"

"Until your sister gets dumped again, yup."

"Don't even joke like that, Terri. You have no idea. Okay."

The door shut behind her and then she was alone in a cell with Torg Skarpsvärd. As the leader of the Rolling Figueroas, Torg was a genuine anomaly. A lone blond Anglo heading a small army of vicious Indian gangbangers, he thrived in the shadowlands of the skyscrapers. Once every sixteen months or so, he got himself arrested on a misdemeanor with the intention of meting out punishments to those who'd eluded him in the free world. Using complex channels of bribes and outside pressure, he navigated his way in and out of most cells and facilities he wanted, improvising through the penal system. His reputation gave the impression of a man comfortable inside or out.

She'd seen Torg plenty of times, although never in person. Terrifying footage had made the rounds, and still circulated among rookies. Torg had fought a half-dozen cops, guys from Devonshire she'd never met. In the melee, he'd received two fantastic hits with Maglights, one to the back of the head, one to the solar plexus. And yet he'd kept on fighting. She hadn't been able to watch without wincing. In the inevitable remixes, Torg had been assaulted with larger and larger weapons—assault rifles, surface-to-air missiles, falling pianos—never quite faltering or giving up. It was as if the remixers, cops all, would have felt disrespectful depicting his loss.

Sitting across the cell from him now, she realized he had no body fat. Although his freshly shaved head and a small Sanskrit tattoo on his throat gave him an artificial air of serenity, a holy man falsely imprisoned. She opened a lie detector box in the space between them.

"Alright. First question. Are you acquainted with Dio 'Froggy' Sarin?"

Torg leaned against the wall of his bunk and sighed. He produced an Asian pear from a small paper bag. For a moment she wondered if he'd already had a weapon smuggled in.

"Nope."

The lie detector said otherwise.

"Mr. Sarin double crossed one of your deputies, Mr. Achindra 'Nailer' Sankaran."

Torg shrugged, looked down to the fruit, rotated it to an angle he liked, and took a bite.

"Are you telling me that you don't know anything about that?"

He smiled. "That is what I am telling you, Detective Pastuszka. What's your first name?"

"How about Farrukh Jhadav?"

Torg tilted his head just slightly, a plane in the smooth surface of his scalp catching the light. "I have no idea who that is."

You had to hand it to the guy: if she didn't have the lie detector bipping along true north, she'd have sworn he was telling the truth. It was the mark of a genuine sociopath.

This next question was just for reaction. "Do you have any knowledge of who killed Farrukh Jhadav on the morning of January 5?"

He squinted just for a second.

"No, I do not."

Torg was an orphan. Both parents had been murdered while he was just a toddler, hiding under a duvet and listening to the screams. Although the mythology he'd subsequently built around himself had many facets, this detail held at least as much weight as his adult exploits. Any child placed in terrible physical peril, or who witnessed terrible carnage, was tagged, by various networks and systems, so as not to "go Torg."

She'd always wondered if this tale was entirely cautionary. He'd certainly emerged from childhood a master of cruel efficiency. Skarpsvärd was as efficient a manager as anyone in the ranks of corporate America. If he or his deputies had been crossed, by anyone, at any level of the gangland hierarchy, Torg knew and arranged an appropriate response. He did an admirable job of downplaying a retention for names and faces that bordered on photographic. She hoped this reputation would help her now.

"And do you know the whereabouts of Rujuta Jhadav?" This was the crucial question. Regardless of anything else, Farrukh had gotten himself close to an enemy of Torg. Even though Farrukh had dispatched this enemy, the social physics of skyscraper life made Farrukh a possible target as well. She knew Torg had nothing to do with Stacy Santos—on either end of the gun—but she had no assurance that Rujuta wouldn't take the fall for some unknown offenses committed by Farrukh.

"No, I do not." The lie detector smoothed out; he was telling the truth. Her relief at this factoid was tempered by the utter similarity with which he'd offered her a lie and a truth and made both look like the same thing.

On her way back out, passing through the airlock, she had to rotate around a buxom young blonde with neon pink lipstick. As they slid past each other in the tight little antechamber, the woman's byline popped up with a string of prostitution-related arrests and Terri understood that this woman was intended for Torg. She glanced up at the woman's name just as the door was shutting behind her, and for a split second seemed to read KRISTA SPRIZZO. Standing back in the hallway with the Christmas decorations, she slapped herself once to wake up, the crack of her open palm echoing off the marble walls.

In the car, Terri sat and let the shakes pass. She recalled a rumor from five or six years ago, the ancestor of the blinding story that had so terrified Bottlecap. For six months, criminals of all stripes had persuaded themselves that the LAPD could somehow remotely tap into EyePhones and see, in real time, what the wrongdoers themselves saw. It'd been a wonderful fear to exploit. Now that she no longer trusted her PanOpts, she appreciated how stressful it would be to believe that someone could always see what you were seeing. She needed a new pair of eyes.

And anyway, she'd need a few things if she was actually going to be temporarily homeless. Searching for a pharmacy, she reduced the city to a high-contrast outline, with mammoth mortars and pestles floating over its drugstores. In the distance, she saw a cluster of these. Did LA have a pharmacy district? She wondered whether, if she kept this layer active, she'd see these mortars and pestles loom, huge, over whatever store she finally selected. This led to the image of Farrukh, desperately searching for a pharmacy in Panama. This was still his case, even with the hunt switched to his killer's killer's killer.

The pharmacy was an underlit, forlorn little space in the Fashion District. Terri grabbed toothpaste, sunscreen, hand moisturizer, floss. In one aisle she hesitated and then selected a pair of disposable EyePhones, the force-issued disposables in her jacket being as conducive to paranoia as the PanOpts themselves.

That word—"disposable"—had always irked her, being a weird inversion of its former meaning, always making her flash back to all those extinct throwaway luxuries of her youth: sporks, tin foil, fabric softener sheets. These disposables had to be "disposed" of in seemingly ubiquitous purple and yellow receptacles, or roving jump dumps, or back at participating stores, each unit being smart enough to tattle on its former owner if discarded improperly.

At the counter, a miniature landscaping trellis framed the cash register, its funereal arch decorated with fake roses and pulsing Christmas lights, connected to the drop ceiling by dusty strands of cobweb. A pursey-lipped, bald little clerk appeared under this gloomy ornament, ringing up her purchase and handing over a receipt without saying a word. She walked to the corner of the front window and slipped the flimsy shades onto her face, the miniscule ridged border creating a tight seal and a disconcerting blackness. It was strange that something so thin and light on the bridge of her nose could bring about such total darkness. There was a pause and then a glowing pyramid arose from the darkness, flying up from the maw of nothingness to face her. As a teenager, her sister had suffered from optical migraines, baffling, half-hour episodes of blindness that left her couch-bound and morose. Tammi had described the lights that crossed her field of vision as neon zigzags and triangles, and Terri wondered now if this was close to what she'd seen.

The pyramid unfolded into a menu. She tagged this to her debit account and pinged a box that filled in her personal information. Then she was back in the drug store, seeing the shelves and floor and front window overlaid with a flurry of banners and commercial Easter eggs that would erupt into more boxes and banners and dancing animations if given a chance. In her upper-center field of vision, a hot-pink drop-box read ONE PERSON ON THIS BLOCK HAS JUST TAGGED YOU.

Back in the waiting car, she turned off and pocketed her PanOpts, trying to gauge how alert she was. The relief at not having to worry about her cop glasses was offset by the effort of trying to figure out what she had to worry about with the civilian glasses. Her face still came up as cop. No one could contact her directly, but they could still harass her with pop-up messages.

The pink drop-box faded into view again, alerting her that now three people in her immediate neighborhood had tagged her. What constituted a tag? She tapped the box, unscrolling it into a snazzy ad for a service she didn't understand. In the middle of a mass of candy-colored link buttons, bright red letters announced, SEE WHAT THEY'RE SAYING. She clicked this, reading,

I just sold this bitch a pair of throwaway shades three minutes ago. Maybe she went renegade? If this was Sweden, I could've just fired her.

Terri circled the car back to the pharmacy. The bald little clerk stood framed by the small arch, talking with a pair of citizens, all three heads snapping up in sync as she barreled down the aisle. He raised both hands, perhaps thinking he was under arrest.

"You got a fucking *problem*?" she growled.

"No problem."

"I've got a problem," one of the shoppers said. He was a young kid in a frizzy afro and turtleneck. "I've got a problem with cops who kill people who tell the truth."

"What?"

"Nuestro *Quin*tiglio?" a frumpy college-aged woman said in righteous outrage.

"What about him?"

"He was trying to get to the bottom of the Tournament of Roses story. Now he's dead."

"So?"

"So we all saw the footage," the afro kid said with steely self-confidence. "We all saw the footage of cops executing him on his own lawn. And we all saw you there, laughing at the whole thing."

"Easy," she said.

"Easy or what? You gonna kill and frame us, too, now?"

She turned and saw another small flock by the front door, drawn to the drama in real time. Who knew how many people were watching this scene unfold on the networks. The hot pink drop-box read, EIGHT PEOPLE ON THIS BLOCK HAVE JUST TAGGED YOU.

"Easy or you're going to be under arrest for threatening a police officer. Is that clear?"

"How about me?" the frumpy girl said. "You going to arrest me too?"

A chorus of "me too"s erupted from the doorway, a dozen or so citizens of wildly different ages and backgrounds gathering by the entrance to the store.

With affected deliberation, she strode in silence back out through the small, glaring crowd, wondering if anyone had the balls to get in her way, then reaching the car and whispering, "That's what I thought."

Ten blocks away, she pulled over and tried to figure out a destination. An idea came to her. Rujuta wasn't where Liney had said, but the odds were low that she'd left the city. Knowing her backstory, there wasn't much of anywhere else to go, especially for someone with no registered identity, and double especially for a young female with no registered identity. Rujuta's vulnerability would have made her hunker down somewhere.

There was something else besides the EyePhones. The niece might be eligible for a California Victim Compensation Program handout, especially if Farrukh had been supporting her. If Terri could just get the word out about possible compensation, that would go a long way toward finding the missing niece. Human beings would crawl out of any woodwork for a cash money payout.

Crawling out of the woodwork: the phrase seemed somehow apt for the events of the last week, and especially the last twenty-four hours. Ever since the reporter's house, any problem she could have had had crawled out of hiding. She yawned and rested her head against the car's headrest, wondering if there was some way Nuestro Quintiglio could have booby trapped his own death, maybe arranged for a series of baffling and borderline terrifying things to happen to whatever police officer found him murdered. In her fatigued funk, the thought almost made sense. After India and China had murdered each other, dead-hand programs had launched massive cyberattacks against India's biggest ally, crippling America in one afternoon; the world's biggest booby trap. If it was good enough for America, it was good enough for her, she thought with a drowsy distance, leaning against the glass of the window.

The car honked her awake ten minutes later, as she'd instructed it to. She woke surprised that her mind had cleared space for a plan of action. Terri attempted to open a map box, realizing she was in the Overlay, not PanOpt; different interface, different everything. She brought up a dashboard box and set a course for the LAUSD, the school-district building half a mile down the freeway from the Temple. In motion, she peered at the sharp red neon reflected in the back window of a passing car, watching, transfixed, the way its electric squiggles rolled off the glass, realizing she was looking at the car through a public layer, viewing the reflection of fake neon that floated over the city.

Ads spilled in on her peripheral vision. Billboards changed every time she blinked. Some walls turned into female body parts; huge, glossy lips, a bare shoulder, the top of a bikini bottom, giant eyes that followed her motion, a massive pair of shapely women's legs, grotesque, perhaps a half-mile tall, with panties stretched between the ankles. Working in PanOpts, it'd been easy to forget how much of the Overlay was dedicated to sex. There were private-pay layers that were nothing but raw copulation, nonstop, everything an orifice, the air filled with squawks and groans of delight, like bird tweets.

The opportunities were endless for truly anonymous sex, people who met up for brief sessions in secluded spots, both seeing each other as anonymous hardbodies, sometimes exotic, sometimes fulfilling a specific erotic requirement. She imagined these people reaching for a bare thigh and finding seemingly supple flesh having far more slack and elasticity than it should have, or reaching for a waist and finding their hand connecting an inch above the seen.

As she approached the LAUSD headquarters, she saw a clean Helvetica Student Of The Month announcement floating over the rooftop, barely distinguishable between the jumble of floating neon and block-high banners. Her brain fired off a random epiphany: your good deeds may be tallied, but they weren't banked. A person's Virtue Points were just another invisible limb, no more or less important than one's bank account, or credit score, or family history, or married life, or web of friendships. Although most people had a few more of these phantom limbs than she.

In the lobby of the district building, shiny metallic balloons for twos and fives and zeroes bobbled along the ceiling. Most of the back wall was taken up with a photo of one of the main cricket stadiums, somewhere inland. The space featured beautifully crafted wooden bleachers, and soaring, solar-powered sodium-vapor lamps. Two police chiefs ago, a concerted effort had been made to eradicate the public cricket courses, an exercise in futility and group tone-deafness. These days, refugee teams had snazzy uniforms and official sponsors, intramural sports being one of the very few legal outlets for refugee youth besides religious protests. The LAUSD had arguably the most solid connections with the refugee community of any governmental agency.

A half hour later, she sat in Sam Bustamante's office, watching as he scrolled through his own databases, seeming to peer through her and the wall behind her.

"Well . . . all you got is a name and a scar?"

"Yeah. It's a thin ID, I know."

She'd dealt with Bustamante years ago, when she and Zack had been on the hunt for a vicious psychopath SSK hitman. They'd wanted this guy so badly they'd picked up his younger brother, a mostly straight-arrow tenth-grader, on the hopes that the suspect would dispatch someone to bail the kid out, providing some sort of trail back into the ether. They nabbed the poor teen on an attempted murder charge after he'd posted a classmate's name as the last in an online game of "fuck, marry, kill." It hadn't been her proudest moment, but she'd been up for anything to get her man, and Bustamante had negotiated the takedown without asking for a quid pro quo, able to see the big picture in the whole ugly scenario. It was funny: she remembered Zack and her being ferocious about that case. But she was already in so much deeper on this one.

"Nah, sorry. We can't track deformities. That'd be, you know, a big red flag. You understand."

"Sure. Long shot. Let me ask you. A kid like this, no registered name . . . there's no way this girl, Rujuta, that she would have even made it into the school system to begin with, right?"

"She could be going under a different name. But yeah, she'd need at least an immunization card, and some sort of quasi-proof of residence. If she lives in a skyscraper, then she'd have to do this through RALA."

Terri shocked herself by yawning. "Oh man, sorry."

Bustamante looked at her sternly, and for a moment she thought he was genuinely angry for wasting his time. But then he pointed to a poster on the wall reading GET A GOOD NIGHT'S SLEEP BEFORE COMING TO SCHOOL and she realized she actually had wasted his time; she could've done all this legwork in her PanOpts in ten minutes. How to remedy that situation?

Just after dusk, she pulled into the teardrop-shaped parking area of the forensic science division and had the car park near the curb, as far from the brassy lot lights as possible. A cluster of stragglers had gathered at the other end of the lot, waving to each other as a formation of cars gracefully swooped in and popped their passenger doors. Two of the men slapped hands as they ducked into their vehicles and zipped off toward the Friday night excitement of the civilian world.

She'd tried calling Carla Morales five times with the disposables, and each time she hadn't gotten any farther than the webroom foyer for the science division. The logic of coming here in person was slippery, although she supposed Carla would have to emerge sometime, and when she did, she'd have to come up here. Or maybe not. Who knew how many entrances and exits this unit had.

From somewhere past her left side field of vision, Santa Claus lumbered across the parking lot with weary steps, finally lowering himself to squat on the curb twenty feet away, perfectly illuminated by the streetlight, his shoulders slumping as if he simply could go no further. She sighed. This ad campaign had been dogging her all day. Buying the disposables, she'd steeled herself for an onslaught of dating ads, all the subtle cues and lures of automated matchmakers that found her face an irresistible target. Instead, she'd been barraged with the annual post-holidays anti-depression campaign that had come to feel like as much of a Christmas tradition as discarded tree fires, so prevalent that it felt like she was hearing about it every January.

Although the campaign took many forms—graphics, walk-ons, signage that attached itself to every possible public surface—it adhered to a rigid script: Kris Kringle, having done his duty, had been consumed by clinical depression. Sometimes he appeared sprawled in an empty toy shop, sometimes slumped in front of a roaring fireplace, staring down into a mug with parted lips. She'd never been sure if this was an ad campaign targeted at overwhelmed first responders, or to the public at large, and the one time she'd remembered, years ago, to ask her sister if she'd ever seen any of the ads, she'd felt self-conscious and weird, as if she were trying to retell a bad dream.

Over Santa's head now, a floating band of red-and-green neon read THERE'S NO SANTA FOR SANTA. As she watched, the neon fluttered and then read HELP IS ONLY A PHONE CALL AWAY. She'd never once seen a contact number for this alleged help. Maybe she'd have to ask him for the number. Because the disposables tracked her eye motions, every time she glanced over at Sad Santa, or read, for the fortieth time today, his sad, two-stage message, he'd look back up at her with red-rimmed, beseeching eyes. She raised her hand to give him the finger, got spooked, and lowered it again.

She stepped out of the car, opening a call box in the chilly space before her, trying Carla Morales one last time. The floating cubicle showed her a one-eighth-size version of the phantom waiting room of the SI Division, or maybe just an empty version of a real room somewhere below the parking lot. She again punched in Morales' extension and was again rebuffed by a stern, androgynous voice telling her to leave a message.

"Hey, ah, it's Terri Pastuszka again. Just wondering if you'd have a moment to help me with a pressing technical issue. It's actually kind of urgent, so, yeah. You can call me on this number, not my department line."

Commercial blowback was, by far, the worst part about using disposable shades to place an actual phone call. As if to spite her solitude, the parking lot suddenly swelled with dazzling banners and rectangles, the world of commerce grasping onto each individual word of her message, desperate to connect her with a product or service. A neon border around the call box erupted into a dozen free-floating bubbles, each jostling for airspace as they offered her time management seminars, dry cleaners, service plans, mechanics. The phantom luminescence of these bulbous announcements lit up the asphalt below, itself erupting into a riot of zig-zaggy lines and cascading alphabets. Over the low hill and the dark outlines of neighboring houses, a distant, mile-high billboard read TECHIE STRESS? SKIP THE MESS! Far above that, the almond-shaped half moon sprouted eyes and lips and chubby cheeks, looking down on her with benevolent concern, and when the silvery words VALLEY STYLE BIKRAM 1ST MONT/$300 spilled out of its mouth, the giant Helvetica letters tumbled toward the earth's surface, edges glowing red as if actually smoldering as they entered the planet's atmosphere.

Terri yawned and pulled off the disposables, using this same hand to grasp both temples between outstretched thumb and middle finger. When she looked again, the lot was empty: no banners, no boxes, no onslaught of glowing alphabets. Sometimes this job required a "close sesame." How do regular people interact with the Overlay like this?

Turning to lock the car, she spotted a small rabbit in the weeds near where Santa had crouched, laughing when she realized this was an actual thing her eyes were actually seeing.

At the door to the bunker entrance, she found a buzzer. The same no-sex voice said, "Scientific Division."

"This is Detective Pastuszka from Central Division. I'm here to see Carla Morales. In NR."

"Do you have an appointment, Detective?" Appointment: like a reservation? The question confused her.

"Yes."

The voice said nothing, searching the bowels of the complex. She wondered how far down the building extended, trying and failing to remember something about a European police force that had recently relocated below ground, on the theory that this would make them less vulnerable to the bad guys. But which bad guys? Organized crime? A rebel army? Maybe it was a show she saw. Her mind was slipping. She'd need something soon; a pot of coffee at the least.

"Yep."

"Carla? This is Terri Pastuszka. Got a minute?"

"Uh, yeah, sure. Why didn't you just call me?"

"I did. On the . . . never mind. Just buzz me in."

Down in the office, she found Carla surrounded by the same pile of clutter she'd seen last time, maybe even wearing the same sweatshirt, swirling a mug of oily coffee with a stained wooden stirrer that obviously held some sentimental value.

"I need my shades set to zero location," Terri said. "Is that the right term?"

Carla removed the coffee stirrer and slipped it into her mouth.

"I have no idea. Whaddya wanna do?"

"I need my PanOpts configured for basic undercover field work."

"Are you *doing* 'basic undercover field work'?"

"Not exactly."

"Not exactly. Huh. You sure you know what 'zero location' means?"

"It means I can't be located."

"Right. Meaning you are literally on your own. The force can't see you. The Wall can't see you. You have no backup. Pass by anything in progress, and you're solo. The cavalry wouldn't be any closer than 911 by way of Layer one. And you're at a distinct disadvantage in public, since everyone can still see you're a cop, unless you go with a full-face dust mask."

"I won't be in public, so it won't be an issue."

"Zero location is used maybe twice a year by Internal Affairs. Otherwise, there's no reason for anyone to fool with it. I'm not trying to stick my nose in your business, and I can *make* a waiver, but . . ."

"I just need it."

Carla rubbed the back of her neck, muttering, "Christ, I'm tired." As if by transference, a wave of fatigue passed over Terri as well, hollowed her out, and she tried to lean against the door jamb as nonchalantly as possible.

"Sure. Okay. Gimme."

Terri reached for her empty breast pocket and actually felt a stab of panic until she realized she was holding the PanOpts in her left hand.

"How long does something like this take?"

"Maybe . . . ten minutes. I just have to do the I/O box. Take a seat," she said, motioning to the vinyl sofa and then disappearing into the back workroom. Even if this hadn't been occupied with stacks of mysterious packing boxes, she couldn't imagine sitting down and staying awake, so thorough was this new wave of fatigue.

On the desk Carla had been working on, almost lost amongst piles of rubber-handled tools that had no obvious meaning outside this room, a photo frame of dull brass sat on its side. She picked this up, seeing it was a picture of Carla on a deck or back patio, flanked by two teenagers, boy and girl, obviously hers. In the photo, Carla wasn't exactly smiling. But something about her eyes and pinched grimace made her look entirely different, like someone captured during a fleeting brush with serenity.

Terri smacked her lips and placed the picture back on its side. Up until this moment, she'd never actually thought of Carla as another fully-formed human being with thoughts and emotions and a life outside of this low-ceilinged bunker.

Terri had the car drive her to a shabby strip mall. She ate dinner in the back corner of a Hawaiian barbecue joint with muted overhead lighting that gave the place another dirty aquarium vibe. Afterward, she had the car drive her around the Eastside for a half hour, finally finding a seemingly identical strip mall to land in, someplace to make a few calls before she crashed for the night. The car circled around a bankrupt and boarded big box store, bringing her back to park alongside dumpsters that appeared to have been padlocked and forgotten years ago. A bank of security lights lit a long corridor of weeds, hearty plant life rising triumphant through the weathered asphalt. It was perfect for her scenario: too thin for anyone to effectively hide in, too thick for a lone cop car to attract any sort of attention.

The obvious thing would be to send drones to peek in on her apartment. Too obvious, she decided. She'd already established that her place was being watched, that strangers had been traipsing in and out at will. Drones would be the most predictable move she could make. She pictured the view through her window, a rogues' gallery of creeps and perps partying it up in her living room.

She dialed Zack, who answered on the first ring. In zero location, he came up audio only.

"Jesus, I thought you were going to call me!"

"I am calling you."

"This isn't a joke. I was worried. Where are you?"

"On the Eastside. I'm fine. What'd you dig up on your end?"

"Something's happening. I don't know what. I bought some kids' drones at 7-Eleven, cheap crap no one would think twice about if they got spotted. Set one for Reynoso, one for Blanco, two more for your place . . ."

His pause went on too long. "My place," she said.

"Shit, I'm sorry to have to be the guy who tells you this, but yeah. It's trashed. I got a good look through the living room window, and, from what I could see, it didn't look tossed. It looked like someone slipped an orangutan in there. Like, punitively trashed, not seeking-something trashed. Someone's trying to send you a message."

She was quiet for a moment, realizing the news didn't affect her as badly as she'd assumed it would. The few things she actually cared about were back in Jersey. All she felt was pissed.

"What about Blanco?"

"Nothing yet. The best I can tell, she's been in her office all day. But there's something else. Remember that piece of shit lawyer from the shoe store stabber thing?"

"Yeah. 'Red' something."

"Red Oquendo."

"He was disbarred not long after, right? Moved up north?"

"Well, he's back now, and reinstated, too. A little after noon, he walked into the Temple. So I looked him up. And guess who's his only legal client now? That 'I'm Sane' kid."

"Mansaray? That makes no sense. The kid is barely felony."

"And then, when I sped the footage up, I see Red exit two hours later, practically arm-in-arm with the Assistant Chief."

She tightened her mouth and ran a hand slowly over the top of her hair. It was a bad combo; genuinely scared and deeply tired.

"So where exactly are you, anyway?"

"I told you. The Eastside."

"And why are you audio only?"

"I got my shades zeroed out."

"Oh shit. Hey, that's not the . . ."

"Look, let's skip the warning talk. I know what I'm doing. Whatever it is that's happening, it's obvious that someone inside the department is watching. So I need to be able to move around anonymously." She thought of Reynoso: go on the low. That prick.

"You're not staying in a hotel or anything, right?"

"No, I'm parked."

"Listen, I don't mean to be the voice of doom, but . . . parked where? Somewhere you can be seen?"

"Jesus, Zack. I'm behind a boarded-up Romance Outlet near the reservoir. There's no one here."

"You in a gumball? You got a people alarm set up?"

"Yes. Stop. I have the proximity alarm on. I'm totally safe."

"Okay. Alright. Good. Call me tomorrow. Stay vigilant."

"Yeah," she yawned. "Vigilant."

"Good," he said with a surprising tenderness. "Good. Sleep well, Terri." He hung up, the whisper of ambient noise coming from his end going mute with a strange finality.

Terri pulled her PanOpts up onto her forehead, halfway popping out the earpieces, absorbed in silence. The car had parked itself directly facing the backside of the abandoned strip mall. Even without headlights, she could make out the dim outline of a loading dock, a forsaken, sunken square that reminded her of a stage in an elementary school assembly room. All it needed was the theater lighting back on the equally desolate Mulholland Drive.

The lane leading to the loading dock was scattered with an assortment of mini-liquor bottles and discarded hobo detritus and flattened home appliance boxes that had themselves served as homes. The bend that once allowed trucks to pull around the mall and back into the dock had been coated with hard tarmac. Almost nothing grew in this channel. But the rest of the wide lane had been set with porous concrete, capable of absorbing rainwater, and in its abandonment, plant life had snuck up through the pores. Each hearty, waist-high weed stood immobile and sculptural in the still-air silence.

Even though she'd picked the general location—"behind that mall"—it still felt as if the car had brought her here for the sole purpose of contemplation, forcing her to mull her actions, to weigh self-correction. It dawned on her that this was the first moment she'd been able to sit and mourn Mutty. If that was indeed appropriate. She'd never known him that well. In many ways, Mutty Posada had functioned as a caricature for everyone in her social circle, the amiable stoner in a crowd of angry drunks. Had Mutty's highness gotten him killed?

A sudden heaviness seized her throat, making her audibly swallow. Of course not: she'd gotten Mutty killed. Her single-mindedness, her stubborn bullshit tunnel vision, had flushed a good person out of this world. Mutty was gone because of her. She'd erased him, would never see him again. This fact settled down on her, oppressed her, squeezing out a feeble whimper as she bent over and prepared herself to sob.

An alarm shrieked. It was a high-pitched sizzle, not as deafening as the falling objects alert, but startling enough that she'd yanked her shades down and replaced both earpieces before consciously registering that she was doing so. A red banner read PROXIMITY WARNING with multiple arrows pointing off into the weeds. She squinted and saw two figures, maybe three, crouch-walking up on her, the closest producing a long, L-shaped object as she thought, *Don't go into shock just move*. Seeing this object come up in the stranger's hand, she heard herself say in a soft, agreeable voice, "Wait."

The crack of the gunshot knocked her off the seat, hitting the car floor as she reached up and pulled the control box down, wondering, strangely, if the floating box itself could shield her from bullets, hearing the second deafening crack overhead, the ricochet echoing off the walls of the loading dock. The car roared to life as a third figure pulled up to her starboard side, aiming down just as she roared out, the forward motion knocking her back onto her head. A third and fourth gunshot sounded, something tinking off the metal frame of the vehicle, and Terri crouched low, holding her skull, trying to make herself as absolutely small as possible, still whispering, "Wait, wait, wait . . ."

She arranged for a car swap at LAX. It was the most secure and heavily populated public spot she could think of at this time of night. Because she didn't have a dust mask with her,

Terri zipped up her arlando jacket and pulled the neck up to her nose. It looked out of the ordinary and certainly wasn't comfortable, but made her a hard trace while she waited for the replacement car at the terminal curb.

Rich people flowed past her, thin with wealth, jetting to or from whatever professions allowed them to whiz across the globe. No one gave her a second glance. Nearby, a child in an expensive miniature pea coat moved his little arm in a see-saw motion, finally saying to someone unseen, "I'm not fist bumping you, I am slowly punching you out."

Terri turned to take in the concourse on the other side of the glass, her own hot breath steaming up the jacket neck. She'd heard that one could get a passport remotely in less than a half hour. She had enough in her bank account to just leave. It was a jarringly real thought. All she had to do was do it.

A sleeper car crept to the curb. It was a long pod with one glorious reclining bed, plush, padded walls, recessed reading lights, and a retractable moon roof. Pulling out, she glanced back at the bright apparition of the terminals, the county still shoveling cash into its airport—even now that it was only a port of call for the world's wealthiest—still determined to prove that the city was functional long after it had resumed functionality. She directed the sleeper to drive at full speed in a huge clockwise freeway loop, 405 to 605 to 210, a holding pattern for its rootless occupant.

A light drizzle fell as the car picked up speed. Terri felt blank, and oddly awake. As a kid, her dad used to take her out on long, aimless drives. Would this even be possible now? Probably not: unless you were a cop, all car services would almost definitely require a destination. Tonight's loop was a perk of the job, one of the few left for her. Perhaps the Overholsers, as owners of cars, could still order any of the vehicles in their fleet to drive them around without a target.

She passed automatons designed to sweep up debris on the freeway, and larger automated vehicles, huge, lugging giant slabs of drywall and lumber. A truck synced with her car, and she caught a flash of a dirty plush teddy bear lashed to its bumper. A city bus passed in a blur, its illuminated interior vacant. Another car synced, a compact, its curtained mystique making her nervous.

Rain surged. Traffic flowed as smoothly and orderly as a factory assembly belt. She thought of the network of cars, watching, judging their operatives, communicating with every other car on the road, exchanging load and speed info, alerting each other who was in danger of hydroplaning, how to take the turns, how much to adjust gearboxes for an incline or decline and when to hold the gear through a bend, which car posed any variety of subtle but statistically real dangers to its fellow vehicles, a million different brains holding a vast, unheard, ceaseless conversation. The rain let up to a light sizzle, the windshield wipers groaned once and then shut themselves off.

She leaned back, trying to will herself asleep. Terri hated lying awake in bed, alone with her thoughts. There'd been so many nights of staring up at the ceiling, replaying loops of disaster footage, people screaming and running from the hideous flashes lighting up the night sky. No matter how hard she'd tried to contemplate pleasant things, she always came back to that stark choice, global horror or local horror.

When she'd been married, it seemed like she was always contemplating their deaths, exhaustively churning over scenarios. There'd be a bad biopsy, or a blood test gone wrong, or a lump detected in the shower. This would be followed by weeks or months of suspense, then the final goodbye in a hospital room somewhere, a scene that resisted, in its bottomless misery, actual contemplation, registering as an abstraction no matter how hard she'd tried to conjure its actuality. Or there'd be a phone call in the middle of the night. Or there'd be a call during the day. Or a fellow cop would approach, hat in hand. Then she'd picture one of them alone in their house as a very old widow, tottering about like Gabriella's senile grandfather in Houston, never sure if his late wife was gone forever or just in the next room. In all these scenarios, Terri had pictured both of them as the survivor, each circumstance having a different emotional edge. But she'd never pondered desertion. It'd never crossed her mind.

Of course, she was avoiding thinking about Zack. In zero location, no one else could have known where she was. She'd only told him. Terri probed around his betrayal, finding it something else that registered only as an abstraction. He'd been her partner for six years, the guy who complained about his kid's attitudes and friends and tuitions, who'd saved her ass twice from three hundred-pound berserkers, who'd had to get drunk, as a rookie, to put his dog to sleep. How could this man not be this man? The enormity of it made it impossible to conceive, although she knew when it clicked—when her brain finally did admit his treachery—the grief would be cataclysmic.

At some point, she woke with a jolt from a lack of motion. For a moment she wondered if it was a dream, her mind clearing as soon as she heard a faint fumbling around the side of the car, feeling for her gun in the curtained darkness. Terri parted one drape with the muzzle, doing something she had seen in many movies, peeking out and realizing that the car had driven itself to a fuel island. She watched the reedy nozzle of a power cord reach out tenuously toward the vehicle, finding its tiny port and connecting with a barely audible snap.

When the car pulled out again five minutes later, her heart was still thudding from the action of drawing her gun. She was sure she wouldn't be able to fall back asleep. But then she was climbing down a steep embankment, the loose dirt clouding around her ankles because she was underwater, and she found herself in a cave the size of a cathedral, surrounded by seahorses, and when she touched the walls, she realized they were made of leathery brown fungi which broke off in her hands, and the bottom of the cave was carpeted with thousands of tiny pigtails that had drifted down to the ocean floor.

To be sure she caught Carla as she entered the complex, Terri camped out in the scrubby forensic parking lot at dawn, unsure if the front entrance was even the right one to watch. She'd been left so acutely paranoid from the night before that she'd used the civilian shades to subscribe to three different pay-service face alerts in the neighborhood. As the first long shadows crept across the asphalt, she watched a homeless woman, white, a non-refugee, totter from one end of the lot to the other. There had been a point in her life when she'd felt strangely envious of people with nothing left to lose. She realized now she had become such a person, set apart from this nameless street urchin only by the shelter of a car.

A rush of vehicles entered the lot all at once, a synchronized procession of cars slowing and disgorging. She heard the chime of a Face Alert from her disposables on the seat even as she saw Carla disembark and walk toward the entrance kiosk, squinting into the oblique early morning sun. She was again struck by the woman's rugged unhandsomeness, her face chapped, like she'd just flown in from the Arctic. Terri intercepted her at the door,

Carla seeming to accept her presence with inscrutable silence, as if they'd already had a prearranged meeting.

Downstairs, the cluttered office smelled of fried meat and ketchup. Terri laid out her case again, giving the same presentation she'd delivered to Zack, but with the slight compression of practice. She included Stacy, Nuestro, the bag, the shirt, adding the one new coda of Zack's own betrayal. Halfway through, she wondered why she was taking in Carla as a confidant, then realizing that she needed someone inside the force, not just for her own sanity but from the sheer truth that she simply could not go it alone. If others inside the department were gunning for her—if the entire city was gunning for her in one way or another—she would have to have someone helping on the backend. She'd have to trust that she could trust.

During the entire monologue, Carla had skinned a tangerine in one peel, eating the fruit in two bites and then flopping the orange rind back and forth like a tiny animal hide, seeming more interested in the scrap of trash than the story. When the whole ridiculous tale was finished, she looked up from the peel and said, "What is it you want me to do?"

The question struck Terri as borderline autistic, a swell of self-pity welling up and washing over her before she got that it was a face-value sentence. What had she wanted from Carla?

"I guess . . . I need to know how worried I should be."

"Do you mean from physical harm? I'd say very, based on what you just told me."

"Okay. But, more precisely, I'm wondering . . . how reliable are my PanOpts? How worried do I need to be from the technical side?"

"I don't follow."

"Well, this maybe sounds crazy, but I don't know if I can trust my PanOpts at this point."

"If you're in zero location, you should be safe from detection. Zack pretty much confirmed that last night, just before you were attacked."

"What about the thing at my apartment? With the lack of surveillance protection?"

"Yeah." Carla had carefully refolded the tangerine skin back into a mauled sphere. "That's a puzzler. It's not a slam dunk that this involved collusion on the Wall side, and if it did, it could easily have been just one rogue operator."

"Is there a way that someone could have gotten into my apartment without technical support from up on high?"

"Well, anything's possible, sure. I can think of some scenarios with trace blockers that would allow someone to pull this off. But that's besides the point. There's no logical motive here."

"Okay."

"You've got a cascade of situations that have no rational motive."

"Yeah . . ."

Carla flattened the tangerine skin on the table's free space, squashing it with one thumb. "So what you need to do is figure out what it is that's happening. What about Farrukh's EyePhones? The original ones?"

"I'd assumed the niece, Rujuta, would still have them."

"Unless something's happened to her, that seems like a safe bet. She'd guard those things with her life, even if they didn't have all kinds of memories of her uncle on them."

"But she's gone. I hit a brick wall yesterday. If she's still in the county, she's faceless. I can only hunt her as far as she's on the grid. If she was never on the grid, there's no way for me to find her."

"That's not really true, though, is it?"

"How so?"

"Switch over to human intelligence. The odds are in your favor that she's still in the city. All you have to do is reach out and find her."

"Easier than it sounds."

"It's been done."

They were silent for a moment and then something in Terri's stomach audibly contracted. Carla tossed the tangerine peel into the trash can overhand.

"You do that. I'll work the Nuestro end. You should be running both sides of this story."

"Zack was trying to steer me off the front end . . ."

"So let me handle that part for now."

Terri nodded. Carla suddenly raised her eyebrows and whistled, a high-pitched note that hurt Terri's ears. "This is some shit. We need to act quick."

Terri cruised downtown, trying to think, her car crawling, drawing attention to itself even in the slow lane. Five blocks in, her car got edged into the next lane out by an idling bus, its sides shivering and jiggling like cellulite. She passed a Salvadoran restaurant drenched in purple neon, the surging, dinging music coming through its open door sounding like the sped-up clang of a train crossing signal. On every block, men with nowhere to go and nothing to do stood on street corners or squatted in doorways, watching traffic, watching people with jobs come and go, solemnly observing the entire world slide by. They were vessels of inherited emptiness.

The contrast south of Ninth Street was jarring, not just because of streetwalkers and candy girls, but also from the sheer volumes of trash. The city's anti-littering program had been a huge success in other parts of the city. Kids were encouraged to pick up debris in a citywide game where everyone got points for each piece of litter, each point tallied by the city's grid of eyes, redeemable for treats at participating stores, JoyRide coupons, shirts, probably a whole small universe of prefab swag that would become next month's litter. But the program worked, largely because people like playing games, and liked working games into their lives.

In downtown, none of the game's demographic groups—children, pensioners, the chronically unemployed—had any way to play the game. They could pick up as much trash as they wanted, accrue as many points as their hearts desired, but at the end of the day they had no way to redeem anything. More importantly, they had no reason to trust that redemption didn't mean any one of any number of mythical traps the city, state, or federal government was always allegedly laying out for them. She called Carla on the disposables, not trusting her own eyewear or judgment.

"I've just been circling. Should I continue this? I was thinking about street connects, and I remembered there'd been an article in one of the street papers about undocumented refugee girls. Maybe if I could locate the author, see if I could work this from that direction . . ."

"That sounds like a lead." Terri squinched her eyes in frustration, her only confidant an emotional automaton. Hanging up, she figured out who Carla reminded her of: the veterinarian. The afternoon her dog, Congo, had died, Terri had found him on his side. She'd called the vet, an eccentric, frizzy-haired German lady who refused to address the humans in her office, speaking only in a strange falsetto directly to the animals. But when Terry had the vet look over Congo remotely, the woman had done so with an efficient thoroughness, then looked straight at Terri and said, "I'm so sorry." There was something similar in Carla's expression, a familiar remoteness.

In reality, her street connects were rusty. She stopped at a downtown newsstand, buying every English-language paper for less than the cost of a cup of coffee. There were only five now: *Voice of The Towers*, *Figueroa Free Press*, *The Downtown Express*, *The Downtown Sun*, and the stripped-down revamp of *The Times Of India* that had failed and rebooted a half-dozen times. In the car, she spread these out on the seats, each printed on the coarsest pulp paper, with bright graphics whose ink stained the reader's hands.

In refugee newspapers, an almost antiquated politeness pervaded. The ones that thrived often sold their entire front page, and even the name of the paper for a day. Despite the almost comical reliance on advertising, each paper served several vital community functions, including classified ads and sports news. One of the leading refugee newspapers had hit upon a successful innovation: daily themes, cycled throughout the week. Tuesdays were cricket, Thursdays were soccer, Fridays were all about obituaries. Other, smaller dailies had followed suit.

Not that she'd read any without a solid investigative reason. Their national and international stories were pulled from wire sources, if not badly rewritten press releases.

There were no stories about gang life, and almost never any mentions of the war, the two plagues of refugee life omitted as cleanly as any act of censorship on the Overlay. What few stories did concern refugees were often written by citizen stringers, hard luck men like Nuestro Quintiglio. English-language Indian newspapers thrived among a population with no means of networked news and a waning literacy.

Terri didn't know why she felt so superior. She'd given away her own meager collection of beach paperbacks after the divorce. And if she counted the two daunting shelves of palm tree books at the Zendejas house, Zack owned several dozen times the volumes she'd probably read in her lifetime.

The layout from the *FFP* looked about right. She remembered that some higher up had bought multiple copies and taped the article up in every workstation downtown. She'd tapped a finger on one paragraph as she'd read it, her finger coming away with a cheap bluish ink, as it did now. She called the listed number, surprised that this wasn't audio only, accepting the check box, and finding herself in a simulation of their cluttered office. An elderly Indian man with a fantastic waxed mustache answered.

"I'm a homicide detective with the LAPD,"—she listed her badge number—"Your paper ran an article on unregistered female refugees. A few years back. I need to contact the writer."

"We have no archives," the man explained in a regal, thickly accented voice. "Except what you see . . ." He motioned toward a bank of brown metal filing cabinets at the back of the room. "If you can wait, I'll gladly search."

"That would be wonderful, thanks."

The call went on hold, Terri wondering what possible reason a newspaper might have for not having macros, trackers, at least an internal, instantly searchable system, how even a refugee business could operate like this, one foot in the Middle Ages.

She looked back down to the papers, wondering if their simplicity in any way reflected the refugee experience. The compromises and omissions of immigrant papers were transparent; every online news source involved daunting layers of opaque complexity, of meaningless razzle-dazzle to hold public opinion. "Participation" had become such a byword of modern media that she'd almost forgotten what it had been like to just *receive*. Watching the news now meant negotiating endless offers to share and connect with other viewers. Personalization was crucial to individual identity, people basing their public persona, in part, around their news choices, the way they themselves reacted to and remixed the stories of the day. Some news outlets went so far as to allow their audience to vote entire subjects out of coverage.

Terri's generation wanted curated news. The postwar generation wanted enthralling news. As best she could tell, friendships dictated the information people received from the outside, objective world. Young people only trusted stories recommended to them from their friends. It took work for Terri to get updates on the situation in Turkey, a place she would surely never visit herself. It made her feel like she was the one seeking out news from the fantasy world.

The man returned. "I'll have to call you back."

Inertia was the enemy. She'd need to set out on foot, to find something to jog her mind, to spur her on. Terri was back to where she'd started on the force, doing footwork, labor both honest and futile. Back on the pavement, she faced a faded mural of long-dead Mexican soccer stars, the paint having peeled from the eyes, hanging down in hard-to-look-at flaps, too pathetic to vandalize. Above this, an ancient, sun-worn sign read VIDEO TAPING IN PROGRESS.

She walked behind one young guy eating a burnt elote, corn glistening with chutney and chili powder, nodding his head to an unheard beat, probably soundtracking his entire life. She'd once heard of a sicko who just walked around all day listening to applause. As much as she liked to poke fun at personalized scoring, Terri always acknowledged that it had an important function in certain moments. She thought of the Zeppelin song in Leimert Park. The kid suddenly looked up, seeing something private, and she flashed back on the witness kid with his death butterfly.

Walking, each block formed a mini-district. On Broadway to Seventh, it was competing street dentists, each flaunting public health laws; kiosks for eyebrow threading and foot massage; a barber who'd set up shop on the sidewalk, complete with chair, mirror, and nearby standpipe done up in red and blue crepe paper. One block up, she passed a red-and-green nopalito booth; three different mango-on-a-stick huts; tiny, movable chai houses establishing themselves in all sorts of improbable nooks and just as easily evaporating.

Terri had never noticed how thoroughly the sidewalks had been dotted with black gum spots. It was history as stain. She thought of the yard out behind her grandmother's house in Jersey, pavement under a sprawling oak tree that wept sap every summer, stepping on the sticky black dots in her bare-foot, running around collecting leaves and debris with her sticky soles. In hindsight, it was kind of gross. Fifteen feet away now, a barefoot child stood with eyes wide, receiving some sort of admonition in rapid-fire Hinglish. From this angle, she could see the corner of a storefront church, its vinyl banner advertising a blessing of the animals.

After the war, her quietly devout mother had stopped going to church entirely. Terri had thought it was something her mom had needed to process on her own, but then one day, maybe a few months later, she'd passed the boarded-up church. There'd been more church closings in the months to come, a mass boycott of a God who could allow such carnage. Later, in hindsight, Terri had been deeply grateful for the mass loss of faith. Not because she herself had any strong feelings in any direction—she'd retained her vaguely Episcopalian self-identification in the face of Gabby's stubborn atheism—but because it almost definitely forestalled the kind of mass revivals that'd swept the Deep South and Russia. Immediately after the war, scapegoating had almost entirely followed political lines, meaning ethnic lines. But as ugly as that had gotten, it had at least followed a rational playbook. Not so elsewhere in the world.

The war had loosed so many self-supporting, self-replicating errors of thought. There was a persistent rumor that, somewhere deep in the bowels of Nano Alley, someone was putting the final touches on a radiation eraser, and that eventually, soon, Indians could return to their homeland and rebuild. She'd heard Indian political analysts praise the war as an instant reset on all the stifling dysfunctional inefficiencies of the Indian state. It was as if the war had been merely a natural disaster.

The world seemed destined, doomed, to repeat India and China's mistake. Turkish rebels were still threatening to nuke Istanbul, to kill themselves if they couldn't have their country. Years ago, there'd been a tremendous push to abolish the world's remaining atomic arsenals. But those days were long gone, everyone trying to scramble by, the next generation too submerged in their own endless artificial worlds.

On the sidewalk, someone had written RECOGNIZE in strong chalk letters. For economic reasons, there was incredible pressure for the United States government to recognize the government in exile of India. Hundreds of billions of dollars in Indian money sat in offshore accounts held by nationals who had seen the writing on the wall. The key to unlocking that money, to spurring investment in Los Angeles and the revitalization so desperately needed after the Slide began, was in this simple act of recognition. Which would, of course, necessitate recognizing China in exile and, subsequently, the trillions of dollars in Chinese debt that had evaporated nearly overnight.

The entire refugee experience seemed summed in that one word—RECOGNIZE—all the self-reliance pitted against all the indolent apathy, no one making the first move, everyone waiting for recognition. When she intersected with the refugee world, it took a conscious switch for her to remember that it wasn't a culture without networks, but rather one with its own networks: rumor, vigilance, memory; everything but oral history, the next generation having come up as removed from their parents as if they were cavemen or space lizards.

She didn't totally blame these kids. They were pressed on all sides. Even two decades into the Slide, there were always fresh tales of parents who refused to obey local child labor laws, who had themselves toiled in mines or sweatshops and expected no less from their offspring. She'd once arrested a mother who'd migrated from an area in Meghalaya that had been strip mined to moonscape even before the war. The woman had worked her two youngest sons to death and sold all her hair for money; she seemed entirely unfazed by the universe.

Terri had never been sure how much of this self-reliance was imported and how much was thrust upon the refugees by circumstances. Or genetics, as Zack once asked, straight faced, of a skeletal little man attempting to carry a broken motor scooter on his shoulders. The thought of Zack pained her, made her alert.

The newspaper man called her back and she paused on the sidewalk outside Clifton's Cafeteria.

"You are very patient," he said, curling his *W*, sounding winded from digging through folders. "I did find the article you mentioned. The author's name was Nuestro Quintiglio. I'm going to need to spell that for you. That's Q-U-I-N . . ."

Someone had reheated taquitos in the corner kitchenette of the Fourth Street workstation, a nasty smell, sharp and vaguely chemical. She found a chair in the farthest corner of the L-shaped room, not so much sitting as simply allowing her body to fall into it. Something about prolonged street work always exhausted her in a way that no amount of jogging could equal. Running: the thought seemed like an ancient memory, something she'd done when she'd been very young.

This corner of the room held two rows of tan cloth seats. Across from her and one row away, Travis Contreras sat brooding. Travis was a housing cop whose own life had soured through divorce. She'd heard he'd taken to crashing random parties whenever he had the opportunity, wandering the rooms of strange houses, knowing he'd be identified as police and thus immune from confrontation. She'd also heard he'd made a point of finding at least one book in each house and ripping out the last page, some random but highly focused act of aggression at the world. She'd seen him just last week, at Uganda, but he'd looked completely miserable and not open to any acknowledgement of their mutual existence, let alone their mutual predicament.

She opened up her notes, fanning them out into the air and aligning them with the plane of her lap. Even as she made the gesture, she knew it was nothing more than a ritual, like taking off and tossing her shoes at home. She closed her eyes, holding her head in her hands. She thought of all those people living in the feudal corners of civilization, unable to view their own lives as anything but static, knowing nothing of the past, having no framework for conceptualizing the future. And yet here she was, knowing no more about the location of one anonymous stranger than a cop would have a thousand years ago. Her phone rang. It was Blanco. On instinct, she clicked to reply before she could think through what she was doing.

"I thought you were going to call me yesterday," Chief Blanco said with a flat tranquility Terri found impossible to read in audio only.

"Yeah, that," she said, feeling utterly buffaloed, lost, unable to think up any plausible reply.

"And now I see you've intimidated a prisoner in an unrelated case."

"What?"

"You questioned Torg Skarpsvärd yesterday morning."

"Yeah, but there wasn't any . . ."

"You didn't think to obtain my go-ahead?"

"Go-ahead? This was done in the course of my mainline investigation. And who said anything about 'intimidation'?"

"Skarpsvärd is filing a dismissal because he said his council wasn't present during questioning."

Terri weighed hanging up, aware that the entire premise of the phone call—she should have answered in the first place—was flawed. "He . . . well, I guess if we're being technically accurate . . ."

"If we're being accurate, a lethal psychopath is probably going back out on the streets because you couldn't be bothered to follow the simplest of protocols."

She considered replying that there would be more safe people inside the prison system, thought better of it, and instead said, "Can I call you back later this afternoon? I'm actually following up on several vital leads as we speak."

"Actually, you're no longer following up on anything. I'm taking you . . ."

"Oop, wait, hold on, I have to call you back!" She raised a hand into the call box and actually hung up before she gave herself time to reconsider.

She lowered her hand, seeing it flutter for the first time since this entire mess had ensnared her. The tremor of adrenaline hadn't kicked in during the whole time she'd been betrayed, or inside the skyscraper, or even when she'd been shot at. It took this direct threat to her livelihood for it to activate. She sat motionless, paralyzed, watching another incoming call cycle through three more attempts, each going to her Dupe. She felt fluttery, hollowed-out, her mind doing that awful stammer-loop of doubt and self-assurance.

"Hey."

Travis Contreras had said this, but he was looking away from her, to a trio of uniformed male cops who stood off to her left.

"Anybody seen Mutty?"

"Naw, I haven't seen 'im," one of the officers, the largest, said with exaggerated loudness.

"Yeah . . . I wonder where he could've gotten to?"

All four turned to face her.

"How's about you, Detective? Any insights into where Mutty could've gotten to?"

She stared.

"It'd be a goddamn shame if anything were to happen to that guy because some dumb ass had to make some sort of a political point with her case."

"Whaddya say, Detective?" The largest officer stepped toward her. "Pretty fucked up, huh? For a cop to actually be that careless?"

Someone yelled something else as she fled out to the parking lot, the phone ringing and ringing and ringing.

She had the car drive her in an aimless circle, changed her mind three blocks later and decided to see Carla, thinking of those *Thin Man* movies, cops having to cross physical space to confer. The scene at the workstation had been raw, stingingly so, but not really worse than her worse average weekly street scene. Terri found she'd arrived at a spot where her choices were clear, and she craved structure, lack of ambiguity, freedom from limbo. All she could do was to stay on the case and crack it, to use whatever leverage she had to clear her own name, to make everyone see the big picture, or at least the few puzzle pieces she'd been made privy to. It was simple. She'd probably be dead if she couldn't do that, the thought coming to her flat, an intellectual assessment made without sensation. And yet when she pulled into the forensic science division, a fear gripped her that Carla had seen her coming. Carla would be down below, waiting to haul off and stab her with one of a dozen sharp esoteric instruments lying around her office.

Instead she found Carla animated, clearly waiting for her arrival.

"I thought about what Zendejas told you. About the 'chain of shit extending back into the mists of time.'"

She nodded, realizing Carla had tapped into Terri's shades and watched the conversation from Friday morning.

"So I went back to see if I could find whoever it was this Froggy guy killed with the same gun. I thought about the shades trace you tried. Did you know you can do the same thing for weapons?"

"I asked Pearly about that. Pearly's Dupe. He said it couldn't be done."

"Yeah, well. If you know how to tell the Basement what to do, you can pretty much do anything. I've done all kinds of custom traces. I went back to the shooting, on the bridge, stitched together three scenes as your guy walked, like this," she said, holding an imaginary gun in her left hand, just behind her hip.

"My thought was that I could get some distinguishing marks on the weapon, try a trace, see if anything came up in the backlog."

"If the Basement can do that, why isn't that done?"

"It's rare that it works. Manufactured guns have to have some seriously identifying scratches to track on physical characteristics alone. Not that it matters, because when I pulled up the gun, there was the serial number, right on the chassis. It never got filed off."

"No." Terri licked her lips in recall. "We would've seen that. In the Farrukh shooting."

"Stacy Santos had two fingers covering the serial when she shot. Used her ring finger for the trigger. She'd probably never fired a gun before."

"Then what about when Froggy himself got shot?"

Carla shrugged. "Tony Collazo probably didn't know enough to stitch together the serial number from multiple vantage points. Overseer oversight. Or who-gives-a-shittedness oversight. Anyway, you'll never guess who the gun is registered to."

"Christ. *This* case? The Pope?" Terri said, trying to come off conversational but already feeling that deep trench of fear open up again.

"One Dio Sarin. He bought it himself, in Riverside, three weeks ago."

"*How?*"

"Walked into a gun shop and paid cash. The kid might've been low-level SSK, but he put in his paperwork for a green card. Took the time to get a driver's license and everything."

"Huh. So . . . not a chain. Just four links."

"Actually five and counting. I found the shooter on Nuestro Quintiglio."

"You did this all since I left this morning?"

"It wasn't that hard, once I had that serial. You didn't catch her in the Basement because all those raised foundations around his house made a nice getaway channel. But she spent some time walking around with the gun sticking out of the back of her pants. All I had to do was narrow the search. First I found a Browning HP grip sticking up out of the back of her jeans. Two blocks later, she was walking with it out in the open, striding up Crenshaw Boulevard with the thing swinging from one hand. She dropped it in a tight alley with no good coverage, presumably for the next person to come get it." Carla's neutral expression didn't give away any hint of pride in the morning's accomplishments.

"So this shooter . . ." Terri said, steadying herself on a wall, "What's her name?"

"Lucy Cardenas."

"Walking around with a gun in the open like that . . . is this Lucy Cardenas a crazy?"

"Kind of. She's an AMAST follower. Remember them?"

"Ouhhhgggh . . . 'Azusa Ministry of something or other.' The soap guy one?"

Carla nodded and cracked a knuckle. "That's them."

She'd seen their work for years, colorful parodies of the various melanoma clinic ads, imploring citizens to Fight Sin Cancer. For a long time, she'd thought they were a mainstream church with a decent sense of humor. But then she'd seen their logo, a ghostly galleon with three bare, bloody crucifixes for masts. Sometime in the last decade, they'd gone from being a quaint, one-note joke to a franchise, with distinctive, bright blue-and-white branches all over southern California. Then Zack had showed her footage of the group's founder, John Crosley, a handsome young preacher who cried tears of soap bubbles. She got a little nauseous whenever she thought of his followers, laughing with childlike zeal as they washed their hands in the sudsy lather leaking out of his face.

"And you have an address? Am I rounding her up?"

"There's no urgency. She's down in front of City Hall. Probably seen a hundred different protests at this point. I ran her backward in the Basement. A guy in a gorilla costume shot her last Monday. She's been dead for the last five days."

For some reason, the full significance of the gorilla-man attack, the imagery of it, didn't click until she was in the car. Then she doubled over laughing. It was perfect: there probably wasn't a single protest outside city hall that didn't involve at least one joker in a pilgrim or superhero or Biblical costume. A rampaging primate was the next logical step. He'd come up from the toilet tent half a block away, done the deed, and slipped back to execute a perfect costume change. Nobody would've given a giant ape a second glance.

Just the thought of all that forensic canvassing—recreating exactly which bottom feeders had come and gone from that tent five days ago, finding and then interviewing each and every one—made her dizzy with fatigue. The car pulled onto the off-ramp, bringing her past a brilliantly lit baseball diamond on Arcadia, a flash of kids practicing, a major city asserting its normality. Zack called as she disembarked at City Hall. He went straight to Dupe.

Terri was only half disguised. She'd slipped on a dust mask below her PanOpts. Meaning, she'd be identifiable as cop, but not as herself, the hope being that she could get to the body before her PanOpts raised too many red flags. A lone authority figure in a riled-up protest was always a security risk, and she knew several cops, officers and detectives, who'd walked into some severe beatings in circumstances very similar to this.

A blocky pedestrian footbridge covered this portion of Main. Most times of day, the spot was shaded, as if providing a dank breeding ground for the 24/7 protests it sheltered.

Every time she'd attempted to deduce the gripe of the day, the effort had left her confused. Everyone decried "gridlock" on the refugee question, as if a clean solution to the entire mess were merely a management issue. It'd become a constant of Southland politics for the last twenty years: group after group emerging from the woodwork to condemn shadowy "elites" that benefited, through increasingly nefarious, complex, and Rube Goldbergesque schemes, from the ongoing and chronic refugee skyscraper nightmare. Knowing she'd regret it, Terri raised a hand and riffled through the lower civilian layers, finding one that showed all local protest boxes. Over one large man's head, she read,

Isn't it curious that we know more about Nuestro Quintiglio in two days than we do from two weeks of cover-up at the Tournament Of Roses?

In the comments below this, someone had just posted,

why is NO ONE questioning why a man with NO MOTIVE would want to kill the DA's daughter????????!!!!!!!!

She groaned and looked longingly down the street, in the direction of Jazz Hands, one infinity away.

Finding a body seemed like an easy task. And yet the shifting mob made close-range visibility bad. Two separate crowds claimed each side of Main, each abutting the very edge of the busy street. It was surprising someone didn't get pushed straight into traffic. She crossed to the east side, only realizing halfway across that the vehicles routing around her said far more about her being cop than her choice of shades. She could already feel the first eyes on her, the surrounding air probably blooming with fresh totem poles of abuse.

Terri made a beeline for the back of the crowd, but fifteen feet in, she saw two bare feet sticking out from under a dark coroner's blanket. She pushed her way through the swarm, up to the head of the body, only then seeing that the blanket actually did say Los Angeles Coroner with a little cartoon tombstone. A voice in the throng roared, "We deserve what?" The crowd chanted back, "An-swers," and a hand shot up from under the blanket as if in rigor mortis, a clenched fist raised high, some outraged citizen who probably didn't know or care that the surging mob had engulfed his or her protest.

The crowd thinned thirty feet away from the street, people dispersing around her, news of a cop's arrival having transmitted in real time. A gaggle of street people sat along the far wall of City Hall's eastern campus, utterly detached from the clang of consternation all around them. She inspected the row and saw one hooded figure slumped in the middle, a hand outstretched in petition. Terri squatted on her haunches and tipped up the hood, hit by that familiar stink of perfumed meat. The woman's face was ashen, the face of a dead body. Below this, a dingy charm necklace read John 9:25. A hobo man sat next to the corpse, almost touching it.

"You didn't *smell* this?" But the dust mask and the chanting crowd muffled her.

She stood, pinging for backup. It was the ultimate comedy death, having a guy in an ape suit come up and pop you and no one give your dead body a second thought. This dust mask was turning into a good thing; no one in the crowd could see her chuckling, lest the protest shift to focus on her and her lack of sensitivity.

Waiting, she called Zack back, first setting her voice to filter out the crowd noise, making it sound as if she were alone somewhere in a car or a room. He answered on the first ring.

"Hey, I was getting worried." There was a slight note of surprise in his voice.

"I'm right here."

"And where's that?"

"Around. Around town." She wasn't going to mention the ambush, instead letting it ride out in silence.

"Oh-kay. Well, you'll never guess what I found out."

"Yeah, what's that?"

"That shithead lawyer? He's representing Mutty's shooter now."

"Do tell," she said, feeling a physical relief as she saw the red-and-blue flash from two blocks away.

"You don't sound surprised. How'd you already know?"

"No, that's exciting." She weighed hanging up, the chat feeling masochistic.

"Look, Terr. I know this is some difficult shit you're in. You think I don't know that? I'm trying."

"Uhn-huh."

"Seriously, what else do you want me to do? You want me to come meet you? Just give me a place, I'll be there."

"You hold down the fort on the home front, Zack. Make sure Hyperion doesn't get scalded."

"Wait, what? Out by the airport?"

Not sure what to make of this, she said, "Hyperion Waste Eatment almost getting it. From the other day."

"Oh yeah, I think I saw something about that on the news."

She didn't know how to reply to this. The first pair of uniformed officers were already weaving through the crowd, generating an upsurge of boos and catcalls in their wake.

"Goodbye, Zack."

She followed the crowd's nearly unified gaze as the group followed the officers over to her position, everyone staring expectantly at the three of them now, like they were going to bust into some street theater themselves. A fresh chant started at the periphery, back by the curb. She pointed down to the corpse. The bum who'd been sitting next to the body stood quickly, uncomfortable with attention. As he turned to skitter off, she saw his dreads had fused into one rounded lock, a hair helmet.

"The body's been down for five days. If the shot went through her, the bullet could easily have gotten moved or blown around since then. So I want a thorough sweep."

The chanting intensified, and the closer of the two uniforms, twenty-something, female, clearly intimidated by the crowd, leaned in, cupping one ear.

Terri repeated herself, yelling through the dust mask. Finally she said, "Fuck it," pulled down the mask and repeated the order a third time.

The cop nodded and the crowd noise intensified. She looked up, seeing shock radiating out from her own recognized face. A blurry, smeared boo sounded from the throng, maybe two hundred strong. A chant started, *Nuestro, Nuestro, Nuestro . . .*

She looked back at the officers, who seemed dazed, grabbing the closer one, the woman, and motioning rudely to the body again. The crowd surged forward, two protesters falling into her and then backing up again. She instinctually placed a hand over her holster as someone yelled, "Another one?"

"You kill another?"

In her upper-left view, she pulled up her car and furiously triple-tapped the icon. An elbow pushed her from behind, knocking her down, and Terri caught herself with both hands, scraping her palms, hearing the car honk in rapid bursts for everyone to clear out. The honks mixed with shouts as the car bullied its way through the crowd. She could see headlights through a thicket of legs. Twenty feet away, it sounded an alarm, 130-decibel bursts that hurt, the last tapering off as the car trundled up and flung its door open, Terri scampering in, the two cops clambering in after her, a jungle of arms and fists pounding on the windows like a bad dream she must have had at some point in her life.

At midnight, palms still smarting, Terri waited on Broadway for the downtown Feeler team, perched against the sloped hood of a passenger car she'd rented with her own money. She'd spent the evening in this car, circling the city, fitfully napping, waking every ten minutes with a fresh suspicion, some new configuration of puzzle parts that might make the last forty-eight hours seem plausible.

City Hall blazed with light, its cherry-topped ziggurat affirming civic authority. All around her, Saturday nightlife surged, tipsy twenty-somethings bar hopping, stumbling under trees that had grown large around their host streetlights, seeming illuminated from within. Below the tidal drone of surface street traffic, she heard synchronized crickets.

The skyscrapers towered over all this. Seen this close, the towers were dark, imposing, with only a few flickers coming from a tiny fraction of the hundreds and hundreds of blacked-out windows. She found the nighttime skyline unnerving, as if this prosperous, well-lit metropolis existed in the foothills of a dead city, built by giants thousands of years ago. She'd once watched an immersive documentary about Bunker Hill, showing her all the run-down Victorians and squalid grandeur of the neighborhood erased by the city a half century before she'd been born. Could they have imagined that the skyscraper building boom would one day facilitate exponentially larger and broker surges of humanity? In PanOpt, she set these buildings to appear the way they did in movies, their offices lit by late-night commerce or cleaning crews, a random but seemingly significant assortment of windows still blazing with the exertions of some midnight oil-burning entrepreneur, struggling into the wee hours to propel the economy even further.

Whatever Chief Blanco was going to do, Terri had at least tonight, a genuine last stand before her PanOpts were shut off, suspension, who knew what else. As she acknowledged the self-pitying tone of the thought, she saw the Feeler team—hulking Angel, the even-larger Vincente, and petite Alejandra—emerge from around the corner, lit up by the Christmas lights some enterprising person had strung up thirty feet of nearby palm tree. The Feeler team were a specialized plainclothes unit tasked with going after any nocturnal wrongdoing that crossed their paths. The detachment functioned largely as a nighttime cleanup crew, handling narcotics, vice, robbery, anything and everything but homicide.

As they approached, she heard Vincente's booming voice first. "So this human beluga looks at me and says, 'I just came over here to fry up some onions. It stinks up my place too bad.' Then he goes and gets the onion, like that's his alibi. The Onion Defense." Alejandra laughed like a secretary. Terri had never been sure how such a polite woman worked this particular shift. She raised her scraped-up palm in a greeting.

Vincente did a war-whoop and tomahawk chop.

"Going after a no-name, huh?" Alejandra asked.

"Yeah. Long shot, but . . . you know." She figured everyone was too polite or, far more likely, too overwhelmed to give a shit about the Mutty shooting. Maybe they hadn't even heard about it yet.

"How does this work? Do you all go out as one unit, or . . ."

"I gotta do that thing," Alejandra said to Vincente. "So we'll catch up on the other side." They slapped hands, then she waited for Terri to do the same, Terri suppressing a wince at the smack on her raw flesh.

"So just you two guys, then?" Terri wanted to make a joke about having large males escort her through the underbelly, then realized it wasn't that far off the mark.

"I'm due back over at the Dolson, having some drinks." Angel already seemed well into boozy. "Got a one-week time out."

"For what?" She yanked up her PanOpts to confirm that he meant figuratively, that he hadn't just magically projected his VT and made it seem like his physical self.

"Ah, I got caught relinquishing some cock taco of his petty cash. I'll be back in on Wednesday. Who else is going to do this shift?" Both men guffawed in a low pitch, slapping hands fiercely.

She used to assume all of them had gotten busted down to Feeler team for the sin of indiscretion, for being unlucky enough to have gotten caught doing something stupid. Everyone she knew had met opportunities to separate scums from funds. Once, before making homicide, she'd assisted in the bust of two pimps, twin albinos from Ghana who ran a stable of women in Eagle Rock. After all the hooplah of the raid, she'd found herself in a room with five bankers' boxes full of hundred dollar bills. She hadn't taken any, there being too big an asterisk on money earned by helpless immigrants. But just a month later, she'd had a smaller experience with a two-bit coke crew, and she'd wound up splitting a thin wad of cash with the other responding officer. She had been struck by how easily it could have been the same bills, circulated through four weeks worth of human misery. That weekend, she'd hesitated depositing the modest take in her joint checking account, not because she was worried about Gabby noticing, but because it felt like the cash would somehow taint the rest of their money. She wound up buying a $2,200 Lojas gift certificate and sheepishly placing the inappropriately expensive present in that year's Secret Santa box at work.

Alejandra set out. Vincente said, "Shit shift, baby," as he led Terri in the opposite direction. They passed sidewalk chess games played by men with nowhere to go, cardboard and cloth vagrant nests, exhausted people sleeping in doorways, or on baled sacks of laundry, or slumped against alley walls. Tea merchants slept curled around their meager kiosks. They stumbled upon several sad family tableaus, groups of sleepers flanked by overfilled shopping carts wrapped in fluttering garbage bags. Did any of these carts lurch back to life and roll on home to their stores?

At Grand Hope Park, one lone, lean hobo did shirtless pull ups on a festively painted jungle gym, his bent legs brushing against a brood of inert street hens. Years earlier, there'd been a nasty rash of avian bronchitis, dead birds piled all around downtown, as if the Dead Chicken Fairy had visited the entire city overnight. The episode had provided a dramatic reminder of why tower life was so untenable, of how quickly a pandemic could rip through a skyscraper. Not that any steps had been taken.

Terri queried anyone conscious about Rujuta. No one knew anything. For the first hour, Vincente seemed content to walk alongside her, alert but not seeming actively interested in meeting any sort of quota or rounding up any particular bad guys. At one point they rounded a corner as another overmuscled street personality yelled, "Yo man, I thought you was *broke*!" as he bullied a frail elderly man, a wisp of a human. Vincente calmly strode over to defuse the scene. It was hard for Terri to imagine what these older refugees had to endure just to make it here, the lowest rung of Heaven.

It was 2:40 a.m. when they entered Pershing Square and Terri realized they'd nearly made a large circle. Vincente blinked like a jungle explorer coming into a clearing, saying, "Mothership." The largest of the downtown toilet tents took up nearly half the plaza. In the daytime, the tent didn't merit a second glance. At night, it was floodlit, luminous, its huge cloth walls billowing with the fury of galleon sails. Two unisex lines, each several hundred people long, curled from both sides in a spiral pattern. She wondered where the mystery hole was that the housing cop had told her about over a week ago. The thought somehow connected to Mutty, to feelings she needed to sequester until this was all over.

She worked the lines dutifully, asking every single person about Rujuta, a refugee without a known face, someone she knew only by name and scar. And this was assuming Liney hadn't gotten the scar part wrong. She made sure to keep Vincente within her line of sight. Working with an audience bereft of eyewear, she could only prove her authority with her shield, a symbol not universally recognized. One homegrown drunk, perhaps mistaking her for a health inspector, grabbed her arm and pointed toward the tent's interior, saying, "Thersh an outbreak of Sisyphus."

Refugees' endurance for queues perfectly balanced their total disdain for personal space. Squabbles flared over spouses jumping line to be with spouses, children with parents, cousins with cousins. Barging, skinny touts shouted out sad little bargains. Women worked their elbows like fighting cocks, forcing their way through the horde, fending off adolescents versed in squeezing between adults. Some refugees appointed themselves queue leaders, springing from the horde to direct the flow of humanity into orderly rows. These invisible codes of conduct were survival skills, born in the old world but reinforced through years of camps.

On the far side of the square, someone had left a perfectly nice couch, perhaps to commemorate the spot where she and Zack kidnapped Sanjiv Goswami. Two shirtless, clearly zonked-out Indian teenagers sat on its sinking cushions with spacey gazes directed toward Vincente, who stood posed with one leg up on an armrest. She heard him say, "You goofed up on drugs, Tonto?"

Terri leaned against a light pole, always interested to learn the latest in illicit kicks among the city's underclass. Skyscraper kids tried just about anything, getting high on laughing gas, or candy canes dipped in brake fluid, or grinding and snorting prenatal vitamins. For six months last year, the big thing had been Smiles, those black bouillon cubes that only affected people under twenty-five.

During her entire career, only two drugs had remained consistent: Overlord and opium. Cops had been fairly effective in strangling the supply of the former, which did away with the need for sleep, food, and any other logistical constraints not rooted in the immediate present. They'd been nearly as effective with their inaction toward the latter, tacitly allowing opium to continue as a tool of pacification. Apathy among refugees was never discouraged.

Not hearing an answer, Vincente sighed and said, "Look. Me and my partner here,"—he pointed toward Terri—"are gonna find it anyway. Instead of you making us strip search you in front of all your buddies here, making us make you waggle your junk in public, how's about you just give up the goods. C'mon guys, okay? Scout's honor," he said, raising his hand without having actually promised anything. Terri had always heard Vincente did his lowly nocturnal shift for the sheer bossy thrill of it. His husband was a major star in the world of high-end glass art; he certainly didn't need to work.

Slowly, underwater, the two kids glanced at each other, nodding just slightly, one reaching down into his sock and producing a small glassine baggie.

"There. *See?*" Vincente said, snatching this and letting the crumbly black stuff spill down into a small puddle on the sidewalk, the empty baggie drifting down to the gutter. Nearby, an older refugee man eyed the puddle, and she pictured the guy lapping up its nastiness as soon as they left.

Instead, this man said, in a voice crisp with anger, "Aren't you going to arrest him for the opium?"

"Hey, opium is the opiate of the masses." Vincente smiled widely, the tip of his tongue peeking out. "Who are we to impose our value system on you guys?"

"That is bullshit! If an American kid gets caught with opium, you pound his head into the curb, teach him a lesson. If one of us gets caught with opium, you laugh it off." As the man's speech grew heated, he lost his cultivated street accent and slipped into old world patois.

"You want me to pound your head?"

"I want you to behave like you behave with any other basic human being!"

Vincente laughed. "You sound like a cartoon character, you know that? 'Ah Beep Bah-beep-a-beep-a-beep-a-beep . . .'"

They continued up West 5th, coltish candy girls meandering down the sidewalks in widely spaced pairs. In contrast to daytime streetwalkers, these girls really were girls, their garish rouged faces contradicted by short statures. Most were in the fourteen-to-sixteen age bracket, but looked even younger because of malnutrition, stumbling along in jeans cut into short-shorts, pockets poking out from underneath the ripped fabric, a substitution for actual fashion.

Night altered the geography and demographics of downtown prostitution. In the daytime, candy girls provided a good barometer of the younger generation's buying power, hookers, refugee and otherwise, targeting high school kids. Seeing these streets now, Terri realized she and Vincente were the only citizens on the sidewalk. At night, did refugee hookers hook to other refugees? In a city flooded with lost or stolen daughters, Terri had a strange realization: she was hoping she didn't find Rujuta.

"How do you *cope* with all this?"

"You really want to know?" Vincente smiled. "Try 6220."

She switched to this sandbox layer, seeing nothing. An old woman with ulcerated facial lesions passed and Vincente said, loud enough to be overheard, "Hey, check out perpy with the herpes." Laughter erupted, swelling and fading, and Terri had to fight to not laugh out loud as well.

"I don't leave my house without a laugh track. Makes every little thing alright."

"I don't know why I'm surprised." She didn't. If a growing number of regular people could only muddle through their mundane desk jobs by overlaying constructions on the world—seeing their humdrum environs drenched in ivy, nine-mooned, medieval, tribal, the skies filled with swooping dragons—it made perfect sense that a night cop would find some relief in the same.

Vincente looked off into the distance. "Alejandra got something. Lez go."

They caught up with her three blocks away, in a street level space that had once been retail. Scavengers had long since stripped the storefront of everything but the chipboard wall covering. Even the carpet was gone, the bare concrete patterned with faint gray squiggles of dried glue. A gaping hole connected this cavern to the next, presumably leading to a tunnel or skyscraper. Terri leaned against one of the open glass doors, seeing a sticker for the Better Business Bureau, their logo showing a curl of Hebrew floating up from a fedora. Had this been a Jewish organization?

Two spotlight drones flanked the front entrance, their beams turned horizontally, illuminating the interior with the intensity of stadium arc lights. In the center of the space, six hapless handcuffed teenagers stood with heads bent low to keep out the glare, their gesture one of shame. Past them, in the washed-out brilliance, she saw a meager tent at the back of the room and long gang markings on the wall in chalk, most likely noting which SSK set collected taxes for that building. Alejandra and Vincente conferred and then the three of them stepped inside, the drone illumination sliding upward, looking now like track lights installed above the pavement.

From certain angles, downtown at night was a demilitarized zone, reminding her of the very worst neighborhoods in the city. Twenty years ago, black flight had essentially abandoned Watts to the most ruthless of refugee gangs, all the old residents fleeing either down—to well-paying service jobs south of the border—or sideways, to Bell Gardens, Cudahy, Maywood, or a half-dozen other shitty sub-cities nestled along the 710. Watts now struck her as an abandoned backlot out of some science-fiction movie. Even though it was infested with humanity, it always seemed as if no one was there. The vast Nickerson Gardens buildings, the third-largest housing project west of the Mississippi, had devolved into something especially eerie. The few times she'd driven through, it'd felt like a reconnaissance sortie, every window a peephole of jagged glass.

Eyes adjusting to the dimness, she realized a campfire smoldered in front of a tent; someone lived a life back there. Vincente said, "Okay. I reach in all your pockets, what do I find? Buncha earlobes?"

The kids laughed nervously. Urban legends of hedge clipper-wielding earring bandits had swirled around downtown for so long everyone could laugh off the reference. The smallest of the bunch apparently took this momentary lightening in the mood to lodge a complaint.

"Hey, what happens to all our shades? I need mine for school!"

"Yeah, what school is that?"

"LAUOED."

"Is that some floating classroom crap?"

The kid nodded with a frown, having already realized his own question was rhetorical.

"In my day, we had to *go* to school, yo."

Another kid chimed in: "She was just gettin' down on the rest of us because we *dint* go to school. Now you're mad at him because he *does*?"

Alejandra cleared her throat, smiling like a meter maid. "You can't win, you can't break even, nor can you get out of the game."

"Move my ass to Sweden," the largest member of the group mumbled.

Terri watched the smallest kid's face for tears. A banger concerned about education: the concept fascinated her. Modern-day gang kids had the least to gain from formal schooling of any generation in human history. If you were a refugee and able to afford EyePhones, you certainly wouldn't feel any truancy pressure. And if you owned a pair of EyePhones, you could basically outsource your comprehension. There were free layers that would read everything aloud. Most adult gang-bangers she'd met had been proudly illiterate.

Vincente was speaking to someone remotely, pointing out attire details on the gathered bunch as if they were anthropological specimens.

"Yeah, shoulder blade and temple tats. I heard they gotta get their taints, too," he said with a cheery laugh. Terri cleared her throat and asked the group about the girl with the vertical scar, barely waiting for the chorus of head shakes.

Alejandra murmured something that ended with the word "Mutty."

Terri's head snapped sideways. "What?"

"I didn't say anything."

The handcuffed kids eyed her and then eyed them, sensing a new vibe coming off Terri, somewhere between shock and anger, a conflict between authorities so rare and exotic that they didn't know how to react. She all at once felt her vulnerability, exposed on all sides, in a space more cave than room.

"It's late, I need to hit the road," she said, backing out.

Vincente said something that sounded conciliatory, but she was already speed-walking down the street, the drone lights casting a long thin shadow in front of her, Terri pinning her badge to her jacket to let late-night street creepers know the deal. She yawned once and was unable to stop.

Waiting for a pickup car a block away, she glanced down to the lights of Pershing Square. There'd been a shift in the street life, Saturday night transgressions giving way to Sunday morning labor. Upcyclers already combed the gutters for useful debris. The first raddiwallah of the day rolled past, hauling bundles of carefully twined old paper by pedicab to the recycling plant up by the train yards. These men were just more worker ants, carrying their seeds and crumbs back to the anthill.

A woman in an incongruous gas mask darted into an alley. She pictured Rujuta already starting the day in a sweatshop somewhere, another round black spot stuck to the floor. When she looked away, Terri realized a corner of the sky was already light.

She woke exhausted in Carla's storage closet, unable to sleep more than a few hours, feeling just as shaky and stiff as she had when she'd lain down. Sunlight spilled in from a thick window of reinforced security glass, making a long rectangle on the wall above her, next to the tall shelves of boxed supplies. She thought about how nice it would feel to jog. Reaching for the jacket she'd folded under her head, she fished out the last two breath mints, taking these without chewing, just letting them sit in her mouth.

Lying on her back, staring up at the orderly row of boxes, she thought of *The Shining*, Jack Nicholson coming to in a locked pantry. As a teenager, she'd watched a documentary on the making of this movie. A narrator had discussed all the hidden messages and impossible geography allegedly masterminded by the director. She hadn't gotten around to actually watching the film itself until years later. By then, the art form dissected in the documentary—a story, singular in presentation, masterminded by one person—had ceased to exist. Now everyone was a director, an artistic mastermind. As soon as copyright law permitted—ten years? Five?—there would be a million versions of *The Shining*, each with different endings, new characters, every viewer free to add or subtract to the geography of the hotel as they pleased.

She'd seen a photography exhibit, not long after she'd moved out west, called "Our Common Humanity." The show had focused on the impoverished undersides of every continent, featuring a variety of portraits and slumscapes, each with the huddled masses of the third world staring directly at the audience, matching the camera's gaze with faces leeched of humor or hope. Terri had been haunted by the huge, luminous photos, the entire exhibition composed entirely of prewar pictures, so that all its defiant pain was already anachronistic, a peek backward.

None of those pictures would mean anything to the new generation. Or, more precisely, pictures themselves would mean something entirely different and lesser to the new generation. Photography was no longer about documentation. It couldn't be. Such a show now, less than twenty years later, would be about the show itself, everyone reading artistic intent into each photo, common sense holding photography closer to simulacra than actual representation. Bit by bit, picture by picture, memory by memory, no one could be sure that the past was actually the past.

The endlessness of the networks—the infinity of rooms, plains, hidden pay-per-view civilizations—all of it was slopping over into the physical world, obliterating the rivulets and riverbeds that once defined the one, true past. It wasn't just that the younger generation was bored by the content or format of history; it was that they no longer had any incentive to believe history.

Revisionism had taken root with a supernatural ferocity. People remixed the past like they remixed old home movies. Some people remixed the war, changing battles or outcomes. Terri hadn't kept up on the recent surge in war denial simply because the subject freaked her out too much. But she couldn't deny that such denial was growing in popularity. Every year, she encountered more and more oddballs and cranks who insisted that there had been no war between China and India. Soon, there would be people insisting there never had been an India or China, period.

A door slammed in the next room and a surge of panic shoved her upright, making her scramble for the gun somewhere under one of the flimsy blankets. Carla had let her in last night through one of the emergency exits, and even though she hadn't formally passed through the main entrance, the building, and thus the force, would surely know she was on the premises. Logic gave police property a bit more safety than anywhere else, but she didn't like not knowing how large or small that margin of safety might actually be. And when she realized she'd be sleeping in an unlocked storage room, it'd been a trick to dismiss that this was basically a cul-de-sac.

A shuffle of motion came through the door, somebody moving around stacks of things on the worktable. Knuckles rapped. Terri sat perfectly still.

"Hey," Carla said. "Breakfast. C'mon. It's almost ten."

She cleared her throat and said, "Yeah," absurdly grateful for the spike of fear, more effective than any alarm clock for removing all need for coffee.

But when she opened the door and smelled the roast beans, an equally old impulse kicked in, reminding her that fresh coffee was a privilege, that to refuse its sacrament was disrespectful. She poured herself a cup and, seeing no room on the cluttered sofa, perched herself on the edge of two stacked and solid-looking bankers' boxes in the corner farthest from the entrance.

Carla stood in the opposite corner and looked over her shoulder as she fiddled with a separate pile of boxes, saying, "There's bagels," motioning with her head toward a blue jute bag on the work table.

"Great, thanks." She drank down half the cup, feeling that acidic heat as a rejuvenation. "Any news?"

"Nothing in the last twelve hours. Dead ends all around. Here's some creamers for your coffee."

Terri was about to say she took hers black, but when Carla pressed the little sachets in her palm, she felt something extra, seeing a small note folded into something dense and serious. She unwrapped this and read,

Did you set your VT to say that you had the flu? Cough once if Yes, tell me you need some sugars if No.

She cleared her throat quietly, hoping that wouldn't be mistaken for a cough.

"Hey, did you happen to get any sugars?"

"Yeah," Carla said, sounding distracted. She crossed the room and pressed another few little water-soluble packets into Terri's palm. On another note, she read,

Something screwy is going on. Get out of here, use only disposables, call me in 30 mins. I'll be on SwiftWhisper, off premises.

She crumpled the note, slipping it into her pocket as she downed another mouthful of coffee, thinking she'd been looking forward to that bagel.

"Hey, I was supposed to meet a contact a half hour ago. Let's talk later. Thanks again for the coffee."

"Any time," Carla said as the door swung closed.

Outside, she summoned a private car through her civilian shades, parking three blocks away and finding SwiftWhisper. It was a messenger service she didn't really understand, something probably for teens and adults with illicit intentions. Paying the hundred-dollar signup fee, she wondered if she should keep a receipt, picturing all the expenses from this bizarre, terrifying chapter of her life tallied and itemized on next year's 1040 form. Next to her, a refrigerated minivan pulled up, dipping on its suspension as a delivery boy bounded out the other side and into a meat shop, the vehicle's back end dribbling blood and water onto the pavement.

SwiftWhisper wasn't an audio account, so the two of them sat face to face twenty minutes later, Carla's VT in the car with her.

"I called you early this morning, to tell you I was going out for some food," Carla said. "I was going to leave a message with your Dupe, for when you woke up, so you'd know when I was going to be back. Instead, your Dupe told me that you had the flu."

"That's what I figured from your note. I didn't do that, so . . . how is that possible?"

"It isn't. Unless you set it that way the last time you were sick and forgot about it?"

"No."

"Look, Terri. Um. I can understand the stuff with someone breaking into your apartment—I mean, I don't understand it, but I can kind of get my mind around some scenarios where it might be possible for someone to have set you up from on high. But this is something else. I mean, for someone to have forged your Duplicado . . ."

"That seems like it would be a hard thing to do"

"It's not a hard thing to do. It can't be done. Period. Your Dupe is the foyer to your personal, closed system. In a polycultural network chain, there is no means of outside attack."

"I don't really follow . . ."

"If you were using something on the Internet, sure, someone could, with a good amount of skill, attack you remotely. But that's not possible on the Overlay. That's the point of the Overlay. It'd be like someone coming into your house and changing the locks while you were watching them do it. And then you're not even on a civilian system. I don't know that any American cop network has ever been breached like this."

"Well, someone did get into my house . . ." she said, not sure why she was saying it.

"For someone to change your outgoing, they would basically need your face, your eyes . . . they'd need to be you. Even if you had a twin sister . . . you don't have an evil twin sister, right?"

"I have a twin. Not identical."

"Jesus, no. That wasn't even . . . that was rhetorical."

"Okay, yup."

"I don't know what the hell is happening. Sorry, I don't. I don't know what's happening, I don't know how to proceed, it's fucked."

"I'll call you back," Terri said, shocked by Carla's shock.

She told the car to circle on the freeway, trying and failing to let this dread infect her, viewing the world through the eyes of a civilian. In the commercial layers, there were apps to fill the sky with anything and everything: aurora borealis, biblical locusts, confetti storms, flying saucers, moons, rainbows, zeppelins, lots of zeppelins, so many zeppelins they all crashed into each other and exploded. Some people went about their days with the watchful eye of God peering down from the Heavens. The public Layer two still had occasional fireworks in its sky. But she saw now that these fireworks were only barely discernable behind the mile-high advertising banners, accidentally making the explosions appear colossal, like something occurring far outside the earth's atmosphere.

On the month before her bus ride to California, rumors had run wild that a killer asteroid was on a direct collision course with the planet, and that the United States could no longer afford a space program capable of smashing the thing. She'd heard different versions of this story for a week, each slowly reassuring her, in their increasingly overblown shades of implausibility, that the earth would continue. One version held that the space program did have enough money, but that political gridlock had doomed humanity. Other versions said that the asteroid would destroy the moon, or graze the moon, sending it tumbling into the Pacific Ocean, or that a generation of presidents had known about the asteroid but had been too spineless to deal with it.

She remembered those nights, trying to sleep while confronting the traces of this idea that the world may not continue. The rumor had surely thrived in the new era of postwar uncertainty. No one could pretend that God wouldn't allow such a thing to happen, when He apparently had room in His grand design for all kinds of horror. After the rumors had subsided, she'd looked back on those nights as her low point. But things had continued. She'd come out the other side. Terri pulled up her call box with a fresh resolve. Carla materialized on the third ring.

"Weren't you saying earlier that you could do a custom trace on anything?"

"Yeah. I mean, don't hold me to *any*thing, but yeah."

"Then do one for the gorilla."

"How so?"

"Even in a county this size, there are still a finite amount of gorilla costumes, right?"

Carla let out one dry little chuckle, "It doesn't really work like that . . ."

"No, but you could do a trace on a mask, right?"

"Well. Huh. Yeah, I suppose."

"So maybe this shooter did us a favor. They came and went through the toilet tent, but they must've gotten the suit from somewhere. Maybe you can locate all the gorilla suits in Los Angeles in a set time period, narrow down the search, find some distinguishing characteristics off the footage of the city hall shooting. Worst case, it'll be something mass-produced. But even that gives us one piece of information more than we have now."

"I'll get back with you." Carla vanished again.

The car swung onto the 101 and Terri yawned uncontrollably, removing her shades and leaning against the vibrating glass with her eyes closed. Even with the road humming below, she wondered why it was so easy to fall asleep in a car when it wasn't a sleeper. In the sync of traffic, cars matched up, locking into each other's slipstreams, creating patterns of hums. Head bobbling, examining the light behind her eyes, she pictured Carla furiously flipping through boxes and boxes of information, searching the entire metropolis for a gorilla face, one eye ordering a million eyes to comb through streets and alleys and parks.

She jolted upright, rubbing her lower lip in a fresh fear. After a careful weighing of her options, she and Carla had decided that her workstation was the safest place for Terri to sleep. Whatever outside mercenaries were involved, they couldn't get into the building if they weren't on the force. And Carla's office was double locked. There was no way someone could get into the front room without being heard in the second room. It'd been an imperfect fix for an indefinable problem.

She'd only stepped twenty feet to get into the waiting car, but she'd done those twenty feet in the wake of Carla's cryptic note, preoccupied, with her face uncovered. Anyone using the Basement would have had a full-view shot. With some bad luck, she might have been picked up by a commercial face-spotting network as well. Dumb: there was a dust mask in her jacket pocket.

A gangbanger had once told her that his biggest fear was getting locked in sync with a car holding rival gang members. It had resonated with her, but mostly in the Sucks To Be You category. Now she sat low, feeling his fear, just her eyes coming up over the jump seat upholstery, peeking out at the synced traffic behind her, the faces of strange, intent men peering back. They could be anyone. She resisted powering up her PanOpts and finding out.

She ducked low again, sitting on the floor, feeling vulnerable, weak, stupid, and even stupider still for hiding in this position. In all the depths of dumbassery to which an average citizen could sink, one of the most common and absurd mistakes was the belief that car doors were impenetrable to bullets. She was a sitting duck on the freeway. But where wouldn't she be? If she'd exposed her face, she'd need to arrange another car switch.

Another thought came on the heels of this. What if Krista or Tammi called her line? Whatever faceless enemy was after Terri, would it pursue her sister or niece? She tried to extinguish this panic loop, finding she couldn't. She moved the car's floating control box over to rest on the floor next to her, instructed the car to pull out of sync, to pull off at the next exit, and as it dipped down onto surface streets, she instructed it to loop around, heading north, not sure if she really was being followed or not.

Fifteen minutes later, parked under a tree on a side street, Terri tried to sit and concentrate, ignoring the car interior that blazed with wraparound ads for tire companies and bath salts. She needed reassurance that her messages couldn't be plundered, instinctually knowing that she had already crossed over into territory where Carla wouldn't be able to reassure her of anything. At the church across the street, a robot and vampire-themed Quinceañera was wrapping up, and she experienced a familiar disconnect, an anger at the inappropriateness of people going on with their lives, disrespectfully oblivious to the chaos of hers.

A car passed and slowed, edging up and parking two spaces ahead. Carla appeared on the seat opposite her. Being on the floor, Terri instinctually felt like she was about to get chewed out.

"Okay, I found him."

"Found who?"

"The gorilla guy."

"Already?"

"Hold on, I gotta . . ." She heard a fumbling in the audio as Carla's VT stared out at the church steps and then abruptly vanished.

"Okay. I got two sets of shades on."

"Huh?"

"You're in audio, on my head, I got PanOpts in visual. Yeah, I found the gorilla guy. It looks like he's dead too."

"Who is he?"

"Uhm . . . name is . . . Clay Tejada, forty-eight, pretty clean family man, although I'm seeing some youthful wild oats stuff twenty-five years ago. Listen. This guy dresses up as a gorilla full time . . ."

"A fetishist."

"It's his job. He does gorilla-gram stuff. Balloon deliveries. Parties. I think he sings."

"That . . ." She whistled and gritted her jaw in exasperation. "How could somebody be that *stupid*? To do a shooting in plain view in their work outfit?"

"Yeah, I thought about that. Whatever motivated this guy, it must have been a serious motivation. Serious enough to override all judgment."

"Scared stupid."

"That would be it. And if you think about it, that would cover all these killings. Froggy was the dumbest of the bunch. The rest of these people showed a general level of prudence in their daily lives, and yet three out of the five shootings went down in public. I think these people were scared shitless. Whoever it is that arranged for the gun to get passed from one person to the next . . . whoever this person is, I think they have a hell of a lot of leverage over each perp-slash-victim."

"Three out of five. So where's gorilla guy now? Besides Heaven."

"He's in a parked car in the valley, in a Radio Shack lot. The window was rolled down when he got shot. My guess is he was trying to clear his head after the City Hall shooting, to make sense of whatever mess he'd gotten himself into."

"I know the feeling," she said, freshly nervous, glancing again to the car parked ahead of her, to the figures who seemed to be examining her through the glass of the intervening vehicle.

"One more thought. This guy's three days dead . . ."

"That should smell good," Terri said, realizing that if his suit had AC—as a full-body animal costume surely would—it might actually not be so bad.

"The point I'm trying to make is that there's not such a wide spread on the duration between shootings. Four days between Froggy and Farrukh, a day between Farrukh and Santos, but then three days between each following shooting. I think Santos is the glitch in the timeline because Quintiglio was a reporter and knew how to track down subjects quickly. Which means there's a good chance that the person who shot Gorilla Guy is still walking."

"Oh shit."

"I'm in the Basement right now. I'm closing in. So be ready to move as soon as I call."

"Wait . . . there's something else on my end." She sank down below the dashboard, resting on the floor of the car "I think someone might be tracking me."

"Tracking how?"

"Following me," she said, nearly whispering. "I need you to do an overview in ghost."

"I don't know where you are."

"Right. I'm just across from . . ." She peeked up over the window line long enough to see the church signage obscured by teenagers in cardboard costumes. "Shit, um . . ."

"Terri, *breathe*. Upper-left-hand corner. You're wearing shades."

"Okay." She exhaled, "Okay."

"Ping your location and flip it to me. Upper-left corner."

She did this. "Okay."

"Gimme a moment," Carla said.

Squatting now on the floor of this car, she understood that this was the lowest possible station in the depths of depression. No home, no safe haven, hiding in the bottom of a motionless vehicle. She made herself remove her pistol, placing it on her lap, staring at this object and for a moment seeing it as an unknown artifact, the chemicals of panic and inertia buffeting her into confusion. Slowly, tentatively, she reached up to ping the car's control box and slide this down to her level, terrified of getting shot while executing a getaway, terrified of getting executed herself.

Carla laughed. "Yeah, you're surrounded, alright."

She froze, was frozen, caught in the finality of the cruel laugh: the only person she could trust had been against her all along.

"I'm seeing the full roster of news-hawks and knuckleheads: Tina Bravo, Shep Lyra, Kofi Agyeman, Pedro Stelter from *LA Doings* . . ."

"Reporters."

"You're a celeb. I guess somebody grabbed your face on the way out of the building. I should've thought of that."

She rose to sit on one of the seats, blood thudding, livid in embarrassment, seeing the group of familiar faces milling around on the sidewalk, conferring with each other, nobody veering too close to the car.

"Why aren't they approaching? I'd think they'd want footage of me cowering."

"If the story is you had a hand in Nuestro Quintiglio's death, then, yeah, that makes sense."

"Or they actually believe I'm on the hunt for reporters."

"Back to my own hunt," Carla said. "I'll call."

She had the car pull out, seeing Kofi and a few more young go-getters jump in their own waiting cars to give pursuit, as if she were some bygone starlet fleeing the paparazzi. She'd heard of this happening before, journalists hunting cops, although the more prudent course would've been to track a car with drones and catch up on the other side. Maybe they were doing that as well. As evasion, she dropped herself off at the Toluca workstation, the closest with two street entrances, striding through the building before any coworkers could snipe at her, out the back door, crossing the fifteen feet of pavement to the next waiting car as if it were a perp walk, covering her head with her jacket with one hand, her mouth and nose with the other.

Carla called on the freeway.

"Tejada, Gorilla man, was shot by . . . this lady." A display box materialized over the dashboard, framing a mousy brunette.

"Paula Pineda. No priors, lives fancy, at least according to her listed street address. Young. As best I can tell, she's still with us."

Eight minutes later, the car parked itself on a deserted residential side street in the Hollywood Hills, next to an aquatint-tiled wall. The silence here seemed meaningful, only the fronds of one palm tree fluttering high overhead, like the tarp-covered shopping carts she'd seen the day before. She was about to dial Carla when she realized they'd never disconnected.

"I'm here, but there's a two-car garage coming straight out of the side of the hill, meaning there's a private entrance from inside the house. Anyone could come or go and I'd have no way of knowing."

"This has to be your call," Carla agreed. "If I do backup, you're back in the system and back to being an active target. If you go in solo, you're a target without backup."

Terri ran a finger through her hair, participant in and punchline of a vast conspiracy. Cosmic joke: creeping chaos.

"I'm going in on my own."

"Okay. Obviously I'll corroborate you on Exigent Circumstances. Keep your PanOpts on your person but turned off. Call me if you need the cavalry."

"Yeah."

She made a sucking sound through her teeth as the alert box for her SwiftWhisper account blinked on and off. When opened, it showed all the overhead footage Carla could get of the property. It was a decent spread: main house, side wing, some sort of small atrium, nice pool, everything bordered with thick walls of shrubbery and treeline. The place was rich, but not crazy person rich. More importantly, there were no toys or swing sets or other evidence of children, which was good. Or at least as good could be in this situation, essentially an action that would require official approval in hindsight.

Heart knocking, she glanced at the owner information long enough to register that the property didn't belong to Paula Pineda. Of all the seven perps in this chain of death, Pineda was by far the least threatening, a slender, pale wisp of a twenty-two-year-old probably smaller than even Stacy Santos. Although Terri had to remind herself that every person in the chain was just as lethal as the Browning HP they brandished. She pictured this gun now, somewhere inside the posh grounds, a wasp she didn't want to sting her. Still, the geometry of one gun was preferable to another ambush.

The map showed a grade in the landscaping, to the right of the front entrance and slightly out of view from the street. The driveway to the next house was almost entirely out of sight from this angle, but a place like this would probably have a contract with some rapid-response security firm. If someone called the cops, she'd just have to improv.

She crossed to the gate, sidestepped into foliage, hoisted herself over the wall, and scrambled up an incline of dense landscaping, emerging next to the swimming pool. A cleaning machine sat deactivated at the bottom of the water, the curve of its hose forming a huge, pool-sized question mark, rising in three dimensions and then going flat with the distortion of the surface. Some bouncy bebop played distantly, and Terri put a hand to her chest, feeling her heart slam with illicit knowledge, the old "Open sesame" of her profession placing her somewhere she should not be.

The muted jazz suddenly swelled, and through a picture window she saw someone emerge from the sliding door just around the corner, the effect similar to seeing through the wall with her PanOpts. For the second time in less than two days, she drew her gun. The small figure rounded the corner like a penitent monk, almost entirely shrouded in an oversized bathrobe.

"LAPD! Hands! Let me see your hands!"

The stranger stopped, the sides of the hood flopped in wild confusion, and even when knobby, blue-veined hands emerged from the sleeves and revealed the face of an elderly woman, Terri was so primed to see Paula Pineda that she blurted another command on momentum-primed autopilot, the Tourette's of control.

"Police! Against the wall! Now!"

The old woman saw her and gasped once, a pained half squeak, tottering backward and connecting hard with the stucco wall, as if the entire property had just been yanked out from under her. Terri raced clockwise around the swimming pool between them, thinking there was no way she'd reach the woman in time, hoping that she'd at least fall to one side or another and not stagger face down into the pool.

And yet she did reach the old woman in time, making it to support one frail elbow as she slid around her, hooking a light metal lawn chair with her foot and sliding it across the patio concrete with a loud jangle. The old woman sat and Terri reholstered her gun, trying to remember where the medical apps were in PanOpt, trying to decide if she should pull them out and look, instead producing her badge from its jacket pocket.

"Did you hit your head? On the wall?"

The old woman raised one hand and cleared her throat with some effort, half-whispering, "I'll be okay," with a phlegmy sizzle. From this close, Terri saw that the woman was older than she would have guessed from the way she'd walked out the door, mideighties at least, although a well-tended octogenarian, with skin less sun-damaged than Terri's own.

"Okay. I'm okay," the woman said, seeming to calm herself. "You're a cop. Okay."

"I need to locate Paula Pineda. This is her residence?"

"No, it's *my* residence. I'm Rose. I own this house."

"Is Paula your daughter? Or . . ."

"She's my assistant. Oh my," the woman made eye contact with Terri now, her eyes focused and clear.

"Is Paula in some sort of trouble?"

"I'm not sure, ma'am. But I'll need to speak with her immediately. Is she here?"

"I . . . I'm not sure if she's here or not. She stays here half the week, in the back bedroom." Then, to herself, she added, "Oh no."

"Do I have your permission to search the premises?" Terri didn't like asking a question she didn't need to, but it seemed easier than explaining the legality of what she was doing, and she needed to make sure she could leave the owner where she was.

Rose waved a hand dismissively and looked down to the ground, seeming to catch her breath all over again. Not sure what else to say, Terri mumbled, "Stay right here," drawing her gun again and letting herself in through the sliding door.

This was to be a sweep, not a search, the legal distinction between the two bright and unequivocal. Although without her PanOpts recording, she realized, there was freedom to do nearly anything she wanted. Terri thought of all those coppers from the *Thin Man* movies, striding through private doors with barely a grunt. Exigency upon exigency. At least old-timey cops didn't have to worry about house macros.

The layout was both smaller and also far more sumptuous than expected, the decor a pitch-perfect mix of rounded glass and Southwest mission style, the place spotless, Terri instinctually thinking Rich Widow. After sweeping the two bedrooms and each bedroom's separate bathroom, the closets, kitchen, den, and foyer, she crossed back into the small sitting room she'd entered in and raised her eyebrows in appreciation.

Back outside, Rose sat curled in worry, her huge-knuckled hands clutched together.

"Did you find her?"

"No. She's not here. This is very important. Do you have any idea where she would be right now?"

"Right now. What day is today?"

Terri had to think about this for a moment. "Sunday."

"Oh! Sunday she's at the market!"

"Market . . . which market?"

"Well, today it could be the supermarket, or . . . oh! I know! The one with all the fish!"

"The one with the fish. The Zuma fish market?"

"Yes!" Her face clouded for a moment. "Yes, I think she would have to be." Rose was staring at Terri's hand, at the gun.

"Good," she said, reholstering her weapon and producing the business card whose phone number led to her ghostly Dupe, telling everyone she had the flu somewhere.

"Thank you for your assistance."

"I hope she isn't in trouble."

"That makes two of us."

As she made her way back down to the car, a vision came to Terri with forceful clarity: chuck the badge and the shades in the pool and start over somewhere far away.

Back on the freeway, the car synced itself with another vehicle whose thudding bass rattled the windows in 4/4 rhythm. She closed her eyes, trying to focus, to place herself ahead of the urgency instead of behind it, even as the car raced toward her destination, its sheer acceleration giving the opposite impression, that she was late for a deadline that may or may not have already expired.

As she did in all moments of calm sandwiched by commotion, she tried to recap, to focus on the particulars of what had happened, to sift for clues. Yesterday's conversation with Zack in front of City Hall—the stubbornly disorienting weirdness of it—stayed with her. She called Carla in audio, on the civilian shades, filling her in on the scene at the house and the subsequent race to the Zuma fish mart.

"Listen. Also. Something weird is bugging me about my conversation with Zack yesterday afternoon."

"What's that?"

"I made mention of this thing with his dog. It's this . . . it's an in-joke we've bounced around for years. But yesterday he acted like he didn't know what I was talking about."

"If the guy set you up, it stands to figure he'd probably mess with you. Especially in the call where he's verifying that you're still alive."

"Maybe. But I don't think that was it. It was just an afterthought, like he had no clue what I was talking about."

"So what do *you* think happened?"

"I think maybe Zack isn't Zack. Maybe someone is impersonating him. Impersonating his VT. If someone could fake my Dupe, then . . ."

"Wait. Wait, wait, wait, back up. Yeah, the Dupe thing is . . . I don't know what. But cracking Zack's VT is an entirely different universe . . ."

"But what about those bypasses you told me about? The bank robbery in Tarzana where the robbers faked the outgoing call?"

"That was ten years ago. Those bypasses are museum pieces. Literally. We have them locked up in a display case.

When the chief of police from Tokyo or Mexico City visits, that's one of the things we pull out for them to *ooh and ah* over. It's like showing them OJ Simpson or Black Dahlia stuff. It's historical. No one makes bypasses now, they're rarer than, I don't know . . . they're beyond rare. And now you're saying someone's got two of these, one they used on you—although I don't even know how that could be done without you knowing about it—and one used on Zack. It's crazy."

"Carla, this whole thing is crazy."

"Point taken. I guess Zack's identity would be easy enough to verify. Maybe you should call back, give him twenty questions."

"I'm going to be there in a few minutes. Right now, every cell in my body is focused on getting this Pineda person. Which, yeah, she hasn't shown up in the Basement, right?"

"Not yet. But if she came out of an enclosed garage, she could easily drive all the way out there and go shopping without detection. Especially the way that place is set up."

"So that seems like one sign toward her being there."

"How so?"

Terri realized she'd already arrived at the Fish Mart's long sandy parking area. "There aren't many public places with the kinds of security barriers they have in Zuma."

"Good point. Keep me posted. I'll do likewise."

In terms of surveillance, the tent-covered Fish Mart was the same thing as the Santos community, a space outside regular civic detection, where the luxury of anonymity came built into the price. For police purposes, zones like the Zuma Fish Mart posed as much of a pain in the ass as the Swap Meet. Carla had two drones circling far overhead. Both would be of as much use to Terri as the seagulls even farther overhead, swooping in larger circles and then dipping to the nearby waves in sequence.

Without PanOpt's guidance, a pause was necessary to take in the visual disorder. She'd never been here before, and hadn't expected such tightly packed hustle and bustle. Nearby, an oyster bar was done up like a miniature Route 66 diner, all chrome and Formica. Next to this, huge bins of ice held cod and mackerel and Alaskan King Crabs, each one costing two months' salary for a ten-year cop. Terri walked past fat, triangular slabs of tuna, so pink they resembled marbled watermelon, and stacks of smaller fish, red and white, their little eyes gaping in shock, the expression of nearly every murder victim she'd ever seen. That pungent smell—for most of human history a gross, working-class odor—was now the aroma of sheer luxury. It'd been years since she'd even tasted an actual fish. Guards stood at every intersection, smiling but packing sidearms.

Terri set out, scanning the crowd, enduring quick stares and murmurs, everyone knowing her profession, seeing she couldn't see theirs in return. She assumed many of the older clientele here—her age and up—were parents of kids like Stacy Santos, people who sent their offspring to expensive colleges and probably tutted with distaste when they saw displays like the cardboard shantytown at UCPD. But in their private conversations, most of these people probably agreed with the general sentiment, that cops serially abused the poor refugees in their care, like the cruel owners of an orphanage. This perceived critique stung her far more than the usual cop bashing, being both vague and impossible to refute.

Many of the younger adults here were most likely personal assistants. They milled in the aisles, consulting invisible lists of criteria, searching for the perfect cut, or the unique gift. One mobbed booth sold jars of honey as an investment. There'd been huge strides in the manufacture of fake bees, competing armies made in non-compatible formats, each capable of delivering pollen in the contingency that the real ones finally died out. After everything had died, she supposed, these fake bees could still be buzzing around the planet, able to fix each other and build new bees, needing only sunlight to thrive. Maybe someday there'd be fake fish. She squinted and glanced up, realizing that overhead speakers actually played "Ode to Joy" at a soft volume.

Terri arrayed four publicly available face-recognition apps to work over each other, almost instantly regretting her choice. A jumble of name boxes blossomed, quickly filling her visual field, more than half of them commercial bylines opening their own bulbous balloons and animations. She hissed, halting in the middle of the aisle, trying to adjust the parameters for each app as two clashing jingles for dating services blared over each other. She pulled off the disposable EyePhones, wondering, half seriously, if she'd have more luck finding Paula Pineda if she tried to arrange a hookup.

Pineda: why would she come here? Terri walked without shades, trying to see this market from her perp's perspective. Paula was like the others. She'd been terrified into killing another human being. So she would have been left doubly traumatized, once from the shooting, once from whatever made her shoot. Paula would also want to continue with daily routines, both out of a need to reenter her normal life—to make herself believe it'd all been something close to a horrible dream—and a desire to appear as normal as possible. She'd probably be scared of capture, so it would seem advantageous to adhere as close as possible to normal routines, not knowing that those routines would make her that much easier a target.

And who had the gun now? That would be the next step for Carla. The subsequent shooter could easily be here, in the market with her. In terms of lax surveillance, this would be the logical place. Except that would imply that the next shooter had access to face tracking more sophisticated than the pay apps she herself had bought. At a corner between two aisles, Terri paused under a neon sign showing a glowing blue swordfish, smiling maniacally and bucking in an invisible tempest. She glanced down all four aisles, no one direction presenting itself. Her nearsightedness wasn't as bad as some people her age, but she'd definitely had visual help with the PanOpts. She caught herself reaching a hand into space to ghost down to the corners, forgetting again that she was bare-eyed. She paused to stare up at misters twenty feet overhead, standing exhausted to watch the mist drift down in a fine curl of spray, the coil of vapor shaped like the bow of a surfer's trench.

Her jacket pocket chimed. She slipped her PanOpts on, saw it was Zack calling, and glanced around at the slow-moving Caucasian herd, bracing herself for a conversation she didn't want to have. She dinged the box already set back at City Hall, the one scrubbing out background details, then clicked on full view, placing his VT in the narrow aisle with her. Zack appeared agitated, pacing back and forth.

"Whoo boy, you ready to move?"

"Where are we going?"

"I need you over in Pershing Square, ASAP. I got all three of them."

Out of morbid curiosity, she almost asked which three, instead clucking her tongue. "Naw."

"What . . . are you in trouble? Where *are* you?"

"Where I'm at is none of your business. Tell me about Hyperion again."

"That? I don't know, what about it?"

"'It.' Okay."

"Look Terri, don't you want to know what *I've* been up to? I figured it out. All I . . ."

"Tell me about the books in your house."

"Huh?"

"Just tell me the subject of the books in the two bookcases of your *house*."

He paused, then said, "What are you doing, Terri?"

"You heard me. It's a simple question. Tell me about the books in your house."

"I don't know . . . they're books. What the fuck is wrong with you?"

"You can't tell me about Hyperion . . ."

"They're books. Books have all kinds of . . ."

"And you can't tell me the subject of every book in your house."

His VT stood opposite her and glared, an intensity of anger she'd only seen a few times in the six years they'd been partnered, and never directed at her.

"I. Just. Told. You."

"No, you didn't. Because you're not Zack."

He raised a finger to his chin and tilted his head. A slight smile emerged.

"Whoever you are, you're the one who's been setting me up."

His smile grew wider, more confident. Very softly, he said, "Careful."

"Careful or what?"

"Careful." He was nearly whispering. "Because you really have no idea how bad things can get, Terri."

"Who are you?"

Zack—not Zack—smiled. "The right question is *where* am I?" He smiled and vanished. She snatched off the shades, feeling a patch of goose bumps on her neck, looking down at the PanOpts as if she held all the bizarre horror of the last few weeks in one sweaty palm.

"Okay," Terri ran a hand over her jaw. She looked up to a wooden sign depicting a cartoon crab with six human legs, each done up in fishnet stockings, its googly eyes sporting giant curled lashes. This was one of those junction points she'd been vaguely trained for. Except that the crux of all cop training was Don't Go It Alone. She breathed deeply, trying to use the tools at her disposal.

Regulate. Concentrate. Analyze. So the civilian eyewear was all but useless for tracking faces. She could do the job with her own eyes, or she could use her PanOpts. Those were the choices. Were those the only choices? She could leave, that was a choice. And although she didn't have a destination, anywhere certainly felt safer than here. No: that was false. Surveillance was low here. This was her best bet for catching Paula Pineda alive, and Paula Pineda was her best bet for stopping the chain.

Maintain. Breathe. Organize. She'd take her chances with cop eyes. Any incoming calls, even from people she no longer trusted—especially from people she no longer trusted—offered information about whatever it was that was happening. Back in PanOpts, she pulled up the layout of the Fish Mart, seeing it was almost entirely a grid, four rows by five rows with a scattering of kiosks at the entrance and a fringe of restaurants bordering the parking lot. She set up a walking path, setting out with an orderly plan that covered every aisle. Not having a physical photo of Paula on her, she could still question anyone wearing shades, which was maybe a quarter of the clientele.

Rounding the first corner, she set the shades to full alert if Paula's face emerged for just a second, holding out her physical badge for an older couple dressed in all white, standing before a wine tasting booth. Even facing a cop, both continued obliviously sipping on long-stemmed glasses of chardonnay as if the countywide open-container ban somehow didn't apply to them. Which, she supposed, it didn't.

"Excuse me, LAPD, homicide. Have either of you seen this woman," she said, motioning up to the flat photo of Paula Pineda that would be seen at eye level in their own EyePhones.

"No, Officer, we haven't," the older man said, placing an outstretched hand over his wife's shoulder as if shielding her from the indignity of answering. The woman opened her mouth to say something, then took the signal from her husband.

Terri raised a hand to move the photo down below eye level, seeing thick curls of blue smoke spilling out of her fingertips. The effect was so otherworldly that she momentarily turned away from the couple and bumped the shades up to confirm that it wasn't actually happening. Sensing her confusion, the man and woman laughed nervously and walked off. Terri glanced down the aisle and saw that a light dusting of snow fell across the bins and clients, even though all her apps were turned off.

"Hold up," she said, even now letting her irritation with this couple get the best of her. "Ma'am. I need to ask you as well." The couple kept walking.

"Ma'am," Terri called out, holding out a hand, seeing the trail of blue mist left by the sweep of her wrist.

"Excuse me! Sir! Ma'am!" Terri reached out and put a hand on the woman's shoulder, letting out an involuntary yip as her hand continued down, not touching anything, dropping into nothingness where her eyes told her there was a fellow human. She snatched off the shades, seeing no couple, only a few faces turned toward her further down the aisle. Terri realized she was blushing, her body approximating a response to a situation she'd never experienced. She hadn't mistaken the couple for VTs; that wasn't possible. These were counterfeits of living, breathing people. She thought of Carla's words: an entirely different universe.

Returning to PanOpts, she was surprised to see the couple still there, sauntering toward a tabletop aquarium piled three deep with lobsters. She caught up and stepped in front of the couple to see if they'd acknowledge her own reality or simply continue right through her, as if she were the one who didn't exist. They halted, expressions unchanged.

"What is this?" she said. "Showing me what you can do?"

The man smiled, displaying brilliant white teeth, turning slowly to his companion. As Terri watched, her face shifted, curling outward, lines deepening, the nose filling out, drooping, and then she was looking at Nuestro Quintiglio in drag, the shoulder-length blond hair framing his craggy features. But this wasn't Nuestro in life. This face was ashen, with the waxy repose of the gurney.

"Answer your phone," the corpseface said.

A chirp came. It was Zack. She put him on in audio.

"Nope," not Zack said. "VT me. Got something you should see."

She did this, the couple vanishing, Zack appearing in their place.

"Guess where I am."

"Not in front of me," she said, the flutter clearly audible in her voice.

"I'm in Tammi's kitchen," he said with a laugh, then announcing a street address that Terri knew as well as her own. "Isn't that a kick?"

She heard herself say, "What," in a far-off voice.

"Don't worry, she and Rex are out running errands. But look who I *did* find upstairs, trying to hide under a bed."

Not Zack drew a swirled finger gesture in the air, linking VTs, and then Krista was with him, sobbing, held in a moderate chokehold.

"Aunt Terri . . . they found me . . ."

She looked from one face to the next, thinking, *Calm, just stay calm*, then, overlapping this, the significance of that one word: *they*.

"So here's what's going to happen. You're in aisle B2. You're going to go up one, and then left three. Paula Pineda is at the end. You are going to walk straight up to her, and you are going to blow her goddamn brains out in front of everyone. And you're going to do that because you don't want Krista here to die. Nod if that's clear."

She nodded.

"Make an outgoing call, ask for help, deviate in any way, and she's dead. I'll carve her up with that steak set you got Tammi a few years back. Start with her feet and work up. Get marching."

Terri walked, the fake Zack and real Krista hovering alongside her. She turned left where she was supposed to.

"I want to talk to Krista."

"What did I say about deviation, Terri?"

"I want to ask a question."

"You know," fake Zack sighed, sounding just like real Zack. "You're in this whole goddamn mess because you asked too many questions to begin with. You know that, right?"

"Krista. Did they hurt you?" She could see the end of the aisle up ahead, a huddle of shoppers in which Paula Pineda must be included.

"My arm got twisted."

"Listen, the other day . . ."

"Now you're going on two questions," fake Zack said.

" . . . when your school was closed. What was the reason?"

"What?" Krista blubbered.

She was one row away. Not far ahead, Paula Pineda turned, facing toward her, looking down to her hand basket.

"Krista, what was the *reason*?" Terri said, unsnapping her gun holster. "Why did you tell me you had the day off?"

"Enough," fake Zack said.

Krista was sobbing, "I don't wanna die."

Terri halted in place. Paula was fifteen feet away, examining something in an ice-filled bin.

"Just say the words, Krista . . ."

"You've got five seconds, Terri."

Krista blubbered, "Don't let me die, Aunt Terri . . ."

"Yeah," Terri exhaled. "Okay. Okay."

She drew her gun with one hand, simultaneously yanking the PanOpts up and off her face, crossing the three steps and grabbing her prey by the wrist while the surrounding civilians reared back in shock.

"Paula Pineda, you are under arrest for the murder of Clay Tejada . . ."

Mirandized, handcuffed, limp and sobbing, Paula Pineda was entirely compliant. Guiding her the final fifteen feet out into the sunlight, Terri wondered if she'd ever arrested anyone so small. Even the adolescents she'd collared had seemed heavier, more willing to wriggle their low bulk as a weapon. Terri lifted a hand to call for a car, remembering once again that she had no shades, seeing a trembling thumb and quickly dropping her arm. The comedown from an arrest always gave her at least a slight flutter; who knew what the comedown from something like this would be.

She forced herself to systematically inspect each of her pockets, finding the badge and again pinning this on her jacket, then finding the disposables and calling Carla.

"We're here. I got her."

"I'm calling for backup. No signs of the next shooter?"

Terri scanned the faces in the crowd, the pedestrians trying to move around her as quickly as possible, and the gawkers further along both sides of the U-shaped dropoff road, her field of vision rapidly filling with more pop-up bubbles and banners.

"No, we're good. Just get us out of here."

"A car's on its way. Does she still have her EyePhones?"

"I don't know. Hey, Paula . . . shit . . ." Terri pulled up the disposables, her suspect's face getting crowded by ads. As she did this, another dead man zoomed up from the crowd, his movement rendered in that strange slow-motion lucidity she'd only experienced once or twice before. As Froggy raised the pass-along pistol, Terri found herself registering how frighteningly awful he looked, eyes barely open, his face and forearms covered in an oily sheen of sweat that had stained the pits of his light hoodie like cooking oil.

Terri saw Froggy before Paula did, instinctually swinging herself right, around Paula's body as the crack came, all three of them seeming to hit the ground at the same moment, the shock of pain in her wrist pushing time back up to normal speed, Terri thinking, *Why did he fall?*

She kicked the gun away from Froggy's hand and then brought her heel down against his jaw, hard, drawing her own gun and mouthing something loud and authoritative. Her own wrist throbbing, she zipcuffed one of his thin arms to the pole of a bike rack, feeling the fever blazing off him, pulling aside his thin T-shirt and seeing the hideously inflamed wound in his shoulder. A shrill scream started up, but when she turned to tell Paula Pineda to calm down, Terri saw the blood and realized what had just happened.

Paramedics arrived, then backup, red and blue lights playing weakly across faces in the crowd. Terri realized she was still here, that this was actually happening. At some point, a strong hand hoisted her to her feet, draped her with a thin blanket, and ushered her into an empty cop car. She thought, *I'm just shocked, not in shock*, but then felt her legs buckle as she sat.

She patted down her own jacket with deliberate motions, like a blind woman, finally finding the disposable glasses in the same pocket she'd placed them in just a few minutes earlier. It was a Sunday. Krista would be home. She focused through the jittery hollowness as the phone rang.

"Hey Aunt Terri. Hold on?"

"Wait," she said, hearing her own voice warble even as she saw no red letter *D*. "This is *you*, right?"

"Of course."

"And is everything okay there?"

"Um . . . yeah. Should something be wrong?"

"I just . . ." her voice caught and she hung up abruptly, producing a low hoot that was half sob, half chortle.

Of course. Hostage Krista wasn't real Krista. Villain Zack hadn't been real Zack. All those phone conversations with her partner came flooding back, all those suspicious omissions and outright diversions. *Follow up on leads that keep you off this main thread.* She let this sink in. The last time she'd seen Zack in person was at the skyscraper assault. Any phone conversation could be suspect.

Terri stiffened in revelation. Any PanOpt conversation, period, could be suspect. The PanOpts themselves were suspect. She thought back to the lie-detector sessions with Torg and Liney, the readings leading her in the same direction the false Zack had. And she hadn't spoken with Liney in person.

If her cop shades were corrupted, how could she be sure what she'd seen was real?

She rubbed her eyes, then called up her glove box service and dinged the request box. Then she called Carla in audio, condensing the horror of the last ten minutes into a few simple sentences.

"I saw there was a shooting. I'm en route now," Carla said. "I should be there in five minutes."

"Listen, also. There's a guy in Central Housing, Nate Posada. Know him?"

"No."

"I was told of his death. That maybe was . . . false. I need you to call his number in the cop directory, then drop a link over to me."

"Sure. Hold on."

Terri stared down at the light-gray carpeting, rethinking events from the last week. Froggy on the freeway. Debriefing Imsane. The Chief's chew out. Gunshots ricocheting off her fleeing vehicle. Everything had been experienced through PanOpts. She examined the fleshy web between thumb and forefinger, once again experiencing that skipping sensation; her own hands, her real, actual hands.

Carla came back on the line, said, "Here," and then she heard Mutty drawl, "Hey Terri."

She exhaled slowly. "Heeeeey."

"You calling from a pay phone?"

"Where are you?"

"We got a ga-*zelle* watch. What's up?"

"Ahm. Lemme call you back."

She hung up and put a thumb and finger to either side of her throat, trying stop her heart from slamming. Mutty had been there that night, during the skyscraper raid. She'd seen him. No, she'd seen him through cop shades. She thought of the meeting with Chandrika Chavan, on the far side of the building, the only exchange where she hadn't been wearing PanOpts. She hadn't glimpsed any of the cops—outside or inside—with her bare eyes. She thought about the forty-sixth-floor window glazed with dirt, turning to see that she stood in an empty room. One against fifteen thousand.

Carla arrived and said, "Give me a minute," circling back to squat down next to the medical team gathered by the shooting site. Terri again stared at her shoes, trying to find somewhere for her mind to perch that wasn't what had just happened or what she'd just realized. And although the detecting part of her brain felt inaccessible, she knew tumblers were still clicking, the mind still firing up conclusions without her consent. She'd been expertly steered. By who?

Carla rose and swiveled toward her, striding through a cheery hodgepodge of Overlay ad balloons.

"He's dead."

"Froggy."

"Yeah. They called it, just now."

Terri surveyed herself, finding no emotion, surprise or otherwise.

"Acute septic shock," Carla continued. "He's apparently been skulking around with a gunshot wound to the shoulder for two weeks. He definitely hadn't sought out any professional medical help. The walking wounded."

"Something motivated him to make it here out of sheer willpower."

"Yeah," Carla lifted a pair of expensive-looking EyePhones, dangling them from one pinkie. "These."

"They work?"

"He was using them when he died. I'll crack them as soon as I get back to the office. How are *you*?"

Terri shrugged, but she was unexpectedly moved by this slight show of concern, suddenly wondering if she was going to cry.

A vehicle honked from the outer rim of the parking lot at the same moment her disposables dinged. Carla stepped aside to let Terri climb out of the cop car and cross the forty feet of asphalt to retrieve her glove box. To her right, past the flapping crime tape and hovering ad bubbles, she could make out the Fish Market civilians, each watching her through their own shades, every face turning to silently follow her passage. Reporters would be here any minute. When she returned with the smooth metal box tucked under one arm, Carla said, "You need these people cleared out?" Terri shook her head, climbing back into the cop car, placing the glove box next to her and exhaling loudly.

She popped the box lid with a thumbnail, staring down at the dingy gym bag she'd retrieved from the freeway sign three days earlier, feeling the same cold gooseflesh rising on both forearms.

"That's the bag," Carla announced for no reason.

Terri pulled up the disposable shades, yanking down the zipper and producing an expensive-looking soccer jersey, probably tossed up onto the freeway sign by some high school bully.

"My glasses showed me my shirt."

"Yeah."

"This isn't my shirt."

"Yeah."

"This isn't my shirt. I saw my shirt. I was holding this, but I saw my own shirt."

Their eyes met for an uncomfortable moment, Terri trying to phrase her question.

"What *is* this?" she finally asked, dropping the jersey to the floor, patting around her pockets again and retrieving the haunted PanOpts, holding these out in an open palm.

Carla cleared her throat. "Listen, I have a theory."

"Okay."

"It's bad. You're not going to like it."

"Go."

"I linked you to Quintiglio's mail account, Segurança, when?"

"Wednesday. No, Tuesday."

"Everything crazy that's happened to you has happened since then. Right?"

"Maybe." Terri remembered the Godzilla film.

"I charted everything you told me. Unless you left something out, the answer's yes. As soon as you were linked to that account, your PanOpts started making up their own reality. Not all of it. But enough to steer you in a certain direction."

"Steered," she said, her suspicion out in the open.

"Think about it. The conspiracy, unless I'm really, really wrong, was fake. At the same time, public outrage was real. Although you were one of perhaps two dozen cops falsely implicated in the Quintiglio scandal, you were the only one forced by circumstances into a crowded area, and further forced by circumstances to show your face. Reporters gravitated to you because you unwillingly made yourself available. The manufactured crisis created its own gravity, and then it used whatever tools were available to manufacture more crisis. Your PanOpts had unlimited resources. Commercial apps, archives, your own nuances and expressions. Even your lack of sleep . . ."

"My purchase history. Zack—fake Zack—mentioned steak knives I'd gotten my sister . . ."

"Exactly."

"So public outrage was real, but police outrage over Mutty was fake. I was shown a storyline, and then that storyline evolved."

"I'd call it closer to improv than evolution."

"But who did this? *Why*?"

"'Why' is the simple part. A group of random citizens were made to kill each other. Their EyePhones edited input in the service of this goal. I'm guessing Froggy saw the same thing in his shades that you saw in yours. A loved one held hostage. When I linked you to that mail account, your PanOpts were infected."

"Infected. By who?"

"Terri . . . there was no doer."

"Huh?"

"I think this was a self-replicating program. They used to be called reiteratives. Before that, they were known as viruses." Carla pursed her lips just slightly, the only hint that what she was saying had any special significance. "Among its many other security functions, the Wall serves as a final safeguard against these, so that even if a reiterative could operate in the Overlay, which it can't, it would get caught almost instantly by LAPD defenses."

"So when I thought I was talking with Zack . . ."

"You were talking with your shades. With the idiopathic reiterative that had taken up shop inside your PanOpts."

"Eyes edit stuff," Terri said, peering out at the lot, seeing Kofi Agyeman in the distance, already sniffing out some fresh angle in the ongoing saga of cop scandals.

Her head jerked back at Carla.

"Jesus. Froggy got shot just hours before the Tournament of Roses."

"I thought of that."

"This can't be a coincidence."

"I don't think it is."

"Something's arrived." She swallowed, thinking of an emergency room, waiting for terrible news.

"Are the stampedes here?" Her question slipped out as little more than a whisper.

"I just don't know, Terri."

When she'd called Zack the next morning, he'd asked how she'd been. It'd taken an awkward pause to backtrack and figure out he'd meant with the mystery flu her Dupe had come down with. He'd left a message on Thursday to say he'd taken her advice, left his toddler with his teenagers and split town with Janice for San Luis Obispo. His tone of voice had filled in the rest, Zack sounding as optimistic about life as he ever would. The skyscraper assault, the Quintiglio scandal, the scene at City Hall: he apparently hadn't heard about any of it. This being a Monday, Zack was back on the job at the train station, hopped up on some new theory about why this was going to be his lucky week. They'd agreed to meet at a newish place at the mouth of Olvera at nine.

Terri had spent the night at the Ritz, needing someplace safe from reporters, understanding that her own apartment hadn't actually gotten invaded but still feeling a little spooked anyway. She'd gotten herself a nice room, set the windows to southern Italian coastline, and sat in the bath for a long hour, listening to the faint crackles of the bubbles and the occasional muted noises from the hallway, trying and failing to make herself cry.

Before going to bed, she'd called Carla for confirmation of what she more or less knew. Froggy had been receiving instructions from an anonymous shrieking assailant with a cloth bag over his head. This apparition held a terrified little girl—Froggy's daughter or sister—with a sharpened screwdriver to her throat. Pineda hadn't been the final target; Terri was. She'd been perceived as a threat and mixed into the cycle of killings.

A car fetched her, and she rode toward downtown without shades, raising her hands to retrieve them from her scalp anyway, laughing at the impulse. Terri watched the city slide by as it truly was, flat and unadorned. Maybe Farrukh had enjoyed seeing the city like this the day he'd died. She passed commuters already working on their way to work, women applying lipstick even while talking to an unseen client or subordinate, a man wolfing down a crumbly breakfast burrito as he typed into the air. The car slowed, passing the elevated civic sign that'd trumpeted the rebuilding of Chinatown for the last decade, and she could just make out the worn IMSANE tag. As she slipped on her dust mask, she caught a glimpse of the sorrowful mural that always chilled her, large rainbow letters reading MUMBAI YOU WILL ALWAYS BE OUR SISTER.

At the restaurant, she squinted in memory and then stiffened with shock. She'd come here with Gabriella. The place had been called something different then, and they'd come in a group of people, before they were dating. But there'd been that long moment when they were able to meet eyes across a crowded table and smile at each other; the moment she knew her suspicions were real—all those hints and smiles and phone calls made under the flimsiest of pretexts—and that her feelings were rhymed.

She sat at one of the eatery's painted-metal tables flush with the sidewalk, letting this realization sink in. Whatever it was that had happened to Farrukh and Froggy and Stacy and all the others could just as easily have happened to her. If this thing—whatever it was that had reached out and taken seven people with it—had just known who in her past had meant the most to her, she would have done anything it had demanded. If it had been Gabriella in Zack's arms, she had no doubt she would have killed Paula Pineda. She wouldn't have been able to think quickly enough, wouldn't have survived, if Gabby had been involved. It just didn't have the right materials to work with.

A public address system suspended in the nearby tree played some hammy rock song, and a man's voice whimpered through a seemingly endless chorus, *I love you, I love you, I love you, I love you . . .*

"I'm confused. Does this guy love me?" Zack said, pointing up at the speaker with one thumb, visibly pleased to see her. She resisted the strange urge to stand and hug him. Sensing this, he said, "Hey, no hugs, I don't wanna catch whatever you've got." He sat and grimaced, rotating his shoulder in several pained circles.

"What happened?"

"The thing, from last week. From Wade's party. Still healing slow."

"Last week," she said, with a light amused amazement, having to speak up through the dust mask.

"Yeah, well. Old age." He winced again. "I'm gonna comp myself a jet ski out of his college fund."

"How's the train station going?"

"I caught two bathroom flashers on two separate days. That was exciting. Second guy looked just like the first. And you know what he said when I cuffed him?" Zack lifted a finger, saying, "Hold up, Terri," as he turned to face back toward the train station, talking with someone else now.

The waiter brought them each mugs of coffee they hadn't asked for, and she felt that reflex of gratitude, a signal that overrode almost all else, detached from faith or even thought. She was grateful for food. At some point before lunch ended, she'd have to debrief him, one way or another. If she didn't explain the full story, she'd at least have to explain the skyscraper assault from Thursday. There were several plausible versions of the truth that could be offered, up to and including the full truth. But that was for later in their meal. For now, she could enjoy the moment.

Terri sat and watched the crowd, drawn in by its realness, the people actually here, less than a table-length from the edge of her actual table. Viewing these civilians—young, elderly, enfeebled from the past, or striding with great purpose toward some unseen future—she was struck by the realization that people weren't stampeding everywhere, at all times. She stared in insight, a carrier of secret knowledge. One more overlay.

She thought about Paula Pineda. After Terri had disarmed Froggy and handcuffed one of his thin arms to the railing he'd slumped against, she'd folded her own jacket into a thick square, placing this below Paula's head as she gasped for air. Pineda had been hit in the upper-left chest. Terri had heard of gunshot victims refusing to die even when shot in the heart, still able to lurch for a few seconds past their own deaths, the body operating on sheer will. All she could do was call 911 through her civilian shades and wait for the sirens.

She'd uncuffed Paula and rolled her onto her side, into the recovery position, the back of her T-shirt drenched in so much blood that Terri had to steady a hand on Paula's ribcage, lest the weight of wet clothing pull her back down. And when the labored, sucking breaths grew faint, she did roll her back to face up, unclear if she should attempt mouth-to-mouth on someone who clearly had seconds left.

Paula had never closed her eyes. She'd glanced about in confused terror, meeting Terri's gaze, darting off again, locking eyes again. A realization came. Terri had seen into this woman's life from overhead, the components of her final day fanned out like parts in a technical drawing. She'd seen why Paula had been made to kill, why she was dying, truths this twenty-two-year-old would never know, even now, in the last few moments of her existence. Paula was dead before the paramedics arrived.

Terri had sat like this with her dog, Congo, the day he'd died. They'd never gotten any sort of autopsy, so she'd never been sure if he'd been brought down by a stroke or an aneurysm. Whatever it'd been, it'd laid Congo out, so that when she found him on the kitchen floor, he was flat on one soaked side, panting and immobilized. Congo's eye had moved like Paula's, roaming, taking in her face, and then roaming again. She'd felt that the dog was trying to grasp the enormity of what had happened, not just the internal calamity that had felled him, but the entirety of his life. Congo had been reduced to a single eye, taking in the beautiful world he had been thrust into and just as quickly exiled from. The eye had come to rest on hers one last time, beseeching and terrified. The eye seemed to ask, *Why did I have to come all the way here if I just have to leave again?*

THANKS: Lisa Auerbach, Felicia Berryman, Christina Brown, Neil Burke, Noelle Burke, Zack Carlson, Jan Chipchase, Bradley Englert, Laura Fleischauer, Leandra Gil, Oliver Hall, Bob Hardt, Joel Kyack, Ashley Macomber, Mickie McCormic, Amy McPheeters, Tom McPheeters, David Nathanson, Dave Nesmith, Arwen Nicks, Nicole Peeke, Jesse Pearson, Joe Preston, John Skaritza, Mark Steese, Mark Yolles.

SPECIAL THANKS: Anthony Berryman, Scott Gould, John Michaels, Marcus Savino, Tara Tavi.

ABOUT THE AUTHOR

Sam McPheeters is the author of *The Loom of Ruin*. He was born in Ohio, raised in upstate New York, and currently lives in Pomona, California, with his wife.